GUNNING FOR ANGELS

C. MACK LEWIS

DEDICATION

To Dennis E. Lewis
My favorite person in the universe.

ACKNOWLEDGMENTS

Special thanks to:
Mike Lavario for book cover design,
Retroatelier for book cover photography,
Michael Ziffer for editorial expertise,
Dan Hitt for formatting expertise,
and Allen Olson, Laurie Schnebley, Roy Semmons,
Carrie Zerafa and Burt Hopkins for their valuable input

PROLOGUE

Murder is born of love, and love attains the greatest intensity in murder.

—Octave Mirbeau, Writer

The golden necklace was severed. The delicate angel-wing pendant was caught in a clot of blood, resembling hot sealing wax against translucent skin. Her neck jutted to the side in an awkward angle.

Eyes full of empty stared upward as she lay sprawled out like some grotesque pin-up girl. An all-American beauty served up on cheap linoleum, a Jackson Pollock canvas of bullet holes and blood spatter.

A diaper-clad baby girl with blond ringlets sat next to the woman's head, wailing at full lung capacity. The baby's fist spasmodically beat against the dead woman's face, splattering blood in every direction of the tiny kitchen.

One of the baby's hands caught the necklace and clutched it, her body jolting with the violence of her crying. The golden angel wings were sullied red with blood and glinted dully in the late afternoon sun that slanted through the twisted blinds over the sink.

Bloody handprints smeared down the cracked plaster wall, revealing the woman's last gruesome moments as she struggled down the wall, across the floor…

Never no more.

CHAPTER ONE

Even a small mouse has anger.

—*Native American, Tribe Unknown*

When Enid Iglowski hauled off and slugged Joey Wysocki, she hadn't been thinking about anything, she'd been simply reacting. The instant her fist made contact with Joey's nose and she heard the sickening sound of bone and cartilage breaking, she also heard the sound of the last two weeks of her Junior year of high school getting flushed down the toilet.

The rest of the night proved to be a goulash of school officials, police officers and Joey's parents – all punctuated by the glaring absence of her own missing-in-action mother. By the time they located her mother, who had somehow gotten her butt super-glued to a bar stool *again*, Joey's parents had filed a police complaint against Enid and she'd gotten expelled under the school's new zero-tolerance policy.

It was now one week later and, as the Greyhound bus pulled out of Abilene, Enid was feeling the effects of forty hours on the road – and on the run. Her teeth were gritty and she longed to take a hot shower and crawl into her own bed that she had left behind in Florida. She could hardly believe that she had another seventeen hours to endure until she got to Phoenix, where she was determined to find her real father, a man named Jack Fox, whom she had never heard of until one week ago.

Henry Iglowski was the man she had *thought* was her father. Both Enid and Henry found out at the same moment that Henry was *not* her father, that he was simply the man that her mother had duped into believing that he was Enid's real father for the last sixteen years.

Her ears still rang with her mother's drunken ravings on the day Henry had packed up and left.

The way her mother had screamed after him, "You know the kid that you *thought* was your kid? Enid *isn't* yours, you piece of shit! Her *real* dad was a one-night stand in Phoenix! You remember Phoenix, don't you? *Jack Fox, that was his name!* HA! You've been raising another man's kid!"

Enid had stood in the front door, staring at her mother in horror. Henry had been throwing boxes into the back of a borrowed pickup truck. He froze, staring at her mother in shock.

It occurred to Enid that her mother didn't seem to realize what she had said. She had that cloudy, where's-my-drink look as she covered a burp, steadied herself against the Honda, turned and disappeared into the house.

From across the yard, Enid's eyes met Henry's, and she saw that he didn't believe a word her mother had said.

Then he did.

Since that day one week ago, Enid had had the horrible sensation of not just being expelled from school, she felt like she'd been expelled from her whole life.

After three nightmarish days of being stuck at home with her drunk and/or hungover mother, Enid decided to take matters into her own hands. She stole four hundred dollars from her mother's checking account and another forty dollars from her whiskey kitty. She also swiped Henry's Glock 17, which her mother had hidden from him.

Enid wasn't exactly sure why she took the gun except that it made her feel safer. She had no doubt that her mother would report the gun as stolen and would have the police on her butt faster than her mother could dive on a Smirnoff screwdriver on a Sunday morning.

Enid had used up her last chance with Joey's broken nose. Her mother had assured her that her next stop was Juvie detention hall. And the thought of going to Juvie detention, where her archnemesis, Jackie Utton, was currently residing, made Enid sweat harder than a hooker at a Baptist revival.

Since grade school, Jackie Utton had been using teenage terrorist tactics and kicking the crap out of her on a regular basis, and every bit of trouble that Enid had gotten into at school had been directly related to defending herself against what Enid referred to as "the psychopath." Jackie had pushed her, shoved her, pinched her, tripped her and pummeled her so many times that Enid had gotten into the habit of slinking through the school, stealthy as a Navy SEAL.

Not that her mother ever cared or understood or even took her side. According to her mother, Enid couldn't kick a can across a deserted parking lot without running into trouble and coming back with three reasons why it wasn't her fault.

It constantly amazed Enid that, for a kid who got good grades and didn't smoke, drink, cuss or let boys grab her hand and shove it down their pants to feel up their junk, she spent a lot of time in the principal's office.

If I end up in Juvie with Jackie Utton, I am dead dog meat on a stick.

She was relieved to be putting Florida behind her, but at the thought of finding and meeting her real father, she felt queasy. To make herself feel better, she dug her hand into her backpack and gripped the handle of the gun that was as mysterious and dangerous as Joey's *thing* had been.

Boys are scary. Guns are cool!

Enid squeezed the gun's handle and sent a prayer speeding up the highway toward Phoenix.

Please God, don't let my real dad be a crack-head, meth-speed-freak, wife-beating, daughter-beating, sleazebag piece of crap, a woman-hater, racist, homophobic, fataphobic, passive-aggressive, lazy cheapskate loser or a rapist serial-killer pedophile.

Enid bit her lip, afraid that she left something out.

Oh! Or stupid.

"Are you praying?"

Enid whipped her hand out of the backpack. She glared at the chunky kid with the greasy cowlick who had proven nosier than a truffle-seeking piglet.

"What's in your backpack?" he asked, poking at it curiously.

"None of your business." Enid shoved his hand away.

"It looked like you were praying," the chunky kid frowned.

A woman's pudgy hand reached from behind his seat and handed him a sandwich that smelled like sardines. For fourteen hours, Enid had watched the hand appear and disappear as it handed up everything from toilet paper to boiled eggs to burnt snickerdoodle cookies to a kid's book entitled "So Your Daddy's In Jail?" The kid and the unseen woman at the other end of the hand never spoke. Their entire existence seemed to be defined by the hand anticipating what he needed and him accepting whatever was given to him.

Enid watched him chomp into the sandwich. Her stomach rolled with nausea as a tiny sardine face, frozen in "oh my" surprise, peeked out from between his fingers. He swallowed and turned to her. "Show me what's in the backpack or I'll tell the bus driver you stole my five dollars and hid it in there."

Enid's mouth fell open in astonishment. It was a mystery to her why everyone from Jackie to Joey to complete strangers, including this goofball twelve-year-old kid, took one look at her and pegged her for someone that they could push around. It was strange that for all the times she didn't fight back with Jackie, that she finally snapped and hit somebody.

Punching Joey had felt good.

Really good.

"Show me what's in the backpack or I squeal louder than a stuck pig."

She leaned forward and hissed, "Sure as my name is Jackie Utton, if you rat, I'm going to pop that little head off your shoulders, kick it down the highway and use it for target practice."

He eyed her, unsure.

He doesn't believe me!

Hands shaking with anger, Enid unzipped the backpack, revealing the Glock.

"Cool!" His eyes widened with admiration. "Who are you going to kill?"

"Shhh!" Enid looked around, making sure no one had heard.

"Can I hold it?" He asked, reaching for the backpack.

She shoved his hand away and, hoping that she sounded convincing, she whispered, "You say one word *to anyone* and I'll pop you – with the gun, *not* my fist, you little punk."

His eyes got wide as he gave her a new look of respect. He made a "zip" motion on his lips, locked them with an imaginary key and threw it out.

Enid settled back, wishing that she had sat next to anybody but this kid.

I just threatened to shoot him and now he respects me?

A thought occurred to her. She frowned, troubled. Back in school, when Jackie had first started picking on her, what if she had pretended to be tough? Would Jackie have left her alone? Could she have avoided the last four years of torment?

"You are *so* going to end up in jail," the kid said matter-of-factly.

Enid shot him a look, rattled.

"My dad's in jail," the kid said sadly.

"Sorry to hear that," Enid mumbled.

His head snapped toward her in astonishment, "How'd you hear?"

"What?" She asked, confused.

"About my dad! How do you know about *that?*" He eyed her suspiciously.

"You just told me. Duh."

"Oh." He sat back. After a long moment, he asked, "*Your* dad in jail?"

Enid shook her head. Everything she knew about her real father, she had found out from the Internet. He was a private detective, divorced and wasn't on any of the social networking sites. He didn't even have a website for his business. Enid had called his office but, when she heard the secretary's voice, she had hung up.

The hand appeared with a pillow and a blanket. "Bedtime," the kid sighed happily.

Enid watched him tuck himself in and had a jangly-stomach thought.

What if my real dad doesn't like me?

The kid nudged her and whispered, "Thanks for showing me."

Frowning, Enid turned away and stared out the window. In daylight, the landscape had been speckled with gas stations, fast food joints, and billboards. Now that it was night, it was dotted with the neon lights from gas stations, fast food joints and billboards.

She re-focused her eyes and stared at her reflection in the window: a pale heart-shaped face with hazel eyes and shoulder-length brown hair, which was in the habit of confounding her comb and doing whatever the heck it wanted. Last summer, her mother had taken her shopping for a bathing suit and, after giving her a knowing up-and-down evaluative look in the changing room, had shrugged and said, "At least you have a good nose."

Enid was waiting impatiently for the morning she would wake up and her scrawny flat-chested body would magically morph into cute. Or, at the least, something in the same zip code as cute.

She sighed, wondering if her mom would get un-drunk long enough to realize that she was missing a daughter. Enid had a feeling the gun would be missed long before she was.

Probably won't know I'm gone till there's no one there to wake her up in time to go to bed.

Enid kept expecting police sirens to scream the bus to a stop so that cops could drag her off and force her back to Florida where Dad…

Enid felt tears burn her eyes.

She corrected herself.

Henry.

The name sounded foreign in her mouth.

Henry had been her father for as long as she could remember. He'd been to her school plays, read her essays and short stories, and, when she had been so obsessed with winning a trophy and *lost again* in the annual school science fair, he bought her a giant trophy with a winged goddess on top. He had the gold plaque engraved: *Enid Ivy Rose Iglowski, First Place, International Invitational Science Fair.*

He told her that his contest was 'Invitational' and she was the only one invited. Without him, she would've been robbed of her best memories.

Enid was jolted out of her thoughts as the bus hit another pothole. At the thought of meeting Jack Fox, who didn't know she even existed, panic rose up in her throat. Enid stuck her hand in the backpack, grabbed the Glock and sent out another prayer.

Please let my real dad like kids!

CHAPTER TWO

The best way to keep one's word is not to give it.

—Napoleon Bonaparte

I fucking hate kids.

Jack Fox, thirty-eight and not handsome enough for Hollywood but too damned handsome for his own good, stared in horror at Warren's three out-of-control kids who were tearing up his office. A sign on the door read "Jack Fox Detective Agency" and the office décor was two steps ahead of shabby.

Jack glared at his client, Warren Hibbitt. Not only did Jack need to break the news to Warren that his wife of nine years had been cheating on him, he had to tell him that she was cheating on him with his cousin, who was also Warren's business partner. Jack had a folder full of incriminating photos, an office full of Warren's out-of-control kids, and a bad suspicion that Warren was the type to try to eat a bullet — or make somebody else eat a bullet.

Maybe his wife, Sheila? Maybe me?

Warren's ten-year-old daughter wore flip-flops that were held together with duct tape. Ten minutes ago, using a scraggly-haired Barbie, she had walloped her younger brother in the balls with such ferocity that Jack's eyes watered. The boy, deathly pale and sobbing, lay crumpled on the faded carpet, clutching his balls.

"Jesus, Warren," Jack said, waving his hand in the kid's direction, "She's gonna kill him!"

"Cut the funny stuff!" Warren shouted, without releasing his gaze from Jack.

Warren Hibbitt was a squat man in his thirties. He had the face of a bewildered pit bull as he gazed at Jack in bleak desperation. "You have to tell me," Warren growled. "If you don't tell me, I'll go insane!"

"We need to reschedule. We're not discussing this in front of your kids," Jack said stubbornly.

Flip-flop girl ran to her father's side and pointed at Jack. "Daddy says you're a dick. What's a dick?"

"Mr. Fox is a *detective*," Warren said, his face red.

"Can I be a dick?" she asked.

"Go play with your brother."

"*Then* can I be a dick?" she persisted.

Warren pushed her toward her brother. She shrugged and bounced away.

Warren gave Jack an apologetic grimace. "I was calling you a private dick. It's not what it sounds like."

Jack eyed the boy with concern. "Shouldn't you...?"

The third kid, the littlest girl, at least Jack thought it was a girl, was making a game of ripping leaves off his rubber tree plant and shoving them down her pants.

"Warren, who the hell brings kids to...?"

"Had to," Warren said, "Couldn't get a sitter."

"I'm not discussing this while your kids are here," Jack said, standing. "Rachel will reschedule you."

Warren jumped up, eyes gleaming dangerously. "*Look*, instead of using the word we *need* to use, we'll use another word – like..."

"I'm not doing this," Jack answered firmly. "We are not having this discussion in front of your kids."

"If you don't tell me, I'm gonna' go crackpot!" Warren exploded.

"Daddy called the dick a crackpot," Flip-flop girl said, pointing her Barbie at Jack.

"Play with your brother!" Warren snapped.

The girl shrugged and proceeded to sit on the boy, bouncing on him like she was on a hippity-hop and using the back of his pants as a handle. The boy sent a desperate look in his father's direction.

"Warren…!" Jack pointed to the boy but Warren cut him off.

"Did she or didn't she - *go to the store?*" Warren asked, giving him a meaningful look.

Jack frowned, drumming his fingers.

"If she did go to the store, you got proof, right?" Warren asked. "Because, otherwise, I won't believe you."

"Proof that Sheila went to - *the store?*" Jack said skeptically.

"Yeah!" Warren yelled, "What else we talkin' about?"

"Warren, we reschedule or you hire somebody else." Jack stood up, jerking his chin toward the door.

Warren jumped up, "Come on, Jack! I paid good money!"

"You haven't paid me one hot dime."

"You know I'm good for it. As God is my witness, Jack, if you don't tell me – I'm going to…!" Warren's wild eyes scrabbled around the office as if searching for a weapon.

Jack slammed his hands on his desk and leaned forward menacingly, "You're going to *what?*"

Warren blinked, backing down. He got up, paced. He absentmindedly stepped over the little girl rolling on the floor in lumpy leaf-stuffed pants. Warren stopped at the desk and gave Jack a who-stole-my-teeth look. "Did Sheila go to the store? *Yes or no?*"

After a long moment, Jack pulled a file from the drawer and placed it on the desk.

Warren's eyes were glued to the folder.

Jack pressed his fist down on the folder. He said softly, "Not in front of the kids, Warren."

Warren's face quivered like he took a welterweight blow. He sat down heavily. After a long moment, he reached out a trembling hand for the file.

Flip-flop girl skipped over, tugged on Warren's sleeve. "Is mommy a hoe?"

Warren froze. "Where'd you hear that?"

"Gran-ma." She bit down on Barbie's left foot and let it dangle from her mouth as she waited for an answer.

"Don't do that. It's bad for your teeth," Warren said.

She bared her teeth and, laughing, danced away to commence torturing her brother. Warren stared at her, one cheek muscle twitching.

"You hired me to find out the truth," Jack said.

Warren grunted like a wounded animal.

Jack examined him with shrewd but sympathetic eyes. "Are you going to be all right, Warren?"

Warren looked away, wiping the water from his cheeks with his shaking hand. He shook his head.

Jack slid the folder into the drawer.

"Can't trust women," Warren muttered.

Jack shoved a card across the desk. "Here's the card of a good marriage counselor. Mention my name and you might get a discount."

"They're not even my kids," Warren said.

"You're kidding!"

Warren didn't seem to hear.

Irritated with himself for his outburst, Jack assumed his most professional voice. "Warren, if you need the photos, you can have your lawyer contact me."

It took several minutes for Warren to muster the energy to round up the kids and propel them out of Jack's office with a vague promise of a check in the mail. Jack was left in their wake with a bare-assed rubber tree, a pink Barbie shoe and the boy's saliva stains on the carpet.

Jack glanced at the door that Warren had exited through and his breath caught. Sitting in his waiting room were the most amazing pair of legs he'd ever set eyes on. He couldn't see the rest of the woman but the legs were stunning. He felt himself moving toward them with the exhilaration of a surfer caught in the belly of a dream wave.

Please let her face be half as perfect as those legs.

Reaching the doorway, he heard Rachel say, "Mr. Fox, this is Ms. Jennifer Hargrove."

Jack smiled politely, not daring to breathe. The woman turned her face up to him and Jack felt a jolt of horror hit him like a cattle prod. He staggered back, slamming into the wall.

CHAPTER THREE

Bring in the bottled lightning, a clean tumbler, and a corkscrew.

—*Charles Dickens*

Bud Orlean stared at the marriage therapist and his wife in horror. Despite the fact that he adored his wife and was shelling out an obscene amount of money for the counseling, he felt a steely determination to resist.

They were crazy!

He wasn't old and he sure as spit wasn't ready to retire. No power on earth was going to get him to turn in his badge and walk away from being Phoenix's top homicide detective. He loved his job and he wasn't about to don a Hawaiian shirt and cruise the Caribbean playing Bridge with a bunch of old farts.

At sixty-four, Bud had already shrunk two inches from his high school height of six-foot-two. He remembered the shock he had felt when, several years ago, the ridiculously young medical assistant said aloud, "Six-foot-even" like she hadn't just called out the beginning of a slow descent into a grave.

He was shrinking!

It was that moment when he realized that it was all downhill unless he hung on to his manhood with every fiber of his being, and the only way to do that was to *work*.

Sure, he wasn't as young as he used to be, but he still went to the gym three times a week and sweated it out to AC/DC's "Back in

Black" as he struggled to keep some semblance of shape. His muscles were still solid. Only his belly, out over his belt, made him wince when he accidentally caught a glimpse of himself in a mirror. His grey hair was dignified but thinning and he found to his disgust that, as the years went on, he was shaving not just his face but the shaving had now expanded to his ears and nostrils. He wore a light grey suit and white shirt without a tie, which, for Phoenix, was overdressed, but he prided himself on looking the part of the professional police detective that he was.

Bud squinted at Dr. Tanya's diploma that hung on the wall over his wife's head. He still harbored a sharp suspicion that she bought it from the back of Mad magazine. Of course, she hadn't; he had run a full background check on her and she came up clean.

"How do you feel about what your wife expressed, Bud?" Dr. Tanya asked.

Bud grimaced, too irritated to answer. He took a deep calming breath. Losing your temper was the lowest form of human emotion and revealed a weak mind. To think logically and remain in control of your emotions was the sign of a superior mind. To his surprise, as he got older, he was finding it harder to control his emotions and keep his mouth shut.

The last two years had been trying. Bunnie was constantly pushing him to retire and he'd lost his temper on several occasions, which filled him with a deep sense of self-loathing at his lack of control. Being at home with Bunnie was like walking on eggshells, which was another reason why he needed work more then ever. It was all about controlling your emotions and being logical.

It's what separates us from the degenerates.

Dr. Tanya gave him a quizzical look. "Are you listening to your wife, Bud?"

Bud grimaced, knowing that if Dr. Tanya's mother got hacked to pieces and mailed to Peoria, she'd consider Bud her new best friend and sure as heck wouldn't be taking sides against him with his wife.

"I'm not retiring," Bud said in a firm voice.

Bunnie pointed at Bud, "They offered him early retirement and he won't do it! He'd rather be out there with gang-banging meth-murderers than be at home with his wife."

"Are you hearing what your wife is saying, Bud?" The doctor asked.

Bunnie waved her hand in exasperation, "Listening is *not* Bud's problem! He always listens. In fact, I wish he listened less."

Bud made a face. As usual, Bunnie was being overly dramatic because she had a fresh audience.

It always amazed Bud that he married such a tsunami of emotional, illogical feminine energy. Bud's eyes lingered on the curves and rolls of Bunnie's body that were haphazardly crammed in her pink velour bejeweled tracksuit. From her bright blue eyes to her Z-Coil shoes that kept her bouncing through her day like the force of nature that she was, Bud was disgusted to find that he was as attracted to her as the day he first saw her when she was eighteen years old.

"Do you have any hobbies, Bud?" the doctor asked.

"Ha!" Bunnie exclaimed, "His only hobby is murder!"

The doctor smiled nervously, "Are there any other, uh, activities you enjoy?"

"A man should have a hobby, right?" Bunnie looked at the doctor, who was examining Bud with narrowed eyes.

Don't project, doc. I'm not your daddy or the guy that did you wrong.

"What is it that appeals to you about your job?" Dr. Tanya asked. "Justice? Catching the bad guy?"

The hunt.

"I'm not going to retire," Bud stated.

"What about our marriage? What about *me*?" Bunnie shrieked.

The doctor gave Bunnie a cautionary look. Reluctantly, Bunnie sat back in her chair, tossing her head so that the platinum ponytail bobbed spastically.

"Bud," the doctor looked at him, "Do you have any other interests?"

"Chip," Bud said without hesitation.

"He's in college. He's gone. Get over it." Bunnie crossed her arms.

"He might come back to Phoenix," Bud said.

"Are you crazy? Some girl is going to clap eyes on Chip, drag him off by the short hairs to live near *her* parents in Long Island, Krakow or the burg of butt-spaz-tattoo for all we know."

"Krakow?" Bud asked incredulously. "How did you come up with Krakow?"

"What's wrong with Krakow?" Bunnie demanded. "Don't tell me that big fancy medical school doesn't have girls from Krakow."

"Odds are higher that he'll end up with a girl from the burg of posterior-aspect-spaz-tattoo."

"Okey-dokey now, what's our 'timeout' word?" Dr. Tanya said, nervously holding her hands in a "T".

"Not Krakow," Bud muttered.

"Chip's not coming back," Bunnie scowled.

"What's our word?" The doctor asked hopefully.

Bud and Bunnie reluctantly looked and each other and simultaneously muttered, "Bunion."

"Let's talk about Chip," Dr. Tanya said. "Let's talk about what Chip-not-moving-back-to-Phoenix *looks like*."

Bud and Bunnie glared at each other.

"Okay," the doctor smiled at Bud, "Let's pretend someone has a gun to your head."

Bud shot her a look.

"Figuratively speaking, that is," she continued. "If you had to choose a hobby, what's the first thing that comes to your mind?"

"Spousal abuse," Bud said dryly.

"You and what army?" Bunnie scowled.

"That's good! Bud is expressing his *frustration*," Dr. Tanya said. "Let's explore that."

"I'm sorry to disappoint you, Bunnie. I'm not going to retire."

"I'll leave you!" Bunnie jabbed her finger in the air. "Cha-*ching* goes your pension 'cause Bunnie is gonna cruise!"

"You get seasick."

"My *future* hot young stud boyfriend, *who is a doctor*, will prescribe Dramamine!"

"He's going to *need* to be a doctor so he can wheel you around in your wheelchair while everyone asks him: how's your mother today?"

Bunnie gasped in horror. "Oh - no - you - didn't!"

Did.

Bunnie spun toward the doctor, "Do you see what I put up with? How am I supposed to deal with *that*?"

Bud said, "I've given you a good life, a house, a kid – all I want in return is to keep working. Is that too much to ask?"

The doctor held her hands in a "T" as Bunnie went nose-to-nose with Bud.

"Bunion. *Bunion*," the doctor called out as she jumped up and began moving away from them.

"It's *me* who has given *you* a good life, Bud Orlean! It's *me* who has cooked and cleaned and kept you and Chip in clean socks and underwear! You need to retire! I want to enjoy what's left of our life before we end up shriveled up in some nursing home too damned demented to put in our own teeth!"

Dr. Tanya's back was against the wall, her hands out. "Bunion! BUNION!"

"Shut up!" Bud and Bunnie shouted.

In a scurry of size ten Birkenstocks, the doctor made her escape.

Bud opened his mouth to speak but was interrupted as his cell phone vibrated. Like professional boxers separated by a ref, Bud and Bunnie stepped away from each other.

Bud felt the familiar sense of self-loathing at losing his temper sweep over him. He took a shaky breath and read the message. It was from his partner, Jenson. It was a call to duty.

Murder.

Bunnie picked up her purse and snapped, "You wearing sunscreen?"

Bud nodded.

She grabbed his face in her hands and locked her eyes on his, "Is today a good day to die?"

Bud held her eyes with matching intensity and answered, "*Not today.*"

Bunnie released him. Bud headed for the door.

"Bud?"

Bud turned, impatient to be gone.

"I will leave you," she said softly.

He stared at her.

I can't stop.

He didn't say it aloud but he had no doubt she heard his words.

Her lips tightened.

Bud flinched like she'd struck him. Before she could say anything, Bud was gone.

Adrenaline pumping, he moved as fast as his right knee and his sixty-four years on earth would allow. Once in the sunlight, Bud felt his uneasiness slip away. He hurried toward his truck, his eyes gleaming with raw hunger for the hunt.

I can't stop.

CHAPTER FOUR

Change your life today. Don't gamble on the future, act now, without delay.

—Simone de Beauvoir

Enid snuck another look at the woman's amazingly gorgeous legs. Enid glanced down at her own legs and grimaced at her faded denims and battered Converse sneakers.

If I had legs like that...

"Would you like a bottled water?" the receptionist asked. A placard declared she was "Rachel" and Enid was comforted to see that she was also sneaking looks at the woman's legs.

Leg-woman grinned and patted her huge purse. "You kidding? I don't go to the mailbox without water."

"How about you?" Rachel asked Enid.

Enid shook her head. Rachel went back to her computer.

The bus had gotten into Phoenix three hours ago, which had given Enid enough time to wash up in the bus station bathroom, have a fast food meal and walk the thirteen blocks to the Jack Fox Detective Agency. She had loitered another twenty minutes in the lobby of his building, which was old but clean, until she had gathered the courage to get on the elevator.

Leg-woman jumped in the elevator at the last moment. On the third floor, Enid was surprised when the leg-woman also entered the Jack Fox Detective Agency. Enid hesitated and signed in as Ivanna Hamm, since she was still hungry and envisioning a ham sandwich.

From the sign-in sheet, Enid divined that leg-woman's name was "Jeni", with the 'i' in the shape of a heart.

So ninth-grade!

There were only two chairs in the reception room. Enid and Jeni sat next to each other, their elbows almost touching.

Jeni was stacked four inches higher than her actual height of five-foot-eight with the help of chunky red heels. Even to Enid's untrained eyes, Jeni's outfit had all the subtlety of a bullhorn in announcing that Jeni had more than a passing acquaintance with poles.

For twenty minutes, they listened as a series of loud voices and strange "thunks" emanated from behind the door that they were waiting to enter.

Finally, the door was yanked open and a squall of kids spilled into the reception room. A man trudged out, herding them toward the exit like a worn-out giant trudging after a swarm of alley cats.

Enid's mouth went dry and her heart pounded to the point of hurt, like when she was a kid and sat on the curb watching the parade and the drum section passed too close. The horrible pounding reverberated through her whole body, leaving her feeling like she wanted to run away. She fixed her eyes on the door, not daring to breathe.

Is that him?

The man who came to the door was in late thirties. His thick brown hair and hazel eyes in a bronzed face seemed rather average – until he spoke.

"Hello," he said in a masculine voice that was as smooth as Velveeta. Suddenly, she saw that he *was* handsome. Enid stared at him, looking for any sign of resemblance.

With no warning, the man's face drained of color and he staggered back. Enid glanced at Jeni, who looked equally surprised at his strange behavior.

Enid watched the play of emotions on his face. With obvious difficulty, he gathered himself together and gestured for both of them to come into his office.

Jeni hopped up and went into the office. Jack gave Enid an expectant look. In a flash, Enid realized that the man mistakenly thought that she was with Jeni and was waiting for her to come into his office also.

He thinks I'm with her...

Before she could think better of it, Enid jumped up and followed Jeni into the office. She sat in a chair by the door, several feet behind Jeni.

While Jack was walking around his desk and had his back turned toward them, Jeni shot Enid a questioning glance. Enid leaned forward and mouthed, "I'm with him." She gestured toward the unseeing Jack.

Jeni smiled politely and turned her attention back to Jack.

Jack sat at his desk and gave Jeni a forced smile.

Enid stared at the man who her mother claimed was her real father. To her surprise, she felt a knot of anger tighten in her stomach. Without warning, she could feel her face contorting into a scowl so deep that it hurt her teeth.

What kind of jerk abandons his daughter?

CHAPTER FIVE

All paid jobs absorb and degrade the mind.

—Aristotle

For one horrible moment, Jack thought that Stella-psycho-Monroe had come back to put the squeeze on him and what little bit of money she hadn't already drained out of his checking account. Stella Monroe was a sociopath, a full-fledged psycho – *and his first wife.*

Jeni Hargrove was her spitting image – with better legs. Like Stella, everything about Jeni's appearance was calculated to be the embodiment of a hormonal schoolboy's fantasy. Unlike Stella, a closer look at Jeni left Jack startled to see an aristocratic beauty cleverly hidden under tight clothing, heavy makeup and a bevy of hardcore daddy issues. He could taste her cloying perfume that teased the space between them.

Jack's eyes flickered over Jeni's face, making damn sure it wasn't Stella.

She ain't Stella.

Jack looked at the little nutcracker of a girl that sat by the door. She was scowling at him like he'd ridden her mama hard, put her up wet and left her screwed and tattooed by the side of the barn.

The angry girl looked too old to be Jeni's kid. Jack figured that she was most likely her little sister.

"Join the party." Jack gestured for Enid to join them.

The girl's scowl deepened. She got up and sat down in a chair next to Jeni.

Jesus, she looks like she's trying to pass a bag of antique tacks.

"Do we know each other?" Jeni asked, examining Jack curiously.

"No." Jack answered too fast to sound honest even to him.

Jack opened his mouth to ask the angry kid her name when Jeni shoved a photograph across the desk.

"I need to find my mother," Jeni said, her voice quivering. "My real mother."

He picked up the photo, dismissing any thoughts of the girl.

The photograph showed a smiling woman who was cheesecaking for the camera in a black bikini. Her figure was perfect; her face was not. Jack's attention was arrested by her dark eyes under slanting eyebrows that were like a raven's wings that cut upward on a pale winter sky.

Venus flytrap eyes.

Jack glanced at Jeni, comparing her to the woman in the photo.

Zero resemblance.

"Who took the picture?" Jack said, curious who the "fly" behind the camera was.

"She hadn't met my stepfather yet so I don't think it was him," Jeni's voice faltered. "I thought she was my mother, but that photo was taken one month before I was born."

"You were adopted?" Jack asked.

"She says I'm hers."

Jack turned over the photo, noting the time stamp: July 4, 1988. "She wasn't pregnant with you and you're not adopted. Was there a surrogate mother?"

"She keeps saying I'm hers. She's lying!" Jeni shot Enid an embarrassed look and Enid gave her an encouraging smile. Jeni grabbed a business card from Jack's desk and started tearing off bits of it, dropping the pieces onto his desk.

Jack leaned back, studying Jeni's eyes.

Stella…

Jeni continued tearing at the card. Jack glanced at Enid, who was giving him a look like she caught him raping the family dog.

"Everything okay?" he asked Enid.

She answered with a scowl.

A noise came from behind a door leading into Jack's private office. They were currently sitting in his "client" office that he only used for business clients. A fleeting shadow darkened the cloudy glass that separated his private office from the client office. A frown bit across Jack's face. Just as fleetingly, the frown disappeared. He turned politely to Jeni. "Your goal is to find out the identity of your biological mother. Anything else?"

"I want the truth!" Jeni said, grabbing a new business card and tearing off bits. Her cheeks blotched an unattractive red.

Jack waited with a silence calculated to invite more information.

"I'd rather be crazy on the truth than sane on lies," Jeni said, her voice breaking.

"What do you think the truth is?" Jack's eyes gleamed.

Jeni stared at him, confused. She reached for a card but Jack moved the cardholder out of her reach. He smiled apologetically, "Almost out."

"Cheap bastard," Enid hissed under her breath.

"What?" Jack shot her a look of surprise.

Enid glared at him.

Jack frowned and turned his attention to Jeni.

Jeni took a deep breath and said, "I don't know what the truth is. That's why I'm here."

"Fair enough," Jack said. He pulled a contract out of a drawer, set it on the desk. He decided to run some angles on her, see how she reacted. Jack looked pointedly at her outfit, "What do you do for a living, Jeni?"

Jeni raised her chin defiantly. "I'm in nursing school. Full scholarship."

Jack raised his eyebrows.

Jeni shifted uncomfortably.

Here it comes…

Jeni blurted out, "I've had some troubles but I got my life together. I want to know who my real mother is – why she gave me up."

Artsy. Not a direct hit but winding up to make the pitch…

Jeni shifted forward, turning on the sex appeal like she was flipping a well-worn switch. "I was told you could help me. I was told you're the best."

Money shot. Just like Stella…

Jack felt his stomach twist with disgust.

Whatever school they learn it at – they must have his mug shot up 'cause they know me when they see me.

He took his revenge on Stella by leaving Jeni blinking at dead air. He got up, dug through a file cabinet. He turned, held out a different contract, "We updated our contract." He hit a buzzer. "Rachel will go over my contract and fees with you."

Jeni's mouth fell open in astonishment. "I –I don't have a lot of money. I *am* a student..."

Rachel entered. Jack handed her the contract, nodding at Jeni. "Standard contract, Rachel."

"Oh, I was hoping..." Jeni said weakly.

Jack smiled coldly, gesturing for Rachel to escort them out.

"She said she's broke!" Enid jumped up angrily.

Everyone looked at Enid in surprise.

Jack said, "Red Cross is two blocks over, kid. I'm not running a charity."

"She's a student!" Enid exploded with vehemence that caught Jack off guard. "Give her the student discount!"

"Standard fees," Jack said stubbornly.

Enid looked pointedly around the room. "Don't look like you're rolling in cash to me."

Why you little...!

Enid said, "If you don't give her a student discount, we're walking. We'll hire some other two-bit jerk who isn't rude and doesn't have a bunch of kids out there he doesn't even *know* about!"

Jeni's mouth fell open in astonishment.

Jack turned to Jeni, eyes flashing. "Why don't you take your little sister home, get her back on her meds."

Jeni gave Jack a startled look, "I thought she was with you?"

Enid froze, a jackrabbit caught in the crosshairs.

Jack looked from Jeni to Enid, confounded.

In a shot of motion, Enid made a break for the door but Jack sprang from behind the desk and got across the room with surprising speed. He grabbed Enid by the arm, pulled her to a hard stop.

"What the hell...?" Jack growled.

Enid stared up at him in fury and, before Jack realized what was happening, he howled in pain as she sunk her teeth into his forearm. He stumbled back, clutching his arm and staring at her like she was a demon.

Enid jabbed her middle finger in his face, turned and vanished.

Jack looked down at his arm. Blood was seeping through his shirt.

Psycho punk kids!

Rachel rushed to his side. "Are you okay?"

Jack ran into the hallway as the stairwell door was closing. Jack started to go after her but he stopped himself, breathing hard. What was he going to do once he caught her? Spank her?

"Her name was Ivanna Hamm!" Rachel said, "I thought they were together."

"Don't these brats have parents? They need to lock up the nut-job parents who don't know how to control their kids!" Jack exploded. Grimacing, he examined his bloody arm.

"She told me she was with you," Jeni said, "I thought she was an assistant or something."

Jack shot her an incredulous look. A teenage brat assistant? Jeni Hargrove had great legs but she wasn't the sharpest tool in the shed.

I got fooled too…

Jack said, "They should make people pass a test before they have kids!" He gestured for Jeni to return to the office. "Rachel will go over the contract with you."

"How 'bout what the kid said – about the student discount?"

Jack gave her a "you gotta be kidding" look but she gave him an angelic smile and he felt himself slipping down into the Venus flytrap power of her eyes.

Maybe that is her real mother…

He mentally shook himself. No way in hell he was going for another Stella! He walked Jeni into the reception room and handed her off to Rachel. He escaped into his office.

On impulse, he stalked to the door and shouted to Rachel, "Make a sign – no kids allowed! Under penalty of I will kick anyone's ass who brings in anything that can't vote, drink or cuss out their mama!

I. Hate. Kids.

CHAPTER SIX

A jug fills drop by drop.

—*Buddha*

I won't rest until I hunt down the degenerate that did this to you.

The words echoed in his mind as Bud stood in the desert, looking down at a skull that had been bleached dry by the abrasive desert environment. The thought that anyone could think they had the right to kill another person always filled Bud with a steely determination. Bud was the hunter and the killer was now his prey.

The forensic team was methodically digging, labeling and bagging evidence from the shallow desert grave.

The grave wasn't a grave at all and wouldn't have been found if Celia McCraw, grandmother of four, hadn't overturned her ATV and landed nose to nose-socket with the skull. Bruised and bloody, Celia had refused to seek medical attention until long after the police arrived. She and her husband, Thomas, were still sitting on their ATVs, quietly talking as they watched the police work.

Bud walked the perimeter of police tape and markers that staked out the area where the bones had been found. The area was Agua Caliente and consisted of old mines and an extensive network of narrow washes and sandy trails. It wasn't unusual to stumble onto a landscape of lava or an ancient Native American petroglyph, and the remote setting seemed custom-made for dumping bodies.

Bud observed each individual of the homicide team. It always struck him as an intricate choreographed dance production. Everyone had their part and played their roles to perfection. Photographers were the voyeuristic, anti-social peepers who used their cameras like barbed wire fencing to keep a barrier between themselves and the world. Forensic specialists were the dark-edged academics who solved sinister puzzles in the safety of hidden laboratories. Police were the attention-seeking authority junkies arresting what they secretly desired to be – a rule-flouting member of Joe-Wicked-Public.

Bud smiled to himself at his description of his own profession. Homicide detectives were the curious, unrelenting maggots munching their way through society's rotting flesh to get to the *who* and the *why* and then to surgically excise the offending degenerate.

That's on a good day.

Bud felt the gathering of a million questions that would cut at his waking hours until he had his prey quarried and slumped behind a defense attorney. Bud imagined himself in the witness box, staring into the eyes of…

Who?

Bud tried to visualize the person but saw only a shadow of a person wearing a cheap suit and tie.

"Any thoughts?" Detective Jenson said as he walked to Bud's side, smiling like they were at a Sunday ice cream social.

Bud pushed back his Stetson that protected him from the Arizona sun. "How you doin', Jenson?"

"Never better. How's Bunnie?"

"Bunnie's Bunnie."

Jenson laughed, a pleasant sound.

Bud eyed him curiously. His stylish pairings were a constant fascination. He wore sharply creased khaki slacks, a pink polo shirt and a salmon-colored stitch fedora set at a jaunty angle that only Jenson could pull off without getting his behind kicked up and down a mean Phoenix street.

Jenson was Bud's partner and a shrewd detective. Underneath the silky exterior lay the heart of an expert marksman, an ex-Marine and a scathing intelligence that reveled in anyone who was blind enough to underestimate him.

Bud had never been one of those people.

A thought hit Bud and, with a sharp intake of breath, he bent to examine the skull.

"What?" Jenson gave him a keen look.

"Daniel Hargrove," Bud said slowly, testing out the sound of it.

Jenson let out a low whistle as he eyed the skull. "Mister heart-in-a-box finally shows up. They never found the rest of him?"

"Found is an interesting choice of words," Bud said wryly, thinking about the day the carefully wrapped cardboard box had arrived at the station. They hadn't *found* anything. The evidence that Daniel Hargrove had been brutally murdered had been mailed to police headquarters.

Daniel Hargrove had been a prominent Phoenix businessman and owner of a local bank who had gone missing over three years ago. It had graduated from a missing persons case to a homicide case when, three weeks after Daniel Hargrove's family had reported him missing, someone had taken the liberty of mailing his heart, which had been meticulously cut out of his body, to the police. Bud was convinced the killer was a family member who stood to benefit from an unusually large life insurance policy.

"They found his Masonic ring in the left ventricle of the heart. Is that the top or bottom?" Jenson asked.

"Bottom."

Jenson said, "The killer mails the victim's heart to the police, now we have a body, insurance has to pay out, but - I wonder what it *means*? These things always mean something – even if the killer doesn't realize it himself."

"It was a big ring shoved into the biggest hole in the heart. My money is on the fact it was the path of least resistance."

"After cutting a heart out of a man's body, I find it hard to believe one would then take the path of least resistance," Jenson said wryly.

Bud gave a humorless smile.

Jenson continued, "As if that wasn't enough, we also get the victim's molar in the right atrium and his index finger in the right ventricle. Overkill, I'd say. Like the killer didn't trust us to run DNA. Or thought we were idiots."

"Killers always think the police are idiots. It's one of our main advantages – being underestimated."

"And our prime suspect still shacked up sweet as candy in a Scottsdale mansion."

Bud rubbed his jaw, which throbbed with a sudden dull ache. He reminded himself that he needed to make an appointment with his dentist.

They stood in silence, gazing at the skull. The sun was slipping low. A purple-pink glow was taking up residence in the west.

"I think it's time to pay a visit to our favorite prime suspect," Bud said as he turned and headed toward his truck.

"I'd wait till we get a firm I.D. on the body. You really want to stir up that hornet's nest?" Jenson said, giving him a knowing look.

"That bloodsucker is probably waiting for me," Bud said, surprised at the emotion in his voice.

Driving towards North Scottsdale, Bud's thoughts turned to his last meeting with the person that he was convinced had mailed him the package containing Daniel Hargrove's heart.

At the memory of their last meeting, Bud felt a hot surge of anticipation in his gut. He relished the thought of picking up the scent of the trail that had left off colder than a corpse on ice.

CHAPTER SEVEN

Sometimes I've believed as many as six impossible things before breakfast.

—Lewis Carroll

Her heart thudding with fear, Enid slid into a cracked red vinyl booth of a clean but rundown diner that sat across the street from Jack's office building. She had a perfect view of the entrance and was watching nervously for the police to show up. If Jack Fox had called the police, her plan was to dart out the back of the restaurant and run.

She couldn't believe that she had actually *bit* Jack Fox! Until she felt her teeth chomping into his arm, she would *never* have believed that she was capable of doing such a thing. The rage that she had felt for him had caught her completely off guard. She had imagined their first meeting as awkward but civilized. She hadn't expected that she would completely lose her cool and bite him like some rabid animal!

After she ran out of the building, she'd spent ten hairy minutes hiding in an alley. Curiosity had gotten the better of her and she had decided to go to the diner where she could watch the entrance to his building.

"What can I get for you, young lady?" Mona Ruben was an attractively voluptuous woman in her early thirties. She wore a form-fitting uniform with a red apron that ended in a boisterous bow. Mona was to waitressing what a Flemish Baroque painter was to big chicks: she made it look good.

Enid shook her head, unsure if she had enough money for anything more than an orange juice.

"How 'bout some H2O to wet the whistle?" Mona plucked the menu off the table and handed it open-faced to Enid. "The huevos rancheros will make you miss your mama."

Enid gave her a startled look.

Sensing she hit a chord, Mona smiled pleasantly, "Look it over. I'll be back before you can cut a switch."

Enid watched Mona disappear into the kitchen and dug into her backpack and pulled out an anemic wad of cash. Frowning, she counted the bills. To her amazement, she had blown through the bulk of her money and didn't have enough cash to pay for a meal – much less a decent place to stay the night. She bit her lip, wondering why she hadn't waited the extra two days it would have taken her mother to cash her next paycheck. Her mother's whiskey kitty would've been fat with cash in one of its many hiding places: a plastic baggy duct-taped to the back of the toilet, a mayonnaise jar under the sink, an envelope taped on the dirty blades of the lawn mower…

Or, or, or…

Enid sighed, wondering if her expertise at finding whiskey kitties would ever come in handy in the real world. Luckily, her mother performed her paranoid hiding sprees when she was nine-kites-to-the-dog-faced-wind, which resulted in what Enid dubbed whiskey kitty amnesia, which meant easy pickin's with no explanations. Enid occasionally felt a twang of guilt but reminded herself that she mostly used the money for food and paying bills that her mother neglected.

And bus tickets.

"Made the big decision?" Mona said.

Enid looked up with wide eyes, "I – uh –I'm sort of on a budget."

Mona leaned in confidentially, "What's the ceiling?"

"Five dollars and thirty-five cents."

"You like heuvos rancheros?"

Enid looked sheepish. She didn't want to admit she didn't have enough money for whatever the heck a heuvos rancheros was.

Mona leaned in confidentially, "I don't want to hurt his feelings but Cook whipped up a batch for me special, but all morning I been poppin' wheelies on a Southern breeze."

Enid's forehead wrinkled, unsure.

"You'd be doing me a favor if you ate 'em for me."

Enid started to protest but Mona waved away her words and disappeared into the kitchen.

Enid's embarrassment was overruled by her stomach, which was starting to sound like a NASCAR lineup.

Maybe if I pretend I'm waiting for a bus, I can sleep at the bus station.

CHAPTER EIGHT

If you can't run with the dogs, don't get off the porch.

—Southern Saying

After scrubbing his arm with soap and water and hoping that he wouldn't contract rabies or some other flesh-eating disease from the crazy girl's bite, Jack had returned to the office where Rachel was still reviewing the contract with Jeni. He had briefly contemplated filing a report with the police, but didn't feel up to the hassle.

Once in the client office, he stood in front of the door that separated it from his private office. He hesitated, his scowl deepening. During the interview with Jeni, he had heard a noise coming from within his office and knew that there was trouble on the other side of the door, waiting for him.

He opened the door and stepped in. Past the beat-up desk sat a well-worn leather couch. The couch was usually empty and inviting. Today, Petunia O'Donnell sat on the couch like a curled-up kitten ready to play…

Or claw.

At thirty-three, Petunia exuded an unmistakable, albeit slightly crude, sex appeal. Where Jeni was all tan long legs that reminded one of an impossibly smooth silk road that beckoned to be followed, Petunia was a dangerous combination of compact curves that, as recently as two weeks ago, had left Jack intoxicated with pleasure.

Jack couldn't help but run his eyes over those oft-explored curves. In retaliation, *her* eyes devoured his body with self-assured ownership.

Petunia's green eyes were accented with a masterful application of makeup, her shoulder-length red hair was lustrous and shining, and her lips were painted a rich red that harkened back to a 1950s Hollywood siren. Her dress was black with a red cherry design that was cinched at the waist, and her black heels would, on any other woman, have been thought demure. Petunia, however, had the conjuring power to transform even the most demure dress into something vaguely naughty.

Jack didn't try to hide his annoyance as he stripped off his jacket and threw it on a chair.

"I don't like her," Petunia purred.

"You don't like anybody," Jack retorted. He opened the desk drawer and grabbed his wallet. He frowned, hand scrabbling around the drawer, looking for his keys.

Petunia held up his keys. "I like *you*."

"Keep it in your pants, Petunia," Jack said curtly, shutting the drawer with a snap.

Undeterred, Petunia uncurled herself, slid off the couch and walked toward him. Even in stilettos, she walked softly, which gave her a stealthy approach that Jack found disconcerting.

"I miss you," she whispered, leaning into him.

"It's over," Jack said brusquely, trying to ignore the sensation of her dimpled white hand on his chest.

"You *promised* you'd make me happy!"

Jack scowled, trying to ignore the memory of the day he *did* promise to make her happy.

Shit.

Petunia's eyes glowered, "You *did* promise."

It didn't count – she knew that, didn't she?

Jack compressed his lips, shifted uncomfortably.

"Take me to lunch," Petunia demanded.

"Can't afford your kind of lunch."

"It's on me," Petunia stood on tiptoes and whispered into his ear. "Or under me, or behind me."

Shivers ran down Jack's spine, the purr of her voice echoed softly in his head.

Jack's mind flashed back to the first time he had seen Petunia. She had worn a form-fitting cobalt blue dress and looked more brilliant than the perfect Scottsdale sky that hung like a cathedral ceiling above the crowds at the Phoenix Open. Jack had been working a routine surveillance on a husband whose wife suspected him of cheating. The husband was cheating – with Petunia.

Jack fixed the cheating husband in the crosshairs of the lens of his camera and caught his breath when he saw Petunia licking sugar off the rim of a specialty drink. He had been instantly drawn to her X-rated eyes that gazed up at the sucker that he was there to bust.

The wife got the photos. Not to mention the kids, the McMansion, the pool with the waterfall cascading over giant plastic rocks and a truckload of money.

Jack got Petunia.

Things were good – damned good – for over half a year.

Until the promise racket noise hit high decibels.

Uneasy at the feelings that Petunia was a master of invoking within him, Jack frowned and moved away from her.

Petunia petulantly stamped her foot, "I'm here to hire you!"

Jack shot her a "yeah right" look.

Petunia tossed her hair and feigned a nonchalance that Jack knew she did not feel. "I think my husband's cheating."

"Your husband is not the cheating type," Jack answered, grateful to be on firmer ground.

"I'll pay you," Petunia stubbornly pushed on. "For your services."

"Thanks but no thanks." Jack headed for the door. "You remember how to let yourself out."

Springing forward, Petunia grabbed him, her arms encircling his neck. Her lips pressed into his and Jack felt a punch of pleasure as their uneven breath tangled. Jack found himself trying to break free of the kiss with all the willpower of a bee in hot butter.

Soiled memories fought their way up and Jack pushed Petunia back, scowling, "It's no good!"

Petunia looked up at him, lips open, eyes inviting. Waiting.

Jack scowled, turned on his heels and headed out. He called over his shoulder. "Go home! Try to be a good apple."

Petunia stepped forward, eyes snapping with anger and voice thick with taunting, "Since when do you like good apples?"

CHAPTER NINE

In this world a man must either be an anvil or hammer.

—Henry Wadsworth Longfellow

Bud was five minutes from his destination in North Scottsdale when he got the call. The one call he couldn't ignore. With a sigh, he turned the truck and headed to Phoenix where he arranged to meet Larry at a coffee shop on Thunderbird and Seventh.

Seven years ago, Bud started attending Alcoholics Anonymous meetings to get closer to a suspect. It wasn't his case and he would never have gotten involved except…

Bunnie cried for a week over what that degenerate did.

The degenerate in question, Steve Caldwell, was a mild- mannered CPA in his mid-thirties whose wife and two kids disappeared. The wife, Linda, was a soft-spoken woman who bought Avon products from Bunnie. When Linda hadn't returned her phone calls, Bunnie went to their house.

Bunnie indignantly related the incident back to Bud that night. "That bean-counting butt-wipe stood in the door big as the dick he is and tried to tell me Linda left him and moved back to Maryland to live with her parents. He must think I'm dumber than a bag of hammerheads if he thinks I buy that bunk of bullshit! First off, she'd *never* move back to Maryland because the tire dump five miles down the road is still on fire and they can't put it out and Mikey has asthma so there's no way that is happening. Second, she would never *not* pick up her Avon order – it had the Skin-So-Soft-Bug-Guard and she was desperate to get it because if there's a flea in a five-mile radius, it's on Mikey. She loves those kids and there is no way she'd take them back to Maryland – with burning tires and no bug guard! *Duh.* Besides, he *looks* like a serial killer. His eyes are too close together and he's got that crazy left nostril tic. Why don't you go down there and scare him or something? Let him know *we're onto him!* What's the use of having a badge if you can't push people around every once in a while?"

Bud had tracked down Linda's parents and was surprised to find out they had recently filed a missing person's report. Linda's mother was on the verge of hysteria when Bud explained that Steve said that Linda left him and that she was driving back to Maryland to be with *them.* Steve claimed he hadn't called Linda or her parents because he wanted to give Linda her "space."

Within the week, the local news was saturated with stories about the missing woman and children. Steve was the prime suspect in their disappearance but, after a lengthy investigation, nothing was ever proven and no bodies were ever found.

Bunnie was convinced that Linda was dead and Steve was a cold-blooded killer. Months went by and the story faded.

Bunnie's suffering did not.

It cut Bud to the quick to see Bunnie suffer. He made it a point to get friendly with the detective working the case. When he found out that Steve went to Alcoholics Anonymous, Bud decided to attend several meetings.

Steve put on a show: the heartbroken, wrongly accused husband who pined for his family. He hinted that all had not been well. His wife had a temper and she periodically threatened to leave him, but he had refused to believe it - until it was too late.

Bud tried to become a sponsor to Steve and inadvertently become a sponsor to Larry, a sad-sack guy who was crazy in love with his pretty wife who was a serial cheater and only stayed married to Larry because of his exceptional group health insurance that she couldn't bear the thought of losing. Bud cursed his luck and was determined to get out of the sponsorship at the first opportunity, but the opportunity never arose.

At first, Bud treated going to the meetings like a chore, but to his surprise, he began looking forward to them. He liked listening to people bare their souls. He was used to hearing people bare their souls during the course of a murder investigation. This was different. This was a baring of souls that ended with more hope for the future. Nobody in the group ever confessed murder. They confessed horrible things, but not murder, which proved strangely uplifting to Bud.

He also liked the bad coffee and donuts.

Despite the fact that Bunnie knew nothing about his AA life, Bud's being a sponsor and attending AA meetings became the hobby that Bunnie kept insisting he get. Since he worked irregular hours, he never lied – except by omission. He justified not telling Bunnie about the meetings because he didn't want to get her hopes up about the case but, when Steve stopped showing up, Bud continued to go and simply kept his mouth shut about it.

Bud began to like Larry – if for no better reason than he seemed so accepting of the bad hand life kept shoving in his face. Bud didn't have the heart to back out of the sponsor relationship and spent seven years being an on-and-off sponsor to various members, but mostly Larry.

When Larry called him at home, Bunnie assumed that he was a friend from work with a drinking problem. She had complained on more than one occasion that Larry needed to join AA and stop acting like Bud was his sponsor.

Bud met Larry at a Starbucks on Seventh Street and Missouri where they sat on the patio under the misters.

"I know she's cheating on me," Larry said in a low desperate voice. "I should leave but I can't. I want a drink so bad!"

Bud listened as Larry talked about his wife. He knew better than to try to be a therapist.

After twenty minutes, Larry had fallen into a lull. Bud's cell phone rang. He glanced at the caller's name and said, "I have to take this."

Larry gestured that he was going to get them both refills.

When Larry returned, Bud's face was flushed red and he was rubbing his jaw that was throbbing like it was fractured.

"Everything okay?" Larry said.

Bud looked at him blankly, not registering the question.

"What's wrong?" Larry said, getting scared. "Did somebody die?"

"Not yet," Bud muttered through clenched teeth.

CHAPTER TEN

What do we live for, if not to make life less difficult for each other?

—*George Eliot*

Enid put the last of her cash, five dollars and thirty-five cents, under her scraped-clean plate. She couldn't believe that she had gone sixteen years without knowing that something as magical heuvos rancheros existed!

She knew it was a boneheaded move to leave the last of her money as a tip for Mona but something inside her urged her to it. She felt the need to put herself out and broke on the Phoenix concrete to see what kind of luck she could conjure up.

If I'm desperate enough – maybe it'll give me the courage to go back to the Jack Fox Detective Agency.

She shouldered her backpack and headed out the front door. The Phoenix sunshine struck her as startlingly different from the Florida weather she'd grown up in. The Phoenix sun seemed more honest than Florida's baggage of haze and humidity.

Enid's eyes caught Jeni coming out of the building and Enid furtively followed her. Jeni walked a city block before she reached a Honda Civic with enough dents to qualify it for a Purple Heart.

Jeni slid in and was in the process of grinding the gears to a painful start when Enid knocked on her window.

Jeni jumped like she'd been shot.

Enid made an apologetic face as Jeni rolled down the window.

"Hey," Enid said, feeling like an idiot.

Jeni surprised her by lighting up with a smile. "I owe you a big thanks! You got me a discount."

"How much?" Enid asked, smiling in response.

"Hey, what's up with you busting in like that? Why'd you *bite* him? What was *that* about?" Jeni eyed Enid with sudden suspicion.

"I think he's my dad," Enid blurted out.

Jeni's mouth fell open in surprise. "Wildfire! Does he know?"

"Um…"

"Oh my god!" Jeni interrupted, "*I'm* looking for my mom and *you* – you're looking for your dad! What are the odds?"

"I don't think he likes me."

"I wouldn't either if you took a chunk of meat out of *my* arm."

"I don't think he likes kids." Enid frowned.

"You're not a kid. How old are you? Sixteen? I was payin' light bills at sixteen."

"Would you mind – uh – giving me a lift to the bus stop?"

"You're not going to bite me, are you?"

Enid smiled sheepishly, shook her head.

"Plant the tush in the cush." Jeni waved at the passenger seat.

Enid gratefully circled the car and got in the passenger's side. Jeni hauled baby stuff off the passenger seat and threw it into the back. "Sorry for the mess."

"How many kids do you have?"

"One sweetheart of a little girl. I named her Faith after that chick on that soap opera who fell in love with the monk who had amnesia." Jeni sighed before she started grinding the gears again.

Enid flinched at the sound. "You want me to drive?"

"You have a license?" Jeni asked.

"Um…"

"Chinese fire drill!" Jeni hopped out, ran around the car and pushed a surprised Enid toward the driver's seat, forcing Enid to climb over the shift lever. A shrill catcall came from a passing truck. Jeni ignored it.

"Where to?" Enid asked, excited to be behind the wheel.

"Bus station, right?" Jeni shot Enid a look, "Hey, why are you going to the bus station? Aren't you going to tell him he's your dad?"

Enid checked the mirrors as she said, "I told you, I don't think he likes me."

"Big whup! If he's your dad, he's your dad."

Enid eased into traffic, "Do you like your – uh, fake mother?"

Jeni made a face, shrugged.

Enid hesitated, glanced at Jeni, "Um – would you know – do they…?"

"Spit it out."

"Do you think I'd get in trouble – if I slept at the bus stop tonight?" Enid blurted out, face red.

"Are you shittin' me?"

"Noo," Enid said, uncertain.

"I don't have any money if that's what you want. I'm barely keepin' my own ass above water." Jeni frowned.

"I don't want anything! I just wanted to make sure – I mean – they'll let me – *right?*" Enid gazed at her with worried eyes.

Jeni examined her. After a long moment, she cut loose a sigh. "You can stay with me. Turn right up here."

"But…"

"You babysit?" Jeni asked.

"Are you kidding? I was born babysitting!" Enid exclaimed, happily.

"What ages?"

"Thirty-four," Enid said, thinking about her mother.

Jeni raised her eyebrows in surprise.

CHAPTER ELEVEN

To think of shadows is a serious thing.

—Victor Hugo

Jack didn't know who he was more disgusted with – Petunia or himself. He strode into the reception room where Rachel met his eyes.

"Playing deaf, huh?" Jack said.

"Part of my job description," Rachel said cheerfully, holding out a sheaf of paper. "I already did some preliminary research on your new client, Jeni Hargrove."

"What about the part of your job description that includes keeping my private office *private*?" Jack jerked his thumb toward his office.

"If you can't keep her out of your office, how am I supposed to?" Rachel shot back.

"You're fired," Jack called over his shoulder as he headed out the door.

Rachel smiled and went back to her laptop.

After a moment, Jack stuck his head back in the door. "Get rid of her."

"Oh!" Startled, Rachel jumped up to perform the thankless job of hustling Petunia out of Jack's office.

Jack walked quickly down the stairs and pushed open the door leading to the street. Jack luxuriated in the face full of heat, which never failed to surprise him with its intensity. Cutting through traffic, his eyes caught on a dark sedan. The driver's face was hidden behind a newspaper.

Jack rubbed his chin thoughtfully, frowning.

He entered the diner and took a seat at the Formica counter next to Sam Waterstone. In his early forties, Sam sported a boyish face that was strangely counteracted by a cynical glint in his bright blue eyes. He nodded to Jack, munching on an overstuffed sandwich. On his belt hung his City of Phoenix detective's badge.

Jack said, "I need a favor."

Sam swallowed, roughly wiped his mouth and said, "Kids swore me on a stack of Harry-F-ing-Potters to make sure Uncle Jack comes over. Saturday. Four o'clock. *There!* Now maybe the little punks will get off my ass."

Mona sauntered up with a warm smile. "Hey Jack, the usual?"

"Sure thing. Plus a cheeseburger, well done." Jack eyed her appreciatively. "Lookin' good, Mona."

Eyes sparkling, Mona let out a 'Humph!' and headed toward the kitchen.

"For God's sake, I'm a married man," Sam said as he gripped his stomach and burped. "The last thing I need is to be caught in the crossfire of whatever it is that you two have going on. Go out with her already. You're giving me indigestion."

"You worked the Daniel Hargrove case, right?"

"That case is colder than my ex-wife's…." Sam took another bite of his sandwich, his words lost in his munching.

Mona placed a to-go coffee in front of Jack. She frowned at Sam. "P.G. it, Sam. This is a family establishment."

"How did you hear that?" Sam said, mouth full.

"I know what you said." Mona gave him a warning look as she walked away.

Jack said, "I need a copy of the case file. Anything you got."

"You working it?"

"Wallpaper. Working a fast-and-easy for the daughter."

"Which one? Legs, Brains or The Ghost?"

Jack shot him an incredulous look, "If the one I met ain't Legs – I'm in love with the one who is."

"Then you ain't seen Brains yet," Sam whistled softly. "Brick F-ing shithouse."

"Sam!" Mona threw him a warning look from the other end of the counter.

Sam blew her a kiss, "Love you too, Mona. If I wasn't already taken – you'd be in trouble."

Mona frowned, spun on her heels and disappeared into the kitchen.

Sam turned to Jack, "She wants me. She's sharpening her teeth on *you* to get to *me*."

Mona returned, carrying a take-out bag that she plunked on the counter in front of Jack.

"Ears burnin'?" Sam smiled lasciviously at Mona.

"Sam, you seem to forget that I know your wife and if I told her the things you say and how you act…"

"You mean the burping?"

"She'd lock you in the cellar and never let you out."

"That's how much you know. We don't have a cellar," Sam grinned.

Mona rolled her eyes, "If there were a *real* policeman around – I'd be tempted to file a sexual harassment complaint."

"*And* she's funny," Sam smiled.

Jack got out his wallet, gave Mona cash.

"Thanks, Jack." She smiled appreciatively and pocketed the money. Mona held up the edge of her skirt where a single thread hung. "You mind?"

Jack pulled out his switchblade and, holding it low so no one could see, he deftly sliced off the thread.

"Thanks." Mona smiled at him.

"You need to learn how to sew," Jack said.

"It's so much more fun to have you do it," Mona grinned.

Sam gripped his stomach and burped.

Mona flinched, ignoring Sam and smiling at Jack. "Don't be such a stranger, Jack."

From another table, a customer called out, "Excuse me, Miss?"

Mona hurried away.

"You think you can have the file for me by four o'clock?" Jack asked. "I can meet you here. Coffee is on me."

"Sure. I got nothing better to do," Sam said sarcastically. "It's not like it's *illegal* or anything."

"How're the kids?" Jack asked, ignoring the comment.

"Sharon wants to be a private detective like Uncle Jack. Never mind being a flatfoot cop like Pop."

"How 'bout Ernie?"

Sam makes a wry face, "Ernie's discovered the exciting new world of – *ballet*."

"Really?" Jack asked, surprised.

"Really."

"Is he good?" Jack asked.

"Scary good."

Jack laughed. Turning to leave, he walked past a surprised Mona and headed into the kitchen where a Hispanic dishwasher stared after him indignantly. Jack slipped out the back door that led into an alley. A Goth girl leaned against a brick wall, smoking. She gave Jack the once over, wrote him off and returned to her cigarette with black lipstick stains.

Jack entered a door that read "Ide Mania." He found himself in a storage room, his nostrils assailed by the acrid smell of hair chemicals. Jack straightened and walked with confidence into the beauty salon that smelled as pleasantly aromatic as the storage room smelled acrid. Three stylists were busy working on their clients.

The beautiful owner, Ide Flores, who looked like the Hispanic answer to Rita Hayworth, looked up with a frown as she demanded, "Who are you?"

Jack held up the to-go bag like it contained a rodent. "Call me if you have any more problems."

Jack strode out the front door and into the street. He approached the dark sedan from behind and gave a hard rap on the driver's window.

Frank Ficus let out a yelp and gripped his heart. Scowling, he rolled the window down and exclaimed, "Jesus Christ, Jack! You tryin' to kill me?"

At fifty-eight, Frank Ficus had resigned himself to the extra weight he'd long ago given up trying to lose. His nose showed the signs of early pugilist pursuits and, in his heyday, he'd prided himself on finishing any fight that someone else was daft enough to start. With every passing year, he moved slower but still packed a brick pile of a punch.

Jack held out the to-go bag that held a cheeseburger. "Well done. The way you like it."

Frank eyed it suspiciously.

Jack waved it closer to him so he could smell it.

Frank snatched the bag and suspiciously examined its contents.

"Who hired you to follow me, Franko?" Jack asked.

"I'm not one of your cheap dates who's going to blow you for a burger."

Jack opened his mouth with a slur against Frank's sister but remembered his sister died of breast cancer. It was more fun doing the sister insults when they were younger – before they all got married, fat or dead. "Tell Petunia's husband that he can stop spending his paycheck on detectives. It's over between me and her."

Frank's eyes widened in surprise as he exclaimed, "Jesus, Jack! Aren't you too old to be cattin' around after other men's wives? You never learn…"

"Tell him," Jack said, turning to go back to the office. He turned, pointed to Frank like they'd come to an understanding.

Frank shot him the finger and muttered, "Asshole."

Taking a hearty bite of the burger, Frank made a "this ain't bad" face. Mouth full, he called after Jack's retreating back, "You forgot the ketchup!"

CHAPTER TWELVE

I'm not interested in preserving the status quo; I want to overthrow it.

—*Niccolo Machiavelli*

Bud stared at Chip in horror. After several moments of floundering for something to say, he blurted out, "You can't *quit*!"

"You're the one who said I should," Chip answered calmly, picking up his duffel bag from the baggage carousel at Phoenix Sky Harbor International Airport. He tossed the bag over his shoulder and asked, "Where you parked, Pops?"

Chip Orlean was twenty-six and had a body and face that made straight men look twice. He was what a Southern ex-girlfriend's mother once called a tall glass of hot tea – with muscles. He was in the final weeks of his third year of medical school in Philadelphia and was on track to getting a residency that would allow him to become a cardiologist.

"*I said?* What the blazes are you talking about?" Bud sputtered.

"You told me to follow my heart."

"That's assuming your heart led you to finishing med school!" Bud roared, feeling sick with frustration and not caring that he was making a public scene.

Chip glanced nervously at the heads that were turning in their direction. Chip tried to guide him toward the exit. "Calm down, Pops. This isn't like you."

Bud shook off his arm, "We're not going anywhere until you tell me what is going on! Does this have something to do with a girl?"

"I wouldn't change the entire direction of my life because of *a girl*. What am I in? Seventh grade?"

Bud glared at him.

A security guard walked toward them. Chip nodded toward the exit. "Let's talk about it in the truck."

"You're not getting in *my* truck! You don't deserve to get in a truck. There's no 'soul searching' allowed in my truck. You can't quit med school because you want to soul search. We're buying you a ticket *today* and you're going back to school!"

"Is there a problem?" the security guard asked.

"Lieutenant Orleans, Homicide," Bud flashed his badge.

"You planning one, Lieutenant?" the guard asked with a quizzical smile.

Bud scowled at him, hooked his thumb at Chip, "Top of his class. Third year medical school. Who *quits* medical school in their third year?"

"Better than waiting until my fourth," Chip quipped.

The security guard pushed back his cap, "Sorry to hear that, Lieutenant. I do need to ask you to take the show on the road."

"Yeah, yeah. Thanks," Bud glowered at Chip, who followed him as he strode toward the exit.

Bud didn't trust himself to speak until they were in his truck. He sat silent, looking out the front window. He felt like a Buick was parked on his chest and he was having trouble catching his breath. With a grimace of pain, Bud started the truck. He turned to Chip, "Where am I taking you, because I refuse to take you home. Your mother is going to blow a gasket."

"When I explain everything, she'll understand," Chip said confidently.

Bud stared at him in disbelief, "Son, have you *met* your mother?"

"You're blowing this out of proportion."

A searing pain shot down his left arm. Bud gripped his chest and bent forward, groaning.

"Are you all right?" Chip asked, concerned.

"Never better," Bud said through clenched teeth.

"What's wrong?"

"If you'd made it to fourth year, you'd know," Bud gasped, doubling over in pain.

"Pops!" Chip jumped out of the truck and ran to the driver's side. He shoved his dad over and got behind the wheel.

"I'm fine," Bud choked out.

"Sit tight." Chip gunned the engine and sped toward the exit.

CHAPTER THIRTEEN

Don't tell me the moon is shining; show me the glint of light on broken glass.

—Anton Chekhov

"Sit still!" Jeni said as she jumped off the couch to get Enid a towel.

Enid held Jeni's baby girl, Faith, as far away as her arms would allow. Jeni quickly returned and mopped up the baby puke that had been spewed on Enid's shoulder.

Jeni cooed at the baby, "Doesn't that feel better? Get that bad ole' bubble out of your tum-tum-tummy?"

Enid grimaced in disgust as Jeni took the baby from her. Enid grabbed the towel and worked on getting the puke stain off.

An hour earlier, on the drive to Jeni's apartment, Enid had been thrilled to strike a deal that she could crash on Jeni's couch for babysitting services.

Jeni had given Enid a tour of the tiny apartment, which consisted of a living room whose sole contents were a worn pleather couch, scratched coffee table and a television that sat on the upside-down cardboard box it came in. The kitchen was more cheerful with daisy dish towels and brightly colored dishes. Potted cacti sat on the windowsill, softening the effect of the bars that were on the windows. Jeni had confided to Enid that the only plant she had ever been able to keep alive was a cactus.

Hanging on the wall was a decorative blanket with the image of Marilyn Monroe's fuzzy, but dazzling, face. Jeni proudly told Enid she got it from the parking lot vendors on Dunlap and Seventh for ten dollars.

"You sure you're up to watching Faith?" Jeni said.

"Yeah. Sure," Enid said with false confidence.

It can't be any harder than taking care of a drunk.

"Babies are harder to take care of than drunks," Jeni said.

Enid looked at her with wide eyes.

"I mean, they both throw up on you but you change a lot more diapers with babies."

Enid smiled weakly.

Jeni grabbed her keys and a gym bag. "I can be hard to reach at work. If I'm not answering, Mrs. Lopez next door can help you out." Jeni hesitated, frowning, "But, uh, try not to bother her if you don't have to because, uh, you sort of took her job."

"Sorry."

"Don't be. She's reliable but she *knows* it and overcharges."

"Doesn't she know you're a student?" Enid said.

Jeni stared at her blankly for a moment, "Oh, yeah. No, she is – *not* aware of that."

"Is there anything else I need to know?" Enid asked.

"Whatever you do, no matter what happens – don't let anyone in," Jeni warned, her voice ominous.

"Are you expecting someone?"

"No."

She sounds like my mom does when I ask her if she has money for groceries.

They stared at each other for a few moments.

"Help yourself to whatever is in the fridge but make sure you leave the last Pepsi for me. I need my morning Pepsi."

"Okay," Enid said.

Jeni smiled nervously. "Call me if you need me, right?"

"Right."

Jeni went to the door, stopped, jiggling her keys.

"Is something wrong?"

"Nooo. You – everything – it's going to be fine," Jeni said in an unconvincing voice.

"Bye," Enid said, ready to lock the door behind her.

Jeni glanced worriedly back at Faith, then at Enid, "Mrs. Lopez…"

"Don't worry. I won't open the door for anybody. I won't drink your morning Pepsi. Nothing is going to happen."

With a wan smile, Jeni left. Enid locked the door behind her, gave a sigh of relief.

God! She acts like something horrible is going to happen.

Enid grabbed the remote and clicked on the television. She got her backpack and sat on the couch so she was facing the door. She hadn't wanted Jeni to know, but she *was* scared about being left in a strange apartment all alone. With a nervous look over her shoulder, she got the gun out of the backpack and placed it on the couch and settled in to watch television.

CHAPTER FOURTEEN

We sometimes encounter people, even perfect strangers, who begin to interest us at first sight, somehow suddenly, all at once, before a word has been spoken.

—Fyodor Dostoevsky

Returning from the diner, Jack strode into the reception room. He was looking forward to eating his lunch in the privacy of his office. Rachel looked up with that tight smile she got whenever she was about to derail his plans.

"What's wrong?" he said. "Petunia stole the silver?"

Rachel pointed toward his office and whispered, "Someone's waiting."

Jack raised his eyebrows, gestured around the room. "Hence, the waiting room."

"She wouldn't take 'no' for an answer."

"Damn it, Rachel! What am I paying you for?" Jack walked in the client office. It was empty.

Rachel peeked over his shoulder, surprised. "She was here a minute ago."

Jack jerked open to the door to his private office and stalked in. He stopped short.

Twenty-five and exquisite, Eve Hargrove sat at his desk like she already owned him. Porcelain skin, glossy black hair that fell in lush waves over her shoulders, she had full red lips and startlingly green eyes. She wore a simple summer dress – the kind of simple that only a person in a stratospheric tax brackets can afford; the kind of dress that transforms an attractive woman into a gorgeous woman and a gorgeous woman into a goddess.

Eve examined Jack with take-aim eyes. "Jack Fox, I presume?"

Jack stepped forward, not trusting himself to speak.

She said, "I'm here to hire you."

Jack frowned, pissed that she'd hijacked his chair and expected him to sit in the client chair. Something primal twisted in his gut and with sure-footed animal instinct, he walked to where she sat looking up at him with cool eyes.

Too cool. He didn't like it. Not one bit.

He leaned on the edge of his desk, crowding her. She didn't seem to notice – or care. He put his foot up on the windowsill, trapping her in. It was a move designed to own the space and force her to retreat.

She didn't.

Cool as ice, Eve kept her eyes locked on his. "You *are* a private detective, aren't you?"

Jack stared down into her strangely beautiful yet unblinking gaze.

She was spectacular.

A long-forgotten memory shot to the surface of his mind. He had been twelve and on a school trip to the zoo. As the other kids hurried to get lunch, Jack had stubbornly remained staring through the bars of the cage of a black panther that remained frustratingly hidden from view. He was about to give up when, soft and silent, the panther sprang forward. Jack had stood mesmerized – staring into the creature's coldly glittering eyes. An electric sensation coursed through his body and, for what felt like an eternity, he had the sensation that he and the panther had become one.

The panther vanished.

Jack had sprung forward, gripping the bars. He remembered wanting to break them, wanting to climb inside the cage and *be* the panther.

Jack was jolted back to the present when Eve pulled a bundle of cash from her purse and placed it on his desk. "Ten thousand dollars. The job will require *discretion*."

Jack abruptly stood. He walked across the room, turned. "Let's start over."

"In what way?" Eve said, puzzled.

Jack walked to her, leaned in and said in a menacingly soft voice, *"Get out of my chair."*

Their eyes locked.

A bolt of electricity shot through Jack and he felt the dizzying sensation of being back at the bars of the panther cage.

Jack shivered.

Eve gave a quicksilver laugh. With cat-like grace, she glided around the desk.

Jack looked at her, his eyes greedily drinking her in.

Eve held out her hand, "Eve Hargrove."

Jack's eyes flickered in surprise. Jack recalled how Sam had told him about the three sisters: Legs, Brains and The Ghost.

Eve Hargrove sure as hell ain't no ghost!

"I believe you met my sister?" She sat in the client chair.

Jack remained leaning on the desk, waiting.

Eve raised her eyebrows, "Jeni *did* hire you?"

"Confidential." Jack nodded toward the cash, "What's that for?"

"Ten thousand dollars. I want you to drop my sister's case."

"What you want, you get – is that it?"

She raised her eyebrows in an amused "of course."

"Why?" Jack rapped out.

"I'd prefer not to explain myself," Eve said haughtily.

"I'd prefer you did," Jack retorted.

Eve examined him, sizing him up. "Does it matter?"

Jack raised his eyebrows in his own version of an amused "hell yes."

Eve stood, haughty as a queen. "My *fee* includes you keeping your nose out of my business."

"My *job* includes putting my nose where I damned well please," Jack shot back.

Eve's eyes flashed with indignation. She quickly recovered. "Thank you for your time, Mr. Fox."

"Never said I'd take the case." Jack ignored her outstretched hand.

She stood, stubborn, hand outstretched.

Reluctantly, Jack took her hand. At the touch of her fingertips, heat surged through him. Startled, he glanced at their hands and back up to her face.

She smiled, her eyes glinting with…

Triumph?

She turned and, in a moment, was gone.

Jack leaned against the desk, the air going out of him fast. He looked around the room, which suddenly felt empty.

His thoughts on Eve, he was reminded of the stories his grandmother had told him as a child. Stories of the werepanther – a magical creature masquerading as human.

Rachel entered, her eyes probing his.

He felt too bereft to speak. He might was well be twelve and standing at the bars of the cage – alone.

"Well?" Rachel said, curious.

He looked at her blankly.

"What's wrong with you?" she asked.

Jack pushed himself off the desk, and paced.

Rachel's eyes caught sight of the cash and she gave a low whistle. "Who do we have to kill?"

Jack scowled. "Get me everything you can on Eve Hargrove – the whole family."

Rachel hurried out.

Jack walked to the window. Looking down, he saw Eve crossing the street, moving with fluid grace toward a gleaming red Ferrari that two boys were examining with admiring eyes. She slid gracefully behind the wheel. She glanced up, catching and holding Jack's eyes.

Jack pulled back from the window, feeling like a damned fool.

CHAPTER FIFTEEN

A king should die on his feet.

—Louis XVIII

Bud lay in the hospital bed, listening to the man in the next bed moan in his sleep. His moans were rhythmic and steady, like Chinese water torture. If the guy missed a moan, Bud found himself tensing, holding his breath in anticipation of the next moan.

I have to get out of here!

Bud sensed more than heard the approach of Bunnie. As she got closer, he could hear the telltale Z-Coil heel strike and the pausing of voices in the wake of the Bunnie avalanche, which he knew so well and welcomed. Bud relaxed and forgot the moaning behind the curtain that separated their beds.

"What the hell, Bud?" Bunnie jerked aside the curtain. "You been havin' heart pain and didn't tell me?"

The sleeping moaner woke with a snort.

Bunnie hit the curtain. "Keep it down over there! You're not the only heart attack on the ward."

"I'm okay," Bud smiled weakly.

"Like hell you are!" Bunnie said angrily, lifting an electrode line. "How come Chip has to call me from school – tell me you're in the hospital? How come *he* knows before *me*?"

Behind her, Chip entered the room. He froze with the terrified expression of easy prey.

Bunnie paused, sniffed the air as if sensing his presence.

Bud subtly gestured for Chip to leave.

"Bud Orlean, you are about as subtle as a shithouse on fire!" Bunnie spun around. She gave a cry of joy, sprang forward and grabbed Chip in a bone-crunching hug. "Chip-ster! I thought Bud was waving off a doc he didn't want me to talk to…"

"Good to be home," Chip said, awkwardly trying to plant a kiss on her cheek.

"What are you doin' home? Don't you have some big exam next week?"

Bud sat up, swung his legs over the edge of the bed. He winced, stopped to catch his breath.

Bunnie spun around. "What the hell do you think *you're* doing?"

Bud pulled off an electrode, grimacing. "I'm going home. Against medical advice – yes – but I'll follow up with a cardiologist. I promise."

Bunnie's eyebrows shot into a sharp V of anger. She stepped forward menacingly. "So help me Mother-Mary-Louise, if you get out of that bed, Bud Orlean, I will write you a new one."

Bud tore off another electrode. "Chip dropped out of school. He wants to do some soul searching."

Bunnie's body went rigid, a joint somewhere deep within her body cracked like a knuckle. She did a dangerously slow one-eighty.

Chip's face went grey. "I – I can explain…"

Bud struggled to pull on his pants. "Chip says *you'll understand.*"

Her eyes glittered dangerously. "Yeah, Chip, why don't you explain so I'll – *understand.* "

"Wallet, please," Bud said, pointing to a table.

Bunnie handed it to him.

"Thank you." Bud said.

Chip glanced at his dad, who gave him a "don't-mess-with-me" look. Chip took a ragged breath and, after a long hard moment, turned and *ran.*

Bunnie spun toward Bud. She slapped his hands away from a button that he was struggling with and began undressing him. "He's going back to school."

"We can't force him."

"Speak for yourself," Bunnie said grimly as she continued to undress him.

Bud fought to stop her. "I'll make an appointment with a cardiologist, Bunnie. I can't stay here."

"You're staying." Bunnie said as she relentlessly undressed Bud.

"It was an 'episode' – *not* a heart attack. I promise, I'll make an appointment today."

"Bud, if you die, you're going to die like a man and an officer of the law – *naturally*. Murdered on the street in the line of duty. N*ot* dropping dead of a heart attack like you have a wife who doesn't give a shit and never forced you to eat a stick of broccoli."

"I'm not...!"

"Bud, this is not about you!" Bunnie snapped.

Bud looked at her in surprise.

"Do you remember those 'episodes' *I* had – when I went into menopause?"

Bud nodded, disturbed.

"Well, I'm feeling something akin to that *right now*. So, let's keep in mind that I am *not* on medication anymore. You have a choice: glue your backside to that bed and jump through every hoop Nurse Ratchett and Doc Martin put you through until they give you the green light to come home *or* – check yourself out *against medical advice* and I will personally make sure you drop dead of a heart attack if I have to hand-deliver it myself and *FYI*, I will bury you in the backyard with your ass sticking out of the ground so my new husband has a place to park his bike."

Bud got back into bed.

CHAPTER SIXTEEN

Once upon a midnight dreary, while I pondered weak and weary.

—Edgar Allan Poe

Loud pounding on the door startled Enid out of her doze. She sat up, blinking. For a moment, she felt disoriented and couldn't remember where she was.

"Open up, Jeni!" A man's voice demanded angrily from behind the door. "I know you're in there."

Like cold water in her face, Enid remembered that she was in Jeni's apartment – just her and the baby. She grabbed the gun and pointed it at the door.

"Open the door or I'll kick it in!" the man shouted.

Enid undid what Henry called the "safety" of the gun and tiptoed to the door. There was a window covered with a broken blind, but she was too scared to look through it.

"Jeni's not here," she called out in a hesitant voice.

Silence.

Enid glanced at Faith, who was awake and crying.

"Who's that?" the man's voice demanded.

"The babysitter. Jeni isn't here. Come back tomorrow."

Footsteps stormed down the walk. A car door slammed. Enid cautiously peeked out the blinds. A sports car sat in the street. The flare of a match momentarily illuminated the thick scowling face of the man in the driver's seat. The glow of a cigarette hovered. After a moment, he gunned the engine and sped up over the curb and toward the front door.

Enid's scream was lost in the squeal of brakes. The car stopped three feet from the front door, its headlights harshly illuminating the tiny apartment.

Enid ran to the kitchen and grabbed the bars across the windows, but they didn't budge. Her only way out was blocked. The roar of the engine was deafening and Enid heard him shouting about…

Pissing in my skull?

Enid covered her ears, terrified.

The baby wailed. Enid gasped, realizing that she left Faith behind. Trembling, Enid got on all fours and crawled into the living room. Making her way to the crib, she grabbed Faith and crawled behind the sofa.

The man pounded on the door. "I know you're in there, Jeni! If that's your new *girlfriend* – I'm going to kill you, kill her and then I'm going to kill myself!"

Enid reached over the couch and grabbed the cell phone that Jeni had left her.

The sound of breaking glass reverberated through the tiny room, followed by scraping and thudding. Enid's head shot up over the couch. A baseball bat was knocking out jagged shards of glass, which was all that remained of the window. A thick, hairy hand reached in and tore down the twisted blinds.

Certain she was going to die unless she did something, Enid hid the baby behind the sofa, grabbed the Glock and, with a primal scream, barreled toward the front door. She flung the door open and was blinded by the headlights of his car. She saw a blur of boots flailing in the air. Enid went back in and, hands shaking violently, she pointed the gun at the man's head.

"Stop!" Enid shrieked, tears running down her face.

The man's eyes went from crazy to zero. Balancing himself in the window, he dropped the bat. "Hold up, little girl!"

"I'm the babysitter! *I told you* – I'm the babysitter!" Enid screamed, tears running down her face.

"Take it easy."

Sirens screamed up the street. Through the glare of headlights, Enid could see a knot of neighbors. A police car screeched to a stop, lights flashing.

Enid's hand with the gun dropped to her side.

Cursing, the man wriggled backwards, trying to escape.

Enid darted into the kitchen. She opened the freezer and shoved the gun inside a half-eaten box of ice cream. She ran into the living room as a young Hispanic cop was making his way in.

"Police! Drop your weapon!"

Enid's hands flew up. "I'm the babysitter!"

The policeman's eyes seemed to be everywhere at once. Gun leveled at Enid, his eyes found the wailing baby hidden behind the couch. "Who else is here?" He demanded.

"Just me."

"She tried to kill me! That bitch had a gun to my head!" The angry man shouted from the front yard where he lay facedown as another cop snapped on cuffs.

The policeman shot Enid a suspicious look.

"I'm the babysitter," Enid said, trying to look innocent.

"Stand there," the policeman shoved her to the wall, patting her down. "The man said you had a gun," The policeman persisted.

"Nah-uh. Not me."

"If you have a gun on the premises, you need to tell me," the police officer said.

Bursting into tears, she wailed, "I'm the babysitter!"

CHAPTER SEVENTEEN

Promises and piecrust are made to be broken.

—Jonathan Swift

Jack walked into Mid-First Bank on Central Avenue. A skinny bank teller with big hair and a name tag reading 'Kelly' greeted him. "Welcome to Mid-First Bank, sir. How can I help you?"

Jack pulled the bundle of cash that Eve had given him out of a rolled-up newspaper and placed it on the counter. "I'd like to make a deposit."

"Certainly, sir. Is that over…?"

"Nine-thousand, nine-hundred and eighty," Jack said, aware that depositing ten thousand or more in cash required paperwork.

Kelly smiled and ran the cash through a money counter. Jack enjoyed watching the cash fly and the sound it made. "Hey, isn't this the bank that used to be owned by that guy who got murdered?"

Kelly glanced around, uncomfortable.

"Daniel Hargrove – that was his name, right?" Jack said.

Kelly smiled uneasily.

"Did you know him?" He asked.

Kelly frowned, shook her head.

"If I remember right, the daughter – Eve Hargrove, she sold the bank for a boatload of money. I heard everybody loved her – especially the employees."

Kelly shot him an incredulous look. She leaned closer, hissed. "Everybody *hated* that bitch! Talk about take the money and run. Forget about the people who worked here since the beginning – one of them thirty-three years. To hell with *us*, our *benefits*, our *pensions* – she knew if she sold the bank that a bunch of us would get laid off, but did she care? All she cares about is getting her daddy's money and the rest of us can eat dirt and die."

A sallow-faced manager walked toward them.

Kelly straightened, smiling brightly, "Here's your receipt, sir. Would you like to talk to a personal banker today – about investment planning?"

Jack answered in the negative, thanked her, took his receipt and left. On the way to the car, he dialed the office to find out if Rachel had dug up any info on the Hargrove family. Rachel had an uncanny ability to dig up dirt on even the most elusive persons of interest.

After a brief conversation with Rachel, Jack found himself driving across town to a strip club called The Candy Store, which was a seedy dive specializing in cheap beer and neon-bathed flesh.

Rachel had also told him that it was also Jeni Hargrove's current place of employment.

Jack hadn't been surprised that Jeni had lied about being in nursing school. Her appearance had pretty much pegged her for a stripper – and not a very bright one. Jack knew that the smart strippers dressed like college girls while the dumb college girls dressed like strippers. The dumb strippers – they just dressed like dumb strippers.

What surprised him was that Jeni was working in such a dive. Her legs were her calling card to any skin club of her choice and yet, she had chosen to work in the dregs.

As a rule, Jack avoided strip clubs. He had figured out long ago that he had an irrational and extremely inconvenient urge to "save" the girls, which only got him into trouble – and broke.

Heart broke and bank broke.

Jack entered the dimly lit club. Rhythmic music pounded and a stripper hung upside-down in a gymnast move. Her breasts had the telltale volleyball firmness of an augmentation. A smattering of men and one lone lesbian gazed up at her as they sipped cheap beer.

On a second stage, Jeni was gyrating on a pole in white bikini bottoms and a Candy Striper's hat. As good as Jeni looked in her clothes, she looked even better without.

Jack took a seat at the bar and ordered a beer.

The song finally stopped and another instantly started pounding.

Jack turned around in time to see Jeni's eyes home in on a five-dollar bill suspended in the air. She sauntered toward the construction worker holding the bill.

Jack stepped forward, hoping that she would see him before she landed on the guy's lap.

She did see him. Compressing her lips, she leaned over and whispered in the construction worker's ear. He scowled, watching her walk toward Jack. She grabbed a flimsy wrap from a chair and pulled it around her protectively.

A surly Russian in a cowboy hat leaned on the end of the bar. He scowled as he watched Jeni pass more cash.

Jeni slid onto a barstool next to Jack. "I *did* apply to nursing school. I'm waiting to hear if I get in. It's not like I was lying or anything…"

"You don't owe me any explanations." Jack waved for the bartender. "You want something?"

A bartender appeared, nodded at Jeni. "Ginger ale?"

She nodded, smiling her thanks.

At the end of the bar, the Russian was glaring at Jeni.

Jeni's face twitched. "Give me your wallet."

Jack pulled out his wallet. Jeni expertly plucked out a ten. She tucked it into her bikini strap and gave the Russian a "get-off-my-back" look. Appeased, his attention drifted.

Jeni gazed at Jack earnestly. "I took this job for research – *secret* research. I'm writing my life story – it's going to be funny and sad and, who knows, maybe they'll turn it into a movie. My life could be a movie…"

"Tell me about Eve," Jack interrupted, hating to hear her lie.

Jeni shot him a startled look. "What's *she* got to do with anything?"

"You're here. Your sister Eve is in a Ferrari that could buy this place lock, stock and barrel. What's the story?"

Jeni eyed the stage, hungry to get back on.

"You want me to find your mother?" Jack said. "You need to tell me what's going on. Any reason why your sister wouldn't want you to find your real mom?"

"You find her? Or did she find you?" Jeni said suspiciously.

"I found her," Jack lied.

"She's got nothing to do with me finding my mother."

"Do you love your sister?"

Jeni snorted. "Yeah, I love Eve – like a sparrow loves the hawk."

Jack watched the play of expressions on her face and he got the story – not the details but he got it.

Jeni sighed. "Eve is working off a different rule book than the rest of the universe. In the end, she'll win. She *always* wins."

"What'd she do to you?"

Jeni stood up, gestured to the stage. "Look, I gotta…"

Jack put his hand on her arm.

She looked at him, startled.

He pulled his hand away.

After a moment, she asked, "Can I still get my student discount?"

Jack nodded.

Jeni smiled, headed back to the stage. She extended her hands above her head, her shift slipping to the sides, exposing her beautiful breasts.

Jack walked to the edge of the stage. "Who do you think killed your dad?"

Several clients shot him startled looks.

"*Step*-dad," Jeni flinched. "Don't know. Don't care." She turned her back to him and continued dancing.

Jack watched her for a moment. Turning his back on her, Jack left.

Outside the club, when he was reaching for his car door, Jack heard Jeni's voice.

"Hey!"

He turned.

Gripping a man's jacket around her shoulders, Jeni ran to his side and grabbed his arm. "I was totally joking about the book! Don't tell anybody – 'K?"

"Silent like the grave," Jack said, puzzled at her intensity.

"You *have* to promise me. Promise you won't tell *anyone!*"

"Sure," Jack shrugged.

"No, I *mean it*. Promise me you'll forget I ever mentioned it." Her desperate eyes stared up at him.

Jack nodded, irritated. He didn't know what game she was playing, but she reminded him of Stella and all the times she had lied to him.

Jeni smiled uncertainly and hurried back to the club.

Jack watched her disappear behind the red door. Despite his irritation, he fought the almost overwhelming urge to run after her – get her the hell out of that place.

It's none of my damned business…

CHAPTER EIGHTEEN

It is only for the sake of elegance, I try to remain morally pure.

—Marcel Proust

As Bud rang Eve's doorbell, he eyed the massive oak door with distaste. He reached out, touching the fangs of a ferocious wolf that glared at anyone daring to enter.

He'd gotten out of the hospital that morning. Every test was negative. Bud got a clean bill of health and, after a particularly grueling "discussion" with Bunnie, he returned to work. The doctor warned him the episode was a warning shot across the bow and he needed to follow up with a cardiologist for further evaluation, as there might be a subtler problem at work in his heart.

Truer words were never spoken.

The door swung open.

Eve Hargrove greeted him with a knowing smile. "Who did I murder this time?"

"Since when do you open your own door? Fall on hard times?"

Eve turned and strolled deeper into the cavernous entranceway, her voice echoing off the marble flooring and domed ceiling where an elaborate chandelier hung. "Don't tell me you've found another clue? And it only took you two years."

Bud followed her into a luxurious sitting room with high ceilings and overstuffed furniture. The walls were hung with a series of rare tapestries that depicted medieval life. Bud stopped to gaze at a hunter with a strangely detached expression as he plunged a sword into a fallen stag.

"Ancestor?" Bud said.

Eve sat on a couch, gazed up at him with a pleasant smile. "Forgive me for not offering you refreshments, but I despise you."

"And I'm so fond of you," Bud said as he sat in a nearby chair. He found himself staring at her flawless beauty. She had the kind of beauty that gems have: frozen.

"Take a picture, it might last longer," Eve said, eyes glittering with disdain.

"We found your father."

"Step-father," she corrected, eyes flickering. She rang a small silver bell that sat on the table. "Perhaps I will order some refreshment. This conversation may prove vaguely interesting."

"Don't put yourself out."

A butler materialized.

"One iced tea," Eve said.

"What can I get for you, sir?" the butler asked Bud.

"He's not staying long." Eve waved the butler away.

"You don't seem surprised," Bud said. "Aren't you curious as to how he met his end?"

Eve tilted her head thoughtfully as if divining his thoughts. "You don't have a positive identification on the body. You're fishing."

Bud's eyes narrowed. "It's him."

Eve made a tsk-tsk sound, "Fishing."

"We've got the body. The rest will follow."

"I'm not guilty."

"You're not innocent," Bud snapped, surprised at his short temper and his new inability to control it.

Eve paled, her eyes dark with anger.

"I know you did it and I'm going to prove it," Bud said, voice tight with hate.

"Your slip is showing," Eve sneered.

Bud stood up, strode to the door.

"Bud?"

Bud turned, surprised to hear her call him by his first name. He was startled to find that she was within touching distance. He involuntarily stepped back.

She asked in a softly menacing voice, "How's the ticker, Detective?"

Bud stared at her in astonishment.

How did she know?

Bud struggled to keep his cool. He turned and strode out, almost running down the butler.

Her laughter echoed behind him.

CHAPTER NINETEEN

*"But I don't want to go among mad people," said Alice. "Oh, you can't help
that" said the cat. "We're all mad here."*

–Lewis Carroll

"What did you say?" The policeman asked, staring at Enid in
astonishment at hearing such a familiar name.

Parked in front of Jeni's apartment building, Enid sat in the back
seat of the squad car. She was miserable and scared and trembling so
hard that her teeth were chattering. The police had arrested Jeni's
stalker and, luckily, they hadn't found the gun that Enid had hidden in
Jeni's freezer. A policeman with the nametag "Sam Waterstone" had
put Enid in the back of a squad car while he filled out paperwork.

"What?" Enid asked through chattering teeth.

"What did you just say?" he said in a voice edged with urgency.

"I – uh, I'm here to find my dad – my real dad…"

"Jack Fox? The detective?"

"Do – do you know him?" Enid said, fear curling in her stomach.

"Let me get this straight. Your mother is dead and you came to
Phoenix to find your biological father who doesn't know you exist?"

Enid gave a hesitant nod.

"How do you know he's your father?"

"My mom told me." Enid winced, recalling her drunken rant.

"What was your mother's name?"

Enid bit her lip.

"It's easy enough to check all this out with a phone call."

"Georgianna. My mom met him at some rodeo or bar or something to do with cowboys. That's when they…" Enid's voice trailed off. "I don't think they dated for that long."

"It's a common name. There's probably a hundred guys by the name of Jack Fox in the directory."

"Seven."

"How do you know? You hired a detective?"

"I'm not an idiot! All you need is Google, a cell phone and half a brain cell."

"How do you *know?*" he pressed.

"Can I have my backpack?" Enid said, pointing to her backpack on the front seat.

He checked the contents and then handed it to her.

Enid pulled out her wallet and handed him a weathered driver's license with a photograph of a young Jack Fox. "After she told me he was my real dad, I found this."

"The Jack Fox in this picture – he's got no idea about any of this?"

"I've seen him, but he doesn't know about me. Being his daughter, that is."

The policeman studied her face.

"Are you going to arrest me?" Enid said.

"Did you break the law?"

Enid gulped, shook her head.

"Wait here." He got out of the car and joined the other policeman. Enid watched them talk in low voices. They glanced back. He walked back, opened the door. "Come on." He gestured for her to sit in the front seat, "You graduated to the front seat."

"Where are we going?"

"To meet your relatives."

Enid stared at him in astonishment.

Two hours later, Enid found herself sitting in a lime-green kitchen in Peoria, eating Kentucky Fried Chicken with Aunt Cheryl, Uncle Sam and two cousins, Ernie and Sharon.

On the drive over, the police officer told her to call him Uncle Sam and told her that Jack Fox was his stepbrother. He also tried to tell her how much Jack likes kids.

"He likes kids?" Enid asked skeptically.

"Sure, " Sam said, his face twitching.

They pulled up to a modest ranch-style house with desert landscaping. Two bikes lay in the driveway and Sam stopped the car in front of them and blew the horn.

Nothing.

With a scowl, Sam shut off the ignition and headed for the house.

Cheryl Waterstone, a plump woman in her thirties, looked as soft and comfortable as an easy chair. Enid was surprised when her generous hello hug didn't smell of whiskey.

Her new Aunt Cheryl smelled like *cookies*.

From the moment her new cousin, Ernie, had set eyes on Enid, he was love-struck. He was a scrawny boy of twelve with sandy hair and looked like a normal kid, except he was wearing a blue tutu over his shorts. Enid stared at him in astonishment as he swept into a deep bow and introduced himself, "Ernie Waterstone at your service."

Sharon was one year older than Ernie and wore a long brown ponytail to the side. She had the bad habit of staring at people like she was trying to read their minds. She gripped a detective novel to her chest as she examined Enid with suspicious eyes.

After forty minutes of stilted conversation, the five of them sat in awkward silence at the kitchen table.

"Can cousins get married?" Ernie blurted out.

Enid blushed to her roots as everyone burst out laughing. Sam made a mock prayer motion to the heavens and then shot Cheryl a grateful look.

Cheryl popped Ernie in the elbow. "No."

"You wanna be my sidekick?" Ernie asked Enid.

"Do I have to wear a tutu?" Enid asked.

"Only if you want. I've got a couple others that might fit you." Ernie leaned in, "What's your story, morning glory?"

Enid shot a questioning look at her Aunt Cheryl, who smiled and said, "He's harmless."

"Says you," Sam muttered.

"What's up with the tutu?" Enid said.

"What do you mean?" Ernie said, puzzled.

"How come you're wearing a tutu?"

"How come *you're not?*"

"What's *your* story?" Enid said.

"Ernie Waterstone. Sixth grade. I tested at the ninth-grade level. I opted to stay in sixth grade as a social experiment. *I* can wear a tutu because only a *real* man can wear a tutu."

"Damn right, son!" Sam said.

"He's studying to be a man-ballerina," Sharon said.

"A *real man* ballerina," Ernie corrected.

Sharon nodded earnestly. "Uh-huh."

"A *manarina?*" Enid asked, doubtfully.

A car pulled up in the driveway. Sam shot to the window, gesturing for them to remain seated, which none of them did. Everyone but Enid crowded behind him at the window.

Enid heard Cheryl whisper, "Did you tell him?"

"He never called back," Sam said tensely.

Ernie pirouetted away from the window, "It's Uncle Jack!"

Enid suddenly felt as sick as the time when she was really little and mistook a gallon of her mother's whiskey screwdrivers for the best-tasting orange juice *ever* and drank enough to fill her gut and puke it back out.

CHAPTER TWENTY

I choose a block of marble and chop off whatever I don't need.

—Auguste Rodin

Jack was surprised when Sam not only met him at the front door, but also pushed him onto the front lawn, away from the house.

"What's wrong?" Jack asked, struck by the strange look on Sam's face. "Are the kids okay?"

"Why didn't you call? I told you it was urgent."

"What's going on?" Jack said, alarmed.

"Remember that time you lost your driver's license – back in the nineties?"

Jack stared at him in astonishment.

"What was the name of that crazy woman you met at the Rodeo Bar?" Sam hissed.

"I can't believe *you* remember that. *I* hardly remember that."

"What was her name?"

Jack wrinkled his brow in thought. "Something to do with a state. Georgia? Georgianna? Something like that…"

"You had sex with her?"

"Why?" Jack said suspiciously.

"You talk to her since?"

"Stop being so cryptic. What the hell is going on?"

"What would you say if this Georgianna took your driver's license and…"

"What?"

"Got pregnant."

Jack stared at him blankly. After a moment, he busted out laughing. "Is this some sort of punked thing? Sam, she was a one-night stand! Not even a good one. We were both shitfaced drunk and I barely got it up before she puked on me. I was picking red wine barf-chunks out of the carpet for weeks."

Jack heard a noise and glanced toward the house. Enid was standing in the doorway, staring at him in horror.

"That's the girl that bit me!" Jack shoved up his sleeve and showed Sam a bandage. "That little punk took a chunk out of my arm – cost me a visit to Urgent Care for a tetanus shot! What the hell is she doing *here?*"

"She's your daughter," Sam hissed.

Jack stared at Sam in shock. His eyes were drawn back to the girl's pallid face.

No!

Everything in Jack rebelled against the idea. Who the hell was that kid?

It's a scam!

"Don't be an asshole, man," Sam murmured, pushing Jack toward the house. "I tried to give you a heads-up. You should return your calls."

Jack tried to speak but couldn't. He looked at the girl and was startled to see something familiar in her eyes. His brain scrabbled around and, with a sudden shock, he realized that her eyes, her eyebrows – they reminded him of...

Mom.

It was the same look she used to give me – when she was disappointed in me.

Jack stepped back, light-headed, like someone punched the air out of him. He looked up at the sky, at Sam – to make sure he wasn't dreaming. When he looked back at the door – it was empty.

"You gotta talk to her. *She's yours.* Anybody can see it. She's got your eyes."

Jack reeled away, angry. "What the hell are you talking about? She's not...!"

"Her mother died. She took a bus from Florida to find *you.*"

Jack drew a shaky breath, shook his head.

"The kid has your driver's license. Her mother's name was Georgianna."

"She heard what I said? About the one-night stand and – barf in the carpet?"

Sam grimly nodded, shoving Jack toward the house. "Go talk to her."

Cheryl met him at the door, grabbed his hand and led him down the hallway. Behind a locked bathroom door, they could hear Enid vomiting. Jack made a face and tried to retreat, but Cheryl shoved him toward the door.

"Talk to her," Cheryl whispered.

Jack gave her a pathetically helpless look.

"Say something!" Cheryl urged.

"Uh…"

The sound of vomiting intensified. Jack grimaced, stepping back.

Cheryl pushed him back, hissing, "Jack Fox, you *talk* to that girl! You're her father. Don't you dare do to *her* what your father did to *you*."

Jack looked at her, startled.

Cheryl squeezed his shoulder. "Be the dad *you* should have had."

Jack stared at her. After a long moment, he bent over and puked.

CHAPTER TWENTY-ONE

How can a woman be expected to be happy with a man who insists on treating her as if she were perfectly normal human being.

—Oscar Wilde

"What kind of father makes his son sleep on the floor?" Chip exclaimed as he tried to get comfortable in the sleeping bag that was stretched across the hardwood floor of what used to be his bedroom.

"A father who's married to a mother who doesn't want you to get too comfortable!" Bunnie snapped, appeared in the doorway. Bud felt a pang of regret at letting Bunnie talk him into removing the bed frame and mattress from Chip's bedroom and making him sleep on his musty-smelling sleeping bag from his Boy Scout years.

"This is cruel and unusual punishment," Chip grumbled.

"Being a mother is cruel and unusual punishment." Bunnie grabbed the pillow from under Chip's head.

"What the…!" Chip looked up incredulously.

Bunnie snatched a textbook off a nearby shelf and handed it to him, "Try that for a pillow. Maybe some big words will seep in and you'll come to your senses."

"I'm not going back."

"I know, I know," Bunnie said sarcastically, "You're going to go a-soul-searching and 'find yourself' and write the next great American novel. Just what the world needs – another bum writer."

"Everyone's hungry for a good story," Chip argued.

"Everyone's hungry to be distracted from their impending doom but you don't see me stripping buck naked and dancing a jig in the street. Being a writer – it's a pipe dream! You need to grow up and focus on a real career – like being a doctor."

"I'd rather be happy chasing a pipe dream."

"Yeah, forget about becoming a rich doctor with a gorgeous wife. Who needs that?"

"I don't know if you noticed this, mom, but doctors aren't so rich anymore."

"Finish school, become a doctor and *then* – if you want to be an *artiste* – I won't so much as peep."

"The day you 'don't so much as peep' is the day you start pushing up dandelions, mom."

"You're throwing your life away! I won't stand by and help you flush three years of hard work down the toilet." Bunnie threw her hands up dramatically. "As God as my witness, Chip, twenty years from now you are going to wake up a broken man and you are going to *bitterly* regret this decision."

"I don't expect you to support my decision but I do expect you to accept it." Chip turned to Bud, "Can I shadow you tomorrow? I need to start research for the novel – it's a detective thriller."

Bunnie compressed her lips into a thin, white line.

Bud took Bunnie gently by the arm, "Come on, Bunn, let's leave Chip to his…"

"Hardwood floor. What's for breakfast? Gruel?" Chip adjusted the book under his head. "If I wake up with a neck crick…"

"You'll have to go to *a doctor*. Someone who actually made his mother proud."

"You act like it's the end of the world." Chip said. "I'm not going back and you are just going to have to deal with it."

Bunnie took a menacing step toward Chip. "It's not for nothin' I been married to a homicide detective for forty years. I brought you in this world and I can take you out – and nobody will be any the wiser."

"Bunnie…" Bud admonished.

"Don't you 'Bunnie' me!" She turned on Bud furiously. "I want a doctor-son! These bunions aren't going to fix themselves!"

"A *podiatrist* fixes bunions," Chip said. "I didn't go to med school to be a bunion-fixing podiatrist."

"No," Bunnie snapped, "You're a live-at-home dropout sleeping on a floor other people paid for. Finish school and get your own floor."

"You'll get over it," Chip said wryly.

Bunnie sprang for Chip but Bud grabbed her around the waist. He dragged her out of the room as she yelled, "Get over it? I'll tell you what I need to get over! The ulcer in my stomach that you could drive a truck through!"

Bud slammed the door behind them.

Bunnie grabbed Bud's shirt, tears in her eyes, "He's going to ruin his life!"

Bud touched her on the cheek, smiling tenderly. "Like you ruined your life when you married me."

Scowling, Bunnie pushed him away. "That was different."

Bud steered her toward their bedroom at the end of the hall. "Your dad hated me."

"He didn't hate you."

"He told me he had a chainsaw in the garage and he knew how to use it."

"He was a tad overprotective."

"Before he walked you up the aisle, he told you he had a car waiting if you wanted to change your mind."

"Family tradition. It wouldn't be a proper wedding if the escape car wasn't at least offered." In the bedroom, Bunnie peeled off her clothes and tossed them haphazardly on the floor. Bud stripped down to his boxers and neatly folded his clothes before dropping them into the hamper. "Dad hated all the boys we brought home. He liked you in the end, didn't he?"

"I don't think him saying on his deathbed that 'maybe he's not so bad' constitutes him liking me."

Bunnie smiled wistfully. "I miss him."

"I do too."

Bunnie kicked her clothes across the floor into a walk-in closet. She pulled on a silky nightgown and jerked a brush through her hair.

Bud watched her, eyes glowing in admiration. "Why are you so darned pretty?"

Bunnie softened. "We sure made a pretty baby, didn't we?"

Bud reached out to put his arms around Bunnie's waist but she pushed him away. "Are you going to retire?"

"Stop being so – *angry*."

"I *am* angry! I want to sell the house, right out from under that boy's butt. I want *us* to retire and live on a cruise ship."

"We can't afford that," Bud said, laughing.

"Cheaper than an old person's home."

"I don't think we're ready for an old person's home just yet."

"Have you looked in the mirror lately? You're not exactly a spring chicken."

Bud said, "I've seen it a thousand times. A man retires – he loses his edge, gets old and *dies*. Work is what keeps me young. It gives me purpose. "

"I can't take this, Bud."

"What's changed? We've been doing this for years. You've been happy."

"I'm not happy anymore."

"Seems to me you're trying hard *not* to be happy."

"I want something different," Bunnie said resolutely.

Bud stared at Bunnie, realization sweeping over him.

If she's talking about leaving, she's already gone.

Bud stared at her in astonishment. "You're not serious?"

"It's not you," Bunnie whispered. "There's no one else."

Bud's mouth fell open.

Bunnie said, "You can sleep in the guest room. I'll give you to the end of the week to make up your mind. It's either retirement with *me...*" Bunnie's voice trailed off.

"Bunn…"

"Don't call me Bunn!" She screamed, shoving him into the hallway.

Bud stood dazed, staring at the locked door.

CHAPTER TWENTY-TWO

A wounded deer leaps the highest.

—Emily Dickinson

Enid sat on the couch, arms tightly crossed as she surveyed Jack with hostile eyes. Cheryl had deposited her and Jack in the living room and discreetly moved the rest of the family elsewhere. Jack nervously tapped his fingers and looked as comfortable as a condemned man. After several aborted attempts at conversation, he'd given up.

Silence hung between them like a heavy stone.

"If your sister killed somebody – would you cover for her?" Jack asked suddenly.

Enid stared at him like he'd lost his marbles.

"Well?" Jack said.

Enid scowled, wondering what game he was playing. She couldn't shake the image of him picking her mother's vomit out of his carpet on the night *she* was conceived.

I won't let him get the upper hand!

She forced herself to answer between clenched teeth. "Murder, self-defense or revenge?"

"Your sister calls you at two in the morning and says she's got a dead man on her hands and she killed him. What do you do?"

"I don't have a sister," Enid snapped.

"Hypothetically."

Enid scowled, pushing down the desire to punch the calm expression off his face. "Depends on who she killed. Depends on *which* sister."

"I thought you didn't have a sister?"

Enid banged her fist on the couch, yelling, "You said hypothetically! And *hypothetically,* I have a normal family instead of the weirdo show that seems to be my biological parents!"

Cheryl appeared in the doorway, dishcloth in hand. "Everything okay?"

Enid felt a stab of pleasure at seeing Jack's face flush red.

"Just getting to know each other," Jack said grimly.

Cheryl smiled at Enid. "I'll be in here if you need me." She disappeared into the kitchen.

After a long silence, Jack said, "I'm working a case. I thought you might have some insight."

Enid curled her lip in disgust. "Yeah, right."

"Okay." Jack took a deep breath and began again, "What's the first thing you think when you hear that a daughter hates her stepfather?"

Enid shifted uncomfortably.

"Well?" Jack asked patiently.

"This is dumb."

"Look, we can talk about anything you want. Start a conversation; I'm all ears." Jack's eyes glinted shrewdly. "In the meantime, your Aunt Cheryl suggested we talk about – *our feelings.*"

Enid's eyes widened in alarm and, scared that her Aunt was going to pop out and force her to talk about how she *felt,* she forced herself to answer civilly. "Duh. Step-Monster is beating her, beating mom or…" Enid felt her face flush red in embarrassment and the thought of saying what she was really thinking.

"It's a stereotype, but that's what I was thinking."

"Gross," Enid muttered.

"Ducks and zebras."

Enid looked at him, puzzled. Was this guy for real? Or was he messing with her? She suddenly felt an inkling of curiosity to see where he was going with this.

"When it walks like a duck, quacks like a duck…"

"Don't go looking for zebras," Enid finished. "Who'd my hypothetical sister kill?"

"Probably somebody who had it coming."

Enid bit her lip. "Do you usually catch the bad guy?"

"Sometimes."

Enid thought about this. After a few moments, she said, "I guess you never know what you'll do – until you're there."

"I heard you did your own research and found me. Is that how you found out about me?"

Enid remembered her mother screaming at Henry from the driveway. "I was tipped off."

"How'd you do it?"

"What's it to you? You don't care."

"I'm more than willing to start a conversation about our *feelings*." Jack answered with knowing glimmer in his eyes.

Enid examined his face. She didn't like the smug look in his eyes. Not one bit. After a moment, she smiled sweetly, "Okay."

It was Jack's turn to look alarmed.

"I want to talk about my *emotions*," Enid said with a wicked grin.

Jack made an inarticulate sound and gripped the chair like he'd gotten strapped into a broken roller coaster.

Enid leaned forward, "Let's start with how I *feel* about finding out that my mother was a total lush and my biological dad is a…"

Jack jumped up, hands in the air. "You win! I give up!" He shouted toward the kitchen, "Cheryl, I can't do this!"

Cheryl materialized in the doorway.

"She hates me," Jack pointed at Enid. "I'm not – I can't…"

Enid stood up in alarm. Was he going to leave?

Jack strode for the door. He shot her an apologetic look. "Sorry, kid…"

Enid watched with mounting alarm as he made his escape. She looked at her Aunt in confusion.

Her Aunt looked at her with eyes full of – *pity*?

A car door slammed. Without thinking, Enid shoved past her Aunt and bounded out the front door. She ran pell-mell toward his car. She yanked the handle and, when he didn't stop, she slapped her hand on the window and heard herself yelling. In a blur, through her tears, she was shocked to see the expression in his eyes.

He hates me.

The car jolted to a stop. Enid jumped in and hunched down, too scared to do anything but pretend to be mad.

They sat in silence.

After a long moment, Jack threw the car into reverse and, with shaking hands, Enid snapped on her seat belt. She pulled her hoodie up to hide her face. She hunkered down, not caring where they were headed.

CHAPTER TWENTY-THREE

It is difficult to know at what moment love begins; It is less difficult to know that is has begun.

—Henry Wadsworth Longfellow

Jack stared grimly ahead, waiting for the girl to speak.

The girl?

My daughter.

Jack's mind reeled. He was at a complete loss for how to act, what to do or what to say, so he decided to sit tight and wait for *her* to speak. He considered dropping her off at his house, but decided against it. For all he knew, she might burn the place down just to spite him.

He sighed, remembering what his own father had put his mom and him through – he wouldn't blame the kid if she lit his house up like a firecracker on a birthday cake. He inwardly cringed when he remembered the expression on her face when he said that stuff about her mother.

I might as well have punched her.

He gave her a sidelong glance, but her face was hidden from view.

The houses were turning into mansions that got larger and more elaborate as the car climbed higher into the foothills.

"Where are we going?" Enid asked in a muffled voice.

Jack glanced at her, wanting to say something that would make her feel better, but not knowing how. "Work. You don't mind riding along, do you?"

Silence.

Fair enough.

Checking the address that Rachel had given him, he turned into a driveway that was guarded by a security booth.

A guard with a nametag that read "Horace" stepped out of the booth. "Good morning, sir."

"Morning," Jack said, wondering how much the guard got paid to have such a pleasant smile.

"How can I help you?"

"I'm here to see Eve Hargrove. She's not expecting me and I'd like to keep it that way."

"Last time they had a 'surprise' visit, they hired me the next day."

Enid dropped the hoodie and leaned over. "She's my Aunt. She doesn't know that my mom – her sister – just died."

"I'm sorry," Horace said, taken aback.

Jack hid his surprise as Enid said in a quavering voice, "If she knows we're here, she'll know something horrible happened – we thought it'd be easier on her if we tell her in person."

Horace pressed a button so that the gates swung open. "My condolences."

"Thank you," Enid mumbled.

Jack shot her an irritated look as he drove up the winding driveway. "You didn't need to lie. You *shouldn't* lie."

Enid snorted.

Jack said, "He didn't buy it anyway. I guarantee he told them we're on our way up."

They rounded a corner and both stared in astonishment at the looming mansion.

"Wow," Enid breathed.

A Spanish fortress of stone towered in front of them. It was as if they stumbled into a fantastical fairytale world of wizards and imprisoned princesses. To say it was unusual was an understatement. Jack was used to the typical Scottsdale McMansion of every varying floor plan that somehow always looked the same, but this place was Harry Potter off the hook.

They got out of the car and Jack caught his breath at the spectacular view. He hadn't realized they were so high up – it was gorgeous. All that money could buy.

"Sir?" A man's voice said.

Jack turned.

A butler in formal uniform stood in front of the intricately carved doors.

"Horace ratted us out," Enid whispered.

"Wait in the car," Jack said.

"On 'Bring your Daughter to Work' Day? Not a chance."

Jack began to retort but Enid darted forward and disappeared through the door. Disconcerted, the butler hurried after her.

Jack followed them into a cavernous hallway where his footsteps echoed. On all sides were life-sized sculptures, elaborately framed paintings and what looked like medieval tapestries.

Jack found Enid staring as if spellbound at a painting of a bride and groom holding each other, floating.

"Is that real?" she asked in a hushed tone.

Ignoring her, the butler disappeared through a large door.

A statue of a rabbit guarded the door. From the cool darkness of the mansion, Jack stepped through the door and into a world of white sunshine and heat. As his eyes adjusted, he made out the sparkling blue water of a negative-edge pool with a diving board at the far end.

Jack saw her and drew in a sharp breath.

Eve Hargrove stood on the diving board, gazing at him with a look that he would've given everything he owned to know what the hell it meant. Her black bathing suit set off her porcelain skin to perfection. Her black hair fell over her shoulders, one strand entangled in a necklace of amber stone set in gold.

She dove into the water; her body cut the water like a knife. Jack moved forward, staring at the mermaid mirage that swam toward him under the water.

Eve surfaced in front of him, gasping for air. Wiping her long wet hair from her face, she climbed out of the pool and, water streaming from her body, she walked forward until she stood in front of Jack.

Jack felt his breath quicken as he concentrated on not staring at her. The way her bathing suit clung to every curve, the way her nipples pushed against the thin, wet fabric – making him want to reach out and...

"I'm Enid."

Jack gave a start. He'd forgotten the kid.

"Would you like some lemonade?" Eve asked Enid.

"Sure."

Jack remained silent. He was horrified at the strength of his emotions. He wanted Eve like he never thought it possible to want a woman.

"What would *you* like?" Eve asked Jack.

Jack grimaced. He had the uneasy feeling that she read him like a cheap novel.

"Iced tea for me," a woman's voice called out from behind him.

Jack spun around, disconcerted. He wasn't used to missing things. Especially people.

Laura Hargrove was twenty-two and so pale that she seemed almost translucent. Her light yellow bikini did nothing to diminish the impression of fragility as she tucked a tendril of her baby blond hair behind her ear. Her pale blue eyes shone with hostility and were aimed at Jack's obvious hard-on.

Jack felt his face go hot as he suppressed the urge to kick the chair out from under her bony ass.

"My sister, Laura. Laura, this is Enid and…?" Eve gave him a quizzical smile, like they'd never met.

"Jack Fox." He held out his hand to Laura, who ignored it.

"Laura, can you entertain Enid while Mr. Fox and I talk?"

Laura tilted her head in what might be construed as a nod.

"Nice meeting you," Jack said, sarcastically.

Eve disappeared into the dark interior and, with a quick "stay here" look at Enid, Jack followed. He found himself watching the sway of Eve's hips as she left high arched wet footprints behind her. She led him into a library that had a strangely decadent feel.

Jack's eyes fell on a framed photograph. He picked it up, examining it. It was the three sisters in their early teens. Jeni struggling with a fake smile as a frowning Laura shrank from the camera. Eve was in the foreground, gazing into the camera, eyes dark and challenging.

Eve snatched the photograph from his hands. "Is this your idea of discretion?"

Jack smiled, feeling on firmer ground at the sound of irritation in her voice. He nodded in the direction of the patio and Laura. "Sweet girl. Bit too talky for my taste."

Eve's lips tightened.

Jack reached out, slipped his fingers under her amber necklace and held it up so that it gleamed.

Eve recoiled, clutching at her necklace. "What the hell do you think you're doing?"

"Amber. Like your stepfather's ring."

"They never found his ring," Eve said, her voice sharp as a sewing needle.

"Or nine of his fingers," Jack retorted, suddenly feeling more in control.

Eve eyed him coolly. "Mr. Fox, you work for me. I paid you."

"Too much."

Her eyes widened in surprise.

"*Way* too much," Jack emphasized.

Eve studied him.

"Like you're up to no good." Jack stepped close, his voice soft. "Miss Hargrove, *are you up to no good?*"

Eve's mouth dropped open in astonishment. After several moments, she said in a frigid voice, "Let's get something straight...!"

Jack closed the space between them. "How 'bout we get straight – I ain't your bitch so stop barkin'."

They locked eyes.

He took her in his arms and kissed her. Her lips yielded, kissing back and Jack felt an exultation surge through him. Wave after wave, it wrecked him to the core.

Somewhere, from deep within the mansion, a door slammed. The spell was shattered.

Eve's slap bit into his face. "Get out!" She backed away, rubbing her lips with the back of her hand.

Jack forced himself to give her a slow cool grin. With a mock salute, he strode out.

When he reached his car, he abruptly stopped.

The kid!

He turned as Enid came bounding out the front door.

"Where the hell have you been?" Jack snapped.

Enid's eyes flashed with hurt.

His cell rang and he snapped it open, "What?"

Rachel answered timidly, "Jack?"

"What'd you find out?" Jack asked, trying to ignore the wounded expression on Enid's face.

"Is everything okay?" Rachel asked.

"Yeah," Jack said, feeling like a jackass.

Enid was scowling at him, trying to act like she didn't give a shit.

"Hold on," Jack covered the receiver and said to Enid, "Look, I lost my temper. I'm not used to being tailed by…" His words trailed off – he didn't know what to call her.

"Who's tailing you?" Rachel asked. "FYI, if you think you just apologized – that wasn't it."

"Tell me you got something – I need an address." He listened, frowning.

Jack hung up and got in the car. He gripped the steering wheel, feeling disgusted with himself. He hated losing his temper, losing control. Over the years, he had prided himself on keeping his cool and not letting things, especially women, get to him.

Enid knocked on the passenger window.

Shit!

Jack unlocked the passenger door and Enid hopped in. "Forget something?"

As Jack was pulling out, a truck pulled in. It had the license plate of an unmarked detective's vehicle. Jack stopped, waited.

A sixty-something detective got out and shot him a look that made Jack suspect that he was looking at a man who would question rain falling from the heavens as being rain falling from the heavens – unless it was certified by God himself, DNA evidence and a solid I.D. from Mother Mary.

A disgustingly handsome man in his twenties got out of the passenger side. Jack heard Enid suck in her breath. He found himself glaring at the younger man's perfect physique with a mixture of admiration and envy.

Did I ever even look half that good?

"Are you here to see Eve Hargrove?" Jack called out to the older man.

"Who are you?" The detective walked over.

"Jack Fox, private detective." Jack got out of the car.

"Detective Bud Orlean." His eyes flickered as he shook Jack's hand.

It was the flicker of recognition that Jack knew all too well. Whenever an old-timer on the force heard his name, they might not know him, but they remembered his father. And he knew damn well they all knew the stories.

"What brings you here?" Bud said.

Enid materialized beside Jack. She gazed at the handsome guy with lovesick eyes. "*Hi.*"

Chip took her outstretched hand. "Hi."

Enid held his hand in hers, unwilling to let it go. "Call me Veronica."

Jack shot her a startled look.

Veronica?

Chip smiled with a warmly humble quality that even Jack had to admit was charming. Enid's mouth formed a soundless 'O' of admiration.

Jack made a face, pulled Enid toward the car. "Come on, *Veronica*, we've got to get you back to the nunnery."

Enid allowed herself to be maneuvered to the car, her eyes never leaving Chip's face. Jack met Bud's wry eyes as he deposited Enid in the front seat and shut the door. He locked her in.

Enid tried the handle and found it locked. She glowered at Jack as he walked back and handed Detective Orlean a business card. "In case I can be of any assistance."

"Detective Orlean?" the butler called out from the front doors.

Bud held the card in the air in a "thank you" as he walked toward the mansion.

Jack watched them disappear, wishing he was a fly on the wall. He unlocked the driver's side door, but Enid slapped it down, locking it.

Jack frowned and, using his clicker, unlocked it.

She slapped it again.

"What the hell…!"

"How's it feel?" Enid said tauntingly. "Child locks also work on *immature adults!*"

"Open the door, you little…!"

"*What?*" Enid asked with narrowed eyes.

Jack bent down, enunciating his words, "Open. The. Door. *Veronica.*"

After a long moment, a scowling Enid allowed Jack to unlock his door. He got in.

"No fun being treated like a kid, is it?" Enid sniped as Jack started the car.

"*I'm* not the kid. *You are.*"

"I'm not a kid," Enid said, tossed her head. "I'm a young woman on the verge of *womanhood.*"

"Before you start booking the honeymoon suite for you and Dudley-Do-Wrong over there, you need to step back from the 'verge' before I knock you back."

"Violence!" Enid exclaimed in mock shock.

"Until I can deliver you back to wherever or whoever you belong to…" Jack abruptly stopped, remembering that Sam had told him her mother was dead.

"I'm not going anywhere and you can't make me."

"How old are you?"

"Gee, I don't know, how's your math?" Enid pretended to get out an invisible calculator and punch in numbers, "Let's see, a drunken one-night stand, nine months…"

"All right! All right!" Jack waved her into silence.

CHAPTER TWENTY-FOUR

Almost all our desires, when examined, contain something too shameful to reveal.

—Victor Hugo

"The kid has eyes for you," Bud told Chip, their footsteps echoing under the domed entryway.

"She's just a kid," Chip shrugged.

"What do you want?" Eve's voice came from above.

Bud and Chip looked up.

Eve stood at the top of the staircase, one hand gracefully resting on the rail as she gazed down at them. She had a sheer wrap over her still-wet bathing suit. Bud heard Chip's breath catch and immediately regretted bringing him along.

Why didn't I listen to Bunnie?

Bud felt his alarm growing as Eve sauntered down the stairs, her eyes focused on Chip with the intensity of a cat eyeing a bug.

Bud glanced at Chip and was startled to see he had a besotted expression that could compete with the way the kid had been sopping Chip up with her eyes.

"Should I have the maid prepare a guest bedroom for you, Detective Orlean?" Eve smiled, sweet as saccharin. "You're here so much, I'm thinking of declaring you as a dependent on my 1040."

Bud felt a dull ache in his jaw and realized he was clenching. He took a deep breath and said in a controlled voice, "DNA confirmed the body is Daniel Hargrove."

"Oh!" Eve staggered back.

Chip bounded forward, wrapping his arms around her waist to steady her from falling. She leaned into him, fluttering her eyelashes up at him. Chip gazed down at her, his face flush with emotion.

Bud grunted in disgust, stepped forward and roughly shoved Chip away. Eve staggered, almost falling. She caught herself and glared at Bud with hostility.

"Dad!"

Eve's eyes lit up in delight as she met Bud's eyes and repeated, *"Daddy?"*

"Are you all right?" Chip asked Eve.

Eve was in the process of melting him a smile that Bud instinctively knew would nail that kid's feet to the floor. Bud grabbed Chip, hauled him across the floor and shoved him out the front door like he was an eight-year-old. Bud had a glimpse of Chip's shocked face as he slammed the door behind him, locking it.

"My, my, my," Eve purred. "What a pretty boy you have."

Bud breathed heavily, not daring to speak.

"Why'd you bring him to me? A gift?"

"You sick, twisted…!"

"Don't worry, detective, he's too young for me. I like my men older and…" Eve leaned in, touched his collar where it met his skin.

Bud shivered.

"Wiser." Her breath was hot against his neck.

Bud her shoved away and got out as fast as if he'd been standing in an open flame. He was unnerved by the deeply unsettling sensation of being unsure of who he was trying to save – Chip…

Or himself.

CHAPTER TWENTY-FIVE

Is it not these well-fed long-haired men that I fear, but the pale and hungry-looking.

—Julius Caesar

Enid was dying to ask Jack where he was going to be dumping her off, but didn't want to give him the satisfaction. It didn't matter anyway – she came, she met her "father" and...

I want to punch his stupid face!

Every time she thought about how he locked her in the car like she was some idiot kid, she felt a hot rush of stinging tears. Not only did he humiliate her, he did it in front of the most incredible guy in the entire world.

Chip.

The sound of his name was like honey and butter. His face, his body, the sound of his voice was chiseled in her mind, and she luxuriated in the memory of when she first saw his gorgeousness standing there like he was a normal human being.

Not!

Then she remembered Jack hustling her to the car and *humiliating* her right in front of the only man she knew she could ever love!

She looked at Jack – calmly driving the car – ugh! She wanted to reach her hand into his chest like a ninja-magician-warrior and rip his still-pumping heart out and feed it to his stupid face!

She clenched her fists, unaware that a maniacal smile was distorting her face.

Jack glanced at her. After a moment, he asked, "You need me to stop? You look like you're trying to pinch a loaf."

"How could you embarrass me like that?" Enid yelled.

"What the hell are you talking about?" Jack said, surprised.

"Take me to the bus station."

"You've got no money."

"I'm sure I can find some pedophile who will be willing to defile me for ten bucks!"

Jack clenched the wheel.

"What do you care, anyway?" she demanded.

"Does this have something to do with – *Chip*?"

"No!" Enid snarled.

"Then get your bowels out of a bind and stop acting like a spoiled brat."

Enid crossed her arms, staring forward.

Jack said, "You are along for the ride and I expect you to retain some semblance of a good attitude."

"Good luck with that," Enid retorted. She stared out the window, watching as the scenery changed from upscale manicured lawns and golf courses into something that looked more like how she envisioned the Wild West would have looked. Her stomach rumbled as they passed a "Welcome to Carefree" sign. Jack slowed the car to a crawl through a town of quirky art galleries, kitschy western stores and restaurants with names like "The Horny Toad" and "The Satisfied Frog."

"You hungry?" Jack said.

Enid made a disparaging face that she hoped kept her "eat crap" attitude intact without quite saying "no" to the food. Several moments later, Enid felt her heart sink when she realized Jack had taken her reaction for a "no."

He turned up a dirt driveway. An occasional saguaro jutted out, but the landscape was mostly low brush and mesquite trees. Turning a bend, Enid was startled to see what she could only describe as a homemade Jesus garden. She glanced at Jack and saw that he was as surprised as her.

"Relatives?" Enid asked wryly.

He gave her a look.

It was sheer Christian-crazy – from the store-bought Jesus statues to the handmade signs with dire warnings, Enid stared in amazement. There had to be a hundred of them.

Enid read aloud from a sign in red spray paint, "I will make mine arrows drunk with blood and my sword shall devour flesh."

Jack parked in front of a giant agonized face of Jesus. Enid got out of the car, glanced around nervously. "Seriously, what's up with the...?"

"This time, you stay in the car. This will only take a few minutes."

"How much?"

"What?"

"Like you said – I'm broke. How much will you pay me to wait here?"

"Not one damned dime."

Enid shrugged. "I don't like your odds."

"This is work. Wait here and when I'm done, I'll buy you lunch."

Enid made a face, shrugged. "I don't want to meet your girlfriend anyway."

Jack gave her a look and walked to the house. Enid thought she saw a curtain twitch, but wasn't sure.

Enid got out and leaned against the car, looking up at the giant saguaro cactus that loomed near the house. If it got knocked over in a storm, it looked like it could crush the house. If it got knocked over *right now*, it would squish Jack like a bug. Enid smiled as she imagined the horrified look on his face as it crashed down on him. Enid shaded her eyes to get a better look and was startled to see a hawk perched on top, staring at her like she was prey.

"Turn 'round, hands up!" a woman's voice rasped.

Enid jerked forward, hands flying into the air. Her eyes darted around the yard, unsure of where the voice was coming from.

Maude Brisquet, a wizened woman who looked like sixty going on six hundred, was coming from behind the house, a shotgun pointed at Jack. Her loose-fitting housedress flecked with flour puffed out, revealing spindly legs. Her brown eyes in her wrinkled face reminded Enid of the hawk, which, at the sound of the woman's voice, had taken flight.

Terrified that the old witch was going to shoot Jack, Enid bounded forward, shouting, "Hey!"

The old woman spun around – and the shotgun was pointed at *her*. Enid let out a croak that, in her head, translated to some magical words that would make the old woman drop the gun.

"Take it easy," Jack said, his voice surprisingly soft and calm.

Enid glanced at him, too scared to speak.

He met her eyes and gave her a "let me handle this" look.

"Gov'ment?" Maude barked, aiming the shotgun at Jack.

"No ma'am. I'm a private detective. I mean no harm. I came to ask you some questions and I'll be leaving."

"Be leaving is right!" Maude motioned him to his car with the shotgun. "Git!"

Hands high, Jack cautiously picked his way through the Jesus art. "God bless you, ma'am."

Enid blinked in surprise.

Jack gestured to a homemade statue of Jesus hanging on a twine-tied cross, "In the name of Jesus, God bless you for spreading the good work…"

Maude's eyes narrowed suspiciously.

Jack's face transformed. "Raised up in the blood of Christ – on my knees every morning and night, praising the Good Lord, praising Jesus Christ Our Savior."

Enid's mouth fell open.

The old woman's grip on the shotgun wavered as she called out, "What you want?"

"With all due respect, ma'am," Jack said softly, "I had some questions about – your daughter."

"Don't have no daughter but the one burning in hell!" Maude gripped the shotgun tighter, her finger twitching on the trigger.

Enid's mouth went bone-dry as she watched Jack smile gently. "Yes, ma'am. I hate to bring up painful memories…"

"My conscious is clean! Nothing painful for *me!*"

"Ma'am? May I…?" He nodded toward Enid, "It's my daughter I'm thinking about."

Enid jolted, shocked at the sound of "my daughter" coming from his mouth, but then remembered that he was in the middle of a string of lies – calling her "daughter" was as sincere as the rest of it.

"I was hoping I could trouble you for a glass of water – for my daughter?"

Maude frowned, glanced at Enid.

Jack turned his eyes heavenward and quoted, "Whoever drinks of the water that I give will never be thirsty again. It will become in him a spring of water welling up to eternal life."

Maude's eyes changed from hostile to unsure, the muzzle of the shotgun dropping subtly.

"Well, *devil's nightgown*," Maude said, dropping the shotgun to her side, "I guess if you was up to no good, you wouldn't be bringin' no child."

Enid frowned.

What the frig?!

"Come on then, kiddie." Maude gestured for Enid to follow her.

Enid stood frozen, too surprised to lower her hands.

Maude walked past her, tapped her butt with the shotgun, "Come on now."

Enid jumped forward, sending Jack a desperate look.

"I think *the child* might be hungry too," Jack said with a smile.

Enid scowled at Jack, who didn't even try to conceal that he was laughing at her.

CHAPTER TWENTY-SIX

A casual stroll through the lunatic asylum shows that faith does not prove anything.

—Friedrich Nietzsche

The inside of the shotgun lady's house made the front yard look normal. Every nook and crevice was filled with something religious. Suffering Jesus statues, mournful Mary's and a multitude of religious quotes in everything from embroidery to cross-stitch to notebook paper tacked to the wall on a straight pin.

"Jesus," Jack muttered.

"What?" Maude paused at the door leading into the kitchen.

Jack felt a stab of guilt. The sharp gleam in her eyes reminded him of Sister Mary, the nun at the tiny Catholic Church on the reservation that his grandmother dragged him to for the two years he lived with her – after his mother died. He flinched at the memory of his mother and forced any thoughts of her out of his mind.

Jack stared at the curtains decorated with a repeating pattern of Christ in the bloody process of being crucified.

"Lovely home."

"I know," Maude smiled. "I did it myself."

"Oh." Jack tried to look surprised.

Maude motioned for them to sit at a weathered wooden table. Maude grabbed two Jesus glasses out of a cabinet and filled them with water from the tap.

Jack eyed a salt shaker in the shape of a cross. A suffering Jesus hung on it – an "S" written across his belly and one hole in the top of his head. The pepper shaker was a Jesus, which had a "P" on his belly and multiple holes in the top of his head.

Jack concentrated on drinking the water she set in front of them as he tried to ignore the agonized Jesus face that gazed up at him from the glass.

"Private detective, huh?" Maude put a plate of what Jack could only describe as crucifixion sugar cookies in front of Enid. "I'm Maude Brisquet, but I guess you know that if you came all the way out here."

"Jack Fox." He pulled out his wallet, showing his identification.

She glanced at it. "Is part of your job sneaking around like a thief in the night?"

"I'm sorry about that. I…"

Maude bit into a cookie, leaving teeth marks across Jesus's face. "You here about *Ann*?" She said the name like she was chewing on dirt.

"Yes ma'am."

Maude tapped a finger on a worn Bible that sat on the table. "Can't tell me the Devil ain't alive and well."

"Thriving," Jack said, stealing a glance at Enid. She was nibbling an ear off her Jesus cookie.

"Amen! Ann turned her back on the Lord and run out with that piece of white trash boyfriend – she thought I didn't know but I knew. I drove down there myself – *The Sugar Shack*." Maude spat the words in disdain.

"Serpents and sodomites," Jack answered, feeling the skin under his right eye twitch like fishing wire was jerking on it.

"Little pitchers have big ears," Maude nodded toward Enid.

"Honey," Jack smiled at Enid, "Why don't you take some cookies and wait for me in the car?"

"I'd rather stay with you, *Dad*."

"Please do what I ask, Sweetheart."

"Children don't listen to their parents. It's just the beginning. The devil lurks in all young girls, waiting to come out and fornicate."

Enid pushed the chair back, "I think I *will* wait in the car."

"Sit!" Maude said sternly.

With a gulp, Enid sat.

Hang in there, kid.

Maude pulled the Bible to her chest, eyes drifting toward the window. "I had a vision. Angel Gabriel himself came to me – told me that Ann's baby – spawned in evil and that place of vice – the baby needed to die. The Angel Gabriel told me to leave the baby to die."

Jack glanced nervously at Enid, who was staring in revulsion at Maude's withered trance-like face.

"Angel Gabriel told me the baby would be saved, once it was safe in the arms of Jesus – in heaven."

Jack tried to say "Amen," but couldn't.

"My Ann dying in that car accident was no accident – it was the righteous hand of The Lord."

Jack hesitated. "And – the baby?"

Maude looked him straight in the eye. "With Jesus, praise be to the Lord."

Jack tried to hide his disgust by dropping his eyes. He was surprised that Maude thought Ann's baby, Jeni, had died.

Why did she think Jeni had died as a baby? Who told her that?

"You're *glad* your own daughter's baby *died?*" Enid exclaimed.

"Enid!" Jack shot her a warning look.

Enid stared at Maude, trembling with rage. "How would you like it if somebody who was supposed to love and protect you left *you* to die?"

Jack stood, acutely aware that Maude's shotgun was leaning against the fridge, within her reach.

"Let's go," Jack said to Enid.

Enid stood, her fists clenched to her sides.

Maude turned on Enid, like she was the devil come to life in her kitchen. "Demon! Out! Out!"

Jack grabbed Enid and pushed her toward the door.

Enid shouted,"If you're happy a baby is dead - *you're* the evil one!"

"Go to the car!" Jack shoved Enid through the door and planted himself in the doorway, blocking Maude. He listened as Enid stumbled toward the car door.

Maude moved toward him with a menacing light in her eyes, "She'll break your heart, you know."

Jack heard the car door slam. He backed away from Maude, who followed him into the living room, the shotgun moving in herky-jerky motions with her words. "I saw the devil in *her* eyes and he was laughing at *you.*"

Jack backed through the front door, his feet making the porch boards groan. Out of the corner of his eye, he saw Enid in the front seat, behind the wheel. Jack heard the roar of the engine and sprinted to the car.

Jack, hearing the unmistakable click of the shotgun trigger, dove into the car just as the shotgun exploded.

Enid stomped on the accelerator, which slung Jack sideways. He grabbed the seat and fought to keep from tumbling out as Enid careened up the driveway. He had the fleeting image of an anguished Jesus face in the brush that missed catching him in the face by a hair.

The tires hit the asphalt of the road so violently that Jack hit his head and saw stars. Enid yanked the wheel in a hard right, followed by a left that sent the car screeching into the opposite lane.

Jack grabbed the wheel. "Slow down!"

Enid stomped on the brakes and Jack slammed into the dashboard.

"Don't you know how to drive?" Jack yelled, rubbing his shoulder that was throbbing with pain.

"No! I don't know how to drive! I'm too young. You *jerk!*"

Before Jack could speak, Enid burst into hysterical crying.

Jack stared at her in horror. This wasn't any crying like he'd ever seen. This was hiccupping, gulping for air, tomato-faced *wailing*. He got out and came to the driver's side, where he was able to push her into the passenger seat. Jack eased the car onto the dirt median and shut off the engine.

Her wailing was intensifying. He fought the urge to dump her on the side of the road and bolt.

"Are you okay?" He asked awkwardly.

"WAHHHHHHH!" She garbled out something incoherent.

Jack remembered something his father used to do. He reached over, gave her a medium-powered punch on the arm.

"OW! That hurt!" Enid stopped crying and glared at him indignantly.

"Yeah," Jack said enthusiastically, "But it took your mind off the crying."

Why's she looking at me like that?

"That's the stupidest thing I ever heard!" Enid said.

"You stopped crying."

Enid stared at him a long moment. "Can I have a hug?"

"Uh…" Jack recoiled in confusion.

Enid reached out to hug him and, grabbing a clump of his shirt, she blew her nose into it with a loud honk and used what was left of it to wipe her running nose. "Thanks."

Jack stared down at his snot-covered shirt in horror.

CHAPTER TWENTY-SEVEN

You must look into people, as well as at them.

–Lord Chesterfield

"There's no way Eve Hargrove murdered anyone – especially her own father," Chip said.

"You shadowing me was a bad idea," Bud muttered as he drove toward Phoenix.

"Gorgeous *and* rich. I can't believe some people get that lucky," Chip said wonderingly.

"She didn't get lucky. She did it the old-fashioned way and, by old-fashioned, I mean *medieval.* She murdered her father so she could get her grubby paws on his fortune."

"No way. She looks like an angel."

"Your mother is right. If you want to stay here, you need a job. The sooner, the better."

"I'm going to treat researching the book like a job. It's not like I'll be slacking off – I'll be with you all day, so it'll be like putting in a forty-hour week. At least until I start writing my novel."

"You need to start looking for a job *today* – this shadowing me stuff is not going to work."

"I don't get it. You agreed to it this morning. What changed?"

Bud kept quiet, recalling how Eve Hargrove had sized Chip up like a man-sized hors d'oeuvre. Bud shifted uncomfortably when he remembered the touch of her fingertips on his neck. He always imagined her as ice-cold and was shocked to feel the warmth of her touch. Not in his wildest dreams did he ever imagine he'd be susceptible to her touch.

"We're going home," Bud snapped, "You can borrow your mother's car to look for a job."

"You know, I do have friends I can stay with," Chip said defiantly. "It's not like I'm a kid you can order around. I can stay with Joe Westley – don't let it bother you that he's still smoking crack. Or I can stay with Linda Mottle – I think she broke up with the baby daddy who is a gangbanger, so the way is all clear of *me*."

"Fine! You can stay with us - until you come to your senses and go back to school."

"What's next?" Chip said. "Interrogation? Stake out a suspect?"

Twenty minutes later, Bud had Chip in a tiny file room at the station, buried in files.

"It's an important part of detective work, son." Bud said to Chip's disgruntled look. "One percent inspiration, ninety-nine percent perspiration." Bud headed out the door.

"Where are you going?"

"I'll be back before you get to the B's."

"That soon?" Chip said sarcastically, eyeing the stacks of files.

"I'll bring back lunch," Bud said, grinning his way down the hall.

Twenty minutes later, Bud flashed his badge to a nervous cashier manning the front door of The Candy Store. "Can you have Jeni Hargrove meet me out front? Tell her it's Detective Orlean. She knows me."

Within five minutes, Jeni stood in front of him. She wore jeans and a loose tee that concealed her outfit – or lack thereof.

Bud told her about finding her stepfather's body in the desert. "I'm sorry to break the news to you like this."

Jeni said, "I didn't figure he was alive. Not after all this time."

Bud studied her. There was something different about Jeni, but he could never quite put his finger on it. During the original investigation into Daniel Hargrove's disappearance, he had gotten to know the Hargrove family, and he quickly realized that Jeni was different – she was special. She reminded him of a dangerously ripe peach on a low-hanging branch.

The peach that ripens first is the first to rot.

He wished that someone as fiercely protective as Bunnie could have been her mother – things might have been better for her. There was something in Jeni's eyes that looked…

Breakable.

"How's the baby?" Bud said.

A shadow flitted across her face, followed by a forced smile. "Fine. Why'd you come down? You could have called and told me all this."

"I wanted to touch base with you – find out if anything's changed. Any new information that could help us?"

Jeni looked pensive.

Bud felt his pulse quicken.

"I did find out something," she said haltingly, "but I don't think it has anything to do with anything."

"Try me."

"Vivian Hargrove isn't my real mother."

Bud frowned, wondering why he hadn't come up with that information during his investigation.

"I hired a detective to help me find my real mother."

"Who'd you hire?"

"Jack Fox."

Bud raised his eyebrows.

"You know him?" she asked.

Bud nodded.

"I heard he's the best," she said.

Bud gave a noncommittal smile.

Until that morning, the last time Bud had seen Jack Fox was over thirty years ago – at the funeral of Jack's father. Jack was the illegitimate son who had been carefully hidden and quietly living with his mother "across the tracks". Jack wasn't even supposed to exist – much less show up for his father's funeral. There wasn't a police officer or detective in the city who could talk about the legendary Police Chief Harry Waterstone without recalling the stories of his funeral, which a teenage Jack Fox violently disrupted.

As a young recruit, Bud had been at the funeral. Even after all these years, the image of what Jack had done was seared in Bud's memory. The story had taken on an urban legend quality and Bud expected the stories to diminish but, over the years, the stories intensified. In one stroke, the kid – Jack – had forever destroyed the sterling reputation of Police Chief Harry Waterstone.

"When did you find out you were adopted?" Bud asked Jeni.

"That's just it. Vivian says I wasn't. She swears I'm hers, but I got proof she's lying."

"What proof?"

Jeni described to him the photograph that she had found of her mother, looking slim and fabulous in a bathing suit, when she should have been eight months pregnant. Bud listened with interest.

Bud said, "Has Jack had any luck with finding your mother?"

Jeni shook her head, wrapped her arms closer. "Can I ask you a question?"

"Sure."

Jeni looked down, miserable.

Bud said, "Is everything okay? Anything I can do to help?"

Tears sprang to Jeni's eyes. After a moment, she shook her head and escaped into the club.

Bud watched the red door closed behind her, wondering how Jack fit into the picture. It was too big of a coincidence that Jack Fox knew both the sisters, Eve and Jeni. Was Jack really trying to find Jeni's real mother like Jeni claimed or – was Jack Fox investigating Daniel Hargrove's murder?

CHAPTER TWENTY-EIGHT

Truth uncompromisingly told will always have its ragged edges.

—Herman Melville

Sitting in the passenger's seat, Enid listened as Jack rummaged through the trunk of his car. She could hear what sounded like muttering curses and, after a few minutes, he returned wearing a clean shirt.

"Next time you need to blow your nose, I have Kleenex in the glove compartment," Jack said, starting the engine.

"You keep laundry in the trunk of your car?" Enid said, eying his western-style shirt.

"Boy Scout motto: Be prepared," Jack answered.

"That's the Girl Scouts."

"It's still good advice."

"I'm hungry," Enid said. "Are you planning to feed me anytime this century?"

Within twenty minutes, they were sitting in an ugly orange booth chomping on chicken at El Pollo Loco.

The silence was starting to get to Enid when Jack wiped his mouth and said, "So, tell me about your mom."

"What do you care?" she snapped, before she could stop herself.

"Shift the attitude into neutral. We are going to do this thing. We are going to have a normal conversation. Like two mature individuals."

Enid made a sour face.

If he thinks I'm going to talk for his entertainment, he's got another thing coming.

After several moments of silence, Jack said, "Okay. I'll get this party started. I'll tell you what I remember about your mom…"

Enid's eyes flew open in alarm. She did *not* want to hear this – not any of it!

"I never even knew her last name," Jack said.

"How romantic."

"No. It wasn't." Jack said calmly, "I was as much a one-night stand to her as she was to me."

Enid dropped her chicken wing. "I'm going to barf."

"Listen, kid – you want me to treat you like a clueless moron, I'm happy to oblige. You want to talk in truths – here I am. I'm your dad. Am I happy about it?" Jack made a face, "Are *you*?"

Enid glared at him.

"Your mom had great legs," Jack said, taking a bite of his chicken.

"Doesn't anymore."

"When – *how* did she die?"

Enid blinked, caught off guard. "I'd rather not talk about it."

"First time I met her, she grabbed my butt."

"Gross!"

"She made me laugh. And her hair smelled terrific."

"Is that before or after she blew chunks all over your carpet?"

"We all eventually blow chunks on somebody somewhere."

"Not me!"

Jack smiled.

"Were you ever married?" Enid said.

"Nope."

"You have any other kids?"

"Nada."

"Do I have grandparents?" Enid said, trying to hide the eagerness in her voice.

Enid's mom had grown up in foster homes and Enid had always fantasized about having grandparents. She envisioned them living in a big farmhouse that they would let her explore – an attic where she would stumble onto clues to unsolved mysteries and treasure maps that would lead her into wildly exciting adventures. For Christmas, she imagined they gave her a horse named "Star."

She glanced at Jack and was surprised to see a pained expression on his face. She forced herself to say in a breezy voice, "Is that a 'no'?"

"Dead."

Sharp disappointment made her frown. "How'd they die?"

Jack didn't answer. He suddenly seemed a million miles away and it wasn't in a good way. She cleared her throat.

He looked at her, startled.

"Fair's fair," Enid said, imitating Jack as she repeated back to him, "You want to talk in truths – here I am."

"You're one-quarter Apache."

Enid's eyes widened in pleasure, "For real?"

"Your great-grandmother was a medicine woman – a healer."

"Jeez," Enid breathed, thrilled.

"She helped raise me. I lived with her on the reservation for two years while – " Jack's voice trailed off.

"While what?"

"How did your mother die?" Jack said.

Enid took a bite of chicken, answered with a mouth full of food, "Ee's ot ead."

"What?"

Enid took her time, swallowed. "She's not dead."

"Is that the truth?"

"She drinks too much." Enid watched Jack's face for any signs of pity – any signs of anything that would piss her off. Nothing. But it was a good kind of nothing. "Do you drink?"

"Sometimes. Do you?" he said.

"No!" She shook her head in disgust.

"Does your mother know where you are?"

Enid winced, regretting telling him her mother wasn't dead.

"Don't you think you should let her know you're alive?"

"She doesn't care."

"I guarantee, she does."

"You're not going to send me back!" Enid said angrily.

"I'll make you a deal. We call your mom and tell her you're okay and – aren't you out for summer?"

"Yeah," Enid answered suspiciously.

Jack shrugged nonchalantly. "You can - hang out here. For a couple days."

Enid said, "Do you have any – *horses?*"

"I have a cat and one guest bedroom."

A flush of happiness warmed her face. After a few moments, she pretended nonchalance and shrugged. "Maybe a few days."

CHAPTER TWENTY-NINE

A little more than kin, and less than kind.

—William Shakespeare

As Jack pulled up to his house, he couldn't help but feel a sense of pride. It wasn't much – but it was his. It was built in the 1940s, which, in Phoenix, made it a historical building. Every house on Hoover Street was historic, which was a Phoenix way of saying you lived in a quaint house with bad windows and suspicious plumbing. He never got around to the time and cost of updating the windows and, over the years, found he enjoyed the pleasantly dangerous shaking and rattling sounds they made when a monsoon was brewing. The utility bill was ridiculously high in the summer, but so was the price of putting in all new windows. The clean lines of the house were almost hidden by his poorly tended – yet pleasant – landscaping.

Jack pulled into his driveway to the blare of Katy Perry emanating from Annie Cisco's blinged-out boom box. Annie and her girlfriends were washing her brand-new cherry-red Mustang.

Jack had known Annie since she was a toddler and had been disconcerted when he realized that she was nursing a serious adolescent crush for him.

Her father, Nick, was an ex-Marine with a penchant for guns. He and Jack had been friendly acquaintances over the years – until Annie started showing an inappropriate amount of interest in Jack.

Annie had transformed from a coltish tomboy to a bikini-clad beauty overnight. Between sunning herself in the front yard and washing the Mustang in her bikini – Jack avoided the hell out of her.

"Who's that?" Enid said.

"Neighbor's kid."

They got out of the car.

Annie posed with the hose and gave Jack a look beyond her years. "Hey Mr. Fox! Wanna help us wash the Mustang?"

Two teenage girls lounging on the porch, painting their toenails, erupted in giggles.

"Annie, Enid," Jack said awkwardly. "Enid, this is Annie."

"Hi," Enid said with a polite reserve that surprised Jack.

Jack opened his mouth to speak, but Annie flicked the hose at him, getting his shirt wet. The porch girls dissolved into nervous giggling.

Nick stepped out onto the porch, face dark.

Jack waved politely to Nick, who managed a tight-lipped nod. Jack didn't look back as he walked to his house.

Once behind closed doors, Enid said, "Creep-a-delic."

"Tell me about it," Jack said wryly.

It must've been the right answer, because Enid grinned.

"It ain't much, but it's home," Jack said.

Spare furnishings were interrupted with various ex-girlfriends' half-hearted attempts at decorating. No matter how the relationship ended, Jack made it a point to leave their touches on his house – a reminder of the women he had let through the door.

Sylvia had hung the framed photograph of the sunset from one of their weekends in Rocky Point. An eight-inch wooden nutcracker statue had been a gift from Gretta – it was a "Sam Spade" style detective with fedora pulled low over the eyes and his jaw ready to crush walnuts. His foot had broken off and Jack had left it sitting by the figurine for the day he remembered to glue it back. Mary had bought him burgundy pillows for the couch that were now faded and threadbare, and Mallory gave him the coffee table book of birds that sat on an end table. Stella had left a gash in the wall where she had hurled a coffee mug at his head, purposefully missing his skull – at least he always liked to think she aimed to miss.

A black cat jumped onto a nearby chair. Jack picked Harriett up in one arm. "You like cats?"

"I don't know," Enid said, eying the cat.

"Then you're even. She doesn't know if she likes you either."

Enid made a face.

Jack led her down a short hallway to a tiny bedroom that contained a twin-sized bed, chair, and nightstand with a driftwood lamp. Jack pointed down the hall, "Bathroom's there. Towels in the closet. Use your own bar of soap. Do you have any luggage?"

"At – a friend's house."

"I thought you didn't know anybody in town?"

"She's – a mutual friend."

"That's right," Jack said, wagging his finger at her, "Sam said he picked you up from Jeni's apartment."

Enid nodded.

"Sam also said he thought you had a gun."

"Well, *I don't*."

Jack stroked the cat.

"Do *you* have a gun?" Enid said.

"I don't like guns."

"Aren't detectives supposed to have guns?"

"Detectives are supposed to have *brains*. Much more dangerous than a gun."

"Yeah, right."

"What grade are you in?"

"Why?"

"You going to college?"

"Maybe."

"What's your favorite color?" Jack asked.

"Why?"

Jack sighed. "Because I intend to take this highly dangerous information and use it against you. Isn't that obvious?"

Enid scowled. "Do you have a girlfriend I need to know about?"

An image of Eve's face rose in Jack's mind and the thought of her being anybody's girlfriend, much less *his*, seemed ludicrous. Eve Hargrove was above anything so common as things being someone's girlfriend.

"Why don't you get settled in – I have work to do," he said, abruptly heading for the kitchen.

Jack breathed a sigh of relief when he heard the click of the sparebedroom's door closing behind Enid. He was glad to be alone. He wasn't used to having a kid shadowing him, blowing snot on him, doubling the lunch tab, smashing the hell out of his car and bawling hysterically – not to mention hassling him constantly with her teenage attitude.

Where the hell does she get that moxie?

In the kitchen, Jack fed the cat and brewed a pot of coffee. He sat down to the table with his laptop. Sitting at the kitchen table and looking out the window that overlooked the backyard was his favorite place to think. The backyard had simple desert landscaping and mesquite trees that reminded him of his grandmother's house, which gave him a sense of comfort.

He did an online search for "The Sugar Shack, Phoenix" and smiled when he saw that it was categorized as a "drinking establishment" featuring topless dancers. It opened in 1952 and ran continuously until it burnt down in 1978. The owner, Cormac Delrow, had been suspected of arson for insurance fraud, but no charges were ever filed. A search for Cormac Delrow showed that he was currently living in Apache Junction. Jack entered Cormac's contact information into his phone. It was just after three o'clock and, if he left now, he could be on Cormac's front step in forty minutes.

He hesitated, irritated at the thought of taking Enid with him, but reluctant to leave her alone in his house. He went to her door, knocked softly.

No answer.

He wrote a note and was taping it to her door when she jerked it open.

"What?" she asked, irritably. She snagged the note from his hand and read it. "Apache Junction? Do we have relatives there?"

Jack felt his heart sink.

CHAPTER THIRTY

Whoever fights monsters should see to it that in the process he does not become a monster. And if you gaze long enough into an abyss, the abyss will gaze back into you.

—Friedrich Nietzsche

Lunch in hand, Bud pushed open the door to the tiny room where he had left Chip sorting through files. He was startled to hear a woman's voice and, entering, he stood staring in shock.

Eve Hargrove was sitting – no, *draped* – across Chip's utilitarian desk.

At the sight of him, Chip's face flushed with guilt and Eve's eyes sparkled with delight.

"Daddy dearest," she said mockingly.

Chip shot her a startled look, but Eve never took her eyes off Bud as she playfully said, "Your son's trying to seduce me."

Chip's face burned red.

Scowling, Bud slapped the paper bag lunches on the desk.

"What's for lunch, Pops?" Eve said with a devilish glint in her eyes. She looked in the bag, wrinkling her nose in distaste.

"What do you want?" Bud said through clenched teeth.

"It's a business call. Unfortunately, it's not your business."

Bud said, "Nobody *I* need murdered – so…?"

Eve gave a silky smooth laugh.

"What do you want?" Bud said.

Eve pouted, slid off the desk and stood. Her movement caused her exotic perfume to drift over him. Chills jangled down his spine.

Eve said, "I'm here to see Frank Ficus."

Bud narrowed his eyes, surprised.

What's she up to?

Chip interrupted, "She came here looking for Frank."

"He hasn't been on the force for over ten years," Bud said, his eyes narrowed with suspicion.

Eve shrugged helplessly, "My bad."

"What do you want with Frank?" Bud asked.

"You know, Bud, I'm not sure you're the right person to be confiding in." Eve turned to Chip, caressed him with her eyes, "Tomorrow night?"

Bud grabbed Eve's arm and pushed her out the door. Bud slammed the door behind them and shoved Eve into the wall, "You stay away from – !"

"Old man," Eve hissed.

Bud froze.

Her words seemed to capture vapors – silent fears that shapeshifted up from deep within *him*. She had put a voice to his darkest fears.

Witch.

Eve stepped up to him. He could almost taste her perfume. She leaned in like she was trying to whisper a secret into his mouth – like she was out to kiss him...

Afraid to breathe, Bud had the sensation of being caught on a barbed wire hook. Any motion, any thought – would cause her poisonous barbs to dig deeper into his flesh.

As if reading his thoughts, she gave him a wicked smile that dumped ice water down Bud's spine. An instant later, she was gone and Bud realized that he was trembling.

Old man.

Bud wiped sweat from his brow. Her words, that repugnant smile – they echoed in his head. He clenched his fist and barged into the file room where he grabbed a fistful of Chip's shirt. "You're not seeing her – you're not ever going near her!"

Chip broke free of his grasp and opened his mouth to speak, but the ferocity in Bud's eyes halted him. Chip hesitated and, looking away said, "Yeah. All right."

Bud felt a searing pain race down his left arm and he reflexively gripped it, sagged backwards with a groan.

Chip jumped to his side, "What is it? Your heart?"

A relentless weight hunkered down on his chest and then two blasts of searing pain. Bud heard Chip's voice saying something – frantic – what was it? The ominous, oncoming monsoon – he was out in the open, unprotected. He flinched at the distant sound of Eve's laughter. He reached out, trying to touch it – *her* – his fingers finding purchase on the thickness of nothing as he slipped deeper and deeper into the abyss. The last thing he remembered thinking was…

She is the darkness.

CHAPTER THIRTY-ONE

All universal moral principles are idle fancies.

–Marquis de Sade

Flying down the highway with Jack at the wheel, Enid gazed wide-eyed at the Superstition Mountains that, even to her untrained eyes, looked stark and dangerous. She couldn't imagine anyone wanting to hike up there, unless they had a death wish. They were heading toward Apache Junction, which Jack had told her was famous for being the home of a ghost town and the Lost Dutchman's Gold Mine.

Her imagination fired by the thought of lost treasure, she peppered him with questions until he finally gave in and told her the story. She settled back and let his words flow over her as her eyes rested on the mountains that seemed so aptly named.

"The story my grandmother told me was that a German settler named Jacob saved the life of a member of one of the richest families in the area. To thank him, they told him the location of their mine, which was full of gold treasure. Jacob's business partner got greedy, attacked him and left him for dead. Jacob survived long enough to draw a map to the gold mines and gives it to the doctor right before he died."

"What then?" Enid said.

"Thousands of people for the past hundred years searching for the lost gold – nothing."

"You think it's real?"

"I doubt it. I think Jacob was messing with people's heads."

"Why?"

"Maybe he wanted to be remembered for something and that was his last chance – who knows."

"You ever look for it?"

Jack grins, "I don't think you can call yourself a Arizonan unless you hiked up there at least once looking for the lost treasure."

"Nobody hikes in Florida."

"The whole state is three feet above sea level – what's there to look at?"

"Have you ever been to Apache Junction?"

"A couple years ago. Got hired by a guy who worked part-time re-enacting gunfights at the ghost town for tourists. He thought his wife was cheating."

"Was she?"

"Yeah."

"Was his gun real or fake?"

"Always assume they're real."

"Did he try to shoot her?" Enid said.

"No, but he sledge-hammered the hell out of the boyfriend's car."

"Boyfriend?" Enid asked in a sharp voice.

"What do you want me to call him?"

"Cheating sleazebag! What happened then?" Enid said.

"My check cleared – so…" Jack shrugged.

"How'd you become a detective?"

Jack's lips tightened. "This is our exit."

They found Cormac Delrow's house easily. The whole town seemed to be a series of squat, ugly houses. Cormac's house had the nicest truck in the driveway, which gave it the sense of being the best home in the neighborhood.

"I don't want to wait in the car. It's too hot."

Jack hesitated.

"You won't even know I'm there."

Jack looked at her doubtfully.

She gave her most winning smile, which was rusty.

Jack sighed, gestured for her to follow him.

Before they reached the front door, a cacophony of barking dogs hit their ears. Jack rang the front doorbell and the barking increased to a frenzy.

From within the house, a man's shouted, "Shut up!"

Cormac Delrow opened the door. He shoved the dogs back with his legs.

Enid stepped behind Jack, thankful for the iron-barred door.

Cormac was in his late sixties and would have been six-foot four if he had been able to stand straight, but his neck was bent to the left like a gnarled tree. Enid had the feeling that he might have been handsome – a long, long time ago.

Jack held out his identification, shouting to be heard above the barking dogs. "My name is Jack Fox. Are you Cormac Delrow?"

"What's this about?" Cormac shouted.

"I was hoping for a few minutes of your time."

"Shoot." He made no move to invite them in or quiet the dogs.

"I'm doing a background check on a former employee," Jack shouted.

"Since when do detectives do employee background checks?"

"Ann Smith."

Cormac narrowed his eyes, jabbed a finger at Enid. "Who's *she*?"

"Enid!" she shouted, trying to look harmless. Even with the dogs, she didn't want to wait in the car.

"Wait here." Cormac herded the barking dogs into another room and shut them in. He unlocked the iron grate, motioned for Jack and Enid to enter.

They followed him into a living room, which was filled with the vibrant colors of Mexican art – skeletons with voluptuous breasts, skulls, and flowers in every shape and size.

Enid gazed around the room with wide, admiring eyes.

"You like it?" Cormac said.

"They're beautiful," Enid breathed.

Cormac notched his thumb in Enid's direction, "Kid's got taste."

Enid paused in front of a painting that somehow reminded her of a bullfight – or a teacup.

Cormac smiled proudly, "Paid a pretty penny for that one. Worth every cent."

"What is it?" Enid asked.

"Damned if I know," Cormac answered.

Jack said, "I collect Day of the Dead figurines."

Enid shot him a surprised look. What was that crap he'd been feeding her about not lying? And what the hell was a Day of the Dead figurine?"

"A doll collector, huh?" Cormac laughed.

Jack laughed, "I like 'em."

"You want something to drink?" Cormac asked. "Mountain Dew?"

"No thanks," Jack answered before Enid could say anything.

"Well, then, take a load off," Cormac said, "Fire away."

Enid sat on the couch while Cormac and Jack sank into well-worn armchairs.

"Ann Smith," Jack said. "She worked for you at − ?"

"Yeah, yeah," Cormac waved his hands. "Why you need to do a background check on a dead girl?"

"The dead girl's daughter is my client."

Cormac leaned forward. "The baby?"

"Not anymore," Jack answered with a smile.

Cormac rubbed his stubbly chin, "Yeah, I guess not." He looked at Jack, "How'd she turn out?"

"Fine."

"She's not...?" Cormac glanced at Enid, "Dancing...?"

Jack hesitated.

"Shit!" Cormac slapped his hand on his knee. "I hate to see girls end up on the pole."

Jack raised his eyebrows.

Cormac waved his hand, "Just 'cause I owned it, doesn't mean I want to see a baby grow up and hang off a pole like her mama, does it?"

"Can you tell me about Ann?" Jack asked.

"Sweet as they come. Dumb as a rock-sack."

"How so?" Jack asked.

Cormac shrugged, "Client would feed her a line of shit and she'd buy it − hook, line and sinker. Most girls know better or at least learn quick to know better. Except for the ones who love the bad boys. She wasn't one of those. Ann wasn't like the other girls − she didn't belong there. Didn't know the score. I think she had a falling-out with her family. Fell in with the wrong people."

"You remember any names of the 'wrong people'?"

"Some guy. I don't know. Same guy – different face. They're all the same – like they come off an asshole assembly line. She got knocked up and the asshole cleared out – left her high and dry. That's right! If it wasn't for Viv…" Cormac gave Jack a cagey look. "What exactly are you looking for?"

"Viv – as in Vivian Hargrove?" Jack said.

Cormac pressed his lips tight. "How much do you know?"

"Ann Smith had a baby named Jeni. When Ann died, Vivian took in the baby and raised her."

"You know Viv?"

"Not personally."

"So, you know Viv used to be a stripper." He said it more as a statement than a question.

"I'm not out to ruin anybody's reputation. Jeni wants to know who her real mother is."

"Then you know that Vivian Hargrove has the power to hang you up by the balls if…" Cormac glanced at Enid with a frown. "I'd rather handle a rattlesnake than mess with that woman. *Capisce?*"

"My client simply wants to know who her real mother is."

"Are you supposed to tell me that?"

"No," Jack said.

Cormac frowned. "Viv would have my hide if…"

"You keep in touch with her?"

"Hell no!" Cormac laughed, "Not Ms. High-and-Mighty 'never-knew-nothing-about-being-no-stripper' Vivian Hargrove! She's got a gold-encrusted social register stuck up her ass so far she wouldn't look at me if you had a gun to her head."

"How so?"

"She got a whiff of a higher rung of a ladder, and she lunged on it like a rabid dog. That's one thing about Viv – she never missed an opportunity. She had a knack of getting on the lap of money. I got on her once for taking too many breaks – she took her smoke break on the side of the club and I told her we weren't running an open market – she needed to take her smoke break with the other girls in the break room. She looked me in the eye and said 'I don't smoke.' I pointed at her lit cigarette and said 'What's that? A Johnny Walker?' She laughed and said, 'I'd look pretty funny standing out here without a prop, now wouldn't I?' She nodded toward the parking lot where a beat-up truck was pulling in and she said, 'I choose my laps,' and brother – she wasn't kidding!"

Jack said, "Is that how she met her husband, Daniel Hargrove?"

"That pervert who owned the bank – yeah, Viv zoomed in on him like a heat-seeking missile."

"Why was he a pervert?"

"Viv's thing was dressing up like a baby girl with a lollipop and lace undies. Truth be known, it gave me the heebie-jeebies."

"Why do you think she did that?"

"Every girl had her own angle. I don't care what drives them, as long as the bills get paid."

"How did Viv and Ann get to be friends?"

"They weren't really friends. At least I don't recall them hanging out together. When Ann had the baby and brought her in to show the girls, they all made a big to-do over her. I'm not one to oo-and-ah over a baby, but she *was* the prettiest little thing I ever saw. I forgot her name was Jeni."

"What did everybody think when Viv took the baby – after Ann died?"

"Surprised. Shocked, really. I never saw Viv as the warm-and-fuzzy mother type – even though she already had a kid and, like I said, I never saw that she was that friendly with Ann. The girls raised some money to help Viv with the cost."

"How about Ann's death? Any thoughts it might not be an accident?"

"No way it wasn't an accident! Besides, who would want to kill Ann? She didn't have a pot to piss in. It was pure bad luck – hit a phone pole. I heard she was dead before they could load her into the ambulance." Cormac looked at Jack, "What's she like? Jeni?"

"Gorgeous," Jack said.

Cormac nodded, "Ann was pretty, not gorgeous. That dimwit she took up with – I can't believe he had a decent piece of DNA in his whole branchless family tree. Maybe he had a hot grandmother – you can never figure on these things."

"Maybe."

Cormac smiled sadly, "Time keeps moving, doesn't she?"

Jack stood up and held out his hand, "Thank you for your time."

Cormac stood up and shook his hand, "I can't think that I actually helped with anything."

"You did."

Cormac led them to the front door, "If you run into Viv, could you *not* pass along any message from me? I'd like it just fine if she never knows you and me met."

"Done." Jack handed him a business card, "If you have any more information or if I can be of any help to you..."

Cormac took the card, nodded and waved as he went back into the house.

Heading back to Phoenix, Enid said, "What now?"

"What do you think?"

Enid thought. "Vivian Hargrove?"

Jack touched his nose.

Enid tried to hide her smile of pride.

CHAPTER THIRTY-TWO

A bad peace is even worse than war.

—Tacitus

Jack wasn't surprised that Enid knew the next move was to talk to Vivian Hargrove, but he was surprised at the thoughtful silence that she lapsed into as they drove toward Phoenix. She had been the original Chatty Cathy all the way to Apache Junction and he had expected the same on the trip back to Phoenix. Taking advantage of the silence, Jack flipped open his cell and dialed Jeni.

After several rings, Jeni answered.

"Hi, Jeni. Jack Fox here." Jack eased the car into the exit lane.

"Hey. What's going on?" She said.

"I need to get in touch with Vivian. Are you on good terms with her?"

After a moment of silence, Jeni answered, "I saw in the paper — she's doing one of her charity things tonight."

Enid said, "Can I talk to Jeni?"

Jack made a motion for her to wait.

Jeni continued, "It's her big annual fund raiser for the girls' home — at the Phoenician. Big bucks to get in."

Jack recalled the information that Rachel had already given him on Vivian Hargrove. She was on the board for a charity girls' home — something about orphaned and "wayward" girls. Jack had raised his eyebrows at the name — it seemed outdated and vaguely insulting.

"Need a date?" Jeni said.

"No, but thanks. Got to concentrate on work," Jack said, wishing it was Eve asking him that question.

"Oh," her voice hinting at disappointment. "How are you going to get in? It's by invitation only."

Jack was about to answer when she interrupted him, "You shouldn't talk on the phone when you're driving." She hung up.

Frowning, Jack hung up.

"Hey, I wanted to talk to her," Enid said.

Jack handed her the phone.

Enid hit redial and, when Jeni answered, Jack could hear the surprise in her voice when she realized Enid had called her.

"Are you with him?" Jeni said. "Why are you with him?"

"I – uh," Enid bumbled.

Jack grinned at her discomfort.

Enid scowled, cast Jack an evil look. "Remember how I told you about *why* I came here...?"

"Oh! You told him? How'd he take it?" Jeni asked.

Jack stared straight ahead, listening as Enid changed the subject by asking about Faith. Jeni took the hint and told her how she got Faith back from social services, how the crazy ex-boyfriend was in jail and she apologized for what she put Enid through.

Jack was surprised when Enid glossed over the ordeal with Jeni's ex-boyfriend as if it was no big deal.

"Hey, uh – I left some stuff in your freezer," Enid said tentatively. "I was hoping that you could hold on to it for me."

Jeni agreed and they said their goodbyes.

Enid turned to Jack. "I need to pick up – my stuff – from Jeni's apartment."

"I'll take you."

Enid made a face.

"Well, I am not lending you my car. Are you even old enough to drive?"

"I can drive!"

"I can't drive you over till tomorrow. If you need something tonight, we can go to the store."

Enid irritably stared out the window.

Jack glanced at his watch and mentally went through the assortment of clothes that he kept in the trunk of his car. Being a self-employed detective sometimes called for quick outfit changes. "I'm going to Vivian's charity ball and I won't be able to take you with me. I'll drop you off at home."

"Why can't I go?"

"It's a black-tie event. You won't blend in and you'll get in the way."

"What? I can't pass as a wayward girl?"

Jack gave her a look.

"I want to go," Enid said, a determined gleam in her eyes.

"I said 'no' – so the answer is *no*."

"Didn't you say this is a chance for us to get to know each other?"

"I never said that."

"Yes, you did."

Jack said, "Well, let's get to know each other some other time. I've got work to do."

Enid shrugged, "No problem. I can hang out with your neighbor – the girl next door. Maybe she can give me some tips on picking up dirty old men – or we can go cruising the mall for tattooed tongue-pierced boys who'll be happy to slip us a couple of roofies."

Jack glanced at her, irritated. "Did you *ever* do anything your mother wanted you to do? And if so – how'd she get you to do it?"

"Not likely," Enid sniffed.

"Well, if she's got a ninja-mom secret on how to deal with – "

"Yeah," Enid said in a scathing voice, "Her secret is to marinate in vodka until she doesn't remember I exist."

Jack felt a stab of shock. Even though she told him the situation – he hadn't imagined it was that bad.

How bad was it?

He wanted to ask her, he wanted to know, but was interrupted by the sudden violent urge *to beat the shit out of somebody* – some invisible anonymous "somebody" that was to blame for her pain – for everybody's pain – like that would fix anything! A dim memory pushed its way up, and he felt the ghost of that horrible pain and anger that had been as familiar to him as his own skin and worse than any broken bone...

To be a kid and know you aren't wanted.

Grimacing, he shoved the memory back down and stole a look at Enid. She was red-faced and looked like she was going to burst into tears.

Forcing his voice to stay casual, he said, "All right. Wayward girl it is."

The subtlest of smiles curved at her mouth. A thought flashed through Jack...

Did she just play me?

CHAPTER THIRTY-THREE

A soldier will fight long and hard for a bit of colored ribbon.

—Napoleon Bonaparte

Bud stared at the hospital ceiling, wondering how many other chumps had lain in the that same bed, listened to the same doctor and stared at the same fluorescent lights as their world came crashing down.

How many are dead?

Bud closed his eyes, trying to push down the anxiety that wasn't just "anxiety" anymore – it was no longer just an inconvenient occasional feeling – it was a *symptom* of something that threatened to bump him off – into oblivion.

No more Bud.

Bud forced himself to look into the thought of him no longer existing.

What next?

Where?

Bud's thoughts floundered. All he saw was darkness. Bud thought back to all the Sundays he spent in church, all the prayers, all the hymns, all the checks written to the church – what did it mean? Did it mean that he was going to heaven?

Bud knew he wasn't going to hell.

Hell was a place for diseased souls – murderers, molesters, and abusers – with a subcategory for people who hurt animals and, of course, *Mr. Jenkins* – the neighbor who, when he was in sixth grade, cut down the oak tree that he had hidden in as a shy boy – reading books, eating crackers, watching the clouds and whiling away the hours with daydreams of adventure and romance.

Bud turned his thoughts to what was next and what "next" might look like.

After several minutes, beads of sweat formed on his brow at the blank he was drawing. Bud focused on a new thought – no matter what's next – where he goes – whether it's to some magical heaven or straight into the hard-packed Arizona dirt – he decided to concentrate on what *wouldn't* be there – what he *didn't* see.

Bunnie.

At the thought of losing Bunnie, a flood of panic washed over him so that he could hardly breathe. He would die and Bunnie would remarry. Who wouldn't snap up a gem like his Bunnie? Bud clenched his fists, grimly promising himself he would climb over the pearly gates and cold-cock Saint Peter himself – so he could come back and haunt any man who didn't treat Bunnie like the queen among women that she was.

Chip.

Bud dropped his head to his chest and covered his eyes. Would Chip remember him? Miss him? Tears burned in Bud's eyes as he thought about not being there for Chip, not being at Chip's wedding, not knowing his grandchildren. Would they mention Bud in the toast? Would Chip go through the same thing as *this* in fifty years? Did *I* give him the heart gene that's going to land him in a bed – staring up at an anonymous hospital ceiling, contemplating – eternity? The thought was too painful. Bud forced himself to return to his list of what "no more Bud" looked like.

Degenerate murderers.

Who would make them pay?

Bud felt a stab of helplessness that sent his hand to his heart and his eyes back up to the ceiling as every fiber in his being cried out…

I'm not done!

An image of his father materialized.

He died like a man. He faced the diagnosis of cancer with courage and dignity.

Stoically.

Would it have been better if he'd been less stoic?

Ashamed, Bud chased the thought away with a reminder that what his father had gone through wasn't about him or his mom. His father was the one who had to suffer through all those painful months of treatment that seemed worse than the disease. If his father chose to be stoic – so be it. Who was Bud to say that it would have been better if, just once, his father could have said something that he could have clung to during the tough times?

Did he love us? Was he proud of me? What was he thinking when he was here – like me – facing eternity?

Bud felt a great emptiness open inside of him. It was that same familiar feeling of loss, of a vast emptiness – every time he thought of his father.

Morris Orlean.

From all accounts: good husband, good father and good provider. Married to Clarice Gantry. Fragile Clarice. Soft-spoken Clarice.

Opposites attract?

Stoic Morris plus fragile Clarice – equals Bud.

No more Bud...

Bud turned his eyes to the door, desperately wanting Bunnie to come to him – just to be there with him. He wanted to feel her hand in his.

Maybe she was down the hall – talking to the doctor – discussing his heart. Bud had never imagined he'd include "heart disease" as a description of who he was.

It felt...

Devastating.

No, he sternly reminded himself, it would only be devastating if he *allowed* it to be devastating. He searched for another word that he could somehow live with. He came up as empty as he had when he tried to visualize eternity.

I'm only looking for a word!

Bunnie tiptoed into the room, her voice soft and sweet. "Hey, Sweetie...?"

Bud gripped his heart, alarmed. "Is it that bad?"

Bunnie looked startled, "What? No – it's..."

"Bunnie, don't scare me like that!"

"I was *trying* to be nice!" Bunnie snapped.

"Yeah, well, stop it. *Be yourself.*"

Bunnie scowled, plunked down in a chair. "Your heart blows donkey dicks from hell."

"That's more like it."

"Bud, I hope I'm not going to end up changing your diaper, am I?"

Bud laughed, "We'll hire somebody." He felt strangely comforted that no matter what – Bunnie was always Bunnie. Bud reached out, took her hand and felt a warmth steal over him.

Bunnie said, "I guess leaving you forever – just for this afternoon – is out."

Bud smiled.

Bunnie frowned and said, "At least till I get you pumped full of fiber and back up on your feet – then all bets are off."

"I love you," Bud whispered, squeezing her hand.

Bunnie made a face, failing miserably at her attempt to look uncaring. "You're a fool," she said bitterly.

"For you."

"That and a buck won't buy me groceries, mister." Bunnie cleared her throat and stood up. "Gotta find Nurse Ratchett – find out when you can blow this joint."

"Bunnie, I'm going to be fine."

She turned, hand on the door. "You're not going to retire – after *this*? Not even for *me*…?"

"I'm sorry," Bud said.

She braved a smile and disappeared.

Bud listened to her footsteps echoing down the long hallway, still feeling the warmth of her hand in his.

CHAPTER THIRTY-FOUR

Once you begin being naughty, it is easier to go and on and on, and sooner or later something dreadful happens.

–Laura Ingalls Wilder

Enid stared in awe at the magical beauty of the Phoenician resort. Strategically placed lights and the soft glow of the sunset on the mountains gave her the impression that they were driving up to a fairy kingdom.

Jack drove past the valet parking and self-parked at the far end of the lot. Enid watched in fascination as he dug through the trunk of his car and pulled out a surprisingly sharp suit and shoes. The trunk was neatly packed with everything from a toolbox, a cowboy hat, hardhat, hiking boots and various other "props" as Jack called them.

Enid said, "Like Vivian called the cigarette her prop?"

Jack shot her a startled look. "It's nothing like that."

Enid stood guard at the front of the car as Jack changed his clothes behind the car.

After several minutes, Jack joined her and Enid found herself staring at him. He looked sort of – handsome.

"How do I look?" Jack said.

"Like a mortician."

He made a face.

They walked toward the Phoenician's entrance, which shone like a gem on display.

"What about me? Aren't I supposed to have a costume?" Enid said.

"You're a wayward girl with an attitude."

"What does that mean?"

"Means you had a dress, but you're too badass to wear it."

Enid grinned.

Does he think I'm a badass?

Enid cast a nervous glance at the valets who smiled and welcomed them. She expected them to block their entrance and give them the boot – it was obvious they didn't belong to anyplace this perfect.

Jack leaned down, whispered, "Act like we belong."

She glanced up at him in surprise.

Act.

He knows it too…

Jack strode through the entrance like he owned it.

Enid stopped. She couldn't help but to gawk at the vista of glittering lights that illuminated the palm trees, golf course and sparkling blue of the pool surrounded by yellow bathing tents. A magical world stretched out in front of them, ending at the base of mountains bathed in a sunset of pink and violets. Enid half-expected to look down and see that her faded blue jeans and T-shirt transformed into a ball gown and her Converse sneaks morphed into glass slippers.

"Come on," Jack nudged her toward a wide staircase where a sign read: Annual Fundraiser for The Phoenix Home for Orphaned and Wayward Girls.

"Does 'wayward girl' mean I'm a slut?" Enid said.

An elegantly dressed lady walking up the stairs gasped, appalled.

Jack hustled Enid down the stairs as the woman glared after them disapprovingly.

"A little louder next time – the Queen of England didn't hear you."

"How am I supposed to act?"

At the bottom of the stairs, Jack ruffled his hair so that it stuck up awkwardly. "Welcome to your first undercover case, Enid Iglow...?" Jack stopped, unsure and embarrassed.

"Ski. You're daughter's name is Enid Ivie I-V-I-E Iglowski." Enid said.

"Iglow – ski." Jack said as if trying to commit it to memory.

Enid smiled in mock approval. "Are we bonding yet?"

"Sarcasm ill becomes you," he said.

Enid watched as Jack "nerded up" his appearance. He put on geeky glasses and hefted his pants up so that his previously perfect fit on the suit was now high-watered and wedgied.

"Ew," Enid said.

"We don't know each other," Jack murmured. "Get a soda – I hear they're free for wayward girls."

"Huh?"

Jack nodded to a group of girls standing around a table loaded with drinks and eats.

Enid frowned, suddenly scared. *They* looked like the real badasses.

Jack said, "See if you can find anything out. Remember, you're undercover. Don't blow it."

Before she could protest, he was gone.

Nervous, Enid walked toward the girls and immediately felt the cold eyes of the tallest girl zero in on her. She had a mass of red hair that fell to her shoulders like a cloud of rusted cotton candy and a nose that crinkled like she had picked up the scent of fresh dog crap.

Enid felt her courage falter as she saw the girl she nicknamed "Red" nod toward her and say something that made the other girls laugh.

Palms slick with sweat, Enid was about to veer off when she reminded herself...

I'm a badass.

She locked eyes on Red and sauntered up, doing her best imitation of how she imagined a badass wayward girl would walk.

"What do you want?" Red asked, staring at her with disdain.

"I'm a badass!" Enid blurted out.

Red stared at her incredulously. The other girls fell silent, staring at her like she was mental.

"Checking into motel 'wayward girl' tomorrow." Enid tossed her head like she'd seen the cool girls do it back in Florida.

"How come you're dressed like that?" Red sneered.

"Um..." Enid fumbled for something to say and, coming up empty, was about to fade into silence when she saw Red's eyes flicker with triumph. Without thinking, Enid ferociously burst out, "I do what I want!"

After what felt like eternity, Red shrugged, "Don't worry, they'll get you back on your meds after you check in. What are you, bipolar?"

"Uh…"

Red pointed to each girl, "Tweaker. Spaz. Bones. *Heather.* When Tweaker checked in, she got beat up three times before they got her meds straight. Don't go tryin' to break any records."

Tweaker looked like a twelve-year-old trying to hide coat hangers under her ugly blue dress. She was so skinny that her bones jabbed at the fabric like they were trying to make a run for it.

Spaz had corkscrew black hair and a gap between her front teeth. Her tentative smile was more like a vague plea for mercy – like she was silently begging "Uncle" with every smile.

The girl named Bones had a muffin-top waistline that strained against her dress so that the buttons looked ripe for popping off. She had a nervous habit of twisting a strand of her long brown hair, sticking it in her mouth and sharpening the strand of hair to a point, which she would occasionally stab into her cheek.

Heather had long blond hair and gazed at her with eyes that shone with a cynicism that belied her years. She looked like a typical pretty sixteen-year-old in a flowered sundress – until you saw her eyes. The expression in her eyes reminded Enid of a dog who'd been beaten and starved, but was fighting to stay alive.

"I'm Red," The girl with the mass of red hair said.

Enid grinned, surprised that she had guessed her nickname. "Enid."

"E-*what?*" Red what derisively.

"E-*nid.* Short for 'don't-mess-with-me-*Red*!" Enid blasted back.

Red burst out laughing. The other girls followed with their own versions of nervous laughter.

"What are you in for?" Red asked.

Enid grabbed one of the sodas and popped the tab. "Waywardness."

"No shit, Sherlock."

"Are they going to make me wear a dress?" Enid said.

"For parties – bullshit like that."

"So," Enid asked, trying hard to appear casual, "What's the four-one-one?"

Red's eyes narrowed suspiciously.

Enid said, "Looking for a heads-up. What kind of crapstorm am I walking into?"

They stared at her with such foreboding that Enid looked away. "Who's in charge of the monkey house?"

"Hargrove." Red said, "You haven't met her yet?"

Enid shook her head.

Red made a face, "Total bitch."

"I tried to kill her," Heather murmured.

Enid looked at Heather. She didn't seem to be joking.

"We can't decide," Tweaker said, "Heather wants to shoot her, Bones wants to *slowly*..."

"Meth-odically," Bones chimed in.

Tweaker said, "Boil her alive in her own piss! While Spaz here – "

"I ain't doin' nothing. I'm not going to jail," Spaz growled.

"Spaz is a dink," Tweaker said, "*I* have the best plan..."

"Shut up!" Red said.

Tweaker fell silent, pulling nervously at her dress, which accented the sharp jab of her collarbone.

"What'd she do?" Enid asked.

Red was about to say something when she caught sight of someone in the crowd. She frowned, glanced at Heather, who seemed to understand what was wanted and, with a sigh, dumped her soda onto the ground and disappeared into the crowd of partygoers.

Red said, "You're going to *love* it here. A real home away from home – assuming you grew up *in hell*." Red followed Heather.

The girls followed her and, as Bones passed, she hissed, "Run!"

Cold goose pimples ran down Enid's arms as she watched them disappear into the crowd.

CHAPTER THIRTY-FIVE

A clever, ugly man every now and then is successful with the ladies, but a handsome fool is irresistible.

—William Makepeace Thackeray

As Jack wedged his way deeper into the heart of the party, he wondered again at the phrasing of "wayward girls" – it sounded like Charles Dickens with a splash of soft porn.

Maybe that's what they're going for…

A line of bathing tents was set up around a large pool that reflected glittering lights. It reminded him of the Arabian Nights stories and the Sinbad movies he was so fascinated with as a boy.

A server offered him a flute of champagne and he grabbed a crab puff from a passing platter. Popping the crab puff in his mouth, he scanned the crowd for any resemblance to the woman in Jeni's photo – an older version of the girl with the Venus Flytrap eyes.

It was the typical upscale Arizona shindig. Lots of old white guys with their aging trophy wives and a generous scattering of hot young wanna-be-wives looking for a rich sugar daddy.

Welcome to Arizona.

He asked a woman with a face tighter than a drum if she could point him in the direction of Vivian Hargrove.

She pointed to another woman twenty feet away.

Vivian Hargrove was standing in a knot of people, like an empress holding court. Now in her fifties, she was striking, if not beautiful. Walking toward her, Jack looked for any sign of the girl who had once been a stripper and known a thing or two about crashing parties and trolling for a rich husband. That girl was cleverly concealed behind designer duds, jewelry and hair that looked like it could survive a wind tunnel.

As Jack got closer, he saw the upsweep of her eyebrows that had reminded him of startled birds taking flight from a snowy field when he first saw the photograph.

Jack changed the cadence of his step to something quirky. He cleared his throat with a nasally sound and asked, "Pardon me...?"

Vivian acknowledged him with an aloof nod and returned to listening to a man with pork chop sideburns.

Jack stuck his hand out so that Vivian couldn't ignore it. "Nathaniel Hawthorkin. I think this is a commendable and *highly* worthy cause..."

Vivian raised her eyebrows in apology to Pork Chop as she shook Jack's hand.

Jack pulled out his checkbook. "I've been searching and *searching* for the right charity – I'm rather short on my yearly deductions – *so says my CPA* – whom do I make the check to?"

"It's a silent auction – if you'd like to bid..." Vivian waved her hand toward a series of tables set up with everything from gift baskets to weekend getaways to exotic locales.

Jack pulled out a pen, clicked it. "One hundred thousand...?"

Vivian's eyes lit up and Pork Chop was relegated to the back burner. She took Jack's arm like he was a dear friend, "Make it out to: Phoenix Home for Orphaned and Wayward Girls."

Jack wrote, murmuring, "Wonderful cause – simply wonderful."

"Mr...?"

"Hawthorkin."

"How is it that we've never met?" Vivian cooed.

"My therapist says I need to stop being so *anonymous* with my donations. Deeply rooted mother issues, you know. My therapist says the only way to overcome them is to find a worthy charity and *give, give, give* – until it hurts."

"You're interested in children's causes?"

Jack gave his best nerd smile, "I do *what* I can *where* I can."

"Perhaps we can schedule a tour of the girls' home?"

Jack studied her thoughtfully, "Say, you look familiar – oh!" He snapped his fingers like he was remembering something, but then held himself back, murmuring, "Striking resemblance."

"Everyone has a doppelganger, I suppose." Vivian smiled, eyeing the check. She attempted to pluck it from his fingers, but he pulled it back, seemingly unaware of her efforts.

Jack said, "Did I mention I'm an amateur historian? I'm honored to say I have an article coming out in the Arizona History bimonthly magazine and – believe it or not – oh, it's quite risqué, but that's what drew me to the project, I must admit…"

Viv glanced nervously from Jack's face to the fluttering check.

Jack said, "Have you ever heard of – The Sugar Shack?"

Viv froze, the color draining from her face.

"I came into possession of a photograph that I plan to publish with the article and – my gosh! If you aren't a dead ringer for one of the – " Jack made air quotes, "Unnamed dancers."

The corner of Vivian's eye twitched.

"You could be the same person!" Jack said.

Vivian cleared her throat, "Mr…"

"*Nate.*"

"Nate. Would you care to join me for breakfast tomorrow? At my villa."

"*De*-lighted!"

Viv pulled a card from her purse.

Heather, sullen and staring at the ground, walked up to them.

"Nate, this is one of our best girls. Mr. Hawthorkin, Heather. Heather, this is Mr. Hawthorkin."

Heather nodded but did not meet his eyes.

Vivian said, "What do you say, Heather?"

"Nice to meet you," Heather murmured, holding out her hand. She gave Jack a wilting handshake and wiped her hand on her dress.

"Nice to meet you," Jack said, eyeing Vivian, who had a gleam in her eyes that was causing a prickly sensation down his spine.

"Nine o'clock?" Vivian said to Jack as she made a final reach for the check.

Jack absentmindedly tucked the check into his pocket. "Wouldn't miss it for the world! I'll have my CPA print a nicer check and I'll have it for you in the morning."

Viv opened her mouth to protest, but Jack pretended like he spotted someone and, with a wave, he was gone. Jack spotted Enid and gestured for her to follow him.

In the parking lot, Enid hurried to keep up as she breathlessly asked, "What'd you say to that woman? She about sprinted after you when you took off."

"Hurry up," Jack said, glancing behind him. "If we don't hightail it, she might fender-hop us."

"Why? What'd you do?"

"I like to get while the getting is good."

Driving down Camelback Road, Jack breathed a sigh of relief and said, "What'd you find out?"

"You met Heather?" Enid said.

Jack glanced at her in surprise. He hadn't really expected her to find out anything. He'd given her the assignment simply to keep him out of his hair.

"Heather tried to kill Mrs. Hargrove," Enid said matter-of-factly.

Jack gaped at her. "Vivian Hargrove?"

"Total b-i-t-c-h, by the way. One of the girls wants to boil her in pee."

"You're making that up."

"They said being at the girls' school is like being in h-e-double-hockey-sticks. They hate her. *Big-time.*"

"How'd you find that out?"

"Told them I was a wayward girl checking in tomorrow," Enid said with pride.

"Really?" Jack said thoughtfully.

"Sounds worse than jail," Enid said.

Jack stared at the road leading them back to his house. An idea was forming, but his gut told him it was – *sketchy.*

"Did you like working undercover?" Jack said.

"Yeah, sure," Enid shrugged.

"How do you feel about – working undercover – at the home?"

Enid's head snapped in his direction, her mouth dropping open in astonishment.

Jack said, "Tomorrow *only*. You can check in as a wayward girl, spend the day there, find out what you can and I'll get you out of there before the day is over."

"So, you're willing to use me – as *bait* – in a place I just described as h-e-you-know-what?"

"If it's all right with you."

Enid stayed silent for several seconds. "How much?"

"How much what?"

"You don't work for free, do you?"

Jack shot her a look, "It's not work – it's *bonding*."

"I bond better with cash."

Jack rolled his eyes.

"You'd be paying for my time *and* my expertise," Enid said haughtily.

"What expertise?"

"Forget it." Enid shrugged, "Obviously, the need for my expertise is not that important to your case."

"Considering you're the one who ratcheted down my price with all your 'student-discount-payment-plan' garbage...!"

Enid tossed her head in defiance.

"Do I look like I'm rolling in green?" Jack said.

"Fifty bucks," Enid said, crossing her arms. "And I want some new clothes."

"Twenty-five and we stop at Target."

"Fifty dollars and we go to the *Mall*."

Jack drove for several minutes in silence.

"And *no bonding!*" Enid said.

Jack made a face. "Fifty dollars, Target – *no bonding*. It's a deal."

"You promise to get me before lights-out?"

"Yeah."

"Say it."

"Say what?"

"Say: I *promise* to get you out of that place before the lights go out."

"Why do women always want promises?" Jack exclaimed in exasperation.

"Because we know what we're dealing with!" Enid said. "*Promise*."

Jack sighed. "I promise to get you out before the lights go out."

Enid nodded, satisfied. She pointed to an upcoming Dairy Queen, "Blizzard!"

Jack flipped on the turn signal, "You drive a hard bargain."

CHAPTER THIRTY-SIX

Beware of the man that does not talk and the dog that does not bark.

—Cheyenne

"My father died of a massive heart attack," Jenson said to Bud, smiling pleasantly. "If they had had all this high-tech medical do-dad-er-ee back then, my father would be alive, kicking – and up to his eyeballs in dames."

Lying in his hospital bed, Bud frowned at Jenson, who had set down a "get well" African violet on the window sill. Jenson wore a mint green bowling shirt, grey slacks and – Bud had to ask, "Are those spats?"

Jenson stuck one foot out. "Lovely, aren't they? I wouldn't dare wear them to work, but I thought they had a certain *je ne sais quoi* that you might appreciate."

Bud grunted, a half laugh.

"I heard your son got a social call from our prime suspect."

Bud scowled.

Jenson smiled gently. "There was even talk of them going on – a date?"

"Absolutely not."

"Might want to verify that with the kid, Bud."

Bud shot him a look.

Jenson made a face, shrugged. "I didn't make detective grade based on my fashion sense. Word is, Chip shared dirty martinis at Durant's with our fave femme fatale, Eve Hargrove."

"Do you know Jack Fox?" Bud said, abruptly.

"Never met him, but I've heard the stories – the one about when he was a kid at his father's funeral. Gads! Gives me the willies, just thinking of it."

"Jeni Hargrove hired him to find her biological mother."

Jenson looked at Bud, startled.

"Turns out, Vivian Hargrove 'adopted' Jeni when she was a baby, but never did any official paperwork. Jeni hired Jack to find her biological mother."

"How did we not turn that up in our investigation?"

"Makes me wonder about the other sister."

"Paler-than-paint Laura," Jenson murmured. "She's my nominee for most likely to harken from another pool of DNA. Those three sisters are as different as the seasons."

"I want to talk to Jack Fox – find out if – "

"You're on leave. And a long leave at that."

"Where'd you hear that?" Bud said sharply.

"Oh." Jenson stood up, smiling like a cherub. "Perhaps, you haven't heard…?"

"Heard what?"

"Bunnie was kind enough to put in for a six-week leave while you recuperate."

"What!" Bud sat bolt upright, alarmed.

"In her defense, I think she's spot-on. You need time to recuperate. You know who lives the longest, Bud? *Hypochondriacs.* They're always running off to the doctor to get things fixed before anything even breaks down. It won't kill you to take six weeks, but it may kill you *not* to take the six weeks."

Bud glowered at Jenson, who gave him a jaunty wave. "Must go. I'll check in tomorrow."

Jenson left and Bud reached for the phone, intent on having it out with Bunnie.

"Bud?"

Bud looked up and was startled to see Frank Ficus's bulky figure in the doorway. Frank was sweating and shifting nervously from one giant flat foot to the other as he eyed the monitors hooked up to Bud.

Bud clicked the phone off.

"I – uh…" Frank's eyes were glued on the electronic green line that beeped with Bud's heartbeat.

"Hi, Frank. What are you doing here?"

Frank moved toward the chair, gingerly edging his bulky frame into it.

"Don't like hospitals?" Bud said.

Frank grunted.

"Tell me about it," Bud said.

"When are you getting out?" Frank said tentatively.

It was strange to see the big man nervous as a cat. His eyes were on a constant prowl around the room, like a cootie was going to jump out and turn *him* into the patient.

"Not sure," Bud said.

"Yeah, yeah," Frank said, distractedly.

"How's the private eye business treating you?" Bud said, trying to make him feel more comfortable.

"Same old, same old – you know," Frank mumbled, rubbing his hands together.

Bud sighed. Frank had never been known for his scintillating conversation. During the ten years they worked together as police officers on the beat, Bud couldn't remember talking about anything more than the weather, sports or work. Bud decided the best tack was to wait for Frank to pipe up on his own.

After several moment, Frank said, "I heard they got a positive I.D. on Daniel Hargrove's body."

Bud nodded.

Frank said, "I heard the daughter, Eve Hargrove, came around the station – asking for me?"

"Yeah. What was that about?"

"You don't know?" Frank said, surprised.

"Why would I know?"

Frank contemplated this.

"How do you know her?" Bud said.

Frank abruptly stood up.

A subtle instinct tickled at Bud's brain. He casually threw out, "Didn't you used to work with Jack Fox?"

Frank started like Bud threw a firecracker.

Bud sat up. "Frank…!"

"Hope you feel better," Frank blurted out and darted from the room.

Bud tried to get out of bed, but was pulled back by the multitude of wires that stretched between him and the monitors. Bud stared in frustration at his surroundings – he wanted nothing more then to run down Frank and *make* him talk.

The monitors blinked and beeped at him. A wave of depression swept over him. He got back into bed and stared up at the ceiling, thinking.

CHAPTER THIRTY-SEVEN

"Yes, yes," said the Beast, "my heart is good, but still I am a monster."
"Among mankind," says Beauty, "there are many that deserve that name
more than you, and I prefer you, just as you are, to those, who, under a
human form, hide a treacherous, corrupt, and ungrateful heart."

—Jeanne-Marie Le Prince de Beaumont

Enid sat at Jack's kitchen table, glaring up at him as she said, "A little privacy, please."

Jack crossed his arms. "Dial."

Enid held out the cell, smiled sweetly. "Why don't *you* talk to my mother?"

Jack threw up his hands and retreated to the safety of the living room.

Enid sighed. The last thing she wanted to do was talk to her mother, but she and Jack had made a deal. If she got permission from her mother, then she could stay longer. What "longer" meant, both she and Jack had carefully avoided discussing. She took a deep breath and dialed. It rang twice. Her mother's voice, smoky with drink, answered.

"Yel-lo?"

"Hi mom."

Her mother's ear-splitting screech pierced through the phone. "Where the hell have you been?!"

"I'm fine. I – "

"I been thinking you're hacked up and dead in a ditch – or murdered! You disappear and *not* call? Where the hell are you?"

"Arizona."

"Ari-what-the-freak-a-zona are you doing out there?"

"I'm with – Jack Fox."

Dead silence.

"Mom? You there?"

"How…?"

"You told me."

There was a long silence. "Does he remember me?" Enid was surprised at the childish break in her mother's voice.

Enid made a face, "I don't know."

"Well, you're coming home!"

"He said it's all right – can I stay? Just a little longer…?"

"You sure as hell didn't think to ask my permission before you disappeared!"

"I left a letter."

"You took all my cash!"

"I'll pay you back."

"The hell you will – you're coming home. I'll give you my credit card number – I want you back no later than tomorrow!"

"Why?"

"Whaddya mean 'why'?"

"I mean, *why* do you want me back? You don't pay any attention to me – I *know* you wish I was never born!"

At the silence on the other end of the line, Enid's skin prickled with fear – maybe she'd gone too far. She didn't know if her mother wished she never been born, but it *felt* like that.

Jack appeared out of nowhere, took the cell from her.

He walked into the other room where Enid could hear him talking to her mother. He sounded like a rational adult – not like the jerk that'd been hassling her since she arrived. She bit her nails and curled her legs under her, listening to his voice, which was more soothing than she ever imagined it could be.

Within twenty minutes, he had permission for her to stay for three more days. Jack handed her the phone and Enid mumbled a goodbye, and then realized that her mother had hung up.

The next morning, after insisting that going "undercover" was no big deal and, in fact, a really cool adventure, Enid began to regret not letting Jack talk her out of it. He *had* tried to talk her out of it, but she had insisted that she could do it – and wanted to do it.

Why am I doing this?

Walking toward the two-story brick building, Enid felt her stomach twisting with nausea. What seemed like an adventure was becoming reality – and she didn't like it.

Enid glanced behind her, but Jack's car was nowhere to be seen. She concentrated on the reassuring bulge of the disposable cell phone hidden in her sock. Jack bought it at Circle K before he dropped her off and he promised he would be waiting for her at their meet-up spot at six o'clock that night.

He better!

Enid paused as if waiting for a sign from the universe to turn and run.

I must be crazy…

What kind of father was he anyway? Sending his daughter undercover where, for all he knew, she was going to be kidnapped, tortured and buried in some dank basement by an ax-wielding clown! Feeling the panic rising within her, she did an about-face and started planning her story about why she couldn't do it.

"Enid!" A girl's voice called.

Startled, Enid stopped and saw Tweaker walking a fluffy handful of a dog on a leash.

"That yours?" Enid called out.

"Nah. Pooper-scooper witch-detail. You checking in?" Tweaker stopped in front of her.

Enid bent to pet the dog, which went into a yapping frenzy.

Tweaker yanked the leash, which sent the tiny dog flying backwards. "Don't trust her. She'll take your fingers off. She's not what she appears."

"She doesn't look big enough to poop out a finger – much less eat one."

"She's like a python. Stretches."

"What's her name?"

"Tootles. But we call her Little Bitch."

"Why do they call you Tweaker?"

"My mom."

Enid nodded, pretending to understand.

"You smoke?" Tweaker asked.

Enid shook her head.

Tweaker covertly pulled a cigarette and lighter out of her pocket. She lit up, took a drag and offered it to Enid, who shook her head politely.

Enid said, "Is it really that bad here?"

Tweaker shrugged. "No worse than where I came from – just different."

"How?"

A bell clanged. Tweaker stubbed the cigarette on the bottom of her shoe and slid it back in her pocket.

"Come on," Tweaker grabbed Enid's arm and dragged her toward the building. The dog yapped and lunged for Enid's ankles, but Tweaker gave the leash a tug that sent the dog tumbling backwards again.

Enid hurried to keep up with Tweaker, who led her through the front entrance. A sign above it read: And now abideth faith, hope and charity, these three; but the greatest of these is charity (I Corinthians 13:13).

Tweaker nodded toward a door inscribed "Office" and whispered, "We'll find you – *after*."

Enid watched as Tweaker dragged the yapping dog down the echoing hallway. Enid glanced back at the entrance, itching to head out.

I can leave right now.

Vivian Hargrove walked out of the office and ran into Enid.

"So sorry," Vivian said, placing a hand on Enid's arm. "Oh, you're new? Checking in?"

Enid felt a childish urge to turn and run as fast as she was able.

Vivian smiled reassuringly, her hand clamping down as she guided her into the office, "Did you come alone or did someone drop you off?"

The office was sparely furnished. Its only decorative touch was a series of framed motivational pictures.

"Alone," Enid mumbled.

"Mrs. Hobbs, we have a new girl." Vivian gave Enid a nudge toward the desk.

Mrs. Hobbs looked up, frowning.

Enid wrinkled her nose at the sickeningly sweet perfume that permeated the room and seemed to have Mrs. Hobbs as a nucleus.

Mrs. Hobbs handed her a clipboard of papers and pointed to a chair. "Be as accurate as you can. It helps us in determining your needs."

Two hours later, a dazed Enid sat in a tiny dorm room furnished with a bunk bed, two chairs, two lockers, a table and a battered wastebasket. The window overlooked a dirt field bounded by ragged brush. Enid looked over the items Mrs. Hobbs had given her: sheets, blanket, pillow, towel, soap, toothbrush, toothpaste and a comb. Mrs. Hobbs told her that she would be given an extra set of clothes later in the day.

Tweaker stuck her head in the door. "Hey badass."

Enid grinned, happy to see a familiar face.

"Mrs. Hobbs gave me permission to give you the grand tour."

"Am I going to have a roommate?" Enid nodded at the bunk bed.

"You never know. A girl will come in while you're sleeping and be gone before you're awake. Most girls don't stay long. Spaz just came in last week. Me, Bones and Red been here the longest."

"What about Heather?"

"Four months. I don't think she'll last too much longer."

"What do you mean? Like, run away?"

"It doesn't pay to be too nosy around here." Tweaker waved for her to follow her. Once in the hallway, Tweaker opened a door that revealed a long room of toilet stalls on one side and shower stalls with a plastic curtain in front of each on the other. "You want hot water, get here by seven-o-eight and, unless you want to get your ass kicked, don't ever flush when somebody is in the shower. Shout your stall number and they'll flush for you when they leave. They'll do the same for you."

Tweaker led her down the stairs to the first floor and pushed open a door. "Cafeteria," Tweaker said. Four rows of cafeteria tables were lined up and an older woman with a sour face and two girls were working to set up for lunch. "That's Rosa," Tweaker whispered, "When you pull lunch duty – keep your mouth shut and do whatever she tells you."

"Over there!" Rosa barked, whacking a startled girl on the back of the thigh with a wooden spoon. The girl changed directions, scurrying to pick up a stack of plates.

Enid's mouth fell open in astonishment. "You can't hit students! Back in Florida, one of the teachers got fired – "

"You ain't in Kansas anymore, Dorothy." Tweaker pulled her down the hall and they turned a corner. She pointing to a long hallway and said, "Classrooms."

"Don't you go to school?" Enid asked in surprise.

"Home school – minus the home. Wait till you get a load of Mr. Graves." Tweaker shook her hand like it was blazing hot.

At that moment, a handsome man in his late twenties, with a crew cut and muscles, came out of one of the classrooms. He looked at Tweaker in surprise. "Susan, what are you doing out here? Shouldn't you be...?"

"Mrs. Hobbs told me to show the new girl around," Tweaker said, hooking her thumb at Enid.

"Oh. Well, welcome." Mr. Graves smiled pleasantly at Enid. "Finish the tour and get back to class, Susan."

He disappeared around the corner.

Tweaker sighed in admiration, "He's so hot!"

"I'm in love too," Enid smiled, thinking about Chip.

"Didn't say I was in love! *Yuck.*"

"What's that?" Enid said, pointing to a door that had a "Not in Session' sign.

Tweaker made a face, "One of the requirements of you 'having the privilege' of staying here is you have to do one assigned chore every day, go to class and go to your weekly therapy session with *Dr. Dick.* Believe me, it ain't worth missing."

"Why?"

"Your parents dead – or they just not want you?" Tweaker said abruptly.

Enid started. She hadn't thought about her mother since last night. For the first time, she felt a stab of guilt. She had a mother – none of these girls had a mother – or at least, if they did, their mother didn't want them – and they knew it.

"My mom's a drunk," Enid said.

"She alive?"

Enid hesitated. "No."

"You have a dad?"

Enid made a face, unsure how to answer.

"Me too. Unknown sperm donor."

Enid smiled uneasily.

Footsteps sounded from down the hall.

Tweaker hissed, *"Dr. Dick."*

Enid turned to see a man in his forties striding toward them. He was dressed in a light summer suit and Enid was caught by his manner of walking. It reminded Enid of the way Dusty Russell swaggered around the playground after recess, bragging about how he got to second base with Louise Jenkins behind the middle school garbage bins.

"Enid Smith? I've been looking for you. Mrs. Hobbs gave me your paperwork. How are you settling in?" He stopped in front of them and gave them what Enid could only describe as a "rat-eyeballing-bacon" smile.

Enid glanced at the front entrance that was only a sprint distance away.

"This way," He gestured toward the door. Enid turned to Tweaker, but she was gone.

"Follow me," he said.

Enid hesitated, but entered. She stopped, staring in astonishment at his office, which was as plush as the rest of the school was spartan. From the deep swag of the carpet that seemed to gobble up her feet to the heavy burgundy velvet blinds to what Enid recognized as a fainting couch – the place gave her the heebie-jeebies.

"I'm Doctor Pearce. We're going to be meeting once a week. Have a seat." He gestured her toward a couch that looked vaguely lewd.

She hesitated.

"Sit."

Enid walked stiffly to the couch and perched herself on the edge.

"Are you nervous?" he asked.

Enid raised her chin in an effort to look braver than she felt. "No."

"You're safe here. Everything we discuss is confidential."

"What if I want to leave?"

"You came to the school voluntarily, didn't you?"

Enid nodded, uncertain.

"There's no fences, no bars on the window. You can leave whenever you like."

"Why's your office so fancy?"

"You like it?"

"It's – different."

"Tell me why you're here?"

Enid tried to remember all the lies she had written on the paperwork. She felt a spurt of panic at the thought of him figuring out that she was lying. She blurted out, "My name's Enid Smith. I'm from Florida. My mother's dead and I don't know who my father is."

"Any relatives?"

Enid shook her head.

"So, you're alone in the world? No aunts, no uncles?"

Enid shook her head.

"That must be scary."

Enid shot him a look. There was an edge in his voice that set her nerves tingling. She crossed her arms, trying to stop herself from trembling.

"Thirsty?"

Enid nodded.

He went to a sideboard where he poured water out of a crystal decanter into a glass. He crossed the room, his footsteps silent in the deep carpet. She took the heavy glass and gulped greedily. She hadn't realized how thirsty she was until now. Gulping down the last of the water, she wiped her mouth, handed him back the glass.

He replaced it on the sideboard and sat down. "Tell me about yourself."

Enid sighed, feeling more relaxed.

"Do you have a boyfriend?" he said.

Enid smiled, thinking of Chip. She scratched her lip, noticing for the first time how tired she was.

"What's his name?"

"Chip."

"Does Chip know where you are?"

Enid shook her head and felt a sudden, overwhelming urge to lie down and sleep.

"You look tired."

"Uh-huh," Enid murmured. She looked around, surprised. The plush carpet was moving – swirling around her like dark water – she was on a raft and the purple plush water was lapping the edges of her raft, urging her to sleep…

"Are you all right?" His voice was soft and distant, melting away as she drifted further from the shore. She reached her hand out…

For what?

He asked her something, but his voice was far away – like the summer buzz of bees. Enid felt herself slipping down, the waves gently lapping as they murmured softly, urging her to sleep…

CHAPTER THIRTY-EIGHT

I've already told you: the only way to a woman's heart is along the path of torment. I know none other as sure.

—Marquis de Sade

Jack expected to be relieved that Enid was out of his hair for the day, but was surprised when he couldn't shake a feeling of unease. He had an uncomfortable feeling that maybe he'd done the wrong thing. He promised that he'd meet her at six o'clock and, despite his shabby track record in the promise department – that was one promise he intended to keep.

It was another scathingly blue-sky Arizona day, with the temperature steadily climbing, as Jack drove to Vivian's home in Old Scottsdale. Her Italian-styled villa was hidden by high walls and, at the gated entrance, he pressed a button and spoke with a woman who buzzed him through the gates. Once inside the gate, the landscaping was an expanse of lush green lawn and flowers that didn't have any business existing in Arizona.

Jack parked the car. A maid in a uniform stood waiting for him at the door.

"Good morning," Jack said, smiling.

She nodded, remaining stonily silent as she led him through the villa and onto a patio that overlooked an impressive English garden. Jack gazed contemptuously at the carefully crafted plants and flowers. As beautiful as it was, a garden in the desert struck Jack as self-indulgent and foolish. The desert with its birds and jackrabbits always seemed more alive to him than the green expanse of grass and strategically situated trees and flowers of a carefully landscaped yard. You might as well decide to hold back the tide, as turn the desert into an English garden.

A table set for two sat in the center of the patio and, at the sight of Eve, Jack stopped short.

Eve stood at the edge of the patio with her back toward him. The early morning sunshine framed her perfect figure and made her cream-colored blouse almost translucent.

Jack stood silent and watchful, his heart pounding.

Eve turned, her voice dripping with disdain. "Imagine my surprise – Jack Fox has a date – with my mother."

Jack walked to the table, hoping he wasn't betraying the effect that she was having on him.

"What exactly are you after? *Blackmail?*"

Jack sat down at the table, smiled pleasantly as he lightly quipped, "What's it worth – to keep my mouth shut?"

Eve's eyes flashed angrily.

Jack poured coffee for himself. He held up the pot in a silent offer to pour for her, but she ignored him.

From her flashing green eyes to the swell of her breast under the sheer blouse, he couldn't remember the last time he wanted a woman the way he wanted her.

"Hypothetically," he asked, "how much?"

"*Hypothetically,*" Eve enunciated, "I'll have an army of lawyers up your ass so fast you won't know what hit you."

Jack laughed – a deep genuine thing that seemed to leave her unsettled. He leaned back, loving the way her eyes seemed to shoot sparks. Jack spoke softly, "I like you. I guess you know that."

"You like me so much, you're going to blackmail my mother?" Eve snapped.

Jack's eyes lingered on her face. "Sit down. Talk to me. I'll forget all about my blackmail scheme."

Eve examined him suspiciously. After a moment, she scowled, "You're full of shit."

"*Ahhh*, you like me too."

Scowling, Eve sat. She waved away the coffee pot that he held up for a second time. "Are you working for me or not?"

"Haven't made up my mind."

"What are you after?"

Jack gave her a look that couldn't be misunderstood.

After a long moment, she gave a shrug and surprised Jack by speaking matter-of-factly. "Mother married Daniel when I was eight. Bigger house, better life. He knew about mother's line of work – that's where he met her."

"The Sugar Shack?"

"No. Radio Shack," she said sarcastically.

"What about Jeni?"

Eve surprised him again by speaking thoughtfully, "Mother was friends with Jeni's mother…"

"Ann Smith."

"She died. The grandmother was some religious person who wanted nothing to do with Jeni. Mother adopted Jeni."

"Without bothering with any of the pesky paperwork?" Jack said wryly.

Eve shrugged. "Mother has her own way of doing things."

Ignoring her previous refusals, Jack poured her coffee and watched as her perfectly manicured fingers wrapped around the cup. He shivered, imagining her fingers wrapping around *him*.

"Jeni was an orphan. Mother did a *good* thing."

"Did your father…?"

"Stepfather," Eve corrected.

"Sexually molest you?" Jack asked politely.

Eve froze. After a moment, she gave a low pitying laugh, "Is that for shock value? Am I supposed to melt down in tears, confess all?"

Jack raised his eyebrows.

"My stepfather was a perfect gentleman. An excellent surrogate father," she said calmly.

Jack allowed himself a gentle ironic smile, "And you're a nice girl?"

"Exceptionally."

"What happened to your real father?"

"The reason I paid you to drop Jeni's case – I'm trying to protect her."

"*Liar.*"

Eve gave him a haughty look. "You certainly are intent on seeing me as the nefarious villain."

"Who do you think murdered your stepfather?"

"I don't know and I don't care to speculate."

"What are you doing tonight?"

"Not you."

Jack grinned, liking the challenging edge to her voice.

Eve stood and looked down on him. "Seeing as how you're not blackmailing my mother..."

Jack felt disappointment curling in his stomach. He didn't want to go, he wanted to stay with her – no matter what the cost.

"Jeni's writing a book," Jack blurted out before he realized what he was saying. He felt a stab of regret as he recalled his promise to Jeni – not to tell anyone about the book that she probably wasn't writing anyway.

Another broken promise.

What did it matter, anyway?

Eve was staring at him, unsure.

Jack heard himself talking, even as his gut yelled for him to shut up, take it back, or just plain get the hell out. "Autobiography. Family skeletons – a *tell-all.*"

"Jeni wouldn't voluntarily *read* a book, much less write one."

Jack took a gulp of coffee and forced himself to stand. He stood looking at her for a moment, feeling at a loss, not knowing how to tear himself away.

He opened his mouth to tell her that he made it up – it wasn't true...

"You're lying. I know you are – you're that *type.*" Her voice snapped with contempt.

Pretending a glibness he didn't feel, Jack gave a light laugh. "I'll be in touch."

As he left, he caught her reflection in the glass of the patio doors. She was staring at him, her lips and eyes tight with fear.

CHAPTER THIRTY-NINE

Keep your broken arm inside your sleeve.

—Chinese Proverb

Bud decided that if ceiling-staring were an Olympic sport, he'd have earned a gold by now. He'd been discharged from the hospital and, in the privacy of their home, Bud broached the subject of Bunnie's requested six-week leave. The discussion quickly morphed into an ugly argument that ended with Bunnie crashing around the kitchen baking Rice Krispies treats, Chip hiding out in his room and Bud stretched out on the guest bed, staring glumly at the ceiling. He felt like an old battle horse in a harness of electrodes as "they" monitored his heart rate. He now carried a fanny pack of heart medications, and his new life consisted of blood thinners, a low-cholesterol and heart-healthy diet, nitroglycerin to place under his tongue if he began having any chest pain, cardiologist appointments and – in the midst of all this – he was advised that he needed to decrease any stress in his life.

Bud didn't know what was making him more crazy – living with the knowledge that his heart could turn on him faster then lukewarm milk at a July 4th picnic, the fact that Chip was dating a murderer – or that Bunnie was on the verge of divorcing him.

The doorbell rang and Bud sat up with a groan, listening as Bunnie's heavy heel strike worked its way to the front door. He'd forgotten to tell her he was expecting a visitor, which was going to make her angrier than a bag of wet alley cats because, in her mind, the scrupulously clean living room wouldn't be clean enough for a guest.

He padded downstairs, disconcerted at how out of breath he was.

At the bottom of the stairs, Jack Fox and Bunnie had just finished exchanging greetings.

"Thanks for coming over," Bud said to Jack.

"No problem," Jack smiled.

"Bunnie, this is Jack Fox. My wife, Bunnie."

"We met," Bunnie said, smiling with an artificial brightness she saved for when she was particularly aggravated. She abruptly disappeared into the kitchen.

Bud said, "You want something to drink? Iced tea? Soda?"

"Iced tea sounds good."

Bud waved for Jack to have a seat in the living room. He went into the kitchen and listened to Bunnie's grumbling as he got the iced tea.

Returning to the living room, Bud found Jack examining framed family photographs. Bud handed him a drink. "What'd you deduce?"

"Nice-looking family."

Bud smiled, keenly aware that a private detective looking through the family photos had picked up more information than that. Bud settled with a sigh into the sofa. "They got me wired like a snitch."

"Yeah, sorry to hear about that. How you doing?"

Bud shrugged. "Wasn't it Bette Davis that said getting old isn't for sissies?"

"My grandmother used to say that the golden years were a crock of shit."

Bud smiled, nodded. "I appreciate you driving out here."

Jack sat down, "What's up?"

Bud remained silent for a moment. He'd learned over the years that there was a fine balance between not tipping your hand and shooting straight enough so that people would open up and talk. "I'm investigating Daniel Hargrove's murder. Eve Hargrove is my prime suspect."

Jack took a sip of the iced tea, never breaking his gaze.

Bud said, "I understand you're working a case for Jeni Hargrove – to find her biological mother," Bud watched for any change in Jack's expression.

A-plus on the poker face.

"I need your help," Bud said.

"Aren't you on leave?"

"The rumors of my death are greatly exaggerated," Bud said wryly.

A crash of dishes came from the kitchen – proof positive that Bunnie was eavesdropping.

"My responsibility is to my client," Jack said. "Any information is confidential – you know that."

"I'm not asking you to breach your ethics."

"Good."

Bud sighed, suddenly feeling exhausted. He leaned back, staring at Jack, who gazed at him with casual eyes, which Bud knew was a camouflage. You didn't get Jack Fox's reputation by not having an analytical monster machine of a brain. A sudden uncharacteristic wave of bitter jealousy swept over Bud.

Young pisser – with a great ticker.

"The other day, was that your daughter with you?" Bud asked, like a surgeon sticking a dull blade into what he suspected was a sore spot.

Jack started.

Bud felt a twist of pleasure at the sensation of getting an edge over Jack.

"Yeah." Jack watched him with wary eyes.

"Veronica?" Bud said.

"Enid," Jack said.

"I could have swore she said Veronica," Bud said.

"It's Enid."

Bud smiled. "I think Enid has eyes for my son."

"I hear your son dropped out of med school. That must suck," Jack answered equally blandly.

Bud felt a stab of anger, but managed to hide it behind an easy smile as he stood. "I appreciate you coming out."

Jack stood, "You said that."

"I knew your dad," Bud said.

Jack's lips compressed into a hard line. "Thanks for the iced tea." He headed toward the door, stopped. "What the hell did I drive out here for?"

"Eve Hargrove murdered her father."

"What's that got to do with me?"

"Just thought you should know."

"You certainly are intent on seeing her as a nefarious villain," Jack said, repeating what Eve had said to him.

Bud watched as Jack strode to his car.

Why'd I have to stick it to the kid about his dad?

As Jack drove away, Bud got a sharp spasm of chest pain. He stepped into the house and, with shaking hands, he dug a nitro patch out of his fanny pack and slipped it under his tongue. He sank to the floor, waiting for the pain to ease.

After a long time – it did.

CHAPTER FORTY

Adapt or perish, now or never, is nature's inexorable imperative.

−H. G. *Wells*

Enid swam out of the cold, dark dream that seemed like an evil stepchild to sleep. She lay perfectly still, not daring to blink.

Where am I?

A scratching sound − what was it?

She struggled to sit up and groaned with the effort. Her eyes darted around and she quickly found the source − a cockroach as big as a man's thumb scurried along the edge of where the cinder block wall met the dirty concrete floor.

Enid sat bolt upright, panic rising within her as she realized she was in a cinder block cell. Her first thought was that she was somewhere in the basement of the girls' home, but somehow she knew she wasn't. She was on a disgusting mattress in the middle of the floor. She jumped up, her heart hammering in her throat as every horror movie she'd ever seen flashed through her mind. She threw herself at the metal door, screaming and pounding with all her might. After several moments, a thought hit her and she scrabbled down into her sock − desperately feeling around for...

No cell phone!

She collapsed in a heap, sobbing convulsively. The cell phone − that one miraculous line of hope leading to the outside world − to Jack

– was ripped from her and she was left with a sensation of overwhelming helplessness.

The thin fabric of her T-shirt was no protection from the cold of the metallic door that she leaned against and she found herself shivering uncontrollably. Drawing her knees to her chest, she rocked back and forth, forcing herself to think.

She could hear guttural sounds – some wounded animal…

Me?

For what seemed like an eternity, she rocked back and forth. More than anything, she wanted her mom. *Desperately.* Nothing else mattered – she wanted to be safe at home with mom. Everything she had so flippantly despised about her mom suddenly morphed into the only safe thing in the universe.

A sob caught in her throat and she stared forward, numb with fear.

I'm going to die.

Or worse…

She shut her eyes, forcing herself to push down the feelings of helpless terror. She tried to think, but her thoughts came out in a jumble. How long had she been here? Twenty minutes? Hours? She wondered if Jack would be waiting for her call. What would he think when she didn't call?

Will he look for me?

She felt a twist of regret at being such a jerk and made a silent promise that if she got out alive, she'd make it up to him – and her mom…

A memory itched her mind – a poem…?

What was it?

Ninth-grade English. In her mind's eye, she saw elephants and Indian princesses. It was coming back to her – something about "if." A long poem about "if" you could be the one who didn't freak out when everybody else was freaking out – that would make all the difference. If you could stay calm and be brave and…

What would Jack do?

She forced herself to get up and walk around. She found herself repeating, "If you don't freak out, you might get out." She said it over and over as she forced herself to examine the room.

A single light bulb hung from a cord. She bent over the mattress, feeling around for anything that she could use as a weapon. She flipped the mattress over and jumped back as a bug scurried out from under it and disappeared into a crack in the wall. She pried her fingers into the dirty mattress, looking for anything that could work as a weapon, but there was nothing. No metal, no wires – nothing.

She turned to the door. Whoever was going to come through that door would expect to see a hysterical girl.

I'm probably not the first...

The scum-bucket was probably counting on her being hysterical! Enid clenched her fists and decided she needed to burn her bridges on thinking BIG.

If she wanted to get free, she was going to have to dig deep and turn everything upside-down and force *him* to freak out.

But...

How do you freak out a freak?

CHAPTER FORTY-ONE

There is no truth. There is only perception.

—Gustave Flaubert

Jack glared in the rearview mirror at Detective Bud Orlean's shitty house with his shitty wife and his shitty insinuations. He wanted nothing more then to punch the accelerator, so he could drive back and kick the shit out of him.

Jack forced himself to calm down and slow to the speed limit. Bud Orlean was the embodiment of *why* he quit the force.

Arrogant old-school bastards!

Every last one of the old-timers, including Bud, knew his father and repeated the stories from his father's funeral like they were in some an old ladies gossip club – keeping the story alive so that Jack could never get out from under its shadow.

Jack recalled the last time he had seen his dad…

Dead.

Women in black, the police uniforms, the gold buttons – all those eyes staring at him, whispering.

And then – what happened next…

Jack flinched, forcing his thoughts away from that horrible moment – to happier times. His father's booming voice and his mother's golden laughter – she was always happiest when he was there, which wasn't often.

The Christmas tree had hovered over the gifts for over a week. To eight-year-old Jack, it seemed like Christmas morning would never arrive. His mother refused to let Jack open any gifts until his father came home from one of his many work trips.

His father did come home – loaded down with sloppily wrapped presents, apologies, and hugs. His mother somehow turned their delayed Christmas into Jack's favorite childhood memory.

Elvis Christmas songs played on the stereo as Jack tore open his presents. His mom and dad held hands and drank steaming hot chocolate. She had a bag of Hershey Kisses and laughingly told them she'd give them one chocolate Kiss for each kiss they gave her. Much later, when the bag was empty, Jack lay snuggled on the couch in pajamas, holding the air rifle in his arms as he drowsily watched his mom and dad slow dance around the living room. Her bare feet gracefully slid across the floor as he spun her and they came back in a kiss. He remembered his mother sending a glance his way and whispering something to his dad, who grinned and pulled her even tighter.

That was the happiest day.

Everything after that took them slowly down a road further and further away from that moment when the three of them were a family.

As the years went on, his father traveled more and his mother slipped into an ever-deepening melancholy that left her silently staring out windows.

Waiting. Always waiting.

It wasn't until sixth grade that disaster struck.

It rained that day. Not enough to cancel the game. The pitcher was a chunky kid with a habit of throwing to bean any batter who crowded the plate. Jack was hungry for a home run that would make Vicki Minor look his way. Her blue eyes, flipped-back blond hair and the way she snapped her bubble-gum made him crazy with admiration.

The pitcher threw the first ball fast and hard, and Jack jerked back, barely avoiding getting hit. He glanced to the bleachers and saw that Vicki wasn't looking at him.

She and a girlfriend were giggling and pointing to the pitcher. Jack frowned, got back into the batting stance. The second pitch slammed into Jack's knee. He scowled angrily at the pitcher, who was grinning into the stands. Gripping his knee, Jack followed his gaze and saw Vicki popping her gum and grinning at the pitcher.

A wave of jealousy engulfed Jack, and he stepped up to the plate, determined to smash the ball into the pitcher's stupid face!

On the next pitch, Jack slugged it with all his might. Jack heard a sickening thud and a cry. A moan went up from the onlookers. The pitcher was sprawled on his back, blood soaking through his hands that were clenched over his face.

Jack's eyes found Vicki. Hands over her mouth, she was staring in horror at the pitcher.

Jack looked at the pitcher and was startled to see him running toward him with an animal snarl on his face. The pitcher tackled him so that they landed in the dirt, where they pounded each other with wild punches.

It took five adults to pull them off each other and it was another fifteen minutes of a harrowing drive to the local hospital's emergency department.

Jack broke the pitcher's nose with the ball. The pitcher got his revenge by breaking Jack's hand – with his face.

In the emergency room, the two boys sat glaring at each other from across a fifteen-foot aisle as they waited for their parents to pick them up.

Jack was surprised to hear his father's booming voice. Jack sat up, a rush of happiness coming over him. Despite the trouble he was in, he felt a thrill of happiness that his dad was back early from his business trip and was going to take him home.

"Well, son, I hope the other kid looks worse," his father boomed.

Jack looked up, grinning, but his dad was across the aisle, staring down at the chunky kid.

"Oh, Sam!" A blond woman shook her head disparagingly at the pitcher. "You're filthy."

"Sorry, mom," the chunky kid said.

"We'll talk about this when we get home," Jack's dad squeezed the boy's shoulder.

"Dad?" Jack said in a voice that even he didn't recognize.

They turned to look at Jack.

Without knowing it, Jack had crossed the aisle and stood looking up at his dad.

Harry started like he'd seen a ghost.

The blond woman shot him a questioning look. The chunky kid scowled, looking from Jack to his dad.

"Jack...?" Jack's mother called from down the hall.

Jack turned and saw his mom heading toward him, her eyes focused on his cast. "Oh, honey..." She knelt in front of him, gathered him in a hug. "Is the other boy all right? You know, you're going to have to apologize."

Jack looked up at his dad and his mother's eyes followed his.

She gasped, her face draining to a sickly white.

"Harry?" The blond woman's face was hard as flint. She looked from Harry to Jack's mom. "What's going on?"

"Come on, Sam." Jack's father grabbed the chunky kid and dragged him down the hall and out the swinging doors.

The blond woman followed more slowly, staring at Jack's mom with cold eyes.

Jack watched his mother shrink before his eyes.

A nurse came forward and helped his mother to her feet. She led her down the hall, murmuring something. Jack watched them, unable to move, unable to speak. The look on his mother's face struck terror into him.

He'd never seen her look so...

Not there.

The days that followed were filled the horrible realization that he and his mother were – a dirty secret.

His father's dirty secret.

It was four years after that – two weeks after Christmas. He'd come home from school and found his mother hanging by her neck, one high-heeled shoe on the floor and the other dangling from her toe.

The police left him with a neighbor whose hands smelled like lemons, but he wrested himself away and ran back in time to see two policemen cut down his mother with a hook. He stared in shock as the policeman replaced the hook onto his thick leather belt. He felt sick that *that hook* was part of the policeman's belt – just waiting to cut down some other kid's mother.

He spent two bleak years living with his grandmother in her tiny home on the reservation. She was a medicine woman, but there was no medicine that could cure him of his hatred for his father.

Jack had come home one day and found his grandmother sitting in her chair with her chin down, like she had fallen asleep. There was no noose – there were no tools hanging off a stranger's belt, but she was gone as quickly as his mother.

That's when his father had re-emerged with a grim, guilty look in his eyes that never were quite able to meet Jack's eyes. Harry Waterstone claimed Jack like he was lost luggage. Harry took Jack home to live with his wife and their only son, Sam.

The chunky pitcher, Sam, was his brother from another mother.

For the next year, Jack had watched his stepmother's cold eyes follow his every move. Her hatred for him was only eclipsed by Jack's own hatred for his father.

Looking back, Jack realized that if it wasn't for the friendship that burgeoned between him and Sam, he didn't know what would have become of him. Sam was his brother, his friend – his protector.

When Jack lived with his stepmother, she had beaten him so viciously with the plastic stick she had ripped off the blinds, that he couldn't get off the kitchen floor. He was sure that she would have killed him – except that Sam roared into the kitchen, grabbed a butcher knife out of the block and pushed her into a wall and held it flat-edged to her throat. Not a word was said between Sam and his mother, but she left. She got in the car and came back six hours later loaded down with shopping bags full of clothes and shoes from the mall.

Right after she left, Jack had been so ashamed that he had broken into uncontrolled sobs that made it hard to breathe. Sam sat next to Jack on the kitchen floor and, after the longest time, Sam helped him upstairs to his bedroom and, from that day on, they shared the same bedroom, and Sam was the brick wall that stood between Jack and his stepmother.

The blare of a car horn jerked Jack back to the present. He was sitting at a stop sign, one block from Jeni's apartment.

He pulled forward and parked, wondering if Eve had ever been beaten.

Hasn't everybody?

He desperately wanted to be Eve's brick wall – her protector. He cut the engine, thinking about the curve of Eve's red lips and the way her green eyes shone and he happily imagined himself beating the shit out of anyone who had hurt her.

I'd kill for a woman like that.

CHAPTER FORTY-TWO

I am no bird; and no net ensnares me; I am a free human being with an independent will.

—*Charlotte Bronte*

Bud paused, struggling to catch his breath. He was at the top of the stairs and he was scared. His heart was pounding too hard. He wiped the sweat from his brow and rested. After what seemed like an eternity, he felt his heart slow down and the pressure ease, and he moved forward.

He knocked on Chip's door. "Come on. We got work to do."

Bunnie pounded up the stairs, demanding, "Where the hell do you think you're going?"

"Work." Bud went to their bedroom and changed into his work clothes as Bunnie, hot on his heels, threatened him with everything from divorce to murder in the first.

Chip came to the doorway, unsure.

Bud looked at him, "We leave in five minutes."

Chip disappeared.

"As God as my witness, Bud...!" Bunnie yelled.

"If you divorce me, you divorce me. I hope you don't. In the meantime, I'm going to work."

"Bud!" Bunnie gasped in astonishment.

"If I retire, *I die*."

Bud could feel Bunnie glowering at him from the top of the stairs as he made his way to the garage. Chip bounded after him and Bud pointed him to the driver's seat. "I need a driver. Quit anytime you want – especially if it's to go back to school."

"What's the pay?"

"Write your book."

CHAPTER FORTY-THREE

Fairy tales do not tell children that dragons exist. Children already know that dragons exist. Fairy tales tell children the dragons can be killed.

–G. K. Chesterton

Enid decided that if she was going to die, it wasn't going to be because of not fighting like a mad cat in a corner. She made a grim vow that, no matter what, she was going to get a record-breaking amount of DNA evidence under her fingernails – even if it meant clawing his face off.

If I do nothing, I'm dead...

It didn't matter what she did – *she had to do something.* Anything was better then waiting for *him* to call the shots. She felt panic surging up and, gritting her teeth, she forced it down as she muttered to herself...

If, if, if...

She repeated it over and over again – until it became a primitive song. After a long while, it took shape and, without her willing it, it took form into something resembling a 1950s doo-wop song.

She felt cold and she began to move around – something resembling an awkward dance. She swung her arms, snapping her fingers as she sang, "Shoo-bop shoo-bop-if-a-roo."

When the door opened, she'd been dancing and singing for what felt like forever. She turned to the door and, hoping that he couldn't hear her pounding heart, she plastered a smile on her face, waved a friendly hello and continued to sing and dance her doo-wop song.

"He" was a white man in his forties, well built, with thick black hair and wary eyes. If it wasn't for the gun, he would have looked totally normal.

He stood still, watching her.

She threw back her head and smiled like she was having the time of her life. "Shoo-bop, shoooo-boppity-iffity-boo."

He stared, a glint of something in his eyes.

Fear?

Does he think I'm crazy?

Maybe I am…

"Do you mind if I take off my bra?" Enid said sweetly. She was so startled to hear how calm her voice sounded that she – giggled.

His eyebrows shot up in surprise and one corner of his mouth curled.

Enid followed her instinct like a bird catching a breeze. Reaching under her shirt, she unsnapped her bra.

He stared at her with shining eyes, mouth agape.

Still singing and dancing, Enid reached under each sleeve and whipped off her bra through the neck of her shirt like she'd seen her mother do a thousand times after coming through the front door at the end of a long day at work.

Enid shut her eyes, the bra dangling from her right hand as she sang and danced like she was in her own world. Enid sensed more than heard him moving closer and somehow, she was not just ready, but perfectly calm when he placed his hand on her breast.

Enid whipped the bra around his neck and pulled with all her might. His body went rigid and she saw the black of his eyes flare as his gun clattered to the floor. Enid swung around and somehow got behind him. Enid wrapped her legs around his waist and hung on – knowing that if she let go – she was dead.

His fingers dug into his neck, trying to get between the bra and his flesh as he hurtled them both around the tiny room, slamming her into the wall so hard she felt her teeth rattle and a searing pain shoot down her left side. Enid leaned back, putting all her weight into pulling the bra tighter around his neck that was now swollen and bulging with veins. It flashed through her mind that she might have a chance – if she killed him.

Him or me!

He dropped to his knees, desperately trying to pry his fingers between the bra and his swollen neck. It seemed like she'd been pulling tight for a thousand years when he finally fell forward like a sack of grain. Enid stayed on his back, straddling his body as she pulled and pulled and pulled…

He's not dead! It's a trick – like in the movies.

After a long time, Enid forced her hands to loosen their grip.

Heart pounding, Enid backed toward the door. Her foot hit the gun and it clattered into the wall. She grabbed it and aimed it at him.

Enid slammed the door shut, locking it with shaking hands. She shoved the gun in the back of her jeans, between the fabric and her flesh. There was a key in a second lock and she locked that too. Enid shoved the key in her pocket and looked around. She was startled to see that she was in the hallway of a house.

Enid heard a woman's voice from outside calling out for someone named "Dennie" and she headed in the other direction, which led her to a kitchen where an open box of Cap'n Crunch sat on the counter.

When her eyes landed on the back door, all her panic surged up and Enid barreled through the door and out into the night.

Her foot caught on something and she fell forward, sprawling face first into the dirt. Enid scrambled to her feet and ran toward a road illuminated by streetlights. Terrified that *he* was going to jump out and drag her back to the room, Enid bolted for the center of the street where she ran as fast and hard as she could – until her lungs and legs wouldn't let her go any farther.

Enid fell to her knees, gulping for air. The road felt so welcoming that she lay down on her side, enjoying the feel of the asphalt against her cheek. She brushed the hair from her face and realized she was shaking – worse than shaking; her whole body was convulsed with tremors.

Enid held herself tight and the horrible shaking got better. Her breath came easier. She struggled to her feet and staggered forward.

Enid heard a car and turned. Blinded by oncoming headlights, she froze, realizing, but not able to move as the car's brakes screamed for her to move…

Then, it all went black and Enid felt a terrible pain – a searing horrible pain and every bone in her body hurt.

She blinked.

Where am I?

The sky was above her and – everything hurt. Vaguely, Enid heard a car idling and a screech of tires as it disappeared into the night.

Enid tried to lift her head, but couldn't. She looked at the sky, the stars...

Why do I hurt?

Orion was there, blinking down at her. She could always spot the three stars that made his belt. There's his head...

A man's face bent over her, blocking Orion. He was saying something, but she couldn't make out. Enid watched his lips move, wondering why he looked so scared. The thought blew through her brain like a newspaper caught in the wind...

Jack.

Why wasn't he there for me?

The man was calling to her as if from far away. Enid felt herself slipping out on a black tide, felt it enclosing her, carrying her away.

CHAPTER FORTY-FOUR

You can discover more about a person in an hour of play than in a year of conversation.

—Plato

Jack was surprised to see Jeni's apartment building was even shabbier than he expected. He hadn't expected much, but the contrast between how Eve and her mother were living and how Jeni was living was jarring.

He wondered if Jeni knew that her building was one of the apartments where the county dumped recently released jailbirds and pedophiles. It was an eyesore that smacked of an out-of-state owner. Across the street was a nicer apartment building, and up and down the road were small but decent-looking houses that put what Jack had always referred to as "the pedophile motel" to shame.

Jack parked and walked the short distance to Jeni's front door. The window next to the door had cardboard tacked to it. He knocked loud enough to be heard above the pop music that was coming from within. Someone lowered the volume and he felt the presence of someone on the other side of the door.

"Jeni?" he asked, knocking again.

For a moment, he thought she was going to pretend she wasn't there, but she opened the door and greeted him with an embarrassed smile.

"Sorry to drop in unannounced," he said.

Jeni's embarrassment was palpable as she hurried to pick toys off the floor. She threw them into the makeshift crib and a plush toy hit the baby in the head. The baby stirred, but didn't awake.

Jeni looked casual sexy in jean shorts, a scrub-shirt and fluffy house slippers. "You should have called."

"I was in the neighborhood." Jack sat on the lumpy couch that creaked under his weight.

"It's temporary. Till I find a better place," she said.

"It's nice," Jack said, hoping he sounded sincere, but knowing he didn't.

The baby woke with a start, crying. Jeni picked her up, jiggled her into silence. "You want a beer?"

"No, thanks."

Jeni eyed him eagerly. "Did you find her?"

"Your mother's name was Ann Smith."

"Was?" Jeni said in a small voice.

Jack nodded.

Jeni hugged the baby closer and kissed the top of her head.

Jack said, "Back in the day, your mother worked at a local strip club – with Vivian."

"Vivian – a dancer? No way."

"A place called The Sugar Shack. It burned down."

Jeni blinked several times. "How did – my mother...?"

"Car accident. Nothing suspicious."

"Why would you think it was suspicious?"

"You weren't even one year old when it happened. Vivian took you in."

"How come nobody told me I was adopted? Didn't I have any family – other than my mother?"

"You have a grandmother."

Jeni's eyes lit up.

"She and your mother had a falling out," Jack said quickly.

"Does she know I'm alive? Maybe she doesn't know!"

"She knows."

Jeni stared at him for a long shocked moment. She whispered, "She doesn't want me?"

Jack searched for the right words. "She's religious – not in a good way. She wrote Ann off."

"Do you think…?"

"Vivian took you in, but didn't go through any official routes. She took you home and called you her own. Probably why she didn't tell you."

"How is that even possible? You have to tell *somebody* – social services or…"

"Your mother died in a car wreck and Vivian took you in. That's it."

"Did Eve know?"

"I don't know," Jack said, surprised at the lie that rolled off his tongue. He frowned, wondering why he was telling a lie for Eve.

Jeni sat thinking for a long time before she looked up, perplexed. "Why wouldn't they want me to know?"

"I was hoping you could tell me."

"How would I know?"

"Do you remember anything – maybe somebody said something – something that struck you strange at the time?"

Jeni dashed away a tear with the back of her hand. "My grandmother – I want to see her."

"She's not fit to feed a dog."

"I want to meet her. You can't stop me."

"She'll make you sad."

Jeni stared at him.

Jack stayed silent. He hated the thought of Jeni hearing that her own grandmother believed that she heard from the Angel Gabriel that Jeni was better off dead. He hesitated and said, "Sleep on it. If you want to go – I'll go with you."

Jeni stared at him, her eyes troubled.

"You okay?" Jack said.

"I guess I should be happy Viv took me in," Jeni said with an unconvincing smile.

"Why did you start calling her Viv – instead of mom?" Jack said, relieved to be on firmer ground.

"Do you think my grandmother…?"

Jack abruptly stood, frowning. He eyed the door, itching to leave. "I'll call you if I find out anything more."

"Thank you."

"Well, good luck." Jack cringed at the false note in his voice. In two strides he was at the door, but when he turned to shut the door, he froze.

Tears rolled down Jeni's cheeks, dripping off her face. He stared at her. She was beautiful – Stella, but better.

Jeni walked to him and wrapped her arms around him, hiding her face in his shirt.

Jack hesitated, but her body pressed to his made it too late to leave. He tilted her face up and looked into her blue eyes that were shining with tears. Their lips met and Jack gave a groan, his arms wrapping tight around her. He lifted her off the ground, carried her into the bedroom.

Fast, and they were naked and on the bed, Jeni moving her hips aggressively into him, like she was grinding on one of her customer's laps.

He grabbed her face, "Cut it! I don't need a show – I want *you*."

Jeni's face flushed crimson. She tried to push him away, but he pressed her down in a kiss that left her clinging to him like a vine to a rock.

Jack explored and teased every inch of her, until they both could stand it no longer.

"Make me your own," she whispered.

He did.

The baby cried, the neighbor pounded on the wall, the sun slowly disappeared – leaving long shadows across their bodies until the shadows were destroyed by the night – until they were destroyed by each other.

It was close to midnight when Jack leaned back, exhausted. He examined the water damage on the ceiling.

Jeni was pressed up against him, caressing his stomach. "I don't ever want to leave this room."

He reached out, cupped her breast. "Let me help you, Jeni."

"Is that what you think I want – help? *This* is what I want…" She moved her hand to his heart. "And *this*…" She ran her fingertip downward.

"I can't promise you anything. If I do promise you anything – don't trust me."

"I don't need no promises – or help. I been looking for a man like you. I'll take *this*, thank you very much."

"Let me help you find a decent place. They'll be no strings attached."

She smiled, kissed his hand. "Strings – *I like*. The way you fuck – *I love*."

Jack got out bed and began dressing.

She sat up on one elbow. "Don't tell me there's been *two pussies* in this bed?"

He ran his hand through his hair. "I'm goin' to get us food. You hungry?"

"Lyin' dog," she grinned. "You don't think I know what a man leaving looks like? I figured you for a leg man."

"What makes you think I'm not?"

"If you *were*, you'd be next to me – with your fingers in my pie. You wouldn't be offering to *help me* –like I'm a stray off the street."

"I like you, Jeni." Jack remembered that he said the same thing to Eve.

"I'm not Eve," she snapped.

Jack shot her a look, startled.

Did she know?

"You said her name," Jeni said.

He shook his head, eyeing her warily. "You heard it in your head, sister. I didn't say it."

She gave a short, mirthless laugh. "I'm going to tell you a story. Not because I want to, but because you need to know what kind of person you're up against."

"You – or your sister?"

"Our stepfather was a monster. Whoever cut his heart out should get a medal. He was a Grade-A, certified daughter-fucking pedophile. Eve will never admit it – not to you, not to herself. Me? I never been to de Nile. I call it like it is. But Eve would rather *die* than admit that daddy had his dick up her ass."

Jack looked down, hating that he felt pity for them – all three of them.

"She told you different, huh? Yeah, that's her – her shit don't stink and it never will – not in *her* world."

"Did Vivian know?"

"She didn't want to know so she made sure *not* to know. Eve's special trick was pretending to be sick. Then Laura started playing sick – and sleeping in Eve's room so he couldn't come after them – safety in numbers. I was the easy target – too damned healthy and *stupid* to play sick. I hate them for that. If they weren't always playing sick – it wouldn't have all ended up on me." Jeni laughed, "Literally."

Jack winced.

"Eve didn't ever *not* try to steal anything I ever had. *Except him.* You think I'm living like this 'cause I want to? I'm making a *home* for me and my baby in the only world I know that *she* wants no part of – and that works fine by me. If you want Eve – tell her you fucked me and she's getting sloppy seconds. Don't forget to wrap it up pretty, though – she don't like it dirty, *like I do*. And if you want to *keep* Eve, you better start telling yourself lies as fast and hard as you can – 'cause the truth and Eve go together like a fuckin' hawk and the bitch-ass sparrow."

"Jeni…" Jack said in a voice that was made for easing his way out of front doors.

Jeni jumped up, furious. "You don't fucking deserve a real woman. You want *me* – you can stuff dollars in my cunt like the rest of them." She picked up an ashtray and hurled it at him.

It hit Jack in the forehead, drawing blood. She even had better aim than Stella.

Jeni said, "You think I want to marry you and have kids and live in some…"

"Shit," Jack said, his face changing to alarm.

Jeni stopped, startled.

"*Shit. Shit, shit, shit.*" Jack shoved on his shoes and ran to the door.

"What?" Jeni ran after him.

"I was supposed to pick up Enid."

"You *forgot* her?"

Jack bounded for the door, waving over his shoulder, "I'll call. I promise." He winced, hating that he threw another promise into the world.

"Jack!" she called after him as he ran down the walkway. He jumped into his car, not looking back, not wanting to look back and see her standing in the doorway alone. A part of him wished that he could be the man she needed, but he knew it was no use.

As he sped away, he saw Frank Ficus's dark sedan sitting like a toad on the road. Jack hit the accelerator, watching as Frank K-turned to tail him.

Why is he still following me?

Jack sped toward the meeting place. Cursing, he held his sleeve up to his temple, trying to stop the bleeding. He wasn't in the mood to listen to Enid's lip and he sure as hell didn't want to explain shit to her.

He thought about Jeni, deciding that the smartest thing to do would be to forget her. He found her mother, so he had nothing left to do but cash her check. She'd become a memory – a regret. He didn't need a magic eight ball to know that, no matter how you cut it, Jeni was trouble. That's all he needed – to get involved with a dancer with daddy issues.

Reluctantly, he put his sleeve up to his face and breathed in. He could smell Jeni – and he liked it.

CHAPTER FORTY-FIVE

All truth is simple...is that not doubly a lie?

—*Friedrich Nietzsche*

Groggily, Bud reached for his cell phone that rang relentlessly into the dark room. He glanced at the clock and groaned: two in the morning. His first day back to work had been exhausting. If they weren't so short-staffed, he was sure they would have sent him home. It had taken everything he had to slug it out till five o'clock.

When he and Chip got home, he found all his clothes dumped on the floor in the guest bedroom and Bunnie was giving him the silent treatment. Chip had gone to the store to get them sandwiches, which Bud was too tired to eat. Bud retired to the guest room to "read" but, once the door was closed, he sank into bed and was asleep before his socks hit the floor.

"Detective Orlean," he muttered into the phone.

"Sorry to call so late, Bud," Jenson said peppily. "We have a situation that requires you *and* your chauffeur. John C. on Central, Room 314."

Jenson hung up, leaving Bud frowning into the phone. "John C." referred to the John C. Lincoln Hospital on Dunlap, which was a ten-minute drive.

Bud rousted Chip out of bed, which took some effort. Once Chip was driving, Bud leaned back and enjoyed the view of the city at night.

"I don't understand why I have to be there," Chip said. "What's it got to do with me?"

"We'll find out soon enough."

"I don't think I like being a detective," Chip said.

"You're not."

Bud watched the city unwind, his thoughts turning to Bunnie. The thought of losing her made the city look ugly. He tried to picture himself "retired" and he saw a ridiculous version of himself standing in Bermuda shorts and Hawaiian shirt – doing nothing. He shuddered. Without work, he'd be lost.

Without Bunnie, I'm lost.

"Do you think mom's serious?" Chip said.

Bud frowned. "Word on the street is you and Eve Hargrove are picking out china patterns. Really, Chip? If this is an I.Q. test, you're flunking."

"I called her," Chip said.

"Did she happen to confess to murdering her stepfather? Or is she playing coy?"

"I didn't say she called back. Yet."

"Pretty sure of yourself, huh?"

"I'm sure I want to see her again."

"So, on your date, illuminate me. What constitutes sociopath chit-chat?"

Chip tightened his lips.

"Weather? Price of beans in China? Oh, I know, why she cut her father's heart out and sent it to me."

"There's no way she did that."

"If you don't want to pop your bubble of academia and step into the real world, that's fine, but stop with the pretty-boy playboy crap and start using your brain – or that woman will cut it out and mail it to me. Wake up and stop being so naïve."

"I'm not naïve."

"Then you're an idiot."

"I know more about the real world then you think."

"You were always idealistic. You always see the best in people – even when there's nothing to see."

"She's actually – "

"Don't say sweet."

"I wasn't."

"Are you going to see her again?"

"If she calls back, hell yeah," Chip said.

Bud grimaced, put his hand to his chest.

Chip glanced at him, concerned.

Bud dropped his hand. After several moments, he asked, "Remember how Polo used to run away?"

"Now I get a dog story?" Chip said. "You'd send us walking through the neighborhood, carrying dog food, shouting his name. Yeah, I remember."

"Tomorrow, we're making an appointment for you – with Polo's vet."

"What? To have me fixed?"

"I'm going to have Dr. Flanderhann implant a doggie LoJack in you – so I can find your body after she cuts your heart out."

Chip laughed. "Are you crazy? They won't agree to that."

"He owes me," Bud said.

"You're serious?"

"I don't want your mother wondering whether you're dead or alive – this will simplify matters. Give her closure."

"That's the stupidest thing I ever heard."

"You're the genius dating a murderer."

"I like her."

"I like a butcher knife for cutting meat, but you don't see me taking it home to meet my mama."

Chip pulled into the hospital parking lot. They walked in silence to the third floor. A nurse directed them to Room 314, where Jenson and a policewoman watched as a nurse adjusted a line.

Enid lay in the hospital bed. Both hands were bandaged and her forehead boasted a bruise the size of a cherry tomato.

"That's Jack Fox's daughter," Bud said. "What happened?"

Jenson said, "I didn't know Jack Fox had a kid. You sure?"

"Yeah, I'm sure."

Jenson turned to the policewoman, "Jack Fox. Find him and get him down here."

"I've heard of him," she said as she turned to leave.

Jenson turned back to Bud. "The kid…"

"Enid," Bud said.

"No identification. She didn't ask for her dad – they must not be close," Jenson said.

Bud picked up her chart listing her as "Jane Doe." He crossed it out and wrote "Enid Fox."

"Hit-and-run," Jenson said. "Neighbor found her in the road. Nobody saw the vehicle. No broken bones, but her hands are torn up, a mild concussion. Doctor says she'll be all right."

"Why am I here?" Bud said.

"The kid's been spinning us some stories. They have her on heavy meds, but she has been able to tell us – her boyfriend is, and I quote, "a hunk of hot eye-candy" – also known as Chip Orlean."

Chip looked at him in astonishment. "What?"

Jenson's eyes twinkled. "She described you to a 'T' – eyes the color of the Pacific, lips like an angel."

Chip flushed pink.

"Anything you want to tell us?" Bud said to Chip.

"I met her once and I didn't even really meet her – you were there," Chip said.

"Case solved," Bud said. "Jane Doe is Jack Fox's daughter and she's got a schoolgirl crush." He shrugged, turned to leave, "Next time text me a pic and save me a trip."

"Not so fast, pard'ner." Jenson reached for a plastic bag. "Our little friend was packing heat."

Bud frowned at the Smith & Wesson .357 inside the bag.

"I got to thinking about the Wanda Stills case," Jenson said.

"You can't tell me that's the same gun as the Wanda Stills case. No way they can I.D. it that fast," Bud said.

"My own personal speculation," Jenson said.

"What's it mean?" Chip said.

Jenson nodded at Enid. "Our victim is a chatterbox."

"So what? She cheated on her algebra test, or what?" Bud said.

"She says she killed a man. Strangled him."

Bud stared at Jenson in amazement. "You're telling me this kid, ninety-eight pounds wet and belly-full, is carrying a gun that may be connected to an unsolved murder case and, if that's not enough, she *strangled* a grown man?"

"From what she says, she was locked in a dungeon where she strangled a killer-clown – possibly to death – with her bra."

Bud stared at Jenson, dumbfounded.

"Why would she say I'm her boyfriend?" Chip said.

"That's what's troubling you in all this?" Bud said. "Not wondering about the teenage gun-welding strangling-bra clown-killer but, our concern is, *why* she said you're her *boyfriend*?"

"It doesn't make sense," Chip said.

Bud looked at Jenson, hooked his thumb at Chip, "Jenson. It doesn't make sense."

"Keen observation. Perhaps we should call a detective."

CHAPTER FORTY-SIX

A woman knows the face of the man she loves as a sailor knows the open sea.

—*Honore de Balzac*

Out of the haziness, Enid picked out *his* voice and said, "Honeypie."

The voices stopped. She struggled to open her eyes and was surprised to see her future father-in-law.

"Oh, it's you," she said. Chip's face popped up and she felt a flood of happiness.

He found me.

"Hey, Enid," Chip said.

She held out her hand and said, "Darling."

Chip and Bud glanced at each other.

Enid smiled, happy that she was wearing her chiffon gown and tiara with sparklers.

Chip moved closer to the bed. "I, uh, understand we're dating?"

"I love you," she said, enjoying the sea breezes and the sound of the surf as it crashed against the shore.

Bud stepped forward. "Enid, I understand you told Detective Jenson – you strangled a man?"

"Hope not, but – yeah. He deserved it," she said.

"Enid. Focus on what I'm saying." Bud said.

"'K." Enid blew Chip a kiss, "Catchy-catchy."

Chip grimaced.

Bud nudged Chip. "Catch the darned thing."

Chip awkwardly caught the imaginary kiss.

"Wait in the hall," Bud said to Chip. "You're a distraction."

"I need to hear it – for my research. Besides, it involves me," Chip said.

"Stand behind the bathroom door," Bud said.

"Harold." Enid clapped her hands, "More bubbly."

"Harold?" Bud said, "Is that who you strangled?"

"Don't be silly," Enid said.

"Who's Harold?" Bud said.

"The butler."

Chip rolled his eyes, retreating to hide behind the bathroom door.

"I see you," Enid said, craning her neck.

"Further," Bud said, waving him back.

"We're going to name our dog Daisy," Enid said.

"Enid, about the killer clown?"

"He wasn't a clown," Enid said.

"Good," Bud said, "and you didn't strangle anyone, right?"

"I wouldn't have, but he locked me in the dungeon."

"What dungeon?"

"Not a dungeon – a room."

"Who?"

"I thought he'd be a clown," Enid said. She looked down and saw a bug crawling across her chiffon gown. She knocked it away, uncomfortable on the dirty mattress they were making her lay on. She shook her head, trying to clear it.

"Who?" Bud said.

Enid remained silent, worrying that the crashing waves were getting too close.

"Enid, I need the name of the man who locked you up," Bud said.

"She's on too much medication. Maybe we should wait till later," Jenson said.

"I want my mom," Enid said, tears filling her eyes.

"What about your dad?" Bud said.

"He didn't come for me. He broke his promise," Enid said, chest tightening with sorrow.

Bud frowned, "Did he know where you were?"

"I had to do it." Enid could feel the waves coming to get her, coming to wreck her beautiful dress. She put her hand up to her head. The tiara was gone. The ravens stole it and hid it in their cave. She frowned, knowing they would eat the sparklers and choke to death. "Paris – for the honeymoon."

Bud sighed.

Enid drifted onto the pink beaches of Paris where she and Chip were kissing till her head hurt. She could hear the ravens talking.

Are they talking about me?

"What do you think?" a raven said.

"I intend to take it seriously until proven otherwise," another raven said.

Well, of course we're serious. We're in love.

CHAPTER FORTY-SEVEN

For my part I know nothing with any certainty, but the sight of the stars makes me dream.

—Vincent Van Gogh

Five minutes at the designated spot, twenty more minutes of circling the neighborhood and a phone call that went to Enid's out-of-service phone was enough for Jack to decide to get her out of the wayward girls' home himself.

He rang the buzzer and a woman's voice cracked through the intercom. "What?"

"My daughter Enid checked in this morning, I'm here to get her out."

Silence.

"If you can't rustle up my kid, then you can get Vivian Hargrove out here right now," Jack said.

"She's not here."

The intercom went dead.

Jack walked down the steps and around the side of the building. He picked up a pebble and threw it at one of the windows. He threw more pebbles. The window jerked open. A girl with spikey hair leaned out.

"I'm looking for a girl who checked in this morning – name is Enid. Do you know her?"

"How do I know you're not some perv?" The girl said.

"She's my daughter. Do you know her?"

The girl held a finger up to her lips and motioned for him to wait. She disappeared.

Jack glanced around, nervous. That's all he needed, the police asking why he was lurking under a teenage girl's window.

After what seemed like an eternity, a skinny girl stuck her head out the window. Two other girls hovered behind her.

"Who are you?" the skinny girl said.

"I'm her father. If Enid is here, just get her."

"She said her dad was dead."

"Ladies, I need to talk to my daughter."

"She left."

"When?"

"They took her," she said.

"Who took her? Where?"

"Ask Mrs. Hargrove." The girl shut the window and the room went dark.

Jack stared up at the window, feeling strangely helpless.

They took her? What did that mean?

Regret twisted in his stomach at the thought of having involved Enid in the case.

What if she's in trouble?

He drove the twenty minutes to Vivian's house, which stood dark against the night sky. The gate was locked, so he climbed over the wall and searched the grounds, half expecting to set off a burglar alarm as he tested every door.

The place was empty.

Climbing back over the wall, he barely registered the sound of his pant leg ripping. He jumped down and walked to his car.

He sat behind the wheel, thinking. He called Eve and left a message for her to call back and started driving in her direction.

When he reached her house, Horace was at his post in the guardhouse and said she wasn't in.

"Where can I find her?" Jack said.

"Another death in the family?" Horace said.

"My daughter lied to you, I know." He held up his hands in exasperation, "I don't know, she's missing. I'm trying to find Eve to find her mother, who might be able to help."

Horace stared at him a few moments. "Got a kid giving me trouble, too. You didn't hear it from me, but she's at her sister's gallery."

"Thanks."

"You can thank me by not hearing it from me."

Rachel's research had shown that Laura owned a jewelry and art gallery in the heart of Old Scottsdale.

Within fifteen minutes, Jack stood looking in the illuminated windows of empty jewelry displays. They were closed for business, but a photo shoot was in progress. Eve sat off to the side, her head bent over a book. Behind her, a handsome dark-haired photographer took pictures of Laura as an older man interviewed her.

Laura wore a teal dress that made her skin glow like pearl. Jack looked at Eve who, dressed simpler, eclipsed everything.

Jack walked back to his car and dug his oversized camera out of the glove compartment. Combined with an "I belong here" attitude, the camera gave him the credibility he needed to get into places that he had no right to be.

He knocked on the glass door.

Eve glanced up, eyebrows knitting in irritation. She walked to the door.

"What do you want?" she said, opening the door wide enough so he could talk, but not enter.

Jack heard the interviewer ask Laura, "What was your inspiration behind the Desert Fire line?"

"I need to find Vivian," Jack said.

"I'm not my mother's keeper." Eve tried to shut the door, but Jack shoved his foot into the space and pushed it open.

"I wasn't asking," he said.

"You have ten seconds to leave – or I call the police."

Jack glanced around. The place was classy. Lots of glass and subtle lighting on display cases filled with artfully arranged jewelry.

"Get her on the phone," Jack said.

"I don't like to be bossed. Especially by a paid employee."

"We can do this the hard way – or easy. Take your pick."

Something in his eyes convinced Eve. She pulled out her phone and called. After several moments, she left a message for Vivian to call. She ended the call and gave him a pointed look. "You're not her type."

"I'm looking for my daughter."

"What's Vivian got to do with her?" Her eyes lit up. "Oh! Is your daughter a wayward girl?" Eve laughed and sauntered back to her stool. She picked up her book. "Out of the running for Father of the Year, Mr. Fox? Feel free to stay till Viv calls, but keep your mouth shut and stay out of the way."

Jack removed the lens cap and walked toward Laura. He snapped a burst of pics.

"Who is he?" the photographer said.

"Just do your job, Jerry," Eve said.

The interviewer scowled, "I thought we had an exclusive?"

"You do," Eve said.

Jack took a burst of photos of the scowling group. "An exposé," Jack said. "I guess I don't need to tell you folks what I'm investigating."

The interviewer's mouth went slack with surprise, he stepped back.

"Give me a moment," Eve said to the group. She pulled Jack to the front door. "You want Vivian – you can wait outside."

Jack snapped a picture of Eve's face.

"What the hell is your problem?" Eve said.

Jack turned and took another burst of photos of Laura, who was sitting tensely on the stool.

The interviewer shoved past him and out the front door.

"Where are you going?" Eve said.

Once on the street, the interviewer broke into a run toward his car.

Jack couldn't resist the urge to snap a shot of Eve's startled face.

"Are you mental?" she said, trying to shove him out the front door.

Jack planted himself in the door, so that Eve couldn't budge him. "I know an Italian place – I want to see what you look like there – with me."

"In your dreams."

He grabbed her waist and pulled her close. "Eve Marie Alexandria Hargrove," he buried his face in her hair, spoke softly in her ear, "you're the best damned thing I ever seen."

She stood frozen as his lips moved toward hers, lingering.

Her lips parted and she leaned into him.

"Eve," Laura said.

Eve pulled away from Jack.

Disconcerted, Eve said to Jack, "You're out of your league."

"I know," he said.

"Not interested," Eve said.

"Sure you are."

Eve eyed him. "Aren't you looking for your daughter?"

"You're chicken-shit scared."

Her eyes narrowed.

"Go out with me," Jack said. "If you're still not interested, you'll never hear of me no more."

"Is that a promise?"

Jack grinned, made a "don't count on it" face.

"Eve!" Laura said.

Eve's head snapped in her direction.

The photographer had an iPhone camera on Laura. "What about the rumors that it was you and your sister who murdered your stepfather?"

"We had a deal, Jerry," Eve said.

Jerry pushed closer to Laura, "They say it was you that cut his heart out and mailed it to that detective. Why'd you do it?"

Laura staggered past Jerry as Eve bounded to her side, supporting her.

"Give me that," Eve said, making a snatch for Jerry's iPhone even as she still held Laura around the waist.

Jerry held the phone over his head and behind him, grinning.

Jack came up behind him, took the iPhone, grabbed his wrist and twisted his arm back and put him facedown on the floor.

Jerry gasped in pain.

"You can get up nice and quiet and leave or I break your arm. What is it?" Jack said, pocketing the iPhone.

"Leave," Jerry said.

Jack eased off his arm and watched as Jerry got to his feet and beat it to the door.

Eve rushed to the door and locked it behind him. Laura burst into tears and fell to the floor in a heap of teal.

Eve stared at Jack with hard eyes. "How much do you want for it?"

"Not even a thank-you," Jack said to Eve. He looked at Laura. "You okay down there?"

Laura attempted to pull herself together, gulped down a sob with a nod.

"Get your stuff, Laura. I'm taking you home," Eve said.

Reluctantly, Laura got up and came to Eve.

Eve put her arm around Laura's waist, pulled her close as Laura cried on her shoulder.

"They'll never leave us alone," Laura said.

Jack's eyes lingered on Eve, admiring her fingers as they gently caressed Laura's hair. Eve whispered something to Laura.

Laura's eyes softened. She nodded.

"Get your purse," Eve said to Laura.

Laura nodded and disappeared to the back.

"I want that iPhone," Eve said to Jack.

"I want you. Doesn't mean it's going to happen."

"I don't go out with losers," she said.

"Eight o'clock?"

"Five. Dress nice."

CHAPTER FORTY-EIGHT

For every action, there is an equal and opposite reaction.

—Isaac Newton

"With a father like you, the kid doesn't need enemies," Bud said to Jack with a withering look.

Jack's lips tightened.

Bud felt the satisfaction of knowing he hit a nerve.

Jack Fox is a louse.

"Any other questions, Detective?" Jack said.

"Not till the victim wakes up."

Jack's face clouded and Bud felt a twinge of regret.

"Enid's not a victim," Jack said.

Bud looked at Enid, who was sleeping. She looked like a twelve-year-old in bulky hand bandages.

Bud said, "Whatever happened to her, she got lucky."

"I want to be alone with my daughter," Jack said.

Bud nodded. He retreated to the hallway, where he gave the nurse his number, asking her to call him when Enid was alert.

A pretty twenty-something nurse with strawberry blond hair was flirting with Chip. Bud motioned for Chip to follow and continued down the hall. Chip fell in step with him.

Bud nodded toward the nurse. "Vegas odds she's got her heart set on marrying a doctor."

"She's not my type."

"You prefer brunette homicidal degenerates," Bud said.

"Yup," Chip said.

In the car, Bud told Chip to drive to the station.

Chip shot him a startled look. "We've been up all night."

"Take your pick – the station or the veterinarian."

Chip made the turn that took them to the station – and away from the vet. "If you're going to work me like a slave, you need to at least feed me."

Ten minutes later, they were sitting at a booth in the diner where Bud knew Sam Waterstone was a regular.

"How you feel?" Chip said.

Bud scratched at one of the sticky pads that pulled at his skin. "Like a trussed turkey."

Chip's phone rang and he flipped it open. His face lit up and he signaled that he would be outside.

Breakfast came and Bud watched as Chip paced the sidewalk, his eyes bright and a smile playing around the corners of his mouth.

It's her.

Bud felt a heaviness descend on him. It was inevitable. Chip was going to be stupid and in a big way.

Chip returned and dug into his scrambled eggs and toast.

Bud sighed. His food tasted like chalk. He wiped his mouth and leaned back, examining Chip, trying to remember what it was like to be that young. When the whole world seemed like it was there for your taking and anything was possible. Sex was mysterious – exciting.

Where does it go?

Bud tried to remember when the change happened between him and Bunnie. After Chip was born? After twenty years of marriage? One moment they were in love and making love – the next – she was talking divorce.

"You look weird," Chip said. "You wanna go home?"

"So I can nap?" Bud said.

"You did have a heart attack."

The bell on the diner's front door tinkled. Bud looked up to see Sam Waterstone walk in and take a seat at the counter.

"Wait here." Bud slid out of the booth and made his way to Sam, who was already engrossed in his newspaper. "Sam Waterstone?"

Sam looked up, questioningly.

Bud held out his hand. "Detective Bud Orlean. I'm working your niece's case."

Sam's forehead wrinkled. "My niece?"

"Jack Fox's daughter, Enid."

Sam's eyebrows went up. "What case?"

"She's at John C. – she'll be okay. Hit-and-run."

"Jesus." Sam threw the newspaper on the counter.

"Can I ask you some questions?" Bud inwardly smiled at Sam's wary expression. Cops are the ultimate skeptics.

"Sure. Did she...?"

"We're waiting for her to wake up. She's on meds, making her story garbled. Has Enid ever been involved in drugs?"

Sam shook his head, "Not that I know. Of course, I've only known her for a day."

"Any reason she would have a gun?"

Sam's eyebrows furrowed. He hesitated. "Did Jack tell you – how I met her?"

A waitress set down his coffee and Sam said, "Thanks, Mona."

Bud listened with interest as Sam related the story of how he'd responded to a call for a disturbance and found Enid babysitting for a woman whose boyfriend had tried to break in. They arrested the boyfriend and when he questioned Enid, she told him she came to Phoenix to find her real father, Jack Fox.

"How'd you know she was telling the truth?" Bud said.

"She had names, dates – it fit." Sam shrugged, "I called my wife, we brought her home, then I called Jack."

"How'd he respond to the news?"

"I told you what I know. For the rest, ask Jack."

"I will. Thank you." Bud held out his hand and they shook.

"Who's that?" Sam said.

Bud followed his gaze to Chip. "My son."

"He a cop?"

"He's writing a book. Shadowing me for research."

"Must be nice working with your son," Sam said.

Bud made a face, nodded goodbye and returned to his table.

CHAPTER FORTY-NINE

The weak can never forgive. Forgiveness is the attribute of the strong.

–Mahatma Gandhi

"I'm not lying," Enid said, her face burning with anger.

"I didn't say you were," Jack said. "The cops are canvassing the neighborhood. You don't know where the house was or how far you ran?"

Enid shook her head. "Orange flowers. I remember orange flowers."

Jack remained silent, thinking.

"You think I'm a big fat liar, don't you?" Enid said.

"Look. I, uh – I shouldn't have put you in that situation."

"You should have been there to pick me up – like you promised."

"I'm trying to apologize," Jack said. "Jesus, you don't make anything easy, do you?"

Enid flushed, remembering the promise she made when she thought she was going to die.

I'll be nicer to mom and Jack.

Jack said, "What I'm trying to say is that it was a total asshole move on my part – sending you undercover. I should have never done it. I apologize."

She stared at him in surprise. She felt the anger seep out of her, and she opened her mouth to tell him that she was sorry for being so mean and tell him how she was going to be nicer and…

"You're not bullshitting about the whole strangling thing, right?"

Enid sat bolt upright in bed, anger flooding back. "Why would I make up something like that?"

"To get attention. Put it to me. I don't know. All I know is if you're exaggerating – "

"You mean lying."

"I've heard you tell some whoppers."

Enid sat up. "My jeans. Where are my jeans?" She spotted the bag and pointed. "There."

Jack held it out for her to take.

She gave him a look, held up her bandaged hands. "Duh."

Jack frowned, dug around the bag and pulled out her jeans.

"Check the front pocket."

Jack pulled out a dirty Kleenex. "Jesus," he said, dropping it.

"The key," Enid said as he pulled out a key. "That's the key to the room I was locked in."

Jack cursed, dropping the key. "So much for fingerprints."

"That's a clue, right?"

"Maybe. Maybe not." Jack slid the key into a medical glove.

"What kind of crap detective are you?" Enid said. "I'm handing you a big old honkin' clue and you're like – " She imitated him acting like a doofus, "Dum, dum, dumm-di-dum."

"I'll check it out," Jack said.

"Give it to the detective – Chip's dad," Enid said.

"That's another thing," Jack said. "It's not ladylike for you to go chasing some guy around. He's too old for you anyway. I'd expect a daughter of mine to have a little more pride."

"Look who's talking?" Enid said, even as she felt a burst of happiness at the way he said "a daughter of mine."

"It's unseemly,"Jack said.

"You wanna talk unseemly…?"

"That's different."

"Why? 'Cause you're a guy?"

"Yeah."

"It wasn't different for my mother."

Jack glared at Enid.

"I'm just sayin'…" Enid said, shrugging in mock innocence.

Jack headed to the door. "I need to give Detective Blowhard the key. Why don't you get some rest."

Jack left and a nurse came in. "How is everything?"

Enid held up her bandaged hands, "I gotta go to the bathroom. How does that happen?"

CHAPTER FIFTY

Love is a serious mental disease.

—Plato

Jack drove to the office, irritably eyeing Frank Ficus's car in his rearview mirror.

Dogs aren't this faithful.

Jack wanted nothing more than a hot shower and some shut-eye. He parked and headed to his office, which was unlocked and no sign of Rachel.

He closed the door to his office and stretched out on the couch. He set his alarm for one hour. He listened to the clicking of Rachel's heels returning to her desk and the sounds of traffic and the occasional siren.

The alarm blared, he hit snooze. He closed his eyes and listened as the door opened and softly closed. Rachel checking on him, maybe surprised that he'd been in his office.

His mind drifted and his dream came wafting back.

Eve.

She was flying through the night skies. He was behind her, struggling to get near her, but she was always just out of reach.

He frowned.

There'd been something else.

What was it?

He strained to remember, but it slipped away – elusive as Eve.

The alarm rang again. He slapped it into silence and swung his legs so that his feet landed on the floor.

Rachel opened the door and flipped on the lights, messages in hand.

They spent the next ten minutes going over the messages and arranging his schedule. When they were done, Jack stood up.

"Where are you off to?" Rachel said.

"Too embarrassed to tell you," Jack said, thinking about his date with Eve.

"Sounds promising," she said.

Within the hour, Jack found himself in the Biltmore Macy's, nervously eyeing new suits. He couldn't remember the last time he had been shopping and cared.

I'm turning into a girl.

George, an older man who looked more like a business financier than a sales clerk, glided over and examined him with fond indulgence over his heavily rimmed glasses.

"Hmmm," George said. He rocked back on his heels, hands clasped behind his back as he examined the rack of suits Jack was looking at. "I think not." George deftly replaced the suit Jack had picked and gestured for Jack to follow him.

George walked briskly toward another section of the store with better lighting and plusher carpets. George stopped at a rack with a flourish.

"I'm on a budget," Jack said.

"You are in love?" George said.

Jack grimaced.

"First date with a special woman, eh?" George rubbed his hands gleefully and pulled an elegant suit off the rack, displaying it for Jack to admire.

Jack smiled politely.

"Exactly. You are right – the brown is not for you." George wrinkled his nose as if hit by an unpleasant odor. His eyes landed on another rack and he hurried over.

Jack hesitated and followed him.

George held out an elegant black suit made of lightweight material.

Jack touched it. It felt like cash slipping through his fingers.

George's eyes glowed in triumph. He guided Jack toward a counter, selected a lavender shirt. "Nice, no?"

"Purple?" Jack said.

"Barney is purple, this is lavender. On a man such as yourself – it will be…" George kissed his fingers with a flourish.

Once in the dressing room, Jack looked at his reflection in surprise. It made him look like a better version of himself – a version that might be able to get someplace with Eve Hargrove.

George tapped on the door. "Sir?"

Jack stepped out.

"Perfecto," George said.

Jack looked at the price tag. "I've paid less for a car."

George waved his hand as if waving away a fly. "We have a sale, the real price is – " George adjusted his glasses, squinted at the price tag, calculating. "Five hundred eighty for the suit, shirt is sixty. And this," he ran his hand along the lapel, "does not need a tie – unless you are going formal?"

Jack shook his head, reluctantly took off the jacket.

George stopped him, turned him to the mirror. "Are these business suits, sir? Can they be tax-deductible?"

Jack looked at the three of him in the mirror. He looked like a man Eve might fuck.

"I'll take it," Jack said.

"A man in this suit – is a man a woman takes seriously."

Jack didn't escape George until he had new socks, underwear, a belt and shoes. George insisted that he pay a visit to his barber, who was "the best" and would be worth every dime.

"I don't have any dimes left, George," Jack said.

"Next time you come in, you tell me how it goes, eh?" George gave him a smile and waved him on his way.

Jack would have waved back but he was too laden down with bags.

This settles it. I'm a girl.

Jack looked at a clock, frowning. He'd taken longer than he thought and would have no time to go to the hospital to visit Enid.

From the car he started to dial, but remembered she couldn't answer the phone with the bandaged hands. He dialed the nurse's station and found out that the doctors were keeping her overnight. For a while it looked like they were going to give her the boot, but once her mother gave the hospital Enid's insurance info, she got the go-ahead on an extra night.

He left a message that he would be there in the morning. Hanging up, he felt uneasy.

Driving home, his stomach got jumpier and, at the last minute, cursing, he did an illegal U-turn and headed to the hospital. Taking three flights of stairs, two at a time, he got to her door, breathing hard. She was sleeping.

He walked to her bed, stared down at her, searching for any resemblance to him, but only seeing...

Mom.

The image of his mother's inert body dangling from the noose flashed in his mind's eye and he turned away.

He found a paper and pen and scribbled, "Didn't want to wake you. Will be back in the morning. Sleep well and call if you need me. Jack."

He left the note where she would find it, hoping she wouldn't call. He made record time getting home and into a hot shower, thinking only of Eve.

CHAPTER FIFTY-ONE

When you're wounded and left on Afghanistan's plains,
And the women come out to cut up what remains,
Jest roll to your rifle and blow out your brains
And go to your gawd like a soldier.

—Rudyard Kipling

Bud watched as five grunting policemen dragged the waterlogged garbage bag crisscrossed with duct tape up the steep sides of the canal. Bud stared at it glumly. He didn't feel his usual bloodhound reflexes kicking in and that depressed him. It took zero imagination to know it contained one unlucky son of a bitch who was in the wrong place at the wrong time – or one unlucky son of a bitch who got just what he deserved.

He had to give Chip credit – he was hanging tough. Not only had they been up all night, but Chip had gamely spent three hours following Bud as he trudged through the neighborhood where Enid had been found as they questioned neighbor after neighbor with no results. He was beginning to think that Chip might actually be serious about the writing thing.

Now, under the treeless expanse of the Arizona Canal, Chip showed no signs of fatigue as he periodically took notes in a pocket-sized notebook.

Bud had caught Chip examining him with concerned eyes if he showed any signs of slowing his pace, which had forced Bud to pretend that he felt better than he actually did. His legs felt heavy and he was having trouble catching his breath with the tiniest of slopes – luckily Phoenix was as flat as Bunnie's fallen arches.

Bud pulled his hat lower over his eyes and squinted as the garbage bag thunked to the ground. Dirty brown water squished out as it gave one heavy, sick-sounding roll forward. The garbage bag tore and a big toe, macerated and hairy, jabbed through.

Bud squatted to get a closer look.

Caucasian male – in the water for less than twenty-four hours.

"What do you think?" Chip said, peering over his shoulder, pen poised over his notebook.

"Ingrown," Bud said as he waved over the photographer.

Jenson sauntered over. "Oh dear."

"Can you take over?" Bud said. "I've got personal business."

"Anything new turn up?" Jenson said.

Bud shrugged. "Not much. Talked to the guy who called the police – story thin but reliable."

"You think the kid strangled someone?" Jenson said.

Bud nodded at the big-toe bag. "If we're lucky, this might just be our strangled psycho-clown perp."

Jenson laughed, "If only it were that easy."

Bud waved, trudged to the truck.

Chip caught up to Bud, "You look tired."

Bud ignored him as he got into the passenger seat.

Chip slid behind the wheel, "Where to now? Home?"

"Drive."

Within the hour, Bud sat shivering in a flimsy patient gown, his back exposed to a wicked air conditioning draft.

Dr. Alayon, his new cardiologist, was fifteen years past what looked to be his handsome youth and into a more subdued beaten-down work mode that Bud labeled "married with kids."

Bud watched his mouth move and tried to imagine him smiling – or laughing.

"Do you smoke?" Dr Alayon said.

"No."

Dr. Alayon raised his eyebrows. "Well, if you do, you need to stop. I'd like to send you to our smoking cessation program."

"I don't smoke."

Dr. Alayon tapped something into his tablet and stood, "Let me know if you change your mind. I can't help you unless you want to help yourself. Statistics show – "

Bud said, "What's the next step. What now?"

"Barbara will go over everything with you. Do you have any questions?"

"Yes – "

There was a knock on the door.

Dr. Alayon spun on his heels, pulled the door open to reveal Barbara, a twenty-something girl with Cleopatra eyeliner that looked jarringly out of place with her blue scrubs.

"Four weeks," Dr Alayon said, disappearing down the hall.

Barbara glanced over the tablet. "I see you're signed up for smoking cessation classes."

Bud sighed.

CHAPTER FIFTY-TWO

I can calculate the motion of heavenly bodies,
but not the madness of people.

—*Isaac Newton*

Enid jolted awake.

The morning light slanted through the hospital blinds.

Her arms felt heavy, like they always did after a bad dream. She tried to push her hair out of her eyes but was startled to feel her bandaged hand against her forehead.

Her nightmare came flooding back to her in a nauseating wave. A man who wouldn't die – no matter how many times she killed him. She had clung to his back, her arms going numb with the effort of pulling the rope tighter, knowing that she had to kill him but also knowing that he couldn't be killed. All night, the rope cut deep into her hands, burning like fire.

He won't die.

Enid blew upward, trying to get the hair out of her eyes, desperate to shake off the sickening dream. Her eyes lit on a paper. She hooked her hand around the stand, pulled it closer. She craned her neck to read the message.

Didn't want to wake you. Will be back in the morning. Sleep well and call if you need me. Jack.

She stared at the letter, a dark anger breaking open inside her. He'd been here and left. He didn't bother to wake her. Somehow, it felt worse than anything else he'd done.

She shoved the table away. She wanted to rip the letter into a thousand pieces and shove it down his fat ugly face.

Furious, she bit down on one of the bandages and tried to rip it off. After several minutes of struggle, the bandages were mangled and her teeth hurt. She stared down at them in helpless rage, hot tears springing to her eyes.

She wanted to kill him.

Why didn't he wake me?

"Hello there," a woman's voice said.

Startled, Enid brushed away the tears but not quick enough for Cheryl and Ernie not to notice.

"What's wrong?" Ernie said, darting to her side. "What happened to your hands?"

"Hey, Honey," Cheryl said, gently pushing the hair from Enid's face.

"Why are you crying?" Ernie said.

Cheryl motioned for Ernie to sit down and shut up.

Ernie sat in the visitor's chair, frowning.

"Where's your – where's Jack?" Cheryl placed her purse on the bed and looked around like she expected Jack to materialize.

"Can I go to your house – until I go back to Florida?" Enid said.

"Aren't you staying?" Cheryl said.

"I want to come with you," Enid said, trying to climb out of bed.

Cheryl stopped her. "Not so fast. I need to talk to a doctor – and Jack."

"You can talk to my mom – instead of Jack."

"I need to talk to your dad first."

Enid leaned back, struggling not to cry. She felt like an animal in a trap.

"Has the nurse been in?" Cheryl eyed Enid's torn bandages.

Enid shrugged, miserable.

"I'll be back," Cheryl said, heading out the door.

Ernie said, "I heard you killed a man. Did you?"

Enid stared at Ernie in horror.

Did I?

Enid leaned forward and said, "Ernie, I need your help."

Five minutes later, Cheryl returned.

Ernie sat in the visitor's chair, looking bored.

"Where's Enid?" Cheryl said.

Ernie pointed to the bathroom. "Girl stuff."

Cheryl knocked on the door, "Enid, the nurse said she'll be in to change your bandages. Everything okay?"

Ernie was seized with a coughing fit.

"What's wrong?" Cheryl said.

Ernie gripped his stomach, "I don't feel good. Can we go?"

"We just got here."

Ernie doubled over, coughing.

Cheryl grabbed a basin from Enid's table and held it under him. "Are you going to throw up?"

"It's the smell – it's making me sick."

"What smell?"

"Hospital smell," Ernie said.

"All right, all right." Cheryl helped Ernie to the door. She called out to Enid, "Ernie's not feeling good – we're going to go, but I'll be back."

Cheryl supported Ernie as he coughed his way through the hospital and into the parking lot. When they reached the minivan, Ernie took a deep breath. "I feel better."

Cheryl put her hand on his forehead, examined his face, "What is going on with you?"

"Dunno – but I feel better."

Cheryl looked regretfully at the hospital, "I hate to leave her alone. Who knows when Jack is going to turn up."

"Mom, you left the car unlocked." Ernie said as he climbed into the passenger seat.

"I never forget to lock the car."

Ernie held up her keys, "You left the keys on the floor."

Cheryl got behind the wheel, "How…?"

"What's for dinner?" Ernie said.

Cheryl looking through her purse, confused. "I never forget – what else…?" She turned to search the back seat.

"Vagina," Ernie said.

Cheryl turned to Ernie, startled.

"What's a vagina?" Ernie said.

"Where did you hear that word?"

"I don't remember."

"Try," Cheryl said.

Ernie thought about it.

"Well?" Cheryl said.

"The Food Channel...?"

Cheryl watched him warily as she pulled out of the parking space. "Ernie, I know you know what that word means."

"I don't."

"What do you think that word means – or – is?"

"Pasta?" Ernie said.

Stretched out on the floor of the backseat, Enid gripped her hand over her mouth, trying not to laugh.

"What was that?" Cheryl said, turning.

Enid froze, hoping the sunshade she was partially hidden under wouldn't give her away.

"What?" Ernie said.

"I heard something," Cheryl said, slowing down and looking behind her.

"Penis!" Ernie said.

Enid flinched at the sound of Cheryl smacking Ernie.

Cheryl said, "Now I know you know what that means."

"I need to talk – I got questions," Ernie said.

"Questions are fine. Stop shouting – things," Cheryl said, gripping the wheel.

"Mom?"

"What?"

"Can you drive while we talk?"

"Why?"

Ernie said, "Look at the road and not look at me – or around – or anything – while I ask you – stuff."

"Wouldn't you rather have this talk with your father? Please."

"One would think, but – no," Ernie said.

Cheryl pulled behind a line of cars. "All right, but – no more shouting."

CHAPTER FIFTY-THREE

I love you the more in that I believe you had liked me for my own sake and for nothing else.

—*John Keats*

Dressed in his flawless new suit, Jack stared up the steep rocky trailhead to Camelback Mountain.

Hikers passed him, giving him a wide berth like he was a madman. He was getting every possible reaction – from laughter to contempt to astonishment at his completely inappropriate – and ridiculous – attire.

Eve stood looking down at him from fifteen feet up the trail. She looked like a sexy advertisement for outdoor life in her casual hiking gear.

Jack said, "This isn't exactly what I had in mind."

"Try to keep up." She bounded up the trail and out of view.

Jack looked down at his perfectly polished shoes and mentally wrote them off. Setting his jaw, he started up the trail, his shoes slipping on the packed dirt.

Jack struggled to keep up. Not only were his shoes pinching, but he was lugging her picnic basket – thirty pounds of sliding, bumping god-knows-what.

So much for the reservations at the romantic five-star restaurant.

Jack had climbed Camelback Mountain enough times to know the route and was surprised when, close to the top, Eve gestured for him to follow her and she disappeared into a group of thorny brambles.

He stopped, unsure.

Her hand came out, pulling him past the brambles and into an alcove of rocky outcropping that seemed tailor-made for them to slip past even as the thorns snagged at his suit. He followed her, the basket making it hard going.

A thorn stabbed the back of his hand and he stopped, cursing.

"Come on," she said, calling from somewhere ahead of him.

Pissed, he pushed through the bramble, which was thicker and seemingly impassable. He was on the verge of stopping when it opened onto a narrow trail leading upward. Jack moved cautiously forward and was startled to find himself in a thirty-foot clearing with a sheer rock face at his back and a dangerous, jagged cliff spread out in front of them. Westward, the sky burned with the colors of a magnificent sunset.

Eve stood with her back to him, staring at the horizon.

He walked to within ten feet of her, staring uneasily at the toes of her boots, which were over the edge of the cliff.

Eve said, "Laura and I came here when we were kids. Nobody ever makes that last turn on the trail – not even dogs."

"How'd you find it?"

Eve looked back at him, a smile touched with pity at what he supposed was his stupidity. She turned back to the sunset.

He said, "Too embarrassed to be seen with me in public, huh?"

Eve laughed.

Jack pulled off his jacket, which was crumpled and marred with sweat. He opened the basket and felt a thrill of surprise to see two bottles of wine and two glasses.

She was at his side, reaching into the basket. She pulled out a corkscrew, handed it too him with a knowing smile. "For you."

Jack took it, unable to take his eyes from hers. It was as if he was seeing her for the first time. The sunset cast a glow about her, giving the appearance of an angel's halo.

"Hungry?" Her voice was velvet slipping down his spine.

Jack nodded, feeling the strange and not unpleasant sensation of being out of his depth – and the desire to plunge in deeper.

She poured the wine. Holding up her glass, she looked at him expectantly.

"Us," Jack said.

"Hmmm." Eve drank from her glass with a mysterious smile.

After the sun disappeared and a full moon was rising, they sat on the blanket, the remains of a gourmet meal between them.

Jack had enjoyed letting her lead the conversation around the shallow end, but she had fallen silent. She was staring at the moon and, as he reached out to brush a lock of hair from her face, she sprang to her feet and walked to the cliff.

Jack's stomach flipped with queasiness.

Her foot slipped, sending pebbles careening over the edge.

Jack lunged forward, but she had already righted herself and stood laughing at Jack, who found himself foolishly off-balance.

She reached out, steadied him.

"Jesus," he said. "I thought you were a goner."

"Don't be a pussy."

He gave her a startled look, recalling Jeni's words. It didn't seem in character with how he envisioned her but, somehow, he was even more intrigued.

Eve grinned, as if reading his thoughts. She picked up a rock and threw it over the cliff. She moved closer to the edge, watching intently as it fell.

They listened to the clatter of the rock on its journey downward until it fell silent at the bottom of the steep descent.

"I like edges," Eve said.

Jack remained silent, admiring the outline of her body in the moonlight.

Eve glanced back at him, her eyes daring him to join her on the edge.

Jack hesitated, not wanting her to know he didn't like heights. After a moment, he said, "Were you close with your father?"

"Stepfather," Eve said. "I thought you were off the clock."

"Detective Orlean invited me over – to warn me about you."

"Detective Orlean is a fool," Eve said. "His theory is that I'm guilty and he's not going to rest until he sees me behind bars."

"What's your theory?" Jack said, wishing she'd come away from the ledge.

"Jeni did it."

Jack glanced at her, surprised. He felt a stab of guilt and tried to imagine how Eve would react to finding out that he'd had sex with her sister.

Eve said, "Why do stepdaughters kill stepfathers?"

Jack flinched, knowing the answer.

"He never touched me. Never," Eve said. "He was always watching Jeni. Following her." She shook her head, "You never met anybody with worse luck." Eve faced him, "Is Jeni writing a book?"

"Ask her."

Eve walked over, held out her empty wine glass.

Jack filled it.

Eve sipped the wine, thoughtful. "She'll embarrass herself."

"You afraid of her embarrassing you?"

Eve smiled, amused. "She didn't tell you? I'm perfect."

"Nice work if you can get it."

Eve smiled as if to say "it is."

Jack said, "The newspapers had a field day with you – all the rumors – that you're the killer."

"I got the money. That made me the primary suspect – doesn't mean I did it. People get jealous – they get ugly."

Jack raised his eyebrows.

Eve said, "I'm not the murdering type. I prefer not to get my hands dirty."

"Jeni likes to get her hands dirty?"

Eve shrugged. "I'm not my sister's keeper."

Two bottles later, they cautiously made their way down the deserted trail. He'd stopped drinking, acutely aware that Arizona was not a state where you wanted to get pulled over for a DUI.

The basket bumping against his leg, Eve clung to his arm as they made their way to his car. He opened her door and was startled when she pressed him against the car, moving her hips into him.

Eve said, "You're going to seduce me." It was more a statement than a question.

Jack leaned in to kiss her just as he spotted Frank's car at on the edge of the lot. Cursing, he pushed away from her. "We got company."

"Bullshit," she said, gently biting his lower lip.

Jack saw the burning tip of Frank's cigarette. He pushed her back. "I got a tail. He ain't getting a show."

She pulled a Queen Elizabeth, gave him a cold smile and got in the car.

They remained silent as Jack drove her home. He was ready to invite himself in when he pulled up to her security gate, but her door slammed and she was gone. She signaled for Horace to shut the gate on him and Jack watched as she walked up the long driveway – away from him.

Jack asked Horace, "You always here?"

"Feels like it," he said.

Jack pulled out, scanning the street for Frank, determined to have it out. He was gone.

Why the hell is he still following me?

Driving home, he ran a string of curses that took care of Frank's offspring into the next century.

He'd lost Eve – for tonight – but there was always tomorrow.

CHAPTER FIFTY-FOUR

I have never met a man so ignorant that I couldn't learn something from him.

—*Galileo Galilei*

Bud and Jenson stared down at what used to be a man. Stretched out on the coroner's table, the corpse was a macerated and grotesquely swollen. The neck had a deep cut.

Chip hung back, intently staring at the floor.

"I'll be," Jenson said.

"One strangled, psycho-clown perp, just like the doctor ordered," Bud said.

Jenson said, "Even if our young friend Enid strangled him, I'm having trouble imagining ninety pounds of her wrapping two hundred pounds of him up tighter than a Christmas turkey with a duct tape bow and dumping him in the canal."

"She's a person of interest," Bud said.

Chip said, "There's no way that kid did this." He looked at the corpse and turned away, greenish.

Jenson waved his hand at the corpse, "I thought gross anatomy would have inured you to this."

Chip said, "Big difference between a cadaver and – this."

"Can we get a photo of his face?" Bud asked.

The pathologist, Sarah Nells, serious-faced and pretty, wore a white coat stained with cadaver juice. Her hair was pulled back in a ponytail, which made her look younger than her thirty-two years. She whipped off her greasy gloves and snapped a picture of the dead man's face with a Polaroid. She straightened, "I don't have my official cause of death yet but it's most likely strangulation."

"Ya think?" Chip said, eyeing the neck.

She glanced at him, unimpressed. "I've got fibers in the wounds that indicate man-made materials, nylon rope or clothing maybe."

"Like a bra?" Bud said.

"Possibly."

"Is it common?" Chip said. "I mean – getting strangled by a bra?"

Dr. Nells shrugged, "Wouldn't be the first time; won't be the last."

"Cause of death looks rather conclusive to me," Jenson said.

"I'm not done," Dr. Nells said.

"What else could it be?" Chip said, averting his eyes from the corpse.

She shrugged, "I rule nothing out until my examination is complete."

"Wise woman," Bud said.

"Once burned, twice sure," she said. "He has a penchant for Marvel comics and he's a breast man."

Chip said, "How would you know that?"

"Tattoos," Bud said.

"I only wish they'd include their social security numbers," Dr. Nells said.

"Do you like being a doctor?" Bud said, turning to Dr. Nells. "Are you glad you went to medical school?"

Chip's lips tightened.

She gazed at him in surprise, "I guess so. Why?"

"You ever think of dropping out?" Bud said.

"I didn't realize being a doctor meant I'd spend so much of my time exploring dead people's orifices."

Jenson made a face.

Dr. Nells said, "I always had a hankering for being a country singer – but I couldn't carry a tune if I had needle-nosed forceps."

"But you like it?" Chip said.

Dr. Nells put on her gloves, "Love it."

"We'll let you get back to work," Bud said, holding up the Polaroid photo in thanks and heading for the door.

She glanced at the clock, "I have a blunt trauma I need to get done before lunch."

"*Bon appetit*," Jenson said.

Once in the hallway, Jenson said, "What's the difference between a serial killer and a pathologist?"

"A degree," Bud said.

"Sometimes not even that," Jenson said. "Well, our leads are Superman and big tits. I won't say that narrows it down."

"Oh, I think it does," Bud said.

"How so?" Jenson looked at him in surprise.

"I know who he is," Bud said.

Chip and Jenson stared at Bud in surprise.

CHAPTER FIFTY-FIVE

Any idiot can face a crisis – it's day-to-day living that wears you out.

—Anton Chekhov

Ernie's treehouse that sat twelve feet up was weathered to the point of being dangerous. Ernie sat in the fetal position, groaning and mumbling to himself.

Enid struggled to hold a pomegranate-cherry Popsicle with her bandaged hands. The bandages had been "repaired" with a series of crisscrossing duct tape.

Enid said, "There are worse things then having your mother explain the birds and bees." She pressed her toe into a loose floorboard. "Are you sure it's safe up here?"

"I'd rather fall off a hundred-story building and have my eyelid catch on a rusty nail on the way down than go through that again," Ernie said, curling into a tighter ball.

"It wasn't that bad."

Ernie shot her an evil look.

Enid said, "What's the big deal? You know what sex is all about, right?"

"Yeah," Ernie said, his face reddening. "But a man doesn't want to discuss these things with his mother."

"Your mom was mostly right – I think she was making up the part about – "

Ernie held up his hand, "Puh-leaze! I'd rather be surprised – someday."

From below, Cheryl said, "Ernie?"

They froze.

Ernie scrambled to the hole in the floor. "Yeah?"

"What's going on up there? I hear talking."

Ernie hesitated and said, "I'm practicing my lines for the school play."

"Since when are you in theater?"

"It's mandatory," Ernie said. "I didn't have a choice."

Cheryl said, "I'm going to the store – I'll be back in twenty minutes. Do you need anything?"

"Amnesia," Ernie muttered.

"What?"

"Nothing."

They listened as she got in the car and drove off.

Ernie said, "Have you done it?"

"Done what?"

"What you were talking about."

"Sex?" Enid shook her head. "No, but I'm thinkin' about it."

Ernie's eyes widened. "With who?"

"Guy named Chip. He's – I'm in love."

"He love you?"

"Not yet."

"What grade's he in?"

"He's not in a grade. He's a man," Enid said.

Ernie made a face. "Don't text him pictures, he'll end up in jail."

"Gross."

"So you haven't done it?"

"Not it, but – stuff."

"Like what?" Ernie said.

Enid thought about Joey Wysocki and his thing and how great it felt to slug him after he shoved her hand down his pants.

Did that count?

Enid shrugged, "You know, guys want to do stuff, they chase me – that kind of stuff, but I'm waiting for the right guy. Chip is it."

"What kind of car does he drives?"

"Black Charger."

"Wow. When you gonna do it?"

"He wants to, but – you know."

Ernie sighed, "Yeah, I know. Amber Johnson told me that Mindy Lindd wants to go out with me, but – you know."

"Yeah," Enid said. "I know."

Ernie contemplated this. "You still hungry?"

"Starving."

Ernie led the way into the house, where they raided the pantry for Oreos, crackers, peanut butter, soda and a box of cereal.

"I stink," Enid said, sniffing her armpit.

Ernie led her down the hall to his and Sharon's shared bathroom. "Sprinkle when you tinkle – she'll think it was me."

"Where can I snag a T-shirt and – stuff?" Enid said, thinking about how you never think about how great it is to have clean underwear – until you don't have any.

Ernie pointed to his mother's room, "Pull from the back of her closet. She'll never miss it."

"She hangs up T-shirts?"

"She hangs up socks."

Once in a hot shower, Enid felt like she was getting clean for the first time in a century. She had taken off the bandages, which was a mistake because the soap burned. She gingerly washed herself and removed most of the sticky residue left on her skin by the hospital monitors.

There was a knock on the door. Ernie said, "Hurry up."

Enid stepped out of the shower, grabbed her clothes off the floor and wrapped a towel around her as she made her way to her Aunt's bedroom. She found the closet and thumbed through a row of T-shirts and was startled to see that Ernie wasn't kidding – her socks were neatly pinned on hangers.

Aunt Cheryl is a weirdo.

She chose a black T-shirt with a cracked decal of "Lou Reed Transformer." She didn't know who Lou Reed was, but thought she looked cool.

A car pulled up in the driveway.

She froze.

The front door opened and Sam's voice boomed through the house, "Cheryl?"

Ernie stood in the bedroom door, eyes locked on Enid. His wide eyes moved down her towel-wrapped body. He put his finger up to his lips.

Enid pushed back into the closet until her back was against the wall and socks dangled in her face. She got behind the dresses, which hid her better.

"Cheryl?" Sam said, slamming kitchen cabinets.

"She went to the store," Ernie from the hallway as he headed toward the kitchen.

"Hey, Ern," Jack said.

Enid felt a rush of anger.

What's he doing here?

"Hey, Uncle Jack," Ernie said, his voice unnaturally loud so that Enid could hear him. "What – are – you – doing – here?"

"Nice – to – see – you – too – Ernie," Jack said in an equally unnatural voice.

Sam said, "Did your mother go to the hospital?"

Enid strained to hear the reply but couldn't.

"Was Enid there?" Sam said.

More mumbling.

Enid struggled to make out their conversation but it got more muffled. Another car pulled up and, in moments, Enid heard what sounded like Cheryl's voice.

Enid moved the dresses aside and eyed the window, looking for a way to escape back to the treehouse.

Ernie popped up in front of the dresses, "You won't believe what happened."

Enid almost yelped in surprise. "Do they know I'm missing?"

Ernie said, "Uncle Jack – "

Enid scowled, insulted that they weren't talking about her being gone. "I don't care about him. He's not my father and I never want to hear his name again."

CHAPTER FIFTY-SIX

Once again… welcome to my house. Come freely. Go safely; and leave something of the happiness you bring.

—Bram Stoker, Dracula

On the drive to Sam's house, Jack told him what had happened the night before – it was the least he could do after Sam had bailed him out of jail.

Once in the house, Sam had jerked his head in Ernie's direction and shot Jack a warning look, so Jack had left off anything to do with Eve. What Ernie did hear was shocking enough without adding the truth of what really happened.

The night before, after his date with Eve had come to a screeching halt, Jack came home to a dark, empty house feeling dejected.

He headed up his driveway with a bag of groceries that he'd stopped to purchase.

Annie Cisco bounded out her front door, followed by her father, who sounded like he'd bagged some pints. It was ten o'clock – too early for Jack's date to end, but too late for a kid like Annie to be going out.

Annie and her girlfriend clambered out the front door, her father's voice bellowing behind them.

Annie spun around, high heels digging into the grass and her long legs overexposed in her mini. "Gawd, Dad! Don't worry – we won't smoke, drink – "

Annie caught sight of Jack, flashed him a smile. She called to her Dad, "I'll call if we're late."

"Don't be late!" he said.

Annie and her girlfriend jumped into the Mustang with grins that boded trouble. Annie eyed Jack's ruined suit, "Hey, Mister Fox, how was the prom?"

The Mustang pulled out onto the street to the sound of peals of laughter and squealing tires.

Jack watched as Nick stalked back into his house.

Another fun night polishing his shotgun collection.

Jack unlocked the front door, careful to keep an eye out for Harriett, the cat. He flipped the light switch, but it was dead. He paused, letting his eyes adjust to the dark.

A noise.

Jack froze, looking intently into the shadows.

Harriett?

A woman's voice said, "I hope you don't mind – "

Startled, Jack stepped back.

"I let myself in," Eve said from the darkened corner.

Jack remained silent. In the moonlight, he could make out Eve sitting on his couch. He could just see the white of her neck, rising above the deep V of her dress.

He said, "You rig the light?"

"I'm not that talented."

Harriett nosed open the kitchen door and Eve rubbed her fingers together, enticingly. Harriett bounded to Eve's lap, where she purred under Eve's caressing fingers.

Jack said, "I didn't realize I was such an easy target."

"I'm not accustomed to being turned down."

Jack walked over, standing above her, staring down at her upturned face. Her eyes glinted like shards of glass on a welcome mat.

He bent down, knowing that she expected him to kiss her. He hovered and, with a swift movement, he scooped Harriett off her lap and into his arms.

He stepped away from Eve, caressing Harriett's ears.

Eve's eyes flashed and Jack felt a stab of satisfaction.

It felt good to hurt her.

Eve jumped up, pushed past him toward the door.

Jack dropped Harriett, who landed on the floor with a velvet thud. He grabbed Eve, pulled her close.

She was like a wild thing, pushing him away with vile curses as his lips came down on hers. She pulled away, slapped him.

He slapped her back.

Her mouth formed an "o" of shock.

"Play nice," he said.

She stared at him, unsure. He liked that look on her.

She said, "Why'd you send me away?"

"I never will again."

Eve pulled his mouth to hers, kissing him hungrily. Then she screamed and tore herself from him, cursing. She bent down. Blood trickled from her ankle.

Harriett shot away, hissing and spitting.

Jack crouched down, examining the claw marks on Eve's ankle. "Jealous."

Jack stood, turned to get some soap and water.

Eve put her arms around his neck, pressing close. Her eyes gleamed.

He tried to sweep her up into his arms, to carry her to his bed, but she stopped him. She unbuckled his belt and before he could get his pants off, she'd lifted her skirt, grabbed his dick and shoved it into her.

It was fast and she took without giving – cumming over and over and no damned faking it. On the hardwood floor, he could feel her clench around him as she shuddered and cursed her way through five minutes of cumming.

When she was done, she stared up at him, satiated. "Ladies first," she said.

"Baby, you ain't no lady," Jack said. He'd cum, but – not like anything he ever knew. His felt like a wave lost to her tsunami.

She grinned. "I should have let you fuck me." She reached down, cradled his limp cock in her hand. "First time I saw you, I knew."

"Me too, baby."

Two hours later, in his bed, it was Jack's turn to lay satiated, staring up at Eve as she ran her finger along his face, pausing every time he shivered under her touch.

"I'll make it last longer next time," Jack said.

The second time, she'd been tame – almost cold. He'd still only lasted less than twenty minutes. He tried to hold on, make it last, but – she squeezed down in orgasm – he was done.

"Tell me a story," she said. "You – in a bad situation – how you got out of it."

He smiled. "Poor little rich girl – looking for trouble."

"Once upon a time," she said.

"In a land far, far away," he said as he proceeded to tell her the story of how he nearly got his wings clipped by a cheating husband who turned out to be the original "Shotgun Joe" from Chicago and was broke and hiding under an assumed name. His girlfriend, an aging off-strip Vegas dancer who was bankrolling him, thought he was cheating – and was right, as proven by Jack's photos. It all would have ended there, but Shotgun sent a redneck with a knife Jack's way and got him surprised in a men's stall at the Dew Drop Inn where Jack was taking a shit.

"Is that how you got this?" Eve sketched her finger around a scar that wrapped around his side.

"Dumb luck he never got his knife in me. He slipped on some drunk's piss. I didn't think it – I just did it – played crazy and scared him the hell out of that stall – or else I would've been dead." Jack gave a low laugh. "There ain't a punk in the world that wants to wrangle with somebody who is certifiable."

"That worked?"

Jack grinned at the memory, nodding.

Eve kissed his fingertips. "Tell me about your first case."

Jack's smile faded.

Eve said, "What?"

Jack hesitated. "I'm taking the fifth."

"Tell me. Or are you going to act insane – chase me out of here?

Jack pulled her down in a hard kiss. "Hell no and then some."

Eve nuzzled him, "You might as well tell me. I never give up till I get what I want."

Jack sighed. "I was a kid. I call it the case of the second family."

Eve's eyebrows went up.

He said, "My dad, turns out, had a second family."

"Oh!" Eve stared at him, startled.

"Busted that case wide open," Jack said.

"Did your mother know?"

Jack felt that familiar sickness in his stomach. He shut his eyes, trying to block the memory of his mother's dead body hanging from the noose.

"Hey," Eve gently nudged him.

Jack opened his eyes, tried to smile.

Eve said, "That's what made you want to be a detective?"

"When I saw him with them – I thought I found out the truth."

"What was the truth?"

"*We* were the second family. I thought the old man was hiding them. The truth was – he was hiding *us.*"

"Is he – ?"

"Dead." Jack's mind flashed back to the funeral – the uproar he caused when, with one violent shove, he overturned his father's casket and sent his body tumbling into the first row of mourners.

He winced at the memory. He had no memory of what happened next, but he had been told.

I'd do it again – kick the shit of that worthless bastard's corpse.

"I'm sorry," she said.

"Don't. He's dead – stabbed in some back alley by a two-bit crook – he got exactly what he deserved." Jack brushed the hair from her face. "What are you doing with me?"

"Did you see it?" Eve said.

"See what?" Jack ran his hands along her body, enjoying the feel of her silken skin under his fingertips.

"When he got what he deserved?" She said.

Jack looked at her, startled.

She smiled, "Don't look at me like that."

"Sorry," Jack said, withdrawing his hand.

Is she serious?

Eve laughed, that quicksilver laugh that he'd first heard in his office when he first set eyes on her. He glanced at her, relieved to see her eyes twinkling.

Eve said, "You'll discover all too quickly how boring I am. Let me play the mysterious femme fatale a bit longer. Actually, I'm rather flattered that you thought – "

"I don't."

"I like it," she said.

He gazed at her, unsure.

She leaned in, kissing him with a gathering passion that made him forget everything.

Flying.

In his dream, he was flying and she was there, by his side as they cut through clouds – ever thickening clouds that – stung…

A spasm of coughing brought Jack to abrupt wakefulness. He reached for Eve but she was gone.

Was it all a dream?

Thick smoke plumed under the door. Heart lurching, Jack jumped out of bed, eyes burning and watering. He could hear the crackling flames and feel the –

Heat.

Jack ran to the bathroom – empty. In the bedroom, there was no trace of Eve.

Where is she?

Jack touched the door and yanked his hand away. It was as hot as a stovetop. Jack cursed the barred windows that had been there when he bought the house and he'd never bothered to remove. He ripped the sheets off the bed and shoved them under the door, trying to stop the smoke.

"Eve!" He yelled.

Please let her be safe.

Please let her be gone.

Jack ripped the blanket off the bed and ran to the bathroom. He shoved it in the bathtub and turned on the water. The plumbing groaned but came forth with enough water to soak most of the blanket.

In the bedroom, Jack pulled on his jeans and covered himself with the wet blanket. He crouched down and, pushing his fear down, he jerked the door open.

Smoke billowed at him and he forced himself to stay low and move as fast as he could. The hallway, so short just yesterday, now seemed like a marathon distance.

Lungs burning with the smoke, Jack crawled forward as flames licked at his body. He stumbled forward, choking – suffocating – confused.

Keep moving.

There was no end to it – he sucked in, desperate to breathe – he felt like he was drowning in an ocean of flames.

Where am I?

He inched forward, his fingers scratching against something hard. Drowning in fumes, he made one last desperate lunge forward and felt the fight leave his body.

This is it.

This is how it ends.

Death grabbed him and dragged him out of the oven and straight to hell.

Demons scraped at him – hurt him.

He called out for his mother and she pushed him over, onto his side and slapped him until he was coughing – gasping – a violent convulsion of his body that ended with him puking his guts out.

He heard voices, words – cutting through his consciousness.

Screaming devils – fighting over his soul.

He came to and found himself on the ground, staring up at the night sky. The screaming was sirens – getting closer.

It wasn't demons – it was Nick. His mouth was moving but Jack couldn't make it out.

Jack struggled to sit up but couldn't. The effort brought on another spasm of coughing that left him weak. A fireman ran past him, someone strapped something on his face. He fought against it but oxygen hit his mouth and he sucked it greedily into his still-burning lungs.

"Is anyone in the house?" A fireman was shouting in his face.

He shook his head.

She has to be gone.

He searched the street for Eve and his eyes landed on a silver sports car that he'd never seen.

How did Eve get here? Drive? Chauffeur?

He sucked hard on the oxygen and felt his head clearing.

Nick said, "I called 9-1-1 – I saw a woman leave."

Relief flooded through Jack. He gripped Nick's hand in thanks.

Nick said, "Thank God I was up late cleaning my guns."

Jack was too weak to smile.

The terrible sound of collapsing wood came from the house and they stared in awe as the fire devoured what was left of it.

Jack looked away, overwhelmed at the sight of what used to be his home.

His eyes caught the glowing tip of a cigarette in the silver sports car.

With Nick's help, Jack stood. He walked unsteadily toward the car. He winced as he stepped on a sharp pebble, recognizing it to be one of the demons that had tortured him as Nick dragged him across the ground from his burning home.

Pretending he could see the person in the car, he locked eyes with the darkness within and quickened his pace.

The headlights came on. He shielded his eyes from the glare, still moving forward.

The engine roared to life and sped at him.

He hurled himself backwards, throwing himself over the hood of a parked car, escaping by a hair's breadth as the sports car slammed into the parked car with a screeching sound of metal on metal.

He landed on the sidewalk, a sharp pain shooting from his shoulder – the sick sensation of the wind knocked out of him.

Jack struggled to his feet and staggered forward.

Driving up the street from the other direction was Annie in her Mustang. Her astonished face, mouth agape, was hanging out the window as she drove toward him, her eyes transfixed by the fire.

Jack yanked her door open and pulled Annie out. She stumbled backwards and Jack caught a flash of her shirt, inside out, as he hopped into her still-rolling car.

He hit the accelerator and felt the Mustang jump forward. Jack whipped around the corner and saw the silver car back up and speed away.

Jack slowed only a fraction as he gave chase.

Jack found himself in a nerve-wracking game of chicken with oncoming cars and trucks as the two cars careened through light after light.

The silver car skidded to a stop to avoid hitting an SUV and Jack saw his chance. He slammed his brakes, thinking he could box in the car – between a truck, himself and the pavement. The silver car burned rubber in a spin that left it facing in the opposite direction.

Cursing, Jack reversed out of his position and raced after the car, which was on the verge of losing him. Gripping the wheel, Jack floored it, trying to get close enough to cut it off.

A half a block ahead of them, a minivan stopped in the intersection, making a left turn. Jack realized there was no way they would miss the minivan, which he was probably full of rug rats.

He stomped the accelerator and pulled to the left of the silver car. A violent jerk of the wheel sent the Mustang into the silver car, forcing them both off the road.

Jack caught a flash of the woman's horrified face as they narrowly missed T-boning her minivan.

In slow motion, Jack watched as he and the silver car careened toward a glass-plated storefront.

Every bone in his body jolted and it felt like his teeth would shake out of his head. Glass rained down as they came to a sickening stop.

Jack tasted iron. Reaching up, he touched his head, which was throbbing. His fingertips were red with blood.

A neon sign in the shape of a human palm lay across his windshield, blinking the message at him: Know Your Future, Change Your Destiny.

Someone groaned.

The silver car sat like a panting dog to his forward right.

He tried his door but it wouldn't budge. Climbing over the console, he forced open the passenger door. He got out, wincing as he felt the sharp reminder that he was barefoot and the space between him and the silver car was a minefield of glass shards.

Cautiously, he picked his way forward.

He saw a woman slumped over the wheel, long brown hair hiding her face. The glass was shattered and he reached in, touched her shoulder. The hair moved unnaturally under his hand and he pulled his hand away, her wig coming off.

She was bleeding from a gash above her eyebrow and Jack felt a flood of relief when he saw it wasn't Eve.

The relief was short-lived.

He felt a jolt of shock when he recognized the driver.

CHAPTER FIFTY-SEVEN

A man without ethics is a wild beast loosed upon this world.

–Albert Camus

"Dennie Dutter," Bud said as he paid the cashier for his coffee. The hospital's cafeteria was at a low ebb as he, Jenson and Chip found a table where they could wait for Dr. Nells to finish her autopsy of the duct-taped canal corpse. Bud took a sip of coffee and grimaced. "I have a wheelchair-bound Aunt stronger than this coffee."

"Dutter," Jenson said, "That's feasible."

"Who's Dennie Dutter?" Chip said.

"The corpse," Bud said. "Degenerate specializing in human trafficking."

Chip said, "Human trafficking? In Phoenix?"

Bud said, "Flourishing underbelly industry. Fifteen thousand child prostitutes in Phoenix alone."

Chip said, "I thought that kind of stuff only happened in Thailand or, like, Eastern Europe."

"Ten percent of *all* kids in the U.S. are victims of human sex trafficking," Bud said. "Mostly runaway and homeless – lured in with the promise of food, money, safety – some 'opportunity' – they get trapped in a network of anything from prostitution, massage parlors, strip clubs, to pornography."

"How do you know all this?" Chip said.

"Murder."

Chip raised his eyebrows.

Bud said, "Collateral damage. Human sex trafficking pays well, but it's messy."

Chip hesitated, "So, do you – *not* try as hard – to solve Dennie Dutter's murder – because he's a scumbag?"

"It doesn't work like that," Bud said.

"What's wrong with chalking it up to saying 'thank you very much' to the universe for killing off a scumbag – and move to the next?" Chip said.

Bud said, "It doesn't matter. Murder is murder."

"Most foul," Jenson said as he stirred more honey into his hot tea.

Bud said, "Any person who kills another human being in cold blood – no matter who – Mother Teresa, Charles Manson – deserves getting exposed and being shown for what they are – a cold-blooded killer who deserves to rot in jail."

Chip said, "Mother Teresa versus Manson? You're talking apples and oranges."

Bud said, "Who decides which murder to solve and which to let go? Are you going to make that decision?"

"In this case, yeah," Chip said. "Let the scumbag's case go. Who cares?"

Bud said, "My job is to get to the truth. I don't judge. I reveal."

"I know you, Pops. Don't tell me you're going to work this guy's case the same as some innocent mother of three who got gunned down by some scum-bucket who peddles kids for sex."

"I work them the same," Bud said.

"Why?" Chip said.

"Nobody is innocent," Bud said.

Chip shook his head. "There are good people in the world."

"I didn't say there weren't," Bud said. "One thing I learned in this business is nobody is all good and nobody is all bad. We're all just a messy grab bag of angel and devil."

Jenson said, "It's which side you land heaviest on that counts."

Bud said to Chip, "When you write books, feel free to have everything come out happily ever after. Punish the bad guys, save the innocents. That's not the way it is in real life."

Jenson said, "It is rather buggered out here."

"No black and white," Bud said. "The truth is in the grey. We give each case equal shoe leather."

"I couldn't do it," Chip said. "Don't you ever get mad?"

Bud said, "I harness that energy – put it into finding the killer."

Chip said, "What happens if a good person kills a bad person and makes the world a better place? What then?"

"I find the killer," Bud said.

Chip shook his head. "You're using that as a way to evade the real question."

"An evil baby. Ever come across one?"

Chip made a face.

Bud hooked his thumb over his shoulder, "That thing they dragged out of the canal was once a baby. My job is to find the killer of that baby."

Chip said, "That guy isn't a baby. The baby grew up to be a scumbag who peddles babies for sex."

"That's not my business," Bud shrugged.

"You're talking in circles," Chip said.

Bud said, "I'll concede that this one particular baby grew up to be a human-trafficking dirt bag – but he was once a tiny baby full of big potential. What if solving his case leads to something good? There's no telling what the outcome to anything will be. You do something good and it causes bad, you do something bad and good will come of it. It's useless speculation. All I know is I wake up every morning and do my best to find the killers and let them have their day in court."

"Bring them to justice?" Chip said.

Bud laughed. "Justice? That's none of my business. That's for the legal system to scrape through."

Bud's cell vibrated and he stood, walking away.

Jenson said, "Your father is a good man."

"I guess you feel the same way?" Chip said.

"Goodness, no. Whoever wrapped Dennie Dutter up tighter than a tick did this city a favor."

"Why'd you say it made sense?" Chip said.

"What?"

"About it being Dennie Dutter?"

"Enid is underage," Jenson said.

"She's not homeless or a runaway."

Bud returned to the table, overhearing the last remark. "How do we know that?"

Chip said, "Because – "

Bud said, "Instead of assuming – how 'bout we go ask her?"

"But she has a dad. She's not a runaway," Chip said.

"Facts," Bud said. "Let's go see if we can get some."

Chip sighed, following them out.

In less than an hour, Bud and Chip were at Enid's hospital and Jenson was back at the station house.

The male nurse who looked like he could crack walnuts with his biceps told him that a woman and a boy had paid a visit and they hadn't seen Enid since. They'd been trying to reach her father all morning with no success.

"Did you file a report?" Bud said.

The nurse eyed Bud tiredly, "It was documented in her chart. If we filed a report on every patient who left AMA, we'd spend all day filing reports."

Bud left a message on Jack's cell and, as soon as he hung up, it vibrated that he had an incoming call from Jenson.

"Surprises abound, my friend," Jenson said. "You might want to mosey down to the station and see what the cat dragged in – before he gets bailed out."

Within a short time of Bud arriving at the station, Jenson had filled Bud in on the facts, and they made their way to the area where Sam was finishing the paperwork for bailing out Jack.

Sam looked up as they entered, "Here to get my theories on the Kennedy assassination?"

Bud said, "Stolen car, reckless driving, destruction of private property – possibly arson…?"

"Jack didn't burn down his own house," Sam said.

Bud said, "What I'm interested in – the woman in the other car."

"I don't know anything about it," Sam said.

"You were his one phone call?" Bud said.

"To bail him out. Other than that – you have to talk to him."

"Does he know that his daughter disappeared from the hospital?"

Sam looked at him, startled.

Bud said, "Any idea where she might be?"

"My wife went to visit her – Enid was there," Sam said.

"When?"

A buzzer sounded and a corrections officer entered, followed by Jack.

"All yours, Sam," the officer said as he turned to leave.

Jack's forehead was bandaged and had the remains of dried blood. Wearing jeans, a jail-issued shirt and flip-flops, he looked bedraggled. His eyes hardened at the sight of Bud and he homed in on Chip scribbling notes.

Jack hooked his thumb at Chip, "What's up with Nancy Drew?"

Chip frowned, pocketing the notebook.

Sam said, "Good news is the neighbor's not filing charges – the girl had weed in the car."

Jack eyed Bud, "What do you want?"

Bud said, "Why would Laura Hargrove want to torch your house?"

Jack said, "She confessed?"

Bud said, "I'm working under the assumption you didn't run Laura Hargrove off the road to ask the time of day."

Jack turned to Sam, "I need to borrow your car."

Sam hooked his thumb at Bud, "Detective Orlean tells me Enid is missing."

Jack's neck snapped in Bud's direction, "What? Are you sure?"

"Can we go somewhere to talk?" Bud said.

Jack followed Bud to an interview room, where they sat on opposite sides of the table. Jack stared at Bud with poorly concealed hostility.

Bud said, "We pulled a known human trafficker out of the canal this morning."

Jack shrugged. "What's that got to do with me?"

Bud said, "The cause of death – strangulation."

Jack's eyes narrowed.

Bud said, "With a man-made fiber – perhaps an article of clothing."

"Like a bra," Jack said wryly.

Bud leaned forward, elbows on the table, "Did Enid run away?"

Jack's cheeks flushed red.

"She did," Bud said, leaning back as he watched Jack, who looked guiltier than a hooker in the front pew.

"I can find her," Jack said, running his hands through his hair. "I need time."

"Why? What do you know?" Bud said.

Jack jumped up. "You can't be serious – are you seriously accusing Enid of strangling that – ?"

"How would Enid come into contact with a human-trafficking pedophile who preys on runaway kids – unless she ran away?"

Jack sat down, dropped his head into his hands.

Bud said, "Tell me what you know. Enid could be in danger."

Jack wavered, unsure. He shook his head. "Go to hell."

Jack strode out, the door closing behind him.

Bud sat back, pissed. Jack was hiding something and Bud decided that he was going to dig it out of him if it was the last thing he did.

CHAPTER FIFTY-EIGHT

You don't develop courage by being happy in your relationships every day. You develop it by surviving difficult times and challenging adversity.

—Epicurus

Enid pushed Aunt Cheryl's neatly hung socks out of her face. Hiding in the closet was more boring than she would have ever imagined – not to mention the strange "closet smell" tickling her nose to the point of threatening to force a sneeze out of her. Straining to hear, she struggled to make out what Jack and Sam were saying.

Something about last night...

She heard Sam telling Ernie to go to the backyard, which meant he'd be no help until he got back in or she got out.

Pinching her nose so that she wouldn't sneeze, Enid crept out of the closet, determined to hear what Sam and Jack were saying. Heart pounding, she tiptoed down the hall until she came to the guest bathroom, which was as close as she could get to the living room. She kept the door cracked so she could hear them talking and stepped into the tub, pulling the shower curtain closed behind her.

Sam said, "How could you pull such a bone-headed move?"

"What the hell?" Jack said, "What do I know about taking care of a kid?"

"For starters, don't send them undercover. Jesus, Jack, what were you thinking?"

Jack said, "I've checked the bus station, what's *left* of my house, Jeni's place – I don't know where else to look."

Enid wrinkled her brow, wondering what he meant by what's "left" of his house?

"You need to talk to Detective Orlean," Sam said.

Silence.

"Listen, Jack, this is beyond you not liking the guy. You put Enid – a kid – *your kid* – in a dangerous situation, and you need to do the right thing. Orlean is a good guy – a damned good detective – maybe he can help."

There was a long pause. Jack said, "You think she really is my kid?"

Enid sank down in the tub, face flushing with anger.

"Yeah, I do," Sam said. "Don't tell me – deep down – you never wanted a kid?"

"Never."

Enid compressed her lips, tears stinging her eyes.

Sam said, "Whether she's your kid or not – it doesn't matter. You put her in that situation, you need to get her out."

"I will get her out," Jack said.

"Talk to Detective Orlean – or I will."

"Jesus, Sam."

"You put a kid in danger. Step up to the plate or I do it for you."

"I told you that in confidence."

"This isn't a game, Jack. Your kid is out there alone – scared. From how she tells it, she was drugged, abducted and she may have killed somebody. If what she says is true, what if the guy she killed has friends and they come after her? God knows what she stepped into."

The hairs on the back of Enid's neck stood up. It never occurred to her that anyone would be hunting her. She thought of the gun hidden inside Jeni's freezer and felt a desperate need to get it back in her hands.

Jack said, "I need to talk to Laura."

"I'm not telling you what hospital she's in."

"She burned my house down, Sam."

Enid sat up, shocked.

Who's Laura?

The name rang a distant bell but she couldn't quite put her finger on it.

Jack said, "I need to talk to her."

"Oh, good. *Talk*. I was afraid you might do something stupid like run her off the road into Madame Woo-Fucking-Woo's Palm Reading Emporium. *She*, by the way, *is* filing charges."

"Your car. I'll have it back by tonight."

"Ain't happening," Sam said.

"Not telling me what hospital Laura's at – is just slowing me down from finding Enid."

"Call Orlean."

Silence.

Sam said, "You call – or I will. Pick your poison."

"Fine," Jack said.

Enid listened as Jack left a message for Detective Orlean. Sam grudgingly gave him Laura's location.

Sam said, "I thought you weren't into the Daniel Hargrove murder case?"

"I don't know what I'm into," Jack said.

Enid heard the front door close and, moments later, a car drive away.

Sam let Ernie back in and Enid began plotting how to get Ernie to help her get the gun. The thought of bad guys coming after her made her blood run cold.

An hour later, Enid was back in the treehouse, wrapped in Ernie's Sesame Street sleeping bag and gorged on Oreo cookies. She found herself letting out a series of gentle burps as she gripped the hammer that she swiped from Sam's toolbox.

It wasn't a gun but, in a pinch, it'd be weapon enough.

She felt a smug satisfaction at the thought of Jack being too stupid to figure out where she was. She imagined him worrying and desperate – unable to find her. A contemptuous smile curled her lips as she thought about how he never thought to ask Ernie any questions or search the house.

Doofus.

Her smile faded.

Jack was no fool. He would find her sooner or later – unless she outwitted him. She pulled the sleeping bag tighter in an attempt to rid herself of the emptiness in the pit of her stomach that even the Oreo cookies couldn't fill – and she suspected had nothing to do with hunger.

CHAPTER FIFTY-NINE

Get your facts first, then you can distort them as you please.

– Mark Twain

For the hundredth time, Jack shuddered at the thought of Enid – trapped in the fire and him unable to get her out. As bad as it was that she ran away from the hospital, it was a thousand times better than her being home with him last night when his house burned to the ground.

He'd find her.

Jack pinched his nose tiredly. Everything he owned was gone. He was going to have to start over with nothing – except for one disappeared pain-in-the-ass kid and a shitload of insurance hassle.

He was so tired he could hardly think, and it didn't occur to him till after he'd dropped Sam at the station and was driving off in Sam's car that he'd never questioned Ernie or Cheryl. He should've asked them more questions about their visit to Enid. He was wanting to go home and crawl into bed but – jarringly – kept remembering that he no longer had a home, or a bed.

He called the hospital, verifying that Laura was still there. He drove to Scottsdale Thompson Peak Hospital, which still had a "new car" smell in the plush lobby. The volunteer concierge, who looked to be about ninety, pointed a shaky finger to the elevators and, within what felt like moments, Jack found himself in the hallway outside of Laura's hospital room.

He stopped.

Laura lay in bed. She was partially blocked from his view by Eve's graceful figure as Eve leaned in, intently listening to something Laura was murmuring.

Jack walked in.

Laura's eyes darted past Eve and widened in fear. Eve jumped to her feet and spun toward him, hand outstretched. "Jack, it's not what you think. You have to trust me."

From behind him, a man's voice said, "Well, this makes my task easier."

A man whom Jack could only describe as "dapper" strolled to the foot of the bed, smiled down at Laura.

"Detective Jenson," he said with a smile.

Jack eyed him, curious. He had more the air of a host of a garden party than a Phoenix detective.

Eve said, "Officer, there's been a terrible misunderstanding."

"I didn't do anything!" Laura said, bursting into tears.

Eve said, "Laura thought I was at – "

"My house," Jack said.

Detective Jenson said to Jack, "And you would be?"

Eve stepped forward, "Eve Hargrove. My sister, Laura. He doesn't – "

"Jack Fox," Jack said, holding out his hand.

Jenson shook his hand, "Ah! So nice to meet you, Mr. Fox. You're the private detective?"

Jack nodded, knowing that the police detective, if he was worth his weight in salt, which he obviously was, would know of him – and his dad.

"And were you?" Detective Jenson asked Eve.

"What?" she said.

"At his house?"

"No. I wasn't," Eve said.

Jack shot her a look.

She can lie.

Jenson said, "Is that right, Mr. Fox? Ms. Hargrove was not at your house last night?"

Eve said, "Laura thought I was with him but I wasn't. She was worried about me – that's all."

"Why would she think that?" Detective Jenson said.

Eve hesitated. "She was under the impression I hired him."

"Did you?"

"No."

Jack's jaw tightened.

What is she playing at?

Jenson ticked off the list, "Arson, reckless endangerment, destruction of private property – "

Eve said, "Laura thought I was with Mr. Fox, she was worried and went over and – she certainly didn't set the fire. Jack started chasing her and – she panicked."

Jenson gazed at her impassively.

Eve said, "I'm personally guaranteeing restitution to all injured parties." She pulled a card out of her purse. "This is my lawyer. He'll be handling the restitution."

Jenson turned to Jack, "May I call you Jack?"

Jack felt the weight of Eve's eyes on him, urging him to play along.

"Is there anything else?" Detective Jenson said.

"It's like she said," Jack said, startled to hear his words hang in the air, sharp and untrue. He looked away, certain his lies were as transparent as the air that separated him and Eve in the suddenly oppressive room.

"Excuse me," Jack said, turning to leave. Before anyone could speak, he was out the door and, ignoring the elevators, he made his way to a stairwell, which let him out on the side of the hospital.

I'm not a liar.

A voice deep inside whispered, "Now you are."

He felt a wave of self-loathing.

I don't lie!

That same voice murmured, "Broken promises – they aren't lies?"

With a curse, he spun around, determined to go back and set the detective straight.

He slammed into Eve.

It took him several moments of shock to register that she had remained so close behind him and yet so silent.

She was speaking but he didn't understand what she was saying. His eyes followed the curve of her face, her lips. He didn't want to believe that she would lie.

She looked like an angel.

He tried to tell himself that if she did lie, she would have a good reason – the lie would be for good, not bad.

"I had to – " she said, her voice breaking through his jumbled thoughts.

He grabbed her arms, anger welling up, breaking over him.

"I lied for you," Jack said.

"I'm sorry."

He released her like she was poison, made his way to his car.

Eve stayed hot on his tracks. "Laura's sick! Ever since Daniel – I had to lie. After he got – after he disappeared – you have no idea! Journalists digging into our business – they hounded us. I've done everything – the best doctors – medications – she's – mentally – "

Jack unlocked the door but Eve jumped in front of him, blocking him.

"You can't go – not till you understand – "

Jack shoved her against his car, holding her at arm's distance. "Did she set the fire?"

"I don't know." Eve gazed at him, miserable.

"Last night – where did you go? *Why* did you go?"

"I was worried. I knew…" Eve drew a ragged breath.

Jack examined her eyes, which shone with sincerity.

Or – ice?

Jack said, "She's done this before?"

"She wasn't there when I left. You have to believe me. I would never lie to you."

Jack grimaced as her fingers caressed his cheek. She kissed him softly on the lips.

He closed his eyes.

He didn't kiss her back – he couldn't. A need – too raw to be called desire – flamed up within him and the soft kiss transformed into something white hot and insatiable.

CHAPTER SIXTY

All that we see or seem is but a dream within a dream.

—Edgar Allan Poe

Bud was exhausted.

Chip was driving him home when Bud got a phone call from Larry, his AA buddy. After a brief conversation, Bud asked Chip to drop him off at a nearby coffee shop.

"I'll call you when I need you to pick me up," Bud said.

"What the hell am I supposed to do?" Chip said.

"Write a book."

Grumbling, Chip cleared out and, as Bud waited for Larry to show, Bud checked his messages and was surprised to hear Jack Fox's voice. Short and simple, Jack said he needed to talk in person. Bud called back, left a message for Jack to meet him at the coffee shop in one hour. He'd have to make sure to end the meeting with Larry within an hour, which wasn't AA kosher but – it was what it was.

Larry showed up, his usual hangdog aura percolating with desperation as he described how his wife had threatened him with divorce and he was struggling against picking up the bottle.

Larry said, "I should have never married her – everyone told me not to – especially mother. But I took one look at those green peep-toe shoes tapping, tapping – I couldn't see her face – but I could tell she was gorgeous from the way men were looking at her as they passed. The whole train trip, me sitting behind her, I watched everyone's face as they passed by her – men and women – and before we pulled into Philadelphia, I was in love."

Bud sipped his coffee, thinking of Bunnie as Larry's voice lulled on.

Larry said, "If she wasn't cheating on me – "

Bud looked up in surprise. "I thought she ended it?"

"She said they started up again – maybe she's trying to make me jealous but, as God is my witness…" Larry's words trailed off ominously.

Bud gave him a sharp look, "You own a gun?"

Larry gave a bitter laugh. "I'm not going to kill myself – or anybody else. I'd have to be a real man to do that."

Bud shook his head. This was old territory and he was too tired to get lost in Larry's endless landscape of self-loathing.

Bud said, "You still going to that therapist?"

Larry shook his head, glumly. "Deductible started over."

Bud drank the last of his coffee, which wasn't sitting well with the new pills.

Larry said, "Are you going to the meeting tonight?"

Bud shook his head. "Unless you need me to go."

"No. But – can we hang out – until the meeting?"

Bud fought the urge to look at his watch. "Sure. I have someone meeting me here. Business. Would you mind…?"

"I can wait."

"It shouldn't take long." Bud pressed his hand to his chest that suddenly felt like a mastiff was crouching on it.

"You don't look so hot," Larry said, eyeing Bud.

Bud struggled to catch his breath. He dug into his pouch that held his medications.

"Are you all right?" Larry said.

Bud fumbled through the pouch until he found the right bottle, which he had jokingly drawn a lightning bolt on since it was the one the doctor said would work the fastest. With shaking hands, he slipped the nitro pill under his tongue. Within minutes, he felt the mastiff's weight easing and he breathed easier.

Unsure, Larry watched and waited as Bud returned to normal. During the attack, Bud had waved away his offers to drive him to the hospital and, when he felt better, Bud haltingly told Larry about his newly acquired heart issues.

"Issues?"

Bud shrugged, made a face.

After a long silence, Larry said, "I don't know, Bud. You ever think of retiring?"

Bud sighed wearily. He felt ancient – like a husk of the man he once was. He wanted nothing more than to go home and climb into bed with Bunnie. He wanted to hear her rattle on about her day so he wouldn't have to talk or think – he could just lie back and listen to her voice – like a lullaby.

Larry said, "How 'bout I drive you home?"

Bud smiled gratefully and followed him to the door.

Bud stopped, remembering his meeting with Jack. He looked at his watch and was annoyed to see that the time to meet Jack had passed thirty minutes ago. Bud checked his cell and saw that Jack hadn't called.

Larry said, "No show?"

Bud gave an irritated shrug and they headed out. He sent Chip a text telling him he had a ride home and he was officially off-duty.

Once home, Bud was met with a stink-eye from Bunnie that would have blistered concrete. He waved away Chip's concerned inquiries and went to the guest bedroom. He shut the door, kicked off his shoes and climbed in bed fully clothed. He muted his cell and tossed it on the floor and fell into a fitful sleep.

Bud stood on the deck of an old-fashioned galleon that soared through the sky over Italy. They wouldn't let him land but he had to get Bunnie to the ground where she would be safe. The buckles kept slipping as he struggled to get her fastened into a safety harness so he could lower her to the fields of Tuscany flowers. Her hair blew over her face so that he didn't recognize her and his heart froze as he watched her buffeted in the onslaught of vicious winds as he lowered her from the belly of the ship.

He struggled with the rope, hands blistered and torn, warm blood streaming down the ropes, which ripped from his grasp. He fell back, terrified at what he'd done when a grinning Enid, hair whipping in the wind and strong as an ox with her giant bandaged hands that seemed to have superhuman powers – grasped the ropes and hauled Bunnie back on the ship.

"She'll die!" he cried.

Bunnie sat on the deck, dazed. She was wearing her wedding gown, billowing out like sea foam. Enid pointed over his shoulder. Bud turned and was stupefied to see a mountain growing out of the ocean. The peak of the mountain ripped away as molten lava shot into the atmosphere, followed by flames and billowing black smoke that rolled toward their suddenly tiny and fragile ship.

From behind him, he heard Enid's voice. "Mount Vesuvius. It's the end of the world. We're going to die."

He turned back to her and her bandages were gone. She was wearing a red dress and a bloody bra dangled from her right hand. Dennie Dutter, his neck torn and crusted with blood, sat cheerfully playing cards with Bunnie, who gingerly moved her white dress from the blood running in a gush from his neck.

Bunnie looked at Bud, smiling. "Go fish."

"Go fish?" Bud said, confused.

The ship was shaking – breaking into bits.

"Bud!"

Bud's eyes flew open. Confused, he stared into Bunnie's face, which hovered over his.

Bunnie said, "Did you say go bitch? I *know* you didn't tell me to go-bitch!"

Bud sat up, relief flooding through him. He put his hand to his racing heart and saw Bunnie's face change to worry.

Bunnie said, "I knew it! You didn't take your medication, did you? What am I – your personal 'go-bitch' nurse who has to chase you around and shove pills down your gullet because you – "

"Bunnie." He reached for her but she shoved his hand away. She dug into his medication pouch and found the right pills. Bud opened his mouth and she placed a pill on his tongue.

Bud said, "I had a bad dream."

"Go bitch?"

"Go fish."

Bunnie gave him a skeptical look.

"I almost got you to safety, then I didn't." Bud wrinkled his brow, seeing Enid in her red dress as clear as if she was standing in the room. "Someone helped me save you – then – none of us were saved."

"How'd we bite it?"

"Mount Vesuvius."

"Italy? Were we retired?"

Bud laughed, wiped his sweaty brow. He gazed at her, visualizing her in her wedding gown. After a moment, he nodded to the medication pouch. "Thanks."

"Well, somebody's got to save somebody around here. Sure as hell doesn't sound like it's going to be me."

As she turned to leave, Bud reached out, took her hand. "Stay."

She hesitated, gently disentangled her hand from his. "Like you said: go bitch."

Bud watched her leave with a sinking feeling in his stomach. He didn't want to be alone. He thought about the dream and, as he slipped back to sleep, he had the vague notion that Enid was there, somewhere around the next corner.

CHAPTER SIXTY-ONE

And thus I take my leave of the world and of you all, and I heartily desire you all to pray for me.

—Anne Boleyn

Enid woke up the next morning feeling surprisingly refreshed – considering she'd slept on the floor in Ernie's treehouse and spent most of her night dreaming that she was being chased by faceless bad guys. She pushed back Ernie's sleeping bag and sat up, stretching. She peered into the backyard but there was no sign of Ernie. Stomach growling, she reached for what was left of their food.

She ate the last of the Oreos as she examined her hands. They looked better and hurt less but she still couldn't bend them enough to make a fist.

Ernie's head stuck up from the entrance hole in the floor. "Are you decent?"

She mock-kicked him with her foot, "What if I wasn't, you little perve?"

He clambered into the treehouse. "What am I supposed to do – knock like a visitor when it's my treehouse?

Enid gave a grudging shrug. "Well, next time, make some noise when you come out the back door so I can hear you coming." Enid popped the last of the last Oreo into her mouth.

Ernie said, "Do you think I'm handsome?"

Enid made a face. "Don't be creepy. I'm in love."

"Don't flatter yourself, doll face. I'm asking hypothetically."

Enid said, "What grade you in?"

"I tested at the ninth-grade level."

"How come you always talk like you ate a dictionary?"

"You should take a nibble sometime, might do you some good."

"I'm plenty smart," Enid said.

Ernie shrugged, "Just sayin'. Not too 'plenty' impressed with the vocabulary level."

Enid scowled at him.

Ernie said, "How long are you going to hide from Uncle Jack? Mom is asking me about the missing food and I don't know how long I can keep up the charade," Ernie said, pronouncing "charade" like "sherr-odd".

Enid said, "I've recently discovered that your gross Uncle Jack is not my real father."

"Yeah, right. How many guys did your mom sleep with anyway?"

"More than you're going to sleep with."

"I don't sleep with guys," Ernie said.

"Uh-huh."

Ernie said, "What's that supposed to mean?"

"I don't know. Are you sure you're not living a – 'sherr-odd'?"

"Ernie?" Cheryl's voice said from below.

They froze.

"Ernie?" Cheryl said.

"Yeah?" Ernie called back, not daring to look through the door.

"Who are you talking to?"

Ernie scrambled to the hole in the floor and stuck his head down. "Jeez, mom. Can't a guy rehearse for the school play without getting the third degree?"

"What play are you rehearsing for?"

"What do you mean?"

"I mean, what's the play called? I'm hearing things like – "

"Were you listening?" Ernie said.

"I'm your mother – I'm allowed to listen. What's this stuff about – sleeping with – guys?"

"Mother! If you must know, it's a comedy about a guy who – thinks he's a girl – who is – confused – because he got hit on the head – with a shoe."

Cheryl was silent for a moment. "I'm calling your father."

Ernie scrambled out of the tree, chasing his mom into the kitchen.

Twenty minutes later, Enid spotted Ernie on the side of the house, motioning for her to join him. Making sure the coast was clear, Enid climbed out of the tree and headed for the garage.

Ernie said, "She banned me from going in the treehouse till dad gets home and can have a 'discussion' with me. Thanks a bunch for nothing. Mom thinks I think I'm a girl who wants to sleep with guys and I'm living a *charade*. I don't know whether I'm more offended that she thinks I'm a girl who wants to sleep with guys or that I don't know how to pronounce charade, which, by the way, is how the British pronounce it, so that's the correct way because they had the language before we got hold of it."

"I need your help."

"There are no more Oreos, so don't even try. And, by the way, you could have saved some for me."

"I need to get across town," Enid said.

"Why?"

"To get a gun."

Ernie eyed her suspiciously. "What gun?"

"My gun."

"Why's it across town?"

"I left it at a friend's house."

"You just got here. You don't have any friends."

"I have one friend."

"The guy you're in love with?"

"Him too."

"Him too, what? Him too, he's your friend or him too, he's got your gun?"

"Him too, he's my friend."

"Then who's got your gun?"

"Her name's Jeni. She's a stripper."

Ernie gazed at her for a long moment. "We need to get your gun."

Ernie decided the best way to get there was to bike the seven sweaty miles of Phoenix streets, bike-blind drivers, and a one-eyed bulldog that chased them two city blocks. Before they left, Ernie swiped oven mitts from the kitchen for Enid to wear so her hands wouldn't hurt. On Bethany and 19th Avenue, a cowboy in a beat-up Ford yelled out the window, "Not used to the Phoenix heat?"

Enid comforted herself with the thought that, at the very least, Chip would never see her sweating like a dog and biking around Phoenix wearing oven mitts decorated with hearts and hot chilies.

Once on Jeni's street, Enid tried to get Ernie to wait for her down the street, but she soon realized that he wasn't about to miss his one chance to meet a stripper. Walking up to the apartment, she saw Mrs. Lopez move the curtains aside. Enid waved hello and the curtain dropped back in place.

Enid knocked but there was no answer. She put her ear to the door and listened.

Silence.

Ernie said, "You should have called."

Enid eyed the broken window that Jeni's ex-boyfriend had tried to climb through. It was covered with cardboard. She poked it and one corner came loose.

Ernie backed up. "Are you crazy? My dad is a cop. I'm not breaking and entering."

"Then don't," Enid said.

"Do you have any idea what they do to cops' kids in Juvie? I'm going to the Circle K down the street. Whatever you do, I don't want to know. But I highly recommend against breaking and entering." Ernie grabbed his bike and rode off.

Enid hid her bike behind some trash cans. She looked at Mrs. Lopez's window and noticed the curtain was hanging straight. Using the oven mitt, she stuck her arm through Jeni's broken window blocked with cardboard and unlocked the door.

Heart pounding, she slipped into the apartment, locking the door behind her. She headed for the kitchen and filled a glass with tap water and guzzled it. She opened the freezer and grabbed the ice cream box, smiling with relief when she saw the gun.

That's the nice thing about skinny girls – they don't eat ice cream.

The gun was frozen in the ice cream so she put the box in the sink and ran hot water over it in. While she was waiting for it to thaw, she went to the bathroom.

The front door slammed.

Enid went rigid with fear at the sound of Jeni's heels clomping around the living room as she tried to quiet Faith's crying.

Horrified, Enid jumped up, her brain scrabbling through any excuses she could offer for breaking in. She got in the shower and pressed her ear to the wall.

Loud music blared and she almost fell backwards. The stereo on the other side of the wall banged out a thumping beat. Enid locked the bathroom door, hoping to buy some time and come up with a plan. She quietly turned on the water and washed her hands.

Maybe I can just go out there and be, like, all surprised because…

She stared at herself in the mirror and pretended like she was explaining herself to Jeni, silently laughing and acting like it was this funny thing – that's it! I'll tell her I had to go to the bathroom so bad that I broke in. I'll tell her I came to see her and – I drank way too much water and…

What about the gun?

By now, Jeni had heard the running water in the kitchen and…

But the music is too loud – maybe she hadn't heard it yet.

Enid heard bumping – thudding – over the blare of the music. She stepped into the shower and pressed her ear against the wall. All she could hear was the THUD, THUD of the music. She went back to the mirror and stared at her pale face, trying to get the backbone she needed to walk out there and explain the situation. After a long time, she took a shaky breath and unlocked the bathroom door.

Enid put what amounted to a silly apologetic smile on her face as she walked into the living room.

It was empty.

She turned the stereo down and headed toward the kitchen where Faith was bawling.

"Jeni?"

Enid stopped, her blood running cold with terror.

Jeni lay sprawled on the kitchen floor covered in blood. Enid staggered backwards, trying to scream for help but nothing came out. She hurled herself towards the front door, knocking over everything in her way.

Enid ran headlong into Jack, which sent her sprawling backwards into the apartment. She landed on her back, the air knocked out of her with a sickening jolt. She crawled to her feet and got a glimpse of the bloody handprint she left on the floor.

Jack shoved past her and was in the kitchen. She could see him – his fingers pressed to Jeni's throat, looking for a pulse.

Their eyes met.

He thinks I did it!

Enid jumped to her feet and ran.

She ran and ran until her lungs burned and her legs gave out. She collapsed on the ground in someone's front yard and burst into tears.

Jeni was dead – and she was there when Jeni got dead. They would think she did it. Why wouldn't they? She'd go to jail for the rest of her life. She crawled behind a parked car in the driveway and puked until she got dizzy and passed out.

CHAPTER SIXTY-TWO

No man ever steps in the same river twice, for it's not the same river and he's not the same man.

—Heraclitus

Jack grabbed a dishtowel and gently draped it over Jeni's midsection, covering her where her mini-skirt had come up and she was partially exposed. Jack held the baby as her tiny fists beat against him, splattering blood across his face as she wailed at full volume.

Enid.

His mind struggled to get hold of the fact that Enid had been here. Covered with Jeni's blood.

Jeni stared past him, empty.

The same nightmarish helplessness washed over him like so many years ago when he'd found his mother's lifeless body dangling, dead-weight heavy, from the noose. He was too late. *Again.* There was nothing to be done except call for more people to come share in his helplessness.

His mind flashed back to all the nights he woke up drenched in sweat, his grandmother soothing him with soft Apache words he didn't understand. For years, he was haunted by the same nightmare. His mother lay at the bottom of a deep dark well. Winged demons lunged downward, landing on her frail body, their filthy talons digging into her flesh as they clawed at her over and over. He stood looking down into the well – helpless and horrified. The nightmare was bad but the feeling that came with it was worse.

And now – it was *here.*

The nightmare was here, in this kitchen, looking up at him with merciless eyes. Nauseous, Jack turned away and saw Jeni's bloody handprints hanging on the wall.

Like she's trying to reach out to me.

Jeni had called him, left a message for him to call back. That was yesterday.

Why didn't I call?

He remembered the day like it was a million years ago.

Yesterday.

The best day of my life.

Despite everything – Enid missing, his house gone, everything he owned gone.

Eve loves me.

I love Eve.

Jack stared down at Jeni with her "I'm Your Angel" T-shirt, bright bubble gum lipstick and daisy tattoo peeking out from under the dishtowel.

This is my fault.

Why? Why is this my fault?

It is.

He rubbed his nose and felt something warm and liquid. He drew back his hand and was surprised to see his fingers wet with blood. The baby's wails broke through and he found himself staring at her, trying to piece his jumbled thoughts together.

Jack tried but couldn't remember the baby's name. Like a physical pain, like a lead weight in his gut holding him down to this moment that –

I could have stopped…?

That same feeling – horrible gnawing animal in his gut clawing its way up to his throat. A wave of self-loathing rushed over him. He pulled out his cell phone and made his way to the front door, dialing emergency services. He leaned against the front door and slid down until he was sitting with Jeni's baby cradled in his lap.

A Hispanic woman edged toward him, scared but determined, holding a broom toward him like a weapon. Neighbors gathered behind her as if she and her broom would keep them safe.

Distant sirens sounded.

Jack waited for them to arrive, his mind floating back to the previous day.

It was an eternity ago.

He'd spent the day with Eve. She was everything he'd ever wanted in a woman – and all he wanted was more.

He'd finally torn himself away and left to go looking for Enid. His time with Eve had left him feeling elated and free – like he'd slipped some bonds and floated upward toward something he didn't even know existed.

Jack had called Detective Orlean and left a message – an apology for not meeting him at the coffee shop. He hardly recognized his own voice – it was filled with warmth. He'd been so happy, he could even think of Detective Orlean as a friend. The world looked different. The Phoenix streets looked lovely and inviting. Hookers and junkies couldn't even mar the magically transformed landscape.

The sirens got louder. He looked up and was shocked to see Ernie pushing his bike up Jeni's walk toward him.

Jack jumped to his feet, handing the baby to the Hispanic woman, who grabbed at her eagerly.

Ernie said, "I saw Enid take off up the street – I couldn't catch her."

Jack got his business card, shoved it into the Hispanic woman's hand. "I'll be back."

He hustled Ernie to his car and reached the corner before the first police car screamed up the street.

"Which way?" Jack said.

Ernie pointed to the right, scared. "What happened? Is she all right?"

They drove through the neighborhood, both looking for Enid. Jack was relieved to see the road was through a winding neighborhood with no turn-offs and, if she'd taken the last turn, she would have been like rabbit in a run.

"There." Ernie jabbed excitedly and jumped out of the car before Jack could stop.

Enid lay in a driveway, her face a sickly white. Jack lightly slapped Enid's face and she came to life, giving him a washed-out version of her usual glare.

"Come on," Jack said, trying to help her to her feet. She shoved him away but was too weak to resist when he picked her up and dumped her into the backseat of his car.

Jack drove out of the neighborhood. He paused at the turn to Jeni's street, which was now swarmed with cop cars.

Enid said, "I can't go back."

Their eyes met in the rearview mirror. Her eyes shone with desperation. Whichever way he cut it, those eyes spelled trouble.

Jack gripped the wheel, unsure.

CHAPTER SIXTY-THREE

But which is the stone that supports the bridge?
Why do you speak to me of the stones? It is only the arch that matters to me.

—Kublai Khan

Bud watched as Jack walked from his parked car. His white shirt was blood-splattered and he was gripping Enid's arm, and a boy was tailing them. Mrs. Lopez, who had given him Jack's card and had been talking with a CPS official, began hissing, "That's him. That's him."

At the first sight of Enid, the image of her in his dream punched through his consciousness. Bud glanced at her hands, half expecting to see the bloody bra dangling from her fingers.

"Detective Orlean," Jack said. "Is there someplace we can talk?"

Several hours later, at the station, Bud stared at Enid, who looked pathetically young as she rubbed her hands, which seemed to be bothering her. They'd been in the interrogation room for two hours hashing out her timeline since she'd arrived in Phoenix, especially once she'd gotten to Jeni's apartment that afternoon. He'd had a short talk with Jack, who was lodged in another interrogation room.

"You believe me, don't you?" Enid said.

Bud nodded, knowing that he wasn't supposed to nod but not able to help himself. "Is there anything else you can remember?"

Enid shook her head.

Bud stood. "Give me a few minutes."

"Don't I get one phone call?" Enid said.

"You're not under arrest."

"Oh." She exhaled a sigh of relief.

Once in the hallway, Bud nodded at Jenson, who had watched the interchange behind a two-way mirror. They walked down the hall and stood outside Jack's interrogation room. Through another two-way mirror, they watched as Jack drained the last of the coffee and tossed the styrofoam cup into a trash can like he was playing basketball.

Jenson said, "Outlandish story."

Bud said, "That's the trouble. Makes me think it might be true. I sent the key to the lab – try to lift some fingerprints."

"What about the girl?"

Bud sighed. "Let's start at the girls' home. Talk to the psychiatrist, the owner – "

"Vivian Hargrove owns the place," Jenson said.

"I don't like coincidences," Bud said. "They have a funny way of not being coincidences. Any theories on how this pile of bricks fit together? Or is any of it even related?"

Jenson shrugged, "Not yet."

"Daniel Hargrove – a cold case we've been working for years. Now this guy," Bud nodded toward Jack, "is dating our prime suspect – Eve Hargrove."

"I certainly hope Chip's not batting sloppy seconds with a sociopathic killer."

Bud shot him a look.

Jenson smiled pleasantly, "You can pick the tile in your out-house but you can't pick your relatives. And you definitely can't pick who they decide to sleep with."

"Chip's fine. He'll be – fine," Bud said, his voice sounding anything but sure.

Jenson said, "Then, Jack Fox, the guy who is dating the prime suspect of our favorite cold case – his daughter – who he didn't even know existed until earlier this week – "

Bud said, "Comes to town with a gun that ends up in the murder victim's sink – and the kid is on the premises when Jeni Hargrove is murdered but supposedly hears nothing and sees even less."

"And this occurs two days after her father gets the bright idea of sending Enid undercover at Vivian Hargrove's home for wayward girls, which is Hargrove family member number-four. Then Enid claims she gets drugged and abducted, and only manages to escape by strangling a man to death with her bra – ”

Bud said, “Dennie Dutter shows up duct-taped and delivered to us care of the Arizona Canal.”

“Not to mention the whole story Fox fed us about his high-speed chase with Laura Hargrove – number-five on the Hargrove clan and counting.”

Bud said, “Fox says he was on a date with Eve but ended up in jail the next morning with his house torched and Laura Hargrove in the hospital under suspicion of arson. Fox claims he had no clue where Enid was – why wasn't he out looking for her? In fact, do we have a Hargrove family member that isn't tangled up in this mess?”

“*Voilà!*” Jenson said with a flourish. “What could be more straightforward?”

“I've seen hair in public shower drains less tangled.”

Jenson smiled, tapping his lips with his fingers.

Bud gazed through the mirror at Jack. “We have four – no, five – separate – or not-so-separate incidents, and the person who shows up the most is Vivian Hargrove.”

Jenson said, “Daniel's widow, mother to Jeni, Laura and Eve – and she owns the wayward girl place.”

“See if you can get a search warrant for the home. In the meantime, I'll do Q&A.”

“Fun, fun.” Jenson gave a jaunty nod and headed down the hall. “Let me know if anything emerges.”

“Hopefully not another corpse,” Bud said before he went into the interrogation room.

Jack looked up. “How's Enid?”

Bud sat down. “Scared but she'll be okay. How are you doing? Would you like some more coffee?”

“Cut the crap with the good cop bonding shit. I'm too tired.”

Bud said, “Why didn't you go looking for Enid yesterday – when you knew she was gone?”

“I'm a bad father.”

Bud stared at him. Jack's face was impassive and Bud wondered if he was thinking about his own father. “Jeni told me that she hired you to find her biological mother?”

Jack looked at him in surprise. "Her grandmother is alive and kickin' and as mean as medieval rat's piss."

"Then Eve Hargrove tried to hire you to drop the case Jeni hired you to do?"

"She asked politely. I declined politely."

"Did you sign a contract with either one of them? Did they pay you any money?"

"Jeni signed a contract but didn't pay me. Eve didn't sign a contract."

"But she paid you?"

"Not relevant."

"Humor me."

"She and I are seeing each other. I talk to her before I answer any questions regarding her."

"That's an unusual request," Bud said. "Like you're covering for her."

"Humor me."

Bud was about to speak when he was hit with a bolt of chest pain that made him cry out. He gripped his chest and doubled over, struggling to breathe.

"Jesus," Jack said, coming around the table to Bud's side.

Bud tried to stand, but his legs gave out and he fell back into the chair.

Jack headed for the door but Bud grabbed him, stopping him. Bud reached for the fanny pack, his hand falling from the zipper as he saw fuzzy dots in front of his eyes.

Jack grabbed the contents of the pack and dumped the pill bottles onto the table. "What? Which one?"

Bud pointed weakly to the lightning-bolt bottle. In a flash, Jack had taken out the nitroglycerin.

"Open," Jack said.

Feeling like a child, Bud opened his mouth and Jack stuck the pill under his tongue. Jack watched him anxiously as the medication took effect. Bud's breathing returned to normal and his color improved. He scraped the bottles off the table and jammed them into the fanny pack. He felt self-loathing that he had allowed Jack Fox to see him at his weakest.

Jack sat down, tapping his fingers on the table as he stared intently at Bud.

"Thanks," Bud managed to mutter without looking at Jack. The word tasted like sawdust.

"You want water?"

Bud shook his head. He didn't want to get up yet. He wanted to sit in the tiny grey room and feel the air conditioning blowing down on his sweaty neck.

Jack said, "My dad had heart problems."

Bud looked at Jack in surprise. He'd never expected to hear Jack talk about his dad, considering all the infamous scandals that still stunk after all these years.

"I knew him," Bud said.

"He was an asshole," Jack said with a wry smile.

Bud's lip twitched, the closest he was going to get to a smile.

Jack said, "Were you at the funeral?"

Bud shook his head, remembering the stories that he'd heard over the years – of how Jack had overturned the casket and kicked the dead body, cursing him for killing his mother. From what he'd heard, it had taken three grown men to pull a teenage Jack away from his father's dead body and get him out of the church. The widow, a cold blue-eyed little thing, had practically had a nervous breakdown and Bud always wondered at how Jack and his half-brother, Sam, had remained close. The last he heard, the widow cashed in the insurance policy for a good chunk of change and married a pseudo-cowboy from New York.

Jack said, "I want to help you find Jeni's killer."

Bud opened his mouth to say "no" but Jack leaned forward, eyes burning.

"I can help you. I liked Jeni. She was – " Jack's voice faltered.

Bud said, "She was a good kid. She might have gotten out but she always ended up falling for the wrong guy."

Jack looked away.

Bud remained silent, hoping to get Jack talking.

"And – he's back," Jack said with a smile.

Bud smiled, knowing exactly what he meant. His detective instincts had kicked in – he'd recovered.

"Let me help you," Jack said.

"I already have someone – "

"Your son?"

"You and Chip – " Bud shook his head in a "no."

"I'm a friendly guy," Jack said.

Bud paused, wondering if he should tell Jack that he and Chip were dating the same woman.

Jack sniffed his armpit. "What? Do I offend?"

Bud said, "Conflict of interest."

"Enlighten me."

Bud paused, afraid he would regret his words.

Jack said, "Is it Enid?"

Bud shook his head, knowing that Jack would find out the truth eventually, but it wasn't going to be from him. Bud said, "I'd like to take Enid out to the girls' home."

Jack frowned.

Bud said, "We're in the process of getting a search warrant. We won't have Enid come in unless there's a need. She can wait in the car with Chip. She'll be safe."

"I need to be there."

Bud shook his head.

Jack said, "I'm not leaving her – every time I blink, she disappears."

"I'll personally deliver her back to you when we're done."

"What if she doesn't want to go?"

Bud said, "Are you her legal guardian?"

"No."

"We'll need her guardian's permission."

"Let me talk to her mother. And Enid."

"I'll take care of her like she's my own daughter," Bud said, recalling his dream of Enid in the red dress, saving him from the end of the world.

Jack remained silent for several moments. "Was it easy…?"

"What?"

"When you became a dad?"

"When I became a father – Chip was a baby and didn't know my mistakes from a hole in the wall. You do the best you can."

"What if your best – sucks?"

"It can't be that bad."

Jack said, "I sent her undercover, she got drugged, kidnapped and may have killed someone – because of me."

Bud made a face. "Point taken. Every day is a new starting line."

"I'm seeing my own dad in a new light."

"How so?"

"He was an asshole. He was never there – but – "

Bud waited.

Jack laughed. "Shit. I'm getting soft in my old age."

Bud snorted, thinking of his own age. He stood up but caught the back of the chair, unsteady.

Jack grabbed his arm, stabilized him. "Whoa, there."

Bud pushed him away. "Don't talk to me about getting old."

"Point taken," Jack said.

Bud turning his back on Jack and left him standing alone in the grey room.

CHAPTER SIXTY-FOUR

If you don't love me, it does not matter, anyway I can love for both of us.

—*Stendhal*

Enid sat in the backseat of Detective Orlean's car, staring at the back of Chip's right ear. He had a mole that was in the shape of a tiny pumpkin and she weighing the consequences of leaning up and kissing it.

Detective Orlean and Detective Jenson had gone into the girls' home with a warrant, and Enid was under strict orders to stay in the car with Chip, which was a fantasy come true. She kept trying to think of something cool to say but, instead, sat in dazed silence – staring at his delicious pumpkin mole, terrified of saying something stupid.

I wonder if our kids will have pumpkin moles?

Chip said, "Where'd your dad go?"

"Oh, uh…" Enid made a show of looking around like she cared. "Dunno."

Chip returned to staring out the window with a dreamy look that she could see in the partial reflection of his face in the rearview mirror. Periodically, he would scribble notes in a notebook as Enid tried to figure out a way to start a conversation that would somehow make him fall in love with her.

After much thought, Enid said, "What are you writing?"

"A book."

"What kind of book?"

"Not sure yet."

"A love story?"

"Not really – but yeah."

Enid leaned forward. "Tell me about it."

"I don't have it all fleshed out yet."

"Are you the main character?"

"I guess you could say – I'm all the characters."

"What's she like?"

"Who?"

"The girl you – your character – falls in love with?"

Chip gave her a quizzical look. "How old are you?"

"Why does everybody keep asking me that?"

"Are you a writer?" Chip said.

"Me?" Enid said, "No way! I mean – I wish."

"What do you want to do?" Chip said.

"Now?" Enid said, imagining them kissing.

"For a career, I mean."

"Oh," Enid said, disappointed. "I'm not sure. Something exciting – that will make me rich."

Chip laughed.

"What?" Enid said.

"Nothing. I mean, well, I quit med school, which probably would have been a more stable career choice and now – "

"Could you write me into your book?"

"It's the unexpected that makes characters more interesting – tell me something about yourself – unexpected – and I might."

"Can my name be Veronica?"

Chip wrote the name. "Isn't that what you said your name was the first time we met?"

Enid said, "What if I told you I was a time traveler?"

"Weird. Not super original. What else?"

"What if I told you I've traveled back in time and – ten years from now – you and I…"

Chip looked at her expectantly. "What?"

"You're hopelessly in love – with me."

Chip raised his eyebrows, writing. "That's interesting. Why am I in love with you? Why is it hopeless?"

"Why not?"

"The devil is in the details – tell me more."

Tweaker stuck her head in the window. "Is this your boyfriend?"

Enid and Chip jumped.

Enid said, "Jeez, Tweaker! What the heck? You tryin' to scare us to death?"

Tweaker got in the backseat, shoving Enid over. "Doctor Buttwipe disappeared and the word on the block is you sliced off his *thing* and put it in a blender and made him eat it. Is it true?"

"Gross," Enid said.

Tweaker eyed Chip, "You're even hotter than E –"

Enid elbowed Tweaker. "This is my *friend*, Chip."

Tweaker said, "You're not…?"

"Shut up!" Enid said.

"Sheesh, just askin'," Tweaker said.

Chip stuck out his hand, "Chip. And you're – Tweaker?"

Tweaker shot Enid a "you lying dog" look and shook Chip's hand. "Are you guys casing the joint? 'Cause it's bad timing – there's a diaper-load of cops in there tearing the place apart."

Enid said, "Did they find anything?"

Tweaker said, "Say, where'd you go that day? You took off – "

Angry, Enid said, "I didn't take off! You left me there with that doctor – who freakin' drugged me."

Tweaker said, "What are you talking about?"

"Can you excuse us a few moments, Chip?" Enid said in her most regal tone.

Chip got out of the car and walked away.

Tweaker said, "Is that the guy you were talking about? Gawd, I could fry eggs on his – "

"Remember the party – when we first met?" Enid said.

Tweaker's eyes stayed glued to Chip. "Me wanna take a bubble bath in the deep blue of his eyes. Hey, if he's not your boyfriend – "

"Tweak!"

"What?"

"The party – you remember?"

"Whaddya think – I ride the short bus?"

Enid said, "Bones told me to run. Why'd she say that?"

"How should I know?" Tweaker pushed Enid to the side, her eyes following Chip. "Pardon you, you're blocking the view."

"That doctor drugged me and I woke up in a room where some creep tried to kill me."

"Yeah, right," Tweaker grinned.

"The only way I got out was – " Enid's voice trailed off. She didn't like to think about it – much less say it aloud.

"You serious?" Tweaker examined her face, unsure.

"That doctor drugged me."

"I had a session with that creep plenty of times. Why would he drug you and not me?"

Enid said, "Do girls disappear from here a lot?"

"Girls are always coming and going – there's nothing weird about that."

"You ever stay in touch with the ones that leave? Do they ever come back?"

"No. I guess not." Tweaker reached for the door. "I gotta go."

Enid grabbed her arm, "What are you hiding?"

"Get off! You lied about Chip – you're probably lying about getting drugged." Tweaker jumped out of the car and headed to the school.

Chip got in the car. "What was that about?"

"She thought you were my boyfriend. Says we have chemistry."

Chip laughed.

Enid gazed at him, perfectly serious.

Chip's laughter died and, with a nervous twitch of his cheek, he turned back to scribbling notes.

CHAPTER SIXTY-FIVE

No lover, if he be of good faith, and sincere, will deny he would prefer to see his mistress dead than unfaithful.

—Marquis de Sade

Jack fought the urge to call Eve, knowing that if he did – he'd do his damnedest to get with her. He was scheduled to pick up Enid in two hours and he wasn't going to take any chances. Driving to his office, he'd impulsively decided to drive to Laura Hargrove's house instead. He tried to convince himself that it might prove productive to the case and tried to ignore the nagging hope that Eve would be there. He checked his rearview mirror for Frank Ficus's sedan, which was nowhere to be seen.

The address that Rachel had given him for Laura was a modest neighborhood compared to where Eve and Vivian lived. Jack parked up the street from Laura's house, which looked out of place among the Southwestern homes surrounding it. It had a pale yellow façade with an old-fashioned porch, and its flowerless trellis seemed more like a New England beach cottage than the rows of adobe and low cinderblock houses that were a common sight in Phoenix.

Jack hunkered down to watch Laura's house. He'd long ago gotten accustomed to the long boring hours of a stakeout, and two hours felt like a walk in the park.

His mind drifted back to Eve – the flash of her eyes in the moonlight, the feel of her hands.

A barking dog shook him from his revelry. Eve's car turned onto the street and pulled into Laura's driveway. Jack watched her with hungry eyes, taking in every detail of her appearance, from her elegant slacks to her light, clingy blouse that accentuated the smallness of her waist. She had a key and disappeared through the front door.

Jack got out of the car and, watching for neighbors, he walked toward the house and slipped around the side where he was shrouded from view by high shrubbery. He edged his way toward a window that looked into the living room. He could see but not hear.

Laura sat on a flowery couch, her pale face splotched with the red of recent crying. Eve was pacing in front of her, making an argument.

Jack watched as Eve touched Laura's arm. Jack was startled to see Laura slap Eve away. Eve went down on one knee, pleading. Laura broke into sobs. Jack strained to hear their voices but couldn't.

Eve reached for Laura, who shoved her away. Eve jumped to her feet and said something that, from the expression on Laura's face, was cruel. Eve stalked toward the door and Laura sprang after her.

Laura threw herself into Eve's arms and they kissed passionately.

Jack reeled backwards, stumbling over a pail of tools that clattered noisily into a stack of empty pots. Jack ran to the car and got the hell out of there without so much as a glance backwards.

At the first stoplight, Jack slammed on the brakes. He looked at his hands and realized that he was shaking.

Eve and Laura?

Jack clenched his fists to his head, thinking. He wanted to go back and hurt Eve – hurt them both.

A car horn blared. He looked at the light, now green. He couldn't go back. He didn't trust himself. He needed answers – but not from her. Not yet.

Jack turned left and headed for the person who he was going to get the truth out of if he had to beat her senseless.

Within twenty minutes, he stood in front of Vivian Hargrove's desk at the wayward girls' home.

She stared at him, indignant. Her office was full of framed photos of smiling girls.

Jack said, "Who is Laura?"

Vivian stood. "How dare you barge in here? First you try to pass yourself off as – "

Jack grabbed the edge of her massive oak desk, picked it off the floor and slammed it down. "Who is Laura?"

Vivian jumped back, hand to her throat.

The secretary appeared, alarmed. "Mrs. Hargrove?"

Jack's eyes never left Vivian. "The truth or so help me God."

Vivian looked at the secretary. "Call the police."

The secretary disappeared.

Jack shouted after her, "Tell 'em to haul ass – we got a missing child."

Vivian ran to the adjoining room, snatched the phone from the secretary and hung it up. The secretary stared at her, confused.

Vivian shook her head. "It's all right."

Jack appeared in the doorway.

Vivian looked at him, suddenly old.

The secretary said, "I'm calling the police."

Vivian said, "No. I'll call you if I need you."

The secretary nodded reluctantly.

Vivian returned to her office and shut the door behind her and Jack. She walked to a bookshelf, reached behind a book and pulled out a pack of cigarettes, lighting one with shaking hands.

Jack walked to the window. A group of girls were shouting as they played kick the can.

Vivian blew smoke out her nostrils. "The Girls' Home – it's not a true orphanage. Most of the girls have one parent – some two – who don't want – or can't take care of them."

"Do they know that?"

Vivian paused. "Sometimes."

Jack said, "Laura was one of those girls?"

"Her mother dropped her off – never came back. After Eve – " Vivian's lips tightened. "I couldn't have any more children. I gave Laura a better life – why did she need to know?"

"Does Eve know?" Jack said.

"I never told anyone."

"Not even your husband?"

Vivian shook her head.

"How'd you pull that off?"

"I told him I had a daughter staying with relatives in another state. Once I got settled, I would go get her."

"Any of that true?"

Vivian took a drag, shook her head.

"Why would you go to all that trouble?"

"Why does anyone do anything, Mr. Fox?" She stared impassively at the girls playing.

Jack said, "Is there any way that Eve and Laura would know they aren't really sisters?"

"I destroyed the evidence." Vivian stopped, flushing red. "What now?"

Jack had an idea but he didn't like it – made his skin crawl, but he was determined to find out. He walked to a photograph of a ten-year-old girl, traced his finger along the outline of her face. He turned to Vivian with an enquiring look.

Her eyes flooded with relief. She smiled. "That can be arranged."

Jack forced a smile. He didn't want to tip her off that he wasn't for real so she'd close shop and disappear. He forced himself to play the cautious pedophile. "I'll be in touch."

All smiles, she stubbed out her cigarette and came forward, hand outstretched in friendship.

Jack pretended like he didn't see her and turned to leave. He didn't trust himself to stay. He felt like he was losing his mind.

Her voice followed him into the hallway. "Let me know when is best for you, Mr. Fox."

In his car, Jack gripped the steering wheel, trying to get his hands to stop shaking. He wanted to lock himself away and think. He couldn't go home. It was gone. Destroyed.

He drove to his office, thinking about how good it was going to feel to get Vivian Hargrove locked up for the rest of her miserable life.

Striding into his office, Rachel stared at him as he snapped instructions for her to research missing children, nationwide, 1990 to 1992. "Dig like you never dug, got it?"

She nodded and he locked himself into his office. He lay down on the couch that creaked under his weight. He wanted to think but sank into a thick sleep and when he awoke, it was dark. He turned to his side and saw the papers Rachel had slipped under the door.

He got up and flipped on the lights and found himself blinking at photos of missing children – girls staring out from the page with varying expressions. Halfway into the pile, he caught his breath. A young Laura Hargrove stared out from the page with her unmistakable smile.

Lani Mulberry, 4, snatched from mall, St. Cloud, Minnesota.

Hello Lani.

Jack's cell vibrated. A text from a blocked number read: Meet me outside Jeni's apartment. Frank.

Jack grabbed his keys and wallet and headed for his car.

Jack drove past Jeni's apartment. Her front door was crisscrossed with police tape. He saw Frank's car and parked behind it. He got out and walked to the driver's side where Frank was sitting at an odd angle, hunched over the console.

Jack stopped. The street was empty. A dog barked and the distant highway traffic had the hum of an angry beehive.

Shit.

Jack scanned the empty windows. He might as well have been on Mars for how alone he was. Using his shirt, he tried the door. It was unlocked. He pulled the door open. Frank's head, and the passenger seat, was covered with the dark muck and mess of blood and brains.

Jack's heart pounded. He ran his fingers through his hair, hating that he was here alone. He didn't like that the police would know that Frank had sent him a text message. Everything about it stunk – like a dime-store novel setup.

He got out his cell and dialed the only person who might be able to help him.

CHAPTER SIXTY-SIX

Each player must accept the cards life deals him or her: but once they are in hand, he or she alone must decide how to play the cards in order to win the game.

—Voltaire

"You've hit your quota on dead bodies, Mr. Fox," Bud said as Jack shot him a "no-shit" look. "Why'd you call me?"

"Not to pick up decorating tips," Jack said, nodding to the grey walls of the interrogation room.

Detective Jenson leaned against the wall, idly spinning a Rubik's cube.

Bud sighed. He wasn't interested in wasting time with this jackass.

Jack's face changed. "I'm out of my depth. I need your help."

"How?" Bud said.

Jack leaned forward. "I don't like that Enid was in Jeni's apartment with a gun when Jeni was murdered, and I definitely don't like that somebody went to a lot of trouble to set me up for Frank's murder."

Bud said, "Why do you think Frank sent you a text to meet him?"

"I don't think it was Frank."

"Who then?"

Jack said, "I don't know."

"You have any enemies?"

"Yeah."

"Anybody in particular?"

"Nobody related to this."

Bud said, "Why was Frank tailing you?"

Jack looked up in surprise.

Bud said, "We have his notes."

"Frank didn't keep notes," Jack said.

"How do you know?"

"I worked with the slob – the only time he was forced to use paper was out of sheer necessity – in the stall."

"Maybe he picked up some good habits."

Jack laughed. "Not Frank."

"Why was he tailing you?"

"You got his notes – you tell me."

Bud tapped his fingers rhythmically on the table, trying to hide his impatience.

Jack hesitated. "Most likely hired by the husband of a woman that I was involved with."

"Who?"

"I'm not involved with her anymore. Haven't been for some time."

"I need a name."

Jack hesitated. "Petunia O'Donnell."

Bud started.

Jack said, "You know her?"

"No," Bud lied, thinking of sad-sack Larry. Petunia was Larry's wife, which meant Jack Fox was the man that Larry had been complaining about for the last year.

Jack said, "You act like you know her."

"I don't know her," Bud said.

"You know *of* her then?" Jack said, examining Bud's face.

Bud shook his head, remembering all the times Larry cried into his latte about his wife's cheating. Funny, Larry never mentioned that Petunia's "boyfriend" was a detective. Or, did Larry even know Jack existed? Or – were there more men than Larry knew about…?

Or was Jack lying? If so, why?

Bud's brain sped forward into an avenue of possibilities, a voice inside his head warning him against the improbability of yet another coincidence.

Jack said, "Is that what Frank's so-called notes said – that he was hired by Petunia's husband?"

Bud said, "Your alibi – you were napping?"

"You can verify it with my secretary. Do you really think I'd be dumb enough to shoot Frank – outside of Jeni's apartment?"

Jenson said, "No one else to confirm your alibi? Like, say – the victim's sister?"

"Frank's sister died years ago," Jack said.

"The other victim," Jenson said. "We're not picky about which sister. The one that flamed your house or the one you're romantically involved with – unless you were also romantically involved with Jeni."

"Jeni was a client."

Jenson said, "There is the question of the money."

Bud said, "Nine thousand, nine hundred and eighty dollars. Cash. Deposited in a Hargrove-owned bank on the day you met with Jeni and Eve Hargrove."

Jenson said, "Sounds like hit money."

Jack said, "Somebody's setting me up."

Bud said, "They're doing a good job. Anonymous text from a disposable cell – said the money was a blood-money hit on Jeni and Frank."

Jack said, "If I were a hit man, which I'm not – I sure as hell wouldn't work that cheap."

Jenson said, "We've heard crazier things than somebody icing two people for ten thousand."

"I came to you for help," Jack said. "Why would I be here if I murdered Frank?"

Bud said, "Why did you come here? What do you want from me?"

"I want you to find out who murdered Jeni. And Frank."

Bud said, "What if the murderer is your girlfriend – Eve Hargrove?"

Jack clenched his jaw and sat back.

Jenson lightly twisted the Rubik's cube. "You do realize that your sweetheart isn't exactly exclusive?"

Bud shot Jenson a warning look. When he turned back to Jack, he was startled to see Jack's eyes glittering with hatred.

Jack turned to Bud. "You booking me?"

Bud shook his head, irritated with Jenson for tipping Chip's hand. That's all he needed in the middle of this mess – Jack and Chip fighting over Eve.

Jack stood, turned to leave.

Bud said, "Stay easy to find."

"Thanks for all your help," Jack said sarcastically as he left.

Bud gave Jenson a disparaging look. "What are you trying to do – get Chip killed?"

Jenson nodded after Jack. "You think he did it?"

Bud gazed thoughtfully at the door. "I don't know if he's that stupid."

"He's stupid enough to fall for Eve Hargrove."

Bud sighed, wondering if Chip was the same kind of stupid.

CHAPTER SIXTY-SEVEN

The suspense is terrible. I hope it will last.

—*Oscar Wilde*

Enid watched Chip's face as he tried to figure out a way to get rid of her. He'd gotten a call and, from the way he acted, Enid knew it was some other girl.

"Who was that?" Enid said when he returned.

"A friend." Chip rubbed his lip and looked at her with a cheese-eating smile. "I was thinking – "

"Your dad says I need to stay with you till Jack gets here."

"I need to meet my friend. I was hoping – "

"I can come with you," Enid said.

"You can hang out at a Starbucks, my treat. I'll come back and get you as soon as – "

"You're supposed to be taking care of me."

"Starbucks – "

"I'm allergic to coffee."

"I'll take you anywhere you want to go. I promise, I'll be back within an hour. Or two."

Enid said, "The last time I heard 'I promise I'll be back' – I ended up almost getting killed by a psycho-creep. I'm coming with you."

Within the hour, Enid was startled to find herself at the same mansion where Jack had taken her to talk to fancy-pants rich lady with tits like ice chips that Jack couldn't tear his eyeballs off of.

"Her again," Enid said under her breath as she and Chip followed the butler into what Enid now referred to as "her lair." Enid hoped that the woman Chip was meeting was the pale blonde who didn't look strong enough to wring out a dishrag but, sure enough, it was ice tits.

Enid saw Chip glance apologetically at Eve as he introduced them.

Enid said, "We've met."

Eve smiled at Chip, "The same day I met you. How's your father?"

"Pushing himself too hard, like always."

Eve said, "Tell him he needs to slow down. He's not getting any younger." She nodded at Enid, "How is it that the two of you...?"

"Babysitting," Chip said.

Enid stared at him, horrified.

"She's no baby. She's a young woman. A beautiful one at that." Eve stepped close to Enid, running the back of her fingers down her flushed cheek.

Enid pulled away from her touch, frowning.

Eve smiled at Chip. "In fact, I'm rather jealous that you've been spending your time with such a beauty."

Enid flashed Chip a defiant look.

Chip said to Enid, "Wait here."

Eve said to Enid, "I'll send someone in with refreshments."

Eve and Chip left, their footsteps echoing until they were eaten up by the immensity of the place.

"Shit," Enid said, pleased with the way it sounded. "Shit, shit, shit, shit, shit."

She walked to one of the massive wall hangings. Her eyes were caught by a girl in a blue dress sat in a garden under a rose trellis. A lovesick man was on his knees in front of her, hands clasped. Enid caught her breath in surprise when she saw that in the twisted-tree behind them was camouflaged a creature that looked like a cross between a dragon and the devil. His claws were sunk into a bloody carcass as he eyed the couple.

"Iced tea, miss?"

Startled, Enid spun around.

The butler held out a tray.

"Thanks," Enid said as she took the glass, hating that her hands were trembling.

"Would you like a sandwich?"

She shook her head.

He nodded and left.

Enid circled the room as she examined the tapestries. She leaned in and sniffed one. It smelled old – expensive old.

She looked into the hall, wishing she had asked the butler where the bathroom was located. She walked toward the main entrance, looking for the bathroom. Not finding one, she headed up the marble staircase.

At the top of the stairs, she ducked in a doorway to avoid two maids who were walking out of a nearby room. The younger one was nodding and listening with the expression of someone who was glad to have a new job.

The older lady's orthopedic shoes squeaked as she said, "Her room is off limits. You trip and fall in, you'll get fired, no questions asked. "

Enid watched as they disappeared down the hall and into another room. She tried the handle of the forbidden room and was surprised when it opened. She slipped in, heart hammering.

She stared in amazement. A huge fireplace with intricate carvings of wild beasts in a primeval forest took up almost an entire wall. Enid ran her fingers along the carvings and she found herself mesmerized with the magical animals and plants that seemed out of a fairy tale. High above, a hawk with outstretched wings stared down at her and Enid shivered, recalling the hawk at shotgun lady's house.

She reluctantly turned her eyes away from the gaze of a carved stag and found herself drawn to the massive bed that was a foot and a half off the ground. It was sheltered under a canopy of delicate swaths of spider-web-like material that caught the soft illumination of a chandelier. A French door surrounded by windows that stretched from floor to ceiling led to a balcony.

Enid went to the window and saw Chip and Eve on the far side of the pool. Enid watched as Chip seemed to lunge forward and catch Eve in a kiss.

Enid gasped, watching as Eve returned his kisses. She stepped back, shaking with anger, wanting to vomit.

Eve led Chip to a guesthouse.

Feeling sick, Enid turned back to Eve's bedroom. She clenched her fists.

Chip is going to fall in love with her over my dead body!

Enid hatched a plan. All she had to do was find out something awful about Eve Hargrove and let slip to Chip what kind of person Eve really was and – Chip would dump the rancid old bag of money and Enid would be there to pick up the pieces.

She glanced around the room.

What could she find? Was Eve a drunk? Pill popper? Drug head?

My one special talent – finding things.

All those years of finding her mother's whiskey kitties – if there was something here, she would find it. She checked the obvious places first – under the mattress, the bed, Eve's drawers and her ridiculously large closet. Sweat beaded her forehead as she stood in the middle of the closet and forced herself to think.

What would mother do?

Enid smiled and went to the fireplace. She squatted down and stepped into the fireplace, which was so large that she could stand inside it. She reached up, running her hands around the rough interior edges. Within moments, her fingers glanced off the edge of something crinkly. She reached higher, straining to pry it loose. A small manila envelope with some small object in it fell to her feet.

Eve's voice cut sharply through the air as she was coming up the stairs. "Why weren't you watching her?"

The butler's voice said, "She was in the study."

Enid dropped the envelope and made a run for the bed, which she dove under as Eve entered. She watched as Eve's heels moved from the adjoining bathroom, to the closet and to the balcony where she called down, "Is she down there? Have you found her?"

Chip's voice said, "She's not up there?"

Eve came back, her heels pausing by the bed as she listened.

Enid held her breath and after what seemed like an eternity, Eve left, locking the door behind her.

Enid lay still, hardly daring to breathe. She crawled out from under the bed, half expecting Eve to swoop down. She gently turned the doorknob – it was locked from the outside.

Feeling sick, Enid went to the balcony where she could hear voices. Remembering the envelope, she went to the fireplace and stuffed it in her pocket. She returned to the window.

Chip was walking across the lawn, calling her name. She was about to answer him when she heard Eve's voice, "I'm meeting someone. Could she have left?"

Chip said, "She might have – I don't know."

Eve said, "I'm leaving. Did you try her cell?"

With a gasp, Enid remembered that she left it in the car.

Chip said, "No answer."

Enid watched them leave with a sinking feeling. Enid decided that the only possible thing to do was to hide out till it was night. Once Eve was asleep and the door was locked from the inside, she could sneak out. Heck, it wasn't like she hadn't already been locked in a room with a psycho killer.

She shuddered at the memory of her clinging to the man's back, strangling the life out of him.

If I can survive that, I can survive anything.

If she got caught, she would be humiliated forever but – it's not like she was in any danger, right? Enid tried to calm herself with visions of slipping out of the room to the sounds of Eve's snores. All she had to do was hide in the closet and be patient.

It was a simple plan, she reminded herself.

Seriously, what could go wrong?

CHAPTER SIXTY-EIGHT

The formula 'two and two make five' is not without its attractions.

—*Fyodor Dostoevsky*

Jack left the police station with a bad feeling. It was bad enough that he was a suspect in two murders – but what the hell was Jenson talking about when he said Eve wasn't exclusive?

Did they know about Laura?

He drew a shaky breath as he remembered Eve and Laura kissing.

How did they know?

Or, were they talking about somebody else?

Hearing footsteps, Jack turned to see Sam approach.

Sam said, "They put you with Frank Ficus when he got bumped off? Word is, you're the guy they're looking at – seriously?"

"I'm not getting a lawyer just yet, if that's what you mean."

"To hell with them and a month of ugly Sundays," Sam said, his angry words not matching his worried eyes.

"Anonymous tip on a disposable says I'm the hit man on Jeni and Frank."

"They've got no evidence. It's not like you came into any extra money."

Jack gave him a look.

Sam whistled, fell into step as they walked to Jack's car. "Any way to trace it?"

"What? The money or the disposable cell?"

"How much money?"

"It was a cash payment for a case."

"You got a receipt, right? Have them contact the client."

"It's – sensitive."

"So is your asshole when you get fifteen to twenty. Who are you trying to protect?"

Jack shoved his hands in his pocket.

Sam said, "Do yourself a favor, Jack – steer clear of anything that starts with a 'Har' and ends in a 'Grove'."

Jack was about to answer when Sam raised his hand, "I don't give a crap if you're putting it to the old man's dead carcass, much less the daughter – or daughter*s* – "

"Always the moralist."

"You hear me, Jack? Steer clear."

Jack grimaced.

Sam said, "By 'steer clear,' I don't mean head straight over and bounce her skull off the headboard."

Jack glanced at his watch. "I've got to pick up Enid."

"How's the kid?"

"Detective Orlean's son is playing babysitter. As soon as he calls, I'll pick her up." Jack hesitated, not wanting to invite himself over.

"Cheryl's famous meatloaf surprise tonight if you're game."

"I'm not up for any more surprises."

"Bring Enid. It'll be nice. Downright normal – like out of a Norman Rockhead painting."

Jack smiled wanly. "We'll be there. Thanks."

Sam peeled away. "Remember what I said."

Jack dialed Chip's phone and left a message. Knowing Enid, she probably muted Chip's phone so she could spend more time with him.

Jack stood in the middle of the street, staring up at the streetlights that awoke as day slipped into twilight. He fought the desire to go to Eve. He wanted to confront her – hear her tell him the truth.

He was determined to wait for Chip's call so he could pick up Enid like he promised.

For once, I am going to keep a promise.

Two cups of coffee later and three unanswered messages, Jack drove to Eve's home, swearing to himself that the minute Chip called, he would stop whatever he was doing and go fetch Enid like nice fathers are supposed to do.

Once at Eve's home, Jack was surprised when the butler showed him to the kitchen, which was a decorator's wet dream. Eve sat cross-legged on the counter, holding a steaming mug between two hands as she stared pensively out a window overlooking the grounds.

Jack felt his face flush at the memory of Eve and Laura kissing. He walked forward, forcing himself to remain calm.

Cold.

Eve said, "Do you believe in families – bloodlines – being cursed?"

"No." The words landed like a whip.

She glanced at him, surprised.

Not trusting himself to go near her, Jack leaned on the table. She looked elegant in a kimono of white silk with elaborately stitched battling dragons.

Eve said, "Who would want to hurt Jeni?"

Jack shrugged. "She was a hooker."

Eve's brow furrowed.

Jack walked to a butcher's block that sat on the counter next to her. He pulled a gleaming knife out of a knife holder and stuck it hard into the block.

She remained still, eyes locked on him.

"You and Laura," Jack said, gripping the knife and taking pleasure in how it felt. He glanced at her, admiring that her eyes gave away nothing. "Are you in love – or just fucking?"

The word hung in the air, electric.

Eve stared at him, stunned.

Jack dropped the knife and grabbed her, pulling her off the counter, and set her on her feet in front of him. "Tell me."

Glaring, she shoved him away as she spat out, "Mister man."

Jack found himself transfixed as Eve's persona morphed into something masculine. The Eve he knew was gone. He was looking into the eyes of danger.

A killer?

Jack remained silent, afraid of breaking the spell.

Eve cracked her knuckles like a truck driver. "I turned eighteen – I left. Jeni was gone and I sure as hell wasn't going to leave Laura with him."

Jack wondered if what Jeni had said was true.

Did their stepfather go "down the line"?

As if reading his thoughts, Eve violently kicked a chair at him.

Jack knocked it aside with a clatter.

Her eyes shone wildly. "Not me. Never me. I protected Laura. I protected me."

"Who protected Jeni?"

The masculine was melting away. "I couldn't protect all of us. Someone had to be – "

"Sacrificed," Jack sneered.

Eve stared at him with haunted eyes. The masculine persona was gone.

Jack lowered his voice into soft empathy. "You were just a kid. You did the best you could."

Eve's lips trembled. She slumped over, sobbing.

Jack felt a painful grip on his heart. He wanted to take her in his arms, but he forced himself to remain still as he listened to her story.

"Laura came to me in New York – when I was at NYU. We made it like she ran away. She phoned Vivian – told her she was fine, not coming back, so there'd be no missing person report, no police. She lived with me while I went to school. I told you she has mental problems. I didn't know how serious it was – till…" She shook her head. "Laura got jealous. Not sister jealous – lover jealous. I didn't know what to do – I didn't understand what was going on. A doctor told me it was Obsessive Compulsive Disorder – a love disorder – for me."

Jack gazed at her, unsure.

Eve said, "I swear – my stepfather never touched me."

"When did you find out Laura wasn't your sister?"

Eve stared at him blankly. "Laura's my sister. She's ill but – she's my sister."

Jack gestured for Eve to sit at the kitchen table. He pulled out the missing person reports and photographs of Laura as a child and gave it to Eve to examine.

After several moments, Eve looked up at Jack, shaken. "Laura can't find out. She's too fragile."

"You think she knows?"

Eve shook her head.

Jack said, "Your mother said Laura was dropped off at the girls' home."

"If that's what she said happened – it has to be true."

Jack raised his eyebrows.

"If you're suggesting that mother kidnapped Laura – that's insane." Eve bit her lip. "Vivian gave Jeni a home. She took her in, she didn't steal her."

"Your mother has an interesting way of accumulating children."

Eve said, "Whoever took Laura – that's the person who dropped her at the girls' home. Mother couldn't have known."

"Has it ever occurred to you that Laura killed your stepfather?"

Eve shook her head, emphatic. "Impossible. I know Laura – she's not capable of such a thing."

Jack hesitated. "Are you sure you saved her?"

"You said Jeni was writing a book. Could she have – written – I mean, if she did anything – would she have written it in her book?"

"I haven't read that far," Jack said before he could think better of it.

Eve grabbed his hand. "You have it? You have the book?"

Hating himself for the lie, Jack nodded.

"Thank God," Eve said, relief flooding her face. "If you have it – it's safe. You won't let it out – you would never hurt me – or Laura – now that you know."

Jack watched her, troubled.

"You would never hurt me," she leaned in, gave him a soft lingering kiss.

Determined to resist, Jack didn't respond.

Then he did.

By the time his phone rang with the long-awaited call from Enid, he had already switched it to mute.

CHAPTER SIXTY-NINE

I like whiskey. I always did, and that is why I never drink it.

Robert E. Lee

Bud smiled, trying to look more professional than he felt as he sat in Petunia O'Donnell's off-white living room that was proof positive of a child-free home. "So you have no knowledge about whether or not your husband hired a private investigator?"

Petunia O'Donnell shook her head as she sucked on a lollipop.

Bud couldn't recall the last time anyone had worked him into a schoolboy blush the way Petunia had done in her first three licks. Bud made a show of looking around the room. "Lovely home you have, Mrs. O'Donnell."

"Call me Petunia," she purred.

Bud felt his face get hot. It was the first time that Bud had ever seen Larry's home and he was impressed. Larry was doing well – better than well.

And his wife!

When Petunia opened the door, Bud understood with perfect clarity why Larry was a tortured soul when it came to his wife. Outside of Bunnie, Petunia O'Donnell was the closest thing to perfection he had ever laid eyes on. When she led him into the living room, Bud eyed her swaying figure, envious that Jack had somehow had the wherewithal to get a woman like this.

How in the blazes had Jack, much less Larry, gotten a woman like Petunia O'Donnell?

Petunia turned on him with a smile. "What's this about, Officer?"

"Detective," Bud said, handing her a business card.

She tapped the card on the inside of her wrist, not reading it. "Can I call you Bud?"

Bud nodded. "Do you know a man named Frank Ficus?"

She sat on the couch, curling her legs under her and gesturing for him to sit. "Nada, papa." She unwrapped another lollipop and licked it.

"Does your husband know Frank Ficus?"

"Have you talked to my husband?"

"My partner spoke with him this morning."

"And?"

"Do you know Jack Fox?"

Frowning, she set the lollipop down in a spotless ashtray. "What's this about?"

"This is a murder investigation and – "

"Murder?" She jumped up. "Is Jack…?"

"Frank Ficus was the victim."

She sat down, troubled.

He felt a stab of jealousy when he saw her face reflect concern.

Over Jack?

He said, "What's the nature of your relationship with Jack?"

With a toss of her head, she said defiantly, "Jack was my boyfriend."

"When?"

"When I was married – if that's what you mean."

"Are you involved with him now?"

She picked up the lollipop, tapped it on her lip. "I broke it off with him. At least, I tried to."

"How so?"

"Jack was obsessed with me – wouldn't leave me alone. I told him that my husband and I were trying to work things out. I thought about filing a restraining order but, well, I didn't want to because I thought it might affect his job – him being a detective and all."

"What did he do?"

"He told me he couldn't live without me. Kept raving about how he loved me and how the thought of me being with another man was driving him insane and he was going to kill me and then himself – you know, the usual."

Bud raised his eyebrows.

"I cared about Jack." She sucked her lollipop, eyes drifting toward the window dreamily. "I didn't love him – not like he loved me. With him, it was beyond love – it was like one of those grand passions in a French book, you know? He was desperate and passionate and jealous – he said he'd do anything for me. Have you ever been in love like that?"

"Did you know Jeni Hargrove?"

"Tall blonde, dressed like a stripper?"

Bud flinched, nodding.

Petunia said, "I was in Jack's office when she hired him to find her real mother. I overheard the whole conversation – I mean, if that was her."

Bud pulled a photo from his wallet, showed it to her.

Petunia said, "That's her. The day I saw her – Jack convinced me to come to his office. He wanted to take me to lunch and I would never have gone except he was acting so crazy that I was scared to turn him down."

Bud frowned.

Petunia said, "I wanted to see him, make sure that he was going to be okay. Anyway, she was in the next room and, let me tell you, she was coming on pretty strong, but he shut her down. I was actually sort of hoping he would take her up on her offer so he would leave me alone."

"What offer?"

"She came on to him like a ton of sloppy bricks. She kept saying she was a nursing student – but she was dressed like a hooker."

"When's the last time you talked to Jack?"

"That day. I told him it was all over between us."

"How did he take it?"

"Threatened all sorts of things. He kept saying that if he had enough money – I'd never leave him."

"Money?" Bud said, his pulse quickening. "Did he mention any specific amounts?"

Petunia shook her head, stuck the lollipop back in her mouth. "Are you married?"

Bud nodded, watching her maneuver the lollipop around her mouth.

Petunia said, "What's her name?"

"Bunnie."

"Are you happy?"

Bud stared at her, unsure.

"Marriage is funny," she said, responding like he had answered. "I think we should only get married for three years – a contract for three years – and if you're not happy at the end of three years, you don't renew the contract and you can each go your separate ways. No harm, no foul."

"Doesn't seem fair to the woman. Especially if there were kids."

"Why? Because of some old cliché? The woman gives up the best years of our lives and then the man leaves?"

"That can work both ways."

"I bet you were stone-cold gorgeous when you were younger."

Bud blushed.

"Oh, not that you're not handsome now," Petunia said as she got up and sat next to him. She gently pushed his hair from his face. "I could cut your hair – there, like that." She smiled. "Yes, you are handsome. Quite."

Bud sat frozen as Petunia's fingers tangled deep in his hair. He might as well have been in sixth grade again with Callie May Jones sitting this close and waiting expectantly for him to – do something.

Bud abruptly stood, heading toward the door. "Thank you for your time."

"Don't be a stranger, Bud."

As Bud hurried to his car, a mixture of relief and regret twanged in the pit of his stomach.

CHAPTER SEVENTY

I wonder what fool it was that first invented kissing.

—Jonathan Swift

Enid sat in Eve's closet, hands clamped over her ears. She was torn between laughing hysterically and barfing up a lung.

When Eve had finally come back to her bedroom, the last thing Enid expected was to hear Jack's voice.

Before she knew it, she found herself an unwilling – and horrified – ear-witness to old-people sex.

Why don't old people realize that the only people who should be having sex are teenagers and twenty-year-olds? Maybe an occasional hot thirty-year-old – maybe.

She debated crawling across the wide expanse of Eve's bedroom floor but couldn't bring herself to unclamp her ears.

Finally, the horrible noises had stopped.

Enid eased her hands from her ears and was relieved with the fabulous sound of no sex. She crept to the closet door, determined not to miss any chance to escape.

They were talking and Enid leaned in to listen.

Eve said, "I've been waiting for someone like you."

Enid put a finger in her mouth in a barf-motion.

Jack said, "You don't make love like somebody who's been waiting."

Is that a polite way of calling her a skank?

Eve laughed. "Natural talent. I'm scary that way."

Enid rolled her eyes and looked through the cracked door. The bed was so big and high that she couldn't see them. She eyed the distance between her and the door, estimating her chances of making it without them catching her.

Not good.

Eve said, "You're horrible – at being horrible."

Jack said, "They think I murdered Jeni."

Enid froze, surprised.

Jack said, "And Frank Ficus."

Who's Frank Ficus?

Eve said, "Who's Frank Ficus? Who's 'they'?"

"The police."

"Well, that's silly," Eve said flippantly.

Jack laughed.

Enid frowned, prickling with irritation at how relaxed he sounded.

Eve said, "You have an alibi, right?"

"I was napping."

Enid rolled her eyes in disgust.

She heard kissing sounds, sheets rustling.

She felt panic rise up in her at the thought of them starting up again. She vowed that, no matter what, she had to get out of there. It was getting dark and if she was careful, they would never know she was there.

Heart hammering, she opened the door and crawled into the room. Her plan was to get under the bed and, after that, there was twenty feet and she'd be at the door. If they were going to go at it again, maybe they wouldn't notice the door opening.

Eve said, "You can tell me – did you do it?"

Jack said, "That's a fine question."

Enid inched forward, resisting the urge to go fast. Suspicious sounds were floating down and she felt sick at the thought of getting stuck under the bed during any old-people Olympic sex.

Reaching the bed, Enid rolled over a heap of clothing and almost grunted aloud when she felt the spiked heel of one of Eve's shoes jab her in the ribs.

Eve said, "Have you ever killed anybody?"

Enid edged herself into position to make the final crawl to the door. Luck was with her as the room was getting darker by the minute.

After a loaded silence, Eve laughed, "Forget I asked. It was stupid."

Enid held her breath as she crawled from under the bed and made her way to the door.

The mattress gave a bounce and Jack got out of bed and stepped down – right on the back of Enid's hand.

Enid shrieked in pain and bolted for the door, terrified that they would recognize her. It sounded as if an explosion went off behind her and as she reached for the door, she was jerked backwards. She landed hard on her tailbone and looked up to see Jack staring down at her.

His face was blown up with rage and his hand was clutching a knot of sheets over his crotch.

Enid got an eyeful of naked Eve standing on the bed, eyes glittering like broken glass. She looked like a wild animal ready to rip her to shreds.

"What the...?" Jack yelled. "Are you fucking mental?" Jack grabbed his jeans from the floor and tried to put them on while retaining his grip on the sheets.

His grip on her loosened and Enid made a break for the door. Jack jumped forward and grabbed her so hard that they both slammed to the floor.

Enid gave a violent kick that sent him howling and cursing backwards. She jumped to her feet, jerked the door open and ran.

Her feet caught on a rug at the top of the staircase and, except for grabbing the banister, she would have tumbled down the marble stairs. Enid shot down the stairs and out the front door. She had a flash of the animal eye carvings on the door glaring after her like she was a prey.

CHAPTER SEVENTY-ONE

It belongs to human nature to hate those you have injured.

—Tacitus

Eve said, "She was in here while we – ?"

Still on the floor, Jack looked from the door that Enid had just disappeared through to Eve who was on the bed – naked, gorgeous and – furious.

Jack sat on the floor, flabbergasted.

What just happened?

Jack rubbed his shin. Enid had kicked with ferocity that he found hard to believe came out of ninety-eight pounds of skinny legs and worn Converse sneakers. He shifted his weight, feeling that he was sitting on something. It was a manila envelope with something the size of two matchboxes in it.

Eve leaped from the bed, snatching it from him.

He looked up, confused.

"Get out," she said.

He stared up at her. She had never looked more beautiful. He half-expected her to transform into a panther and devour him.

"Get out!" she screamed.

He jumped to his feet. "You don't think I had anything to do with her being here?"

Eve ran to the fireplace, grabbed a poker and came after him.

Jack reeled backwards, back slamming against the wall as she swung the poker at him. He ducked and the poker wedged into the wall.

She wrenched it free, but before she could swing again, he grabbed her arm, wrestling the poker from her.

She shoved him toward the door, screaming obscenities.

Jack got on the other side of the door and she slammed it behind him, locking it. He stumbled back, stunned. Her curses rang in his mind and he felt dirty and sick. He stepped from the door but was jerked back by the sheet, which was caught. He tried to jerk it free but it only wedged in tighter.

Pissed, he dropped the sheet.

If she ain't worried about embarrassing me, I ain't worried about embarrassing her.

Jack walked down the hallway, descending the staircase like a king born to knock brass nuts to bolts.

The butler, serene as an ice cube, materialized and opened the front door for him, not even batting an eye that Jack was still naked.

"Thanks," Jack said.

Jack winced as his bare feet hit the gravel driveway. Because it was a rental car, he had slipped the key under the mat, which he was relieved to see was still there. He slid into the rental car, adjusting himself carefully on the unforgiving leather seat.

A quarter of a mile down the road, he saw Enid who, hands shoved in her pockets, was trudging up the side of the road.

Jack pulled to a hard stop in front of her.

She froze, like a deer ready to bolt.

Jack popped the trunk from inside the car and said, "Get my jeans and a shirt from the trunk and I'll take you anywhere you want to go – as long as it's a bus stop." Jack had recently purchased some spare clothes and, since his house was gone, he had turned the trunk of the rental car into a mish-mash of clothes and toiletry items.

Her eyes flickered over his bare torso.

Jack watched her in the rearview mirror as she made her way to the trunk and poked around in it.

She approached the window and threw his "nerd pants" at him.

He threw them back, "The jeans, or I leave your ass on this road."

"You don't like it, get them yourself." She threw the pants back at him.

He grabbed them and struggled to pull them on. "What the hell is wrong with you? What the hell were you doing in her fucking closet?"

"You do realize that your girlfriend is – like – with other people, right? You think she's only getting gross with you?"

Jack froze, horrified. "You're a psychotic lying – "

"Don't you wish!"

Jack said, "Prove it. Who then, smart-ass? I want a fucking name or you're a liar."

"Never saw him before in my life."

Jack examined her.

Enid said, "I want to go to Detective Orlean's house."

"So you can hide in his closet?"

"I want to talk to him. I may know something that might be of interest to a real detective."

"Damn it, Enid! I'm not taking you anywhere till you tell me – "

"Take me to the bus station then," Enid said, tears in her eyes.

Jack slammed the car door and went to the trunk to get his jeans. "I don't know what the hell game you're playing, but you'll be lucky if she doesn't call the cops and have you arrested – "

The car gunned forward and Jack got a flash of Enid hunched over the steering wheel. Gravel pelted his legs as he watched his car tear up the road.

"Enid!" He screamed, letting loose a string of curses into the night.

His car had disappeared with Enid and he looked around. No shoes, no shirt – he was alone without a cell phone in rich-people Scottsdale – barefoot and wearing only nerd pants.

The road was empty except for the massive walls that were designed to keep the nerd-pants crazies off their property.

Fuming, he walked gingerly up the road, wincing as the gravel cut into his feet. His only solace was imagining all the horrible things he was going to do and say when he met up with Ms. Enid Iglowski.

And it ain't gonna be pretty.

CHAPTER SEVENTY-TWO

Marriage is like putting your hand into a bag of snakes in the hope of pulling out an eel.

—Leonardo da Vinci

Bud sat at the kitchen table, staring down at the divorce papers. He looked at Bunnie, who was leaning against the sink, watching him with pursed lips.

Bunnie said, "We sell the house, split the money – you go your way, I go mine."

A line from a David Allan Coe song flashed through Bud's mind – when she starts talking about leaving, she's already gone.

How long has she been gone?

He looked down at his hand resting on the paper and saw he was shaking. His heart gave a throb and he felt a stab of fear at the thought of being without Bunnie. "Can't we talk – work this out?"

"I got a Realtor for the house. Movers come tomorrow."

"Movers?"

"I rented an apartment. I'm moving out."

Bud tried to speak but nothing came out.

"I'm sorry, Bud. I have to think about myself. We're not getting any younger. I want to live."

Bud sat a long time, hearing her voice but not comprehending her words. It didn't matter what she said – she was gone. She moved around the kitchen like she had so many times before. She set a glass of water in front of him as her lips relentlessly moved. He watched her face contorting around her words and stared in fascination at the bobbing ponytail cinched up in a pink scrunchie.

She doesn't want me.

"What?" He said, vaguely aware that she had fallen silent and was waiting for a response.

"I'm only asking for half of your pension. I think that's fair."

Fair?

Bud giggled.

Bunnie looked at him, surprised.

Bud clapped his hand over his mouth guiltily. It seemed to Bud like it was the first time she had responded naturally to anything he had said or done since he had come home.

Another giggle escaped.

"What's so funny?" She glared at him, red with anger.

Bud burst into laughter that left him with tears streaming down his face.

"What are you laughing at?" Bunnie yelled.

Bud tried to stop himself but couldn't. He shook with laughter until his sides hurt and Bunnie was purple with rage.

"What's so fucking funny?!" Bunnie screamed.

Shaking with laughter, the words surfaced from somewhere so deep he didn't even know it existed, Bud managed to gasp out, "You – cheating. Me – a detective…"

He howled with laughter, doubling over, unable to control himself. He felt pleasure snake through him in the telling of a bald-faced lie.

Bunnie reeled backwards, bumping to a stop at the sink's edge.

Bud sat up, hiccupping. "I got – a – private detective – follow you."

She stared at him, scared.

Bud hiccupped and said, "He's cheating – on you."

Bunnie glanced at her cell phone on the counter.

"It's finally happened – Bunnie – speechless." Bud wiped his eyes, hiccupping.

Bunnie grabbed her cell phone. "You bastard."

Bud stood, made his way to the front door. He needed to get out. Go someplace – anyplace but here.

Hours later, Bud sat in his office at the station, staring out the window. There was a giant orange moon that hovered to the east over the mountains, gleaming down on the city.

He felt numb, emptier than a tin can.

Tomorrow, strangers would haul their belongings out of the house like wreckage from what was left of his marriage.

She loves somebody else.

For the first time in his life, Bud didn't want to get to the bottom of a mystery. He didn't want to know anything. If Bunnie loved another man – so be it. The hurt that he had expected to feel, that he had been feeling all these weeks – wasn't there. He felt numb, a very lovely kind of numb. His mind flickered back, hovering over the memory of Petunia's lips like a shadow from a cloud passing over the land. He shook his head and leaned back, hand resting lightly on his chest, which had become his new unconscious tic. Bud pressed his hand into his chest, feeling the beating of his heart. He took a deep breath, felt it momentarily slow.

"Detective Orlean?"

Bud spun in his chair and was greeted by the sight of Enid. She was sitting in a chair facing his desk.

"I didn't hear you." Bud sat up straight, clearing his throat. "How long have you been here?"

She bit her lip, eyes troubled.

He frowned. "Chip did take care of you – and your dad picked you up, right?"

"That man I – can you tell me about him?"

Bud shook his head, knowing she was talking about Dennie Dutter.

Enid looked down at her hands, examining the fresh scars. "I keep having the same nightmare. That man – I kill him but he won't die. No matter what I do – he won't die."

"Have you talked to your dad about it?"

Enid took a deep breath, letting it out slowly. "My dad hates me."

Bud opened his mouth to speak but Enid interrupted him. "Does Chip love Ms. Hargrove?"

Bud frowned, unsure.

Enid said, "I think – my dad – is, uh…"

Bud watched her struggle over her words.

"There you are!" Chip charged into the room. "I've been on a wild goose chase looking for you. Where the hell have you been?"

Enid eyes narrowed. "I was in Eve Hargrove's guesthouse."

Chip's jaw dropped, face drained of color.

Bud said to Enid, "What were you doing there? Where's your father?"

"He went for a walk," Enid said.

Bud said, "Have you seen him today?"

"Seen and heard," Enid glanced at Chip, "*lots* of stuff."

Chip groaned, dropped his head into his hands.

Enid said to Chip, "An hour after you left – she was having sex with some other guy."

Bud glared at Chip, "What the hell is this about?"

Chip pointed at Enid. "If anyone has anything to be embarrassed about – it's her."

Bud stood up, hands flat on his desk, "What the hell is going on?"

Chip headed toward the door. "All I wanted to do was shadow you but, no, you have to turn me into a babysitter."

"Babysitter?" Enid shot up, furious. "If anyone here is a baby – it's you."

"Stick a fork in me, I'm done!" Chip left.

Enid ran to the door, shouted down the hall, "Keep chasing that old bag of STD and see if I care!"

Bud went to Enid, guided her to the chair. "What kind of language is that, young lady?"

Enid crossed her arms, tears in her eyes.

The phone rang and, eyes not leaving Enid's face, Bud answered it. His eyebrows shot up in surprise. "I'll be there in twenty minutes."

Bud hung up, gestured for Enid to follow him. "You're coming with me."

"What if I don't want to?"

Bud said, "We can book you for grand theft auto."

Enid grimaced. "I have to go to the bathroom."

"I'll escort you."

"You don't trust me?"

"We're not anywhere you can hijack my car and leave me half-naked on a deserted road so – let's not take any chances."

CHAPTER SEVENTY-THREE

There is nothing so powerful as truth, and often nothing so strange.

—Daniel Webster

"What is this place?" Enid said.

From the driver's seat, Bud said, "One of the few places in town that would let in a half-dressed man with no shoes."

A blue neon sign reading "Nail" decorated a nondescript building surrounded by everything from Mercedes, to Harleys to dust-coated Chevy trucks.

"Wait here," Bud got out and walked to the entrance.

A bare-chested cowboy in leather chaps and a dog collar walked out. Enid's jaw dropped as she saw past him to a bar filled with men decked out in leather, studs and chains.

Jack, dressed in his nerd pants, charged toward the car, his naked chest and feet flashing blue under the neon lights. "What the hell is wrong with you?" Jack pounded on Enid's window. "Do you have any idea of what you've put me through?"

Bud placed a hand on Jack's shoulder.

Jack shot away from Bud's touch. "Back off."

Bud pointed Jack to the front seat. "Remember – "

Jack glared at him, shaking with anger. "No violence."

Bud said to Enid, "He gave his word, you're safe."

Jack said, "For now."

Enid gulped. She was beginning to think that maybe she'd gone a bit too far.

Bud unlocked the door and Jack slid into the front seat, glaring at Enid in the rearview mirror as Bud got behind the wheel.

Jack said to Bud, "Any chance you have a change of clothes on you?"

Bud shook his head. "Where to?"

"His house burnt down," Enid said, trying to be helpful.

Jack shot her a venomous look.

Bud said, "Coffee and clothes – my house. We can talk."

Enid said, "Is Chip there?"

Bud said, "If he's there, he can join the conversation."

Enid slunk down into the seat, feeling nauseous.

Jack said, "You don't want to see Chip? What the hell did you do to him?"

Enid said, "Why do you always assume that all I do is cause trouble?"

Jack said, "Do you have any idea what I had to do to even get them to let me use the phone?"

Enid said, "Ew, you kissed a boy."

Jack said to Bud, "You see what I have to put up with? She's a menace. Since she got here, my whole life has gone up in smoke. Literally! My house is gone – "

"I didn't do that," Enid said.

Jack said, "You couldn't have picked that night to be hiding under the bed with a fire extinguisher, could you?" He hooked his thumb toward Enid. "I'm with my girlfriend – in bed – guess who is crawling around on the floor listening? Who does that shit?"

Bud's eyebrows shot up in surprise.

Enid said, "It was an accident."

"I'll tell you what an accident is – " Jack stopped, fists clenched.

Enid said, "Go ahead and say it – you think I was the accident."

"I didn't say that," Jack said.

"I heard it!"

"I didn't say it so – you didn't hear it." Jack swung around, glaring.

Enid sat forward, shaking with anger, "I heard it clear as day – I don't know how, but I heard it."

Jack turned around.

Enid crossed her arms to try to stop the shaking. He said it in his head and she heard it as distinct as if he'd leaned over and whispered it in her ear. She said, "I didn't ask to get born. You did this to me."

"What did I do to you?"

"Made me. Now here I am. Deal with it."

Jack squeezed the bridge of his nose, grimacing.

Bud said, "My wife is divorcing me."

Jack and Enid looked at him, startled.

Bud said, "I heard some statistic about how high school sweethearts have the lowest divorce rate. She wants to *live*. What does that mean?"

"Sorry to hear that," Jack said.

Bud said, "She's got a boyfriend. I got heart disease."

Enid said, "You mean you have a broken heart?"

Bud sighed, "No, I got the pill-taking, follow up with the cardiologist kind of heart disease that HMO's hate."

Enid said, "Are you going to die?"

"Jesus!" Jack said.

Bud said, "The night is young." He turned to Jack, "Isn't it better she ask than never ask anything?"

"It's not polite," Jack said with a pointed look at Enid.

Bud said, "I think Enid passed impolite miles ago."

"Ya think?" Jack said.

Enid said, "Besides the heart disease that HMO's hate – are you heartbroken? Over your wife, I mean?"

Bud said, "Do you like omelets? I make a mean western omelet – I think I forgot to eat today."

Enid said, "Does Chip know – about the divorce, I mean?"

Bud pulled into his driveway. "Home sweet broken home."

Later, as the three of them sat around the kitchen table, dirty plates cleared and Enid finishing off the last of her orange juice, Enid said, "That was good."

"What do you say?" Jack said.

"I just said it."

Jack said, "How about a thank you?"

Enid made a face. "Thank you."

"You're welcome," Bud said, sitting down with a legal pad. "I want to create a time line."

"What's that?" Enid said.

Bud said, "The three of us know a lot of the same people. I have a hunch that if the three of us combine notes, we might discover something."

"Like putting together a puzzle?" Enid said.

Jack said, "What's your end game, Orlean?"

Bud said, "The bodies are piling up, my friend. If I'm not mistaken, you might be on the hook for one or two of them."

Jack compressed his lips.

Bud said, "If this is going to work – we each need to be completely honest."

Jack said, "I'm in – but the kid can't be here."

"I'm not a kid," Enid said.

Bud said, "She gonna hear anything more shocking than what she already heard – hiding under your bed?"

Jack ran his hands through his hair, sighing. "At least give a man a beer."

Bud shook his head. "No foggy brains."

Jack got up, got a beer out of the fridge, popped the top and took a swig. "Shoot."

Bud said, "Jeni Hargrove."

Jack pulled out his phone, flipped his calendar so Bud could see it. "Here. She hired me to find her real mother. Came to my office."

Bud copied the date.

Enid said, "That's when I met her."

"You were there?" Bud said.

"I was in the waiting room when she went in."

Jack said to Enid, "You lied and pretended like you were with her."

"You assumed I was with her, Mr. Smarty-Pants, and you know what they say about assuming."

Bud said, "We need to stay focused and keep emotions out of this. Can we do that?"

Enid tossed her head, "I can if he can."

Jack said, "Jeni was broke – "

"He wouldn't give her a student discount," Enid said.

"She wasn't a student," Jack said. "She was a stripper."

Enid said, "Duh. But she was also in nursing school. She told me."

"Maybe her application was being processed," Jack said.

Bud said, "This isn't going to work if we pretty up the picture with wishful thinking. Jeni was a stripper at The Candy Store. She had a daughter – Faith."

Enid said, "What happened to Faith?"

"Social Services," Bud said.

"I babysat for her," Enid said wistfully.

Bud said, "How'd you get from pretending to know Jeni at Jack's office to babysitting for her?"

"Oh, uh – "

Jack said, "She got into my office on false pretense and when I called her on it – "

Enid said, "You came after me! What was I supposed to do?"

"She fucking took a bite out of me," Jack said, rolling up his sleeve and showing the scabbed outline of Enid's teeth. "Urgent Care and a tetanus shot."

"You deserved it for scaring the bejeezus out of me," Enid said.

Jack said, "You could have explained why you were there like a normal human being."

Enid said, "Bottom line, I outran you. Not to mention, outwitted you."

Bud held up his hands. "Ladies!"

Enid sighed. "I went to the diner across the street, saw Jeni and asked for a lift. She figured I didn't have any money and said I could stay with her if I babysat."

Bud said, "What about the gun?"

"I got it from my – Henry. My stepdad."

"Got it or stole it?" Jack said.

"Borrowed it," Enid said.

Bud said, "That's the gun the police found in an ice cream box in the kitchen – when they found Jeni. They think it may be linked to a homicide six months ago here in Phoenix."

Enid said, "It can't be involved in anything! I got it from Henry's gun cabinet in Florida."

Bud said, "We're still checking it out."

Jack said to Enid, "The day Jeni was killed – why'd you go to her apartment?"

Enid frowned.

Bud said, "Did Jeni know about the gun in her ice cream?"

Enid shook her head. "Safest place to hide something from a skinny girl."

Jack said, "You went back to her apartment for the gun?"

Enid hesitated.

Bud said to Enid, "You were afraid somebody was after you – like in one of your nightmares?"

Jack glanced at Enid, surprised.

"What?" Enid scowled at Jack, "You think I strangle a new pervert every Tuesday? You'd have a couple of bad dreams too."

Jack frowned, looked away.

Enid said, "So much happened – I'm getting it all confused in my head."

Bud said, "Let's focus on Jeni."

Enid said to Jack, "Did you have sex with her too?"

Jack said, "You got a mind like a sewer."

Enid turned to Bud, "Did *you* have sex with Jeni?"

Bud looked at her, startled. "No."

Enid said to Bud, "You're grilling us, but what about you?"

Bud said, "I met Jeni when I investigated her stepfather's murder. She was a sweet kid, mixed up but, no – I never had relations with her. I'm – *was* – happily married."

"We met Jeni's grandmother," Enid said. She described in overly dramatic detail what happened at the crazy-Christian lady's house.

"Crucifix cookies?" Bud said.

"They weren't that good," Enid said.

Jack said, "The down-low is that Jeni's biological mother was Ann Smith, who worked as a dancer at the same place as Vivian Hargrove, before Viv screwed her way onto the social register. When Ann died in a car wreck – Vivian took the girl in and raised Jeni as her own."

Bud said, "The car wreck was – ?"

Jack said, "Legit. Nothing suspicious. I don't know what else to tell you about Jeni."

"Except somebody wanted her dead," Enid said.

Jack said to Bud, "And you boys in blue think I'm the hit man on her – and Frank Ficus."

Bud said, "Who hired Frank to follow you?"

Jack said, "My money's on Petunia's husband."

"Larry?" Bud said.

Jack looked at Bud, surprised.

Bud said, "I know Larry. I had a conversation with Petunia."

"Who's Petunia?" Enid said.

"Ex-girlfriend," Jack said. "Who has nothing to do with anything."

Bud said, "Your meeting with Jeni at your office –Petunia was there, in the next room. She overheard it all."

Jack's lips tightened.

Bud said, "What if it wasn't Larry who hired Frank to follow you? What if it was somebody else – maybe someone out to set you up for Jeni's murder?"

Jack said, "Or keep tabs on me?"

Bud looked at Enid, "When Jeni was killed – is there anything you can remember? A sound, a smell?"

Enid said, "I heard Jeni come in, her heels. The baby was making noise, nothing weird. Somebody turned on the stereo. Lady Gaga's Bad Romance, I think."

Bud said, "What else? Anything, even the tiniest thing."

Enid said, "I heard voices. I thought it was Jeni talking to the baby."

"Man or woman?" Bud said.

"I don't know." Enid squinched up her eyes. "There was so much blood – and then Jeni." Enid shut her eyes. She opened them and looked at Jack, "The next thing I knew – why were *you* there?"

Jack said, "She left a message – asked me to come over."

Bud said to Jack, "Where were you when you got the message?"

Jack lifted his chin. "With Eve."

Enid made a "gross out" sound.

Jack said, "Well, maybe you wouldn't be so almighty grossed out if you weren't hiding under other people's beds and hearing things you shouldn't be hearing."

"What*ever.*"

Jack leaned forward, "While we're on the subject, why don't you explain exactly what you were doing in Eve's bedroom?"

"We're talking about Jeni," Enid said, "Not me."

Bud said to Enid, "What were you doing there?"

Enid glanced nervously between the two of them. "Well, uh, Chip and me – we were in the car – waiting for you – outside the girls' home and, uh – "

Jack sat bolt upright. "The guy in the guesthouse –was Chip?"

Enid made a face.

Bud leaned back heavily in his chair. "Shit."

Jack turned to Bud, "You knew about this?"

Bud said, "I know – they've met."

Enid said, "Yeah, they met, if by 'met' you mean that their uglies bumped in the night."

Jack stood. "That's impossible."

"The Virgin Mary, she ain't," Enid said.

Jack turned to Enid with blazing eyes, "How the fuck did you end up under her bed?"

Enid stood and the words came rushing out. "She called and he went running, they left me alone there and I needed to go to the bathroom and I ended up in her room and I – I decided to find evidence and expose her for the person she really is and the next thing I know I'm looking out the window and those two are batting around each other's tonsils with their tongues."

Bud said, "You said you were in the guesthouse."

"I was in Eve's bedroom – looking out the window. I needed to find proof that she's a total scum-bucket so Chip would know – "

Jack slapped his hand down on the table.

Enid said, "She came back and locked the door – I hid in the closet so I could sneak out later – when she was asleep."

Jack said, "Sneak being the operative word."

Enid pointed at Jack, "You think I want to hear old people doing it – especially you? I tried to Helen Keller it but you two were louder than a broken blender."

Jack said to Bud, "When we discovered that Enid was lurking underneath the bed – "

"I wasn't lurking – I was investigating."

Jack said, "Eve was upset – so I left."

Enid said, "Ha! She threw you out buck naked."

Jack said, "I stop to help you and you repay me by hijacking my car and leaving me to fend for myself with a group of leather-clad daddies who want to take me home so I could live in a four-by-four box in their Pulp-Fiction cellar."

Enid gave him a thumb's up "no problem" sign. She jumped up, "The evidence! I found an envelope taped up into the fireplace – but I lost it."

Jack said, "I sat on it – right after you kicked my leg from under me. Eve got it back and went ballistic."

"She's so guilty," Enid said.

Jack said, "Of what? Of being freaked out when her boyfriend's daughter is hiding under her bed while we're having sex? Is that your final analysis? Ya think?"

Enid said, "You're not her boyfriend if she just had sex with some other guy."

"Did you *see* them have sex?" Jack said.

"No."

"Then you don't know shit."

Enid jumped up, "That envelope is probably some horrible secret she'd rather die than have anybody find out." Enid turned to Bud, "What if she murdered Jeni because she was jealous of her?"

Jack said, "Just because you can't stand the thought of your wanna-be-boyfriend – who is too old for you – chasing after her – doesn't mean she's a murderer."

Enid glared at him. "You are so sixth-grade."

Bud said to Jack, "I know you're involved with Eve, but if she's innocent, you've got nothing to hide."

Jack said, "I don't care what you think or what she did or didn't do with Chip – I love her – and I don't fucking fall in love with murderers."

A stab of fear shot through Enid.

Jack said to Enid, "She's not what you think she is – you need to give her a chance."

Enid said, "Fairy tales do come true. I've got myself an evil stepmother."

Jack flushed red.

"What's going on?" a voice belted out.

They all looked up.

Bunnie stood in the doorway, hands on hips, glaring. Her black sequin jogging outfit and MBT sneakers made her look dressed up to go K-Mart shopping.

Bud said, "My divorce support group."

Bunnie's eyes lasered in on Jack as she jabbed her finger at him. "Bud hired you to spy on me. That's why you were here that day, you blood-sucking mud-bottom catfish slug."

Jack looked at Bud, who said, "She knows you're the detective I hired to follow her and take photos of her cheating with her new boyfriend."

Jack's eyebrows shot up.

Bud said. "You're also the guy that got photos of my wife's boyfriend – cheating on her."

"Uh-huh," Jack said, nodding.

Bunnie said to Bud, "He said you're a lying sack of shit making it all up to get back at me."

Bud said, "'Cause you wanna live."

"Where's Chip?" Bunnie stepped into the hallway, called up the stairs, "Chip, get your butt down here."

"He's not here," Bud said.

"Oh, I'm here," Chip said from the darkened living room on the other side of the hallway.

Bud jumped up and went to the living room, flipping on the lights.

Everyone followed.

Chip was sprawled across the couch, eyes bleary and a bottle of Jack Daniel's held loosely in one hand.

Bunnie spun on Bud, pointing to Chip, "You did this – you upset our baby!"

"I been in here," Chip said, "writing my very own country song, which, by the way, thank you much, I got enough material for, let's see…" Chip held out his fingers, tried to count on them.

"Chip, honey, you're coming with me," Bunnie said, trying to pry the bottle from him.

Chip said, "Back off, old lady."

Bunnie reeled back. "Chip…!"

"Let me know – what you think," Chip threw back his head and out-of-tune crooned, "Mama cheated on daddy, she got a new man, daddy don't care, my girl, she doing it with – spoiled brats under her bed – with a bag of shit man." He pointed to Enid, "Juvenile delinquent is in lov-lov-lov-oooOOoooOOoVe with meeee." Chip let loose a sloppy burp. "Excuse moi."

"That's enough," Bud said. He stepped forward and took the bottle from Chip.

Chip pointed at Bunnie, "You gots yourself a boyfriend, don't 'cha ma?"

Bunnie glared at Bud. "Fix this." She stormed from the room.

"Don't forget birth control – don't want no little brothers," Chip said as she slammed the front door. He turned to Enid, singing, "Little sister, don't cha' kiss me once or twice, tell me that it's nice and then ruUuuUN…"

Jack stepped forward, fists clenched.

Bud put out his hand, stopping Jack. "Not now – later." Bud tried to pull Chip into a sitting position but stopped, hand on heart. "I can't do this." He sat in a chair.

Jack grabbed Chip, shook him, "What happened with you and Eve? Tell me or I'll bust the teeth right out of you."

"Love her," Chip said.

"Did you have sex?" Jack said.

"Yup," Chip said.

With a curse, Jack threw Chip on the couch. Chip slid off and landed with a thud between the couch and the coffee table and passed out.

Bud shook his head, staring at his son sprawled out on the floor.

Enid sat down and burst into loud sobs.

"What's wrong with you?" Jack said.

Enid dropped her face into her hands, crying bitterly.

After several moments, Jack walked over and patted Enid awkwardly on the shoulder. "He's too old for you."

She shoved his hand away and curled up in the chair, crying until her jaw hurt.

CHAPTER SEVENTY-FOUR

A friend is one who has the same enemies as you have.

–Abraham Lincoln

"I guess I forget what it's like to have a crush at that age," Jack said, taking a pull from his beer. He and Bud sat in the backyard, staring into the starlit night. They had managed to get Enid to bed in Chip's room and they had left Chip sprawled on the living room floor where Bud had turned him on his side and draped a blanket over him.

Bud raised his beer. "Here's to forgetting."

Jack rubbed his eyes, not responding to the toast. He kept visualizing Eve and Chip together, which made him feel like puking – or beating the shit out of Chip.

Bud said, "That's some kid you got there."

Jack gave a short bitter laugh. "Tomorrow, she's on a plane – back to where she came from. The best thing I can do for her is ship her back to Dodge and away from me."

"Movers are coming tomorrow," Bud looked at his watch. "I mean, today."

"Is your – Bunnie – always that mean?"

"Eve Hargrove is such a sweetheart."

Jack flinched.

"Sorry," Bud said.

Jack shrugged.

They sat in silence, nursing their beers.

Jack said, "I saw Eve kissing – her sister."

"What, like, on the cheek?"

"No."

Bud stared at Jack.

Jack shifted, wondering if he would regret telling the story when the beer had been washed away.

Bud said, "Sexual?"

"There was more tongue than a Piggly-Wiggly deli counter."

Bud's jaw dropped. He closed it with a swig of beer.

Jack said. "According to Eve, Laura has mental problems. Claims Laura got diagnosed in New York with love obsession disorder – all of it aimed at Eve. They tried treatments – nothing helped."

"We never turned up anything like that in our investigation."

Jack dug in his back pocket, handed Bud copies of the missing child information with Laura's photo as a little girl.

Bud grabbed the papers and walked under the porch light, where he could get a better look.

Jack said, "From what I can figure – Vivian was a collector – kids."

"Eve was in on it?" Bud muttered to himself.

"She was a just a kid – didn't know shit. She knew her mother adopted Jeni. I don't think she has any idea that Laura isn't her biological sister."

"But she was kissing her?"

"No," Jack said, "*Laura* was kissing *Eve* – not the other way around."

"Are you sure?" Bud said, returning to his seat.

Jack remained silent for a long time. Finally, he said, "I haven't felt this way about a woman in a long time. Never. I can't let go – not yet."

"She's poison."

Jack smiled, remembering the touch of Eve's delicate skin under his rough hands.

Bud said, "She's a bad one to fall for."

"Save it for your kid."

Bud nodded, troubled.

CHAPTER SEVENTY-FIVE

Day and night cannot dwell together.

—Duwamish

In the early morning hours, Enid turned over and pushed her face into Chip's pillow, breathing in the scent he left behind. The night before, she had cracked the window and listened to the low voices of Jack and Bud in the backyard. Unable to make out most of what they were saying, she drifted into a sleep littered with jagged nightmares. When she awoke, her hands hurt from clenching them. She'd been strangling *him* – watching in horror as he sprang back to life every time.

He could not be killed.

Her neck felt clammy on the sheets. She rolled over, feeling the morning air prickle against her skin.

She looked around Chip's room, examining it with hungry eyes.

No.

She stopped herself, turned her eyes away from his bookshelf, miserable.

Why doesn't he like me?

How come I love him so much and he doesn't even like me?

Anger welled up inside her. She jumped out of bed, feeling the urge to destroy everything in the room. She wanted to do something to the room that would match what she felt inside her heart.

She grabbed a trophy from his shelf. The golden boy was swinging a baseball bat – his uncaring face designed to mock Enid Iglowski – reminding her that the golden boy wasn't for a girl like her.

She snapped the statue at the ankles and felt a grim satisfaction as she gazed at the footless golden boy in her hand.

There was a knock on the door.

"Hold on," Enid said, shoving the footless boy into her jean pocket. She set what remained of the trophy on the shelf.

To remember me by...

From behind the door, Jack said, "Movers on their way. We need to get going."

Enid jerked the door open, scowling. "I have girl things I need to do," Enid closed the door in his face and sat on the bed, arms crossed.

Jack said through the door, "Stop putzing around, Enid. We need to go."

"I can't hear you – I'm doing girl things." Enid waited till she heard him go before she gave Chip's room one last look and headed downstairs.

Jack was waiting by the front door for her.

Enid said, "Where's Detective Orlean?"

"Work."

Enid craned her neck, looking in the living room.

"Chip's gone."

Enid gave a haughty toss of her head. "Am I going to get a shower and clean clothes sometime this millennium?"

"You can shower when you get to Florida."

Enid's jaw dropped.

Was he serious?

Jack said, "This isn't working out."

Enid lifted her chin like she didn't care.

A taxi pulled up, followed by a moving truck and Bunnie driving a Honda.

Enid followed Jack to the taxi.

"Sky Harbor," Jack said to the driver, whose face was black as ebony.

Bunnie walked to her house. As she passed the taxi, Bunnie gave Jack the one-finger salute.

"What's Sky Harbor?" Enid said.

The taxi moved forward and Jack said, "I got you a ticket."

"I'm not getting back on that stinking bus," Enid said.

"Airplane ticket."

"What about my stuff?" Enid said.

"I'll ship it to you."

"What about me saying goodbye to Ernie and – everybody?"

"He's your cousin – you'll see him again."

Enid sat brewing in silence. She wanted to ask it but didn't trust her voice to do the job.

What about – us?

"Look," Jack said, "We gave it a try but – "

"You're a lousy stinking father."

Jack's lips tightened, he looked out the window.

Enid said, "What if I don't want to go back?"

"Your mother will pick you up. You can get back to your life – friends, school – "

"It's summer – no school. Second, you may not have noticed but I'm not exactly Ms. Popularity."

"You have friends, right?"

"Scads," Enid said between her teeth.

"I'm sorry, Enid. It – I'm just not dad material."

"No duh."

The taxi driver stared ahead, playing deaf.

Enid leaned forward and said to the taxi driver, "You have kids?"

He ignored her, looked in the rearview mirror at Jack, "Which terminal?"

"Southwest," Jack said.

"Chicken-shits," Enid muttered in disgust.

They drove in silence until the taxi pulled up to the terminal. Enid jumped out and, without a backward glance, marched into the terminal, ignoring Jack's voice as he called to her to slow down. Her stomach rumbled as the smell of cinnamon buns wafted toward her. She hadn't eaten, hadn't showered, was in dirty clothes and her teeth had a film of funk – and he expected her to get on a plane and fly away – never to return.

He hates me.

She stopped, unsure. Jack was by her side, pressing a boarding pass into her hand. She stared ahead, refusing to acknowledge him. She felt his hand on her hair – then he was gone.

Fat tears rolled down Enid's cheeks as she walked blindly forward. People veered around her, their faces registering everything from shock to concern.

I hate him.

I hate everybody.

She turned around, searching for Jack. She felt a need to hurt him. Punch him, kick him – scratch his eyes out of his stupid skull.

I've got nothing to lose.

She bolted after him, barging out of the terminal. She spotted him walking to the taxi that had let them off, the driver leaning against the side, smoking a cigarette.

She ran toward him.

Before she could reach him, Enid saw a hand clap down on Jack's shoulder. She watched as Jack tried to shake it off, then froze.

A gangly middle-aged nerd pushed Jack toward a waiting car. To her surprise, Jack got in the passenger side and slid to the driver's side while the nerd settled into the passenger side.

Enid got within ten feet of the car and she yelled for him to stop, but they drove away.

Enid caught the first three letters of the license JEX, but she couldn't make out the rest of it. She looked up the row of cars and saw the taxi driver waiting.

She ran to the taxi driver who was waiting for Jack to return and said, "Did my dad say he was coming back?"

The driver eyed her impassively.

Enid pointed toward the disappearing car, "He's gone."

The driver reeled off a string of curses in some other language and crushed his cigarette under his heel. He jumped in his taxi and Enid jumped into the back seat as he pulled out with a squeal of tires.

"Watch out!" Enid said as he swerved around a truck, almost hitting it.

He looked at her, startled. "Get out, you little brat!" He slammed on the brakes and stopped in the middle of the road.

"He's getting away!" Enid pointed forward like she could see the car, which she couldn't. "He said you're a filthy foreigner and you should go back to your own country!"

"Motherfucker." The driver's eyes gleamed with fury as he jammed the accelerator with such force that Enid was hurled back against the seat. Within moments, he merged so hard onto the highway that Enid was hurtled to the floor.

Enid crawled off the floor and put on her seat belt. "There's a reward for his capture. He's a wanted man."

"*Jimakplon.* He is the son of his father – like an animal. "

"That's what his parole officer said," Enid said.

The driver pulled a huge machete from under his seat and set it on the dashboard.

"Holy shit!" Enid said. "I made it up! I lied! He's not dangerous – he's just stupid. Stop the car! Let me out!"

They both caught sight of the car that Jack was travelling in at the same moment.

"Let me out!" Enid screamed.

The taxi driver said, "He is impolite!"

"I'm gonna puke," Enid groaned, clamping her hand over her mouth.

Enid wished with all her might she stayed at the airport. She eyed the huge machete that the taxi driver had in a knuckled grip and watched in horror as they caught up with Jack's car.

CHAPTER SEVENTY-SIX

One does not get to know that one exists until one rediscovers oneself in others.

—Johann Wolfgang von Goethe

Jack stuck his eye to the hole where the back brake light had been and saw only the blur of highway. He'd felt safer behind the wheel with a gun aimed at him than he did stuffed in the trunk of a car.

At the airport, Larry O'Donnell had shoved a gun into his side and told him to get in the car and drive. Within a couple of miles, Larry had forced Jack to pull over to a deserted parking lot and made him get in the trunk where the only witness was a mangy dog.

Damn Petunia!

She either flapped her gums to get Larry jealous or Frank Ficus had reported back to Larry before he kicked the bucket. Either way, the cat was out of the bag and the bag was in the river – and the bag was loaded down with one angry cat scratching at a heavy-ass brick.

Jack had tried to talk to Larry but he wasn't having it. Larry's eyes were bloodshot and his gun hand had the tremor of somebody who wanted a drink – and bad.

From inside the trunk, Jack kicked the back of the back seat, yelling, "Pull over, Larry – before this goes any further."

Nothing.

Jack lay silent, thinking.

He sure as hell didn't want to be buried in this asshole's backyard under a slab of concrete. He had just found Eve and he wasn't about to check out now. He couldn't stand the thought of letting Eve go – even in death. Another person would disappear from Eve's life – and he'd be dead. Jack pictured Larry smoking ribs and dogs on the barbecue that Larry would build on top of the concrete slab that would hide *his* body until nobody cared – or remembered.

Enid.

The last memory she'd have of her father would be him dropping her off at the airport with a swift kick in the butt and a "so long and see you later."

How will that be any different from what my dad did to me?

He failed Enid.

Disgust and shame flooded through him. Jack felt a moment of panic and then – rage. He balled himself up and slammed his feet into the trunk wall.

He let out a primal scream that went on till his lungs were empty and his throat hurt.

The car swerved.

Jack dug into his pocket, pulled out his switchblade and hacked into the back seat.

Larry might shoot him but Larry was going to have to do it on Jack's terms. If Larry had a plan of how this was going to go – Jack was determined to fuck it up beyond all recognition.

Jack howled and screamed every obscenity he could think of as he hacked at the back seat. "I'm coming to get you, motherfucker!"

The car swerved – then steadied.

Why hadn't his dad fought for him?

Jack stabbed repeatedly, feeling the fabric give way beneath his knife. Jack screamed threats until he was breathless and slathering.

The car hit what felt like a dirt road so violently that Jack was flung into the front of the trunk where he hit his head and saw stars. After what seemed like a long time, the car stopped and Jack lay still, clenching the switchblade.

The trunk popped open, revealing a slit of light. Jack blinked, trying to adjust his eyes. After a few moments, Jack used his foot to nudge the trunk open.

Blue skies.

Steeling himself, Jack gripped the switchblade so that it was hidden behind his leg. He began climbing out of the trunk.

"Stop!"

Jack froze, anticipating the gunshot that was going to rip through him.

"You got me wrong," Larry said, voice quavering.

Larry stood twenty feet from the car, his gun aimed at Jack.

They were on a dirt road in the middle of nowhere with desert stretching for miles.

Larry looked like he was on the verge of wetting his pants.

Jack stretched his face into his best psychopath smile –like he was having the fucking time of his life.

Larry gasped like he'd seen the devil.

They stared at each other. Larry's eyes wide with fear and Jack's – a killer.

With a jerky movement, Larry turned and ran.

Jack watched in astonishment as Larry ran pell-mell down the long stretch of empty road.

Jack shouted, "Throw me the keys, asshole!"

Without looking, Larry hurled the keys behind him.

Jack climbed out of the trunk, and headed for where Larry had thrown the keys. It took some searching but he found them and headed back to the car.

Jack kept an eye on Larry till he was a speck disappearing into the desert.

Once in the car, Jack gripped the wheel and looked at the broad expanse of desert. Arizona never looked more beautiful.

I'm alive.

And I want to stay that way.

Jack started the engine and headed up the road, thinking.

Two hours later, Jack stood behind the door in Larry and Petunia's bedroom. He'd parked the car on an out-of-the-way street and gotten in using Larry's garage door opener that was in the car.

It was a long time till Larry came home. Jack listened to Larry climbing the stairs.

Jack stayed behind the door as Larry staggered in and collapsed on the king-sized bed covered with a floral comforter.

Jack shut the door.

Larry sprang from the bed. "Oh Jesus – !"

Jack hurled Larry against the wall, pinning him there with his hand pressed over his mouth. "Shut up, fuckhead."

Larry's terrified eyes darted around the room.

Jack pressed his arm into his throat, not enough to cut off his oxygen but enough to get his attention.

"Petunia – " Larry said, voice hoarse.

Jack eased the pressure on his throat. "Did you hire Frank Ficus to follow me?"

"What kind of man tries to break up a marriage? What kind of animal are you?"

"Frank Ficus – !"

"I don't care if you do kill me. Make a lousy joke out of me – I deserve what I get for letting a pig like you – "

Jack shoved him against the wall so hard that he felt his own teeth rattle.

"You're nothing!" Larry screamed.

Larry shoved forward, throwing Jack off balance and threw a punch that Jack easily dodged.

As the punch landed harmlessly in the air, Jack felt a stab of guilt.

I deserve it.

Breathing hard, Jack backed up, surprised at the guilt he felt.

Larry slipped to the floor, racked with sobs.

Jack stood a moment, unsure. "Petunia got with me – to get your attention."

Larry looked up with wet, questioning eyes.

Jack said, "I said something once – she got mad – said you were more of a man than anyone she knew – more than me."

"You wrecked my marriage."

"Frank Ficus – did you hire him?"

With a violent motion, Larry spit in Jack's face.

Jack dragged Larry off the floor and slugged him in the gut.

Larry doubled over, sunk to the floor, gasping for air.

Jack rubbed his aching fist, hating himself.

"Pig," Larry said.

Jack stood for a moment, then turned to leave.

Jack drove aimlessly until he passed Warren Hibbitt's bar. It was a dive on Seventh Street called 'Do Drop Inn' – except it wasn't an Inn. It was barely a shack.

The down-on-their-luck clientele hung over various drinks. A sixty-year-old woman dressed like she was twenty stared at Jack from the end of the bar.

Jack sat at the bar and nodded to Warren Hibbitt, who was the sole bartender. "Bourbon."

"Ran short," Warren said. "I'll send you a check – next week...?" It was more a question than a statement of fact.

Jack shrugged, figuring that "one week" meant maybe never.

Warren set up a beer for a construction worker three stools down.

"How're things going?" Jack said, eyeing Warren.

Warren frowned. "Good. Things going good."

"You got things straight?" Jack said, desperately wanting to hear that everything was good with Warren and his cheating wife.

Warren shrugged, a wary look in his eyes.

Jack leaned forward, so only Warren could hear him. "You and your wife – are you back together?"

Warren's face twisted, a dead giveaway. Warren abruptly turned, busying himself with other customers.

Jack finished his drink. Somehow, he was equating Warren and his cheating wife with Larry and Petunia. Maybe if Warren had managed to get things straight with his wife – maybe what Jack had done – could be undone...?

Fairy tales.

Jack thought about Larry and Petunia. Funny, he had never really thought about them together as a couple. Jack had never visualized Petunia with anyone but him, which was nuts because the first time he had seen her – she was with another man.

Petunia had told Jack that she and her husband had an understanding. She had saidthat Larry understood that he was a wet rag in bed.

No excuse for what I did.

Jack pinched the bridge of his nose between his fingers – trying to rid himself of the terrible sensation of feeling alone and –

Ashamed.

CHAPTER SEVENTY-SEVEN

A woman's guess is much more accurate than a man's certainty.

—Rudyard Kipling

Bud spotted Enid sitting in the open door of the backseat of a police car on the side of the I-10. A police officer was sitting in the squad car writing his report, the wrecked taxi was in the ditch and the ambulance was pulling out as Bud pulled up.

Enid jumped up and ran toward his car. "What took you so long?"

"What happened?" Bud said. "Why'd you tell them to call me – instead of your dad?"

Enid frowned, pushed back her hair.

Bud walked to the squad car with Enid following him. He hooked his thumb at the wrecked taxi and said to Enid, "You were in that? Are you all right?"

Enid said, "The ambulance people checked me out. They said it was a miracle I wasn't dead."

"They should have taken you to the hospital," Bud said.

Officer Roundhouse looked up and nodded toward Enid, "They cleared her."

Enid said, "They said I'm not in shock."

Bud nodded to the wrecked car, "What about the other guy?"

"Fell on his machete," Officer Roundhouse said.

Enid said, "I didn't push him. He fell on it."

"Machete?" Bud said, catching Enid's overly innocent face. "The driver just happened to drive off the road and fall on his machete?"

"It wasn't my machete," Enid said.

Officer Roundhouse said, "He'll live. He's missing an ear though. The EMT's weren't quite sure how he got his ear torn off during the crash. The taxi driver claims – she bit him."

Enid said, "I found his ear and gave it to the ambulance people so they can try to sew it back on."

"Lovely," Bud said.

"She's all yours," Officer Roundhouse nodded at Enid.

"Thanks," Bud said, stepping away as he drove off. Bud turned to Enid, "You bit the taxi driver's ear off?"

"I didn't bite it. I accidently *hurt* his ear and it tore off. There is a difference."

Bud sighed.

Enid said, "You have to help Jack. I was standing there and saw some guy kidnap him."

"Did you tell the police?"

"You're the police and I'm telling you," Enid said.

Bud said, "Tell me what happened. Be honest and don't leave anything out."

As Enid told what happened, Bud's dream flashed through his mind. Enid in the red dress pointing to the volcano behind him that was going to destroy the world.

Enid said, "Didn't you hear me? He's been kidnapped. I got the first three letters of the license – JEX. Can't you run a check or something?"

"Why did the taxi driver pull out a machete? And why was he chasing the other car?"

Enid shrugged. "I don't know."

Bud gave her a look.

Enid made a disparaging sound. "I may have led him to believe that Jack was trying to not pay him."

"Did you stab the taxi driver with the machete?"

"I wouldn't call it stab. More like – accidently poked."

"You accidently poked him – with a machete? What about his ear?"

Enid hesitated and pulled out Chip's golden boy statue from her pocket. "It was the only weapon I had so I poked it in his ear and then grabbed his ear and when the car went off the road – I held on and his head went – " Enid waved her hand in the air. "That way."

Bud stared at the golden boy. "That looks familiar."

Enid pocketed it. "JEX – aren't you going to look it up?"

Bud handed her his phone, "Call your dad."

Enid called and left a message.

Bud led her back to his car. "I'm sure Jack is fine. What time was your flight?"

"It's gone."

"Is your mother expecting you?"

"Probably. Jack arranged everything – to get rid of me."

"Call your mom – tell her you missed your flight. I'll take you to your uncle's house. You and your dad can work everything out later."

"I'm done with that scumbag. And I'm not going back to Florida. I'm going to stay here and get a job."

"You're not old enough."

"I'll run away."

"You already ran away. Now you're running away from running away? Isn't it time to face your problems? You're not a kid anymore."

Enid glanced at him in surprise. "That's right – I'm not a kid."

"You hungry?"

"Big-time." Enid sighed. "I think I stink."

"You're not a bad kid – you don't stink."

"No, I mean I need a shower. I stink."

Bud took her to 'America's Taco' on Seventh Avenue where they found a place in the shade and ate carne asada tacos.

Enid said, "You gonna catch whoever killed Jeni?"

"Gonna try," Bud said, mouth full.

"I think Eve did it," Enid said.

"You don't like her?"

"You think she did it, don't you?"

Bud smiled. "Guilty."

Enid said, "Can't we do a sting or something? Like in the movies?"

Bud's cell rang. He answered it and listened with widening eyes. He stood up, alarmed. "Don't do anything. I'll be there in fifteen minutes – hang on." He hung up.

"What's going on?" Enid said.

"I'll have someone pick you up and take you back to your uncle's."

Enid started to protest but Bud interrupted. "Wait here. You run away, I'll ship you back to Florida myself."

Bud bounded to his car, Larry's voice ringing in his ears as he threatened to blow his brains out.

CHAPTER SEVENTY-EIGHT

Always do what you are afraid to do.

–*Ralph Waldo Emerson*

Despite the fact that Enid had vowed to hate Chip for all eternity, she secretly hoped that he would be the one picking her up.

After all, I can hate him in person, right?

Aunt Cheryl picked her up and Enid found herself scrubbed and deposited safely in her Aunt Cheryl's house in record time. At the kitchen table, Sharon and Ernie stared at Enid with admiring eyes as their mother fed them grilled cheese sandwiches.

Ernie said to Enid, "Mom says she's going to put a LoJack on your butt."

Enid said to Cheryl, "They still don't know where Jack is – what if he's dead?"

Cheryl said, "Your father always lands on his feet. I left a message for Sam to invite him to dinner – you'll see him tonight."

Sharon said to her mom, "But you always say someday Uncle Jack's luck is going to run out."

Cheryl said, "You're all staying in the house until your father gets home – no arguments." She checked to make sure the back door was locked, and headed to the laundry room.

Enid told Ernie and Sharon her story – leaving out the part about Chip not being in love with her.

Ernie said, "Detective Orlean didn't want to do a sting, but we can do it. We can call Eve and tell her we have a copy of whatever was in the envelope that you got out of her chimney – then we go over and spy on her."

Sharon said, "We're not allowed to leave the house."

Enid said, "We can borrow your mom's car and have it back before she knows it's gone."

Ernie laughed. "Yeah, right."

Sharon said, "I'm not going to Juvenile Detention – you know what they do to cops' kids in there?"

Enid said, "Does your mom's phone have that Caller ID blocking thing?"

"Sure," Ernie said. "Doesn't everybody?"

After ten minutes of discussion, Ernie got his mother's phone from her purse and they retreated to Sharon's bedroom.

"All right, Enid," Sharon said, handing her the phone, "Just like we practiced."

Enid took a deep breath. She punched in the numbers and, too quick, Eve's buttery voice said, "Hello?"

Disguising her voice, Enid said, "We have a copy of what's in the envelope – proof that you're a murderer."

Silence.

Unnerved, Enid hung up and they all burst into hysterical laughter.

The phone rang.

They froze.

Enid looked at the phone – it was Eve.

They all jumped up, babbling in terror.

"What is going on?" Aunt Cheryl said as she headed for the ringing phone.

Enid grabbed the phone and, panicking, snapped it in half.

Cheryl snatched the broken phone from her, staring at her in disbelief. "What is wrong with you? Why – ?"

"I'm sorry!" Enid said.

"Your father is going to hear about this!" Cheryl jabbed her finger at her. "You're grounded. You're not leaving this room till your father gets here."

Enid watched as Cheryl herded Sharon and Ernie from the room, wondering exactly how much trouble she was going to get into for stealing her Aunt Cheryl's car.

CHAPTER SEVENTY-NINE

Men in general are quick to believe that which they wish to be true.

—Julius Caesar

Still feeling the effects of the drinks he'd had at Warren's bar, Jack pulled into his parking space at the office.

He'd been surprised at the happiness he'd felt when Eve called him. His happiness had turned to concern when he heard her voice.

She was crying – damned near hysterical. All he could get out of her was that she wanted to meet him at his office.

Rachel was gone for the day. In the doorway of his private office, Jack stopped until his eyes got accustomed to the dark. In the shadows that fell across the couch he saw the outline of Eve's body.

When she stood and stepped out of the shadows, the streetlights through the blinds illuminated her face. Her lip was busted and her left eye swollen a dusky purple.

Jack sprang forward, grabbing her by the shoulders. "Who did this?"

She buried her face in his shoulder, sobbing.

Jack's arms encircled her protectively, hungrily.

"I had to see you," Eve said, trembling.

"I love you," Jack said, feeling like the words had been ripped from somewhere deep inside.

Their eyes met.

Eve said, "Let's go away. Anywhere – together – away from all this."

Jack gently touched her lip. "I'll kill the bastard."

"It's not what you think," she said. The story spilled out of her and, at the end, she looked at him with scared eyes. "Did I do the right thing?"

Jack's arms tightened around her. "You realize what this means?"

"I'll do whatever you say," she said.

"Have you told me everything?"

Eve's lip quivered.

Jack said, "I can't help you unless you tell me everything."

Eve opened her hand, which had been clenched. In her palm lay an amber ring. "It's my stepfather's," she said, "the one he was wearing when he was killed."

"Where'd you get it?" Jack said.

"Laura's house," she said, bursting into tears.

They sped toward Laura's house, Jack driving, trying to keep his mind clear. Eve sat in the passenger seat, face strained.

Jack said, "Tell me again. Don't leave anything out."

"I called Laura this morning – I wanted to talk to her." Eve gave Jack a look, "I was so angry – about your daughter – "

Jack gripped the wheel, too ashamed to tell Eve that he'd sent Enid away.

Eve said, "I went to Laura's house. She wasn't there but I have the key so I let myself in. I know I shouldn't have but – I snooped."

"What were you looking for?"

"After Jeni died – Laura had been acting so strange. I didn't tell her about you and me – I didn't want to. I was afraid."

Jack reached out, took her hand.

Eve said, "She had a silver and turquoise case I gave her – I hadn't seen it in years. She told me she lost it, but it was on her dresser – like she wanted me to find it." Eve turned to him, tears in her eyes. "Promise you won't hurt her – she needs help."

"We'll help her. I promise."

"Laura came in when I was holding Daniel's ring and she went crazy. That's when she attacked me – told me that if I told anyone, she would kill me." Eve shuddered. "She killed them both – Daniel and Jeni."

Jack reached over, gently brushing back a lock of hair that had fallen over her face.

"I've never seen her like that," Eve said in a small voice.

Jack made the turn onto Laura's street.

Eve tensed, staring at the house. "I can't go back in there."

Jack parked.

"She's dangerous. She threatened to kill me if I told anyone. Be careful – for me." Eve leaned over and kissed him.

Jack twined a strand of her hair in his fingers and gently tugged it. "Stay here till I get back."

Eve nodded and handed him the key.

The neighborhood was quiet as Jack walked to the house. He slipped the key into the lock and entered the house. He stood, listening.

Silence.

Jack made his way stealthily through the downstairs, determining that it was empty before he went upstairs. Laura's bedroom was where she had attacked Eve, and a broken lamp and the contents of a nightstand were strewn across the floor.

On the dresser, an envelope that was partially hidden under a handkerchief had "Eve" scrawled on it. Jack tore the envelope open and read:

Dearest Eve,

I hate myself. I hate you for knowing what I've done. I can't look at you – I can't look at myself – I have nothing left to live for. I didn't mean to hurt anybody. No matter what happens – from the bottom of my soul and everything I've ever been or was or wanted to be – I love you.

Laura.

Jack stared at the words.

She did it.

Jack's knees buckled and he sat on the bed, relief flooding over him. He loved Eve but he hadn't been able to shake the image of her face as she came after him with the poker, swinging to bash in his skull. Deep down, he'd thought she was playing him for a chump – maybe even been the killer.

He gripped the letter between his fingers. This was the proof that Eve was innocent.

Or was it?

His eyes settled on the handkerchief, which looked lumpy.

He went to the dresser and opened it. A shriveled and aged severed man's finger rolled out. The ring had left an indentation that was unmistakable.

It was Daniel's finger.

Grimacing, he used the handkerchief and put it in the envelope and rolled it up tightly before putting in his pants pocket.

He thought for a moment and pulled out his new cell phone that he had recently bought and sent a text.

Jack returned to the car and, in answer to Eve's inquiries, he handed her the letter.

Eve read it, her face draining of color.

Jack said, "If she were going to kill herself – where would Laura go?"

Eve read the letter again with growing horror.

Jack grabbed her shoulder, "Where would she go?"

"I don't know. How could I possibly –?" Eve gasped, "Our mountain. Camelback."

Jack typed another text.

"What are you doing?" Eve said, "We have to go!" She reached for his phone as Jack hit "send."

She grabbed the phone and read the message. She looked at him, eyes glinting angrily.

"We may need help," Jack said as he started the car and headed toward Camelback Mountain.

The glint in her eyes gave him the strange sensation that he was a kid back at the zoo – with no bars between him and the panther.

CHAPTER EIGHTY

Being Irish, he had an abiding sense of tragedy, which sustained him through temporary periods of joy.

—William Butler

Bud had met Larry at a Circle K convenience store near his house, where they sat in Bud's car as Larry told his story.

Larry had gotten an anonymous call from a woman who told him that the detective, Jack Fox, was banging his wife, and their affair had never stopped. She told him where Jack could be found and hung up. Larry had tried to call back but there was no answer. Petunia had been in the kitchen drinking coffee and reading a magazine and, as Larry tearfully told Bud, he stormed into the kitchen and would have beaten her half to death but she pulled a knife on him.

"You hit her?" Bud said, taken aback.

"No," Larry said, "But, if she hadn't pulled that butcher knife on me, I think I would have – I felt I could have – "

Bud stifled a smile.

Larry told of how he drove to the airport and found Jack. How he asked him to take a drive with him so they could talk.

Bud listened as Larry described how Jack had attacked him, commandeered his car and dumped him in the middle of nowhere.

Bud said, "Jack hijacked your car? Did he have a weapon – did he hit you? How exactly did that happen?"

Larry said, "He dumped me in the middle of the desert and I hitchhiked and when I finally got home – the maniac was there and waiting for me – he fucking tried to kill me!"

Bud frowned.

Larry said, "I'm filing for divorce tomorrow. This time I'm for real."

Bud nodded. He put his hand to his chest, feeling his heartbeat as his thoughts flitting back to Bunnie.

Larry said, "Are you okay?"

"You're not going to kill yourself?" Bud gave him a searching glance. When he had been at the taco place with Enid, Larry had called him and threatened to kill himself.

Larry said, "I'm sorry. I lost it but I'm okay now. What about you?" Larry said, glancing at Bud's hand resting on his chest.

Bud glanced down, grimaced. "It's turning into a habit. Checking my heartbeat – like that would make any difference."

They sat in silence for several minutes.

Bud said, "I don't think you should be alone. Is there any chance you're going to drink?"

Larry stared glumly at his hands wrapped around the Circle K coffee that Bud bought him. "I thought that bastard was going to kill me."

"Well, he didn't," Bud said.

"I don't want to go back home. She'll be there."

Bud said, "You can stay with me tonight. Until you feel better."

Larry smiled bitterly, "That may be never."

Bud's phone vibrated.

It was a text from Jack that read: Laura Hargrove – written confession to murder. Also suicide note – am going to find her.

"Jesus," Bud said.

"What?" Larry said.

Bud called Jack and cursed when there was no answer. He turned to Larry, "I've got a work emergency."

"No problem – go." Larry got out of the car, shutting the door.

Bud sent a text to Jack: Where are you?

Bud waited for several minutes. He typed in another text: Urgent. Call me.

Larry got back in the car. "I was wrong. I can't be alone. I won't get in your way – I just can't be alone right now."

Bud made a face. Larry didn't know that Bud knew Jack, and Bud wanted to keep it that way, which was going to be difficult with Larry riding shotgun.

Bud gave a fake smile and said, "Sure. Just headed to the office."

Bud headed downtown, thinking of how to get rid of Larry – without Larry going off on a bender.

Bud's phone beeped. It read: Camelback Mountain.

Bud did a U-turn and said, "Larry, we need to talk."

CHAPTER EIGHTY-ONE

I have no pretensions whatever to that kind of elegance which consists in tormenting a respectable man.

—Jane Austen

Enid watched as Chip pulled up to the curb where she was standing. She hadn't been able to talk Sharon and Ernie into "borrowing" their mother's car, but she had been able to convince them to sneak out of the house. She had called Chip and told him that she'd twisted her ankle running away from a mugger and was stranded on the side of the road. When he'd been skeptical and questioned her story, she had started crying and pretended like her cell battery went dead.

Before Chip could get out of the car, Enid opened the passenger side door and waved for Sharon and Ernie to come out of their hiding places. They bounded forward from behind a row of bushes and climbed into the back seat.

"What the hell, Enid?" Chip said, "I thought you were hurt?"

"Sorry, Chip," Enid said, "it was the only way I could get you here fast and I need your help."

"Jesus Christ, Enid! You made it sound like you were half-dead. I was in the middle of something – "

Enid waved her hand as she introduced everyone. "Chip, Ernie. Ernie, Chip. Sharon, this is Chip. Chip, Sharon."

"Hell no," Chip said. "You can all get out and go home because I'm not taking you anywhere."

Enid said, "We need you to drive us to Eve's house."

Chip stared at her, astonished. "I'll drive you to where your meds are – how long has it been since you've been off them?"

Enid said, "I saw a man kidnap Jack right off the street! What if she kills him?"

"Jack gets into a car with a man and you assume that Eve has something to do with it?"

"If you don't drive us there, I'm going to tell your dad that you took it out."

"*What* out?" Chip said.

Enid gave his crotch a knowing look.

Chip gasped. "You're psycho! You are a fucking sociopath evil – "

Enid said, "Cut the melodramatics and drive me to Eve's house."

"You're jealous. That's what this is about." Chip flipped open his cell and dialed.

"Who are you calling?" Enid said, frowning.

Chip said into the phone, "Hey Dad, Enid is trying to blackmail me into driving her to Eve's house so she can play Nancy-Numbskull-Drew."

"Traitor," Enid said.

Chip listened to the phone and then froze, stunned.

Suspicious, Enid watched his face.

Chip said, "Yeah, sure." He hung up.

"What?" Enid said.

Chip looked at her, wonderingly. "Eve's sister – Laura – confessed to murder. She confessed to two murders – her stepfather and her sister."

"It's a trick," Enid said.

Chip said, "She left a note – a confession. And a goodbye."

Enid said, "She skipped town?"

"Suicide."

"She killed herself?" Enid said with a gasp.

Chip shook his head, unsure. "Dad says Jack says – "

"Jack?" Enid exclaimed. "He's alive?"

Chip said, "He's with Eve – they're driving to Camelback Mountain to try to stop her."

"Come on!" Enid said, pointing at the road. "What are we waiting for?"

Chip said, "*We* are not going anywhere. I'm taking you back to whever you came from. The world does not revolve around – "

Enid grabbed his car keys from the ignition and threw them out the window.

"What the fuck!" Chip said. "If you weren't a girl – !" Furious, Chip got out of the car and made his way to the area where Enid threw the keys.

Enid rolled up the windows and locked the doors, sliding over to the driver's seat. She turned to Ernie and Sharon and held up Chip's car keys that she had palmed when she pretended to throw them out of the car.

"Holy crap," Ernie said, scared.

Sharon said, "We'll get in trouble!"

Enid revved the engine and, as Chip ran back to the car, screaming curses, Enid flipped him the bird.

Enid pulled out with a screech of tires.

Sharon started crying. "Let me out!"

Enid said, "You can blame it all on me. Tell your mom I forced you into it, so stop blubbering."

"We're in so much trouble," Sharon said, looking back as Chip disappeared from sight.

Enid gave one last glance in the rearview mirror but Chip was already out of sight. She frowned as she said, "Where's Camelback Mountain?"

CHAPTER EIGHTY-TWO

I am the punishment of God…
If you had not committed great sins, God would not have sent a punishment like me
upon you.

—Genghis Khan

As Jack paused at the entrance to the hidden path that led to the cliff, he had a free-fall feeling of tumbling down the rabbit hole. He stripped off his shirt and tied it to the brush, revealing the entrance that otherwise would be unnoticeable.

Jack had led the way up the trail but Eve had surprised him by pushing ahead and plunging into the brush of the hidden entrance without him.

In his undershirt, he edged his way forward. Thorns pricked his skin and drew blood. He was glad he'd sent the text message to Bud. He couldn't shake the sensation of being in way over his head.

With a jolt, Jack realized that if Bud came after him, there was no way he'd make it up the trail. He'd forgotten about Bud's heart.

It'll kill him.

Jack checked his cell but there was no signal. Cursing, he pushed his way forward, hoping that Bud wouldn't attempt the climb up the steep trail. He couldn't turn back now – he had to help Eve.

Jack heard Eve's voice as he pushed his way through the last of the brambles. He stumbled out of the trail and onto the packed earth of the cliff.

Eve stood twelve feet in front of him, her back toward him as she faced Laura, who stood on the edge of the cliff.

Laura's desperate eyes were locked on Eve, who was walking toward her with outstretched hands.

Laura made a movement toward the cliff.

Jack lunged forward, "No!"

Laura froze, looking at Jack with bewildered eyes.

Jack reached Eve's side as he said, "This isn't the answer, Laura. We'll help you – "

The wind caught Laura's hair, whipped it around her face.

Laura said to Eve, "Did you tell him?"

Jack gestured for Eve to stay where she was as he slowly walked to Laura. "We can talk this through. I promise we'll do everything in our power to help you through this."

Scowling, Laura made a movement away from him.

Jack stopped. "Laura – no."

Laura looked past Jack at Eve, and gasped in shock.

Feeling his opportunity, Jack bounded forward and yanked Laura from the edge. As he reeled them backwards, his heel caught on a root and they hit the dirt. Never letting her from his grasp, Jack rolled over and pinned Laura to the ground.

Relief washed over Jack. He looked up, his eyes seeking Eve.

Eve stood over them, pointing a Magnum revolver at his head.

"Get up," Eve said.

Jack released Laura and got to his feet, his eyes never leaving Eve's face.

Laura scrambled to her feet, "Eve – "

"Shut up," Eve said.

"What are you doing?" Laura said in a quavering voice.

Eve gestured to the cliff's edge with her gun, "Jack tried to save you. You struggled. You both died."

Jack said, "With bullet holes? I don't think so."

Laura gazed at Eve, "I thought you loved me."

"I do love you," Eve said.

Laura smiled, relief springing to her eyes.

Eve said, "Not enough."

Laura stared at her in horror.

Eve pointed the gun at Laura. "You can go over the edge yourself – or I'll make you wish you did."

Jack stepped in front of Laura, shielding her.

"It was you," Laura said to Eve, "You killed Jeni."

Eve smiled contemptuously.

Jack said, "and Daniel."

Laura clung to Jack's arm, tears running down her face.

Jack laughed.

They looked at him, startled.

Jack said to Eve, "It was you."

Eve jerked her chin toward the cliff and said, "You're going over that edge, Jack."

Jack said, "It was you all along – Daniel was fucking *you*."

Eve paled, gripping the gun so that her knuckles looked like bones.

Jack's voice was softly taunting. "Little Miss Perfect is not so perfect. Dirty girl – getting it on with daddy."

Eve stepped forward, spitting with fury. "Liar!"

Jack grinned. "Dirty girl."

Eve's face was a twisted mask of rage. She was on the verge of lunging forward when she stopped. Her face went cold and she backed away.

Jack's heart sank. He needed her to come closer – only a little closer – so he could make his move and get the gun from her.

Eve was retreating, a mean, unforgiving glint in her eyes.

She raised the gun and he saw her finger press down and he saw his mother, father, grandmother – like a chain – moving down until all he saw was Enid.

The truth hit him like a tsunami.

I must survive – for Enid.

He had to live. It was impossible that he would lose his chance to give to her what he had never gotten from his father.

I have to live.

He looked into Eve's eyes. Her eyes shone like dead stones.

This is how it ends.

Jack felt tears running down his face. In his mind's eye, he saw the last expression he had seen on Enid's face when he left her at the airport.

Disappointment.

Jack hurtled forward – to kill Eve.

The explosion of the gun was the last thing he heard.

CHAPTER EIGHTY-THREE

Dying is a wild night and a new road.

—*Emily Dickinson*

Bud parked his car at the trail entrance to Camelback Mountain. There were two trailheads to the mountain, and he hoped he had the right one. He glanced back at Larry, who sat in stony silence.

Bud said, "Wait here."

Bud got out and walked to the trailhead, trying to convince himself that if he took it slow, he could make it up the trail. Thirty feet up, he broke out in a sweat and felt his chest tighten. He stopped, feeling for his fanny pack full of medication, which reassured him.

I am not going to die on this mountain.

Bud climbed slowly upward, his dress shoes slipping on the loose pebbles. Knifelike chest pain brought him to his knees with a groan. With shaking hands, he dug in his pack and got a nitro pill, which he slipped under his tongue.

Bud sat for what seemed like forever. The pressure eased but he felt like shit. He looked down the trail, wondering what was holding up Jenson. He'd called for back-up on the drive over, but hadn't heard back from him.

He forced himself to his feet. He had to get up the trail.

Within forty feet, Bud felt a crushing weight on his rib cage. With a cry, he sunk to the ground. He pulled out his pill bottle, which he opened with difficulty. A gust of wind blew dirt in his face and he felt the bottle slip from his fingers. The pill bottle skittered down the trail.

Bud tried to get up but fell backwards with a grunt of pain. Sweat streamed down his face, dripped off his nose so that he could taste the salt.

He strained his eyes down the trail and thought he saw Jenson.

Or was it Bunnie?

Bud shook his head, trying to shake away the fuzz. The cacti around him were moving and buzzing like bees.

He inched forward, trying to get closer to the pill bottle. If he could get just one of them – maybe the pain would stop.

A searing fire in his chest left him breathless and weak. He stared up at the terrible blue of the sky.

I don't love Bunnie.

The truth broke on him like a stress fracture cracking through his soul.

I want to live.

All his days were behind him. Not one day in front of him.

The pain was crushing.

Like a pebble thrown into the Pacific – he felt himself disappear without a ripple.

CHAPTER EIGHTY-FOUR

I will not let you go into the unknown alone.

—*Bram Stoker*

Enid sped the car up the road leading to Camelback Mountain, ignoring Sharon's demands to let her out as well as Ernie's periodic outbursts for her to slow down. According to Ernie, who had hiked the trail with his dad, they were almost there.

Enid jerked the wheel on a sharp curve and a car materialized out of nowhere. She froze, unable to so much as flinch.

The inevitableness of the crash hung in the air for what seemed like an eternity. The sound of crunching metal and plastic was followed by a sickening impact that knocked the air out of Enid's body.

An acrid smell burned her nose. She opened her eyes.

A man was prying the door open. His voice broke through her fog. "Are you all right?"

Enid looked up, feeling faint and sick. Something smelled like the inside of her mother's purse. She felt tangled up in something and realized that it was the airbag.

Enid looked in the rearview mirror at Sharon's angry face. Sharon's mouth was moving but Enid couldn't grasp what she was saying. Ernie sat with dazed eyes.

Enid climbed out of the car.

The man was opening the back door, unbuckling Ernie and helped him and Sharon out.

Enid remembered why they had come. Jack was on the mountain – with a killer.

Enid stumbled toward the trail. She glanced back, unsure, and saw Ernie and Sharon sitting on the ground. The man was phoning for help.

Ernie met her eyes and gave her a weak smile, waved her forward.

She gave him a grateful smile and started climbing.

For what seemed like a long time, Enid struggled upward. Her breath ragged, Enid looked up the trail and stopped, startled.

A man lay in the dirt, his face down and one hand outstretched as if reaching for something.

Thinking it was Jack, she lunged forward, cold with terror at the thought that she was too late.

She rolled him over and gasped with shock.

Detective Orlean's face was ashen, his mouth lax and drooling.

Enid put her ear to his chest and heard the faint, slow beat of his heart. She shook him violently, calling his name but there was no response.

Her eyes followed his outstretched arm and she saw a pill bottle. She scrambled after it and found it empty. She scanned the ground and saw a pill. She grabbed it and crawled to his side and shoved it into his mouth.

It rolled off his tongue. She picked it up, worried that if she shoved it down his throat he would choke. She put the pill in her mouth and chewed it down to a soft spitball. Her mouth tingled and she felt her heartbeat quicken. Using her finger, she put the glob in his mouth and mashed it onto his tongue.

She went down the trail and got three more pills and did the same thing.

She bit into a fourth pill and felt her heartbeat pound harder.

His eyes opened and he blinked.

Relief washed over her. "It's me – Enid. Are you all right?"

He pressed his hand to his chest and muttered, "Mount Vesuvius."

"Where's Jack?" she said.

"Jenson – he's coming." His jacket fell to one side, revealing his shoulder holster and gun.

At the sight of the gun, Enid's breath caught. Enid grabbed at Bud, forcing him into a sitting position as she struggled to remove his jacket. "We have to get your jacket off – so you can breathe." She clumsily removed his jacket. She threw it aside and tried to unbuckle his shoulder holster.

Bud's hand snapped up. "No!"

"I need to listen to your heart," she said, hoping she sounded convincing. "We learned how in health class."

Bud hesitated but let her remove the shoulder holster. She set it behind him and threw his jacket over it.

Footsteps pounded up the trail.

A man in yellow dress shirt and mint-colored pants bounded up the trail. His eyes looked sharply from Detective Orlean to her and back again. He pushed Enid out of the way and stooped over Bud, loosening his collar and leaning him back on the ground.

Jenson said, "Help's on the way. Hang in there, Bud."

Enid sat back and, when Jenson turned his back, she got Bud's gun from the holster and tucked it into the back of her jeans.

Jenson said, "We have to get him down the trail." He slung Detective Orlean's arm over his shoulder and hoisted him up. "Take his other side."

Enid stood up. "My dad's up there. I have to help him."

Jenson said, "Unless we get him down the trail, Bud is going to die."

Enid wavered, unsure.

"We're wasting time," Jenson said, struggling under Bud's weight.

Enid stepped backwards, shaking her head.

Jenson said. "I can't do this alone. He'll die."

Enid turned and ran up the trail. The man called after her but she forced herself to move faster. She ran until she stumbled and landed on her knees with a painful jolt.

She climbed to her feet and listened. She heard the distant hum of the city and a woman's voice.

Enid walked forward until she came face to face with a man's shirt tied to a bush. She pulled at the shirt and was surprised to see what looked like a hole with a rock ledge to one side and thorny brush to the other.

She heard Jack's laugh.

Enid jumped forward and pushed her way through the bramble. Edging along the rock wall, she winced as thorns dragged along her bare arms.

She stopped, heart pounding. It was Jack's voice saying –

Dirty girl?

Enid got the gun from the back of her jeans and made sure the safety was off. She pushed through the last of brambles, stepping into the sunlight.

Jack and Laura were standing with their backs to the cliff. Eve was pointing a gun at them.

Enid raised her gun and shot at Eve.

The explosion of her gun sent her reeling backwards so that she landed in a group of thorny brambles. Enid screamed in agony as the thorns tore into her from all sides.

Ears ringing, Enid tried to move but even the tiniest movement was agonizing. She lay still, gritting her teeth.

Another explosion.

Pain ripped through her right side. Enid lay still, staring up at the canopy of thorns. The previous pain was now blunted under the new sensation of burning that started at her right side and spread out over her body like fire.

She looked up and saw a bird – was it a bird?

It was in the thorns, staring down at her with eyes that had an impartiality that took her breath away. She gazed into the dark eyes, mesmerized.

Did the bird taste it too?

Blood.

CHAPTER EIGHTY-FIVE

The fallen angel becomes a malignant devil.

—*Mary Shelley*

Jack heard the explosion and sank to his knees. What he didn't expect to hear was Enid screaming. Jack's eyes flew open and he saw what looked like Enid's battered Converse sneakers flailing in the brush. He watched in horror as Eve bore down on her with the gun.

Jack sprang forward and hit Eve with a running tackle. At the same moment, Eve fired the gun into Enid, who lay unnaturally twisted in the thorns.

Jack saw Enid's bone-white face and gasped. Blood seeped out from the right side of her body.

Fury burned through him. He grabbed Eve's arm and twisted it until she screamed. He felt her hot breath as they grappled. He gave a brutal twist that sent her to her knees. The gun fell from her hand.

Eve went after the gun but Jack punched her, sending her sprawling into the dirt.

She tried to crawl away but he came after her, grabbing her hair and dragging her away from the gun.

Eve kicked and clawed at him like a wild animal, twisting from his grasp.

Jack lunged for her and, with a violent effort, she eluded his grasp and hurtled herself away from him – and over the cliff's edge.

She made a mad grab – at nothing.

He dove forward, grabbing her wrist. As she went over, the force of her body dragged him to the edge. He grabbed at a root, which pulled them to a stop with a jerk. His shoulder felt like it was being ripped from the socket and he could hear Eve's feet kicking at the side of the cliff – not finding a foothold.

Using the root as leverage, he tried to pull her toward him but found he couldn't. The root loosened and he slid forward until his eyes were looking over the edge. He found himself looking down on her and the massive drop under her dangling body.

Eve looked up and their eyes latched on to each other.

Like a kick to his stomach, Jack felt the truth combust through every fiber of his being. A stranger stared up at him.

A predator.

Jack gritted his teeth and pulled with all his might. Laura was there, struggling with him, helping him save Eve.

They pulled Eve onto the dirt where she lay gasping – eyeing him with the desperation of a ensnared animal.

There was a click of the gun.

Jack and Eve turned.

Laura was taking aim, her sights locked on Eve.

Eve jumped to her feet, hideous with fury.

Cowering, Laura threw down the gun and backed away.

Eve sprang forward but Jack grabbed her ankle and jerked her back, slamming her into the dirt. He pulled her toward him, her fingernails dragging through the dirt as she resisted.

Jack climbed on top of her, pinning her.

Eve tried to twist free, reaching for the gun.

Jack put his hand around her neck and squeezed.

She stopped fighting and lay still. She gazed up at him, eyes softening.

Jack stared down at her, horrified to feel that he still wanted her. He took his hand away.

"You love me," Eve said.

Her lips were on his and he jerked his head back, hating himself for wanting her.

Eve said, "You and me, we're cut from the same cloth."

Jack said in a hoarse voice, "I do love you."

Her eyes lit up, triumphant.

Jack said, "Not enough."

Eve's face contorted into a grotesque mask of rage. Her curses were drowned out by the sounds of a helicopter that came in from the west and left them in a cloud of swirling dust.

Jack squinted toward Enid, wanting to help her but too afraid to loosen his grip on Eve.

"If Enid dies – I'll kill you," he said.

Eve gave him a look of such tenderness that it took his breath away.

He realized that everything else before that had been cheap acting. This, like her eyes meeting him over the ledge, was real.

It was the only moment she ever loved me.

And then it was gone.

CHAPTER EIGHTY-SIX

Now comes the mystery.

—Henry Ward Beecher, on his deathbed.

"I wish I could have been there," Bud said to Jenson, who stood at the foot of his hospital bed at John C. Lincoln Hospital. "I would have given money to see her face when they cuffed her."

Jenson said, "It doesn't get much better than watching Eve Hargrove cuffed like a common criminal."

"She is a common criminal," Bud said, wincing as he placed his hand over the pacemaker that was lodged under his skin.

Jenson said, "Vivian is facing federal kidnapping charges for Laura – I mean Lani. Not to mention the charges she racked up for running an underage sex trafficking operation out of a girls' home."

Bud said, "Lani Mulberry – what's she going by? Laura or Lani?"

"Laura," Jack said as he entered the room, pushing Enid in a wheelchair. "At least for now."

Jenson tipped his hat and headed for the door. "I'll be going. Nice seeing you all."

Everyone said their goodbyes as he left.

Enid said to Bud, "Am I allowed to say I told you so?"

Jack said, "Say what you want about Eve, but if your mom had been pimping you out to your stepfather you'd end up a sociopath too – so don't go throwing 'I told you so' at glass houses."

Enid snorted.

Bud said, "Eve hired the best defense attorney out of New York – real shark."

Jack said. "I don't care what anybody says – she never stood a chance with a mother that used her as pedophile bait."

Bud said, "What I figure is that Vivian, when she was stripping, was dressing up like a little girl to lure in the pedophiles. Once she found Daniel, she used eight-year-old Eve as bait to get him to marry her."

Jack said, "Upstanding businessman Daniel Hargrove wasn't about to marry a stripper, so Vivian had to sweeten the deal. She took in Jeni – then made up a cockamamie story about another daughter in Oklahoma that she would bring to Phoenix once she was settled."

Bud said, "I wonder if she went so far as to cut him a deal? Give me the life I want and I'll give you three beautiful little girls."

Jack said, "Eve should have cut off his balls." He looked at Enid, "You didn't hear that."

Enid said, "She cut out his heart. I bet she had two special blowtorches made named 'right' and 'left' for his balls."

"Jesus, Enid," Jack said.

Bud said, "Eve and Laura learned that if they faked sick, they could get Daniel to focus on Jeni – until Jeni couldn't take it anymore and ran away. It was Jeni who never stood a chance."

Jack said, "I thought it was Petunia's husband who hired Frank Ficus to follow me. It was Eve. Laura told me that she had told Eve that Jeni asked her for money so she could hire a private detective to find her real mother."

Bud said, "Eve knew that Jeni wasn't her biological sister and didn't want Jeni to find out the truth."

Jack said, "Eve and Vivian must have had a pact – spoken or unspoken – who knows? Eve knew what her mom was doing and, as she got older, was in on the cover-up. Eve hired Frank to follow Jeni, which he did – right to my office. That's when Eve lands on my doorstep, offering me money to drop Jeni's case."

"Ten thousand dollars," Bud said.

Jack said, "You didn't really think I was a hit man, did you?"

Bud said, "I rule nothing out."

Jack said, "If Jeni hadn't told me that story about her writing her tell-all autobiography – if I hadn't told Eve – Jeni would still be alive."

He shook his head, pained. "I might as well be a hit man. I got Jeni killed."

"What do you mean?" Enid said.

Jack said, "Jeni made me promise not to tell anyone she was writing a tell-all book about her family and what do I do? I tell Eve. The one thing Eve can't deal with is the truth. She'd do anything, even kill, to make sure no one ever finds out the truth about her. The thought that anybody would ever even think that she wasn't pure as the driven snow – she couldn't stand it."

Enid said, "But she slept with you and Chip – how does that make her pure?"

"I don't know," Jack said.

Enid said to Jack, "Why'd you tell Eve – after you promised Jeni you wouldn't tell anyone?"

"Because I'm a fucking idiot," Jack said.

Enid looked at Bud, questioningly. Bud was examining Jack with a frown. Enid said to Jack, "It can't be your fault. You're not the bad guy."

Jack said, "Good guys and bad guys are for fairy tales, kid."

Bud said, "No. There's a line."

Jack said to Bud, "Which side was I on?"

Bud remained silent.

Jack said, "A book that didn't exist – I broke a promise and made it exist. I'm the one who got Jeni killed."

Enid stared at him, disturbed. "So you're a scumbag. Don't do it again. Then maybe you won't be a scumbag."

Jack gave a pained smile. "Thanks, Enid. Leave it to you to rub salt in the wound."

Bud said, "We got evidence that Eve murdered Frank. She was setting you up for the murder of Jeni and Frank. She told Frank to be there and, after Eve shoots Frank, she planted bogus records showing that he had been following you for weeks and that you were the last person to see Jeni alive."

Jack said, "Even after she tried to frame me – we were together."

"You were a loose end," Bud said. "So was Laura. Eve planted Laura's suicide note – and Daniel's finger. She told Laura to meet her on the mountain and fed you the story of her fight with Laura –

probably blackened her own eye – and then made damned sure that you went with her to 'save' Laura."

Jack said, "Laura believed that Eve loved her. Like I believed Eve loved me."

Bud said, "You can't blame yourself about Jeni. You broke a promise but you didn't pull the trigger."

Jack said, "First time I met Jeni she told me she'd rather be crazy on the truth than drunk on lies."

Bud said, "We got to the truth."

"Did we?" Jack said with a frown.

Enid said, "What about the guy in the canal?"

"Dennie Dutter," Bud said. "The connection was Vivian. Maybe she started the home to help girls in need – maybe she had bad intentions right from the start – we're not sure. What we do know is that she was high-profile enough to keep the donations coming in, and at some point she needed more money and decided to get into the sex trafficking business."

Enid said, "She was rich. Why would she do that?"

Bud said, "I never met anybody who thinks they have enough money. Vivian had a school full of girls with no one to report them missing, and Dennie was the man on the street with the connections to get the girls trapped into sex slavery."

Enid said, "What's going to happen to them – the girls?"

Bud said, "Child Protective Services."

Enid said, "Eve should have killed her mother."

Bud said, "There's no justification for murder."

Enid said, "Eve murdered her stepdad because he molested her, but her mother was responsible for hundreds of girls getting molested – she's the one who deserved to get murdered."

Bud said, "No one deserves to get murdered."

Jack said, "With Eve it was personal and to hell with anyone else. Vivian was in it for the money."

Enid said, "What about the therapist? The one that drugged me?"

"Gone," Bud said, "but not forgotten – at least not by the authorities."

Enid said, "Was he a real doctor?"

"We're not sure," Bud said. "There is a doctor by that name with all the right credentials but we're not sure it's the same guy."

Jack looked at his watch and said, "I'm meeting with the insurance guy about my house."

Bud said to Enid, "When are they letting you out?"

"Today," Enid said. "They keep telling me how lucky I am to be alive."

Bud said, "You were lucky for me. You saved my life. Thank you."

Enid blushed and looked down.

Jack said, "You've done the impossible – she's speechless."

CHAPTER EIGHTY-SEVEN

There will be little rubs and disappointments everywhere, and we are all apt to expect too much; but then, if one scheme of happiness fails, human nature turns to another; if the first calculation is wrong, we make a second better: we find comfort somewhere.

—Jane Austen

Alone in her hospital room, Enid sat waiting for the doctor to give her the official heave-ho. She felt like her butt was becoming welded to the wheelchair and she was itching to leave. All morning, Jack had been patiently waiting with her, which had surprised her.

Twenty minutes ago, he'd gone to the cafeteria to get coffee, and she was beginning to get scared that he wasn't coming back. His patience had set her nerves on edge — like he was playing nice before he ditched her again.

Ever since she woke up from the surgery, he'd been nice.

Too nice.

The nurses had insisted that she not stand or walk until she started physical therapy, but she felt an overwhelming urge to get out of the wheelchair and go looking for Jack.

She wheeled herself to the side of the bed and, gripping the rail, she stood. She was startled at how shaky her legs felt but she smiled in triumph. She took a step toward the door and felt her legs falter. She grabbed the table and, forgetting it was on wheels, she and the table hurtled forward.

She rammed into something solid and warm. Strong arms encircled her and eased her back to the bed.

"Enid Iglowski. You are fucking dangerous."

She looked up.

Chip was shaking his head in exasperation. "Alone in a room – you still manage to find trouble."

Enid flinched, thinking about the last time she saw him – running up the street after she hijacked his car. She thought of him kissing Eve and felt a stab of jealousy.

Was he still in love with Eve?

Enid cleared her throat and said, "Um, Chip."

"Um, Enid," he said, imitating her.

She looked at him, unsure.

Is he making fun of me?

He was smiling. Not just any smile but the most beautiful smile ever. Like the first time she ever saw him.

Enid said, "I'm sorry I hijacked your car."

"But you're not sorry you wrecked it?"

"That too," she said.

Chip said, "That was a mean trick you played, kid."

Her heart sank at the word "kid."

Chip said, "Dad says you saved his life. I guess I should be the one thanking you."

Enid said, "Are you still in love with Eve?"

"Have you ever pulled a punch in your life, kiddo?"

Enid reached up and said, "Help me up."

"I just helped you not fall down. Shouldn't you stay put?"

Enid said, "You want to thank me? Help me stand up."

Chip helped her stand and, as he turned to get the wheelchair, she grabbed his arm.

He turned to her with a questioning look.

Before she could think better of it, Enid threw herself into his arms and kissed him.

Horrified, Chip's arms flew out to the side as if he was denying any involvement.

Enid held him fast, determined that if she had one stolen kiss – she was going to make it count.

After what seemed like eons, Enid pulled away. She was surprised to see that his eyes were closed and his face dreamy. His hands were gently resting on her hips.

When did that happen?

Chip opened his eyes and looked at her as if for the first time.

"Enid," he said softly.

She smiled, kissed him again. When she was done, she pulled away.

"Jesus," he said in a wondering voice.

Enid grinned and said, "Don't get any ideas, kid."

His eyes widened.

She laughed, feeling suddenly carefree.

Chip leaned in to kiss her and she stopped him and said, "When I'm older – if you try hard enough – I might give you a chance." She grinned mischievously into his startled face, "Maybe."

Jack walked in carrying his coffee. He stopped, frowning. "What's going on?"

Enid pushed Chip away and sat on the bed, "It's about time – I'm starving! Let's get out of here."

Chip stepped out of the way as Jack got the wheelchair and helped Enid into it.

Jack said, "We got the go-ahead to leave."

"Cool beans," Enid said.

Chip said, "Enid, I – "

Jack pushed her out the door and, not able to resist, Enid looked back at Chip – and winked.

Enid decided that the only thing more beautiful to her than Chip's beautiful face – was the startled expression that splashed across his beautiful face when she winked at him.

Two days later, Jack and Enid stood in front of Laura's house. A rental car was loaded with luggage and Laura had Faith buckled into the baby seat when she turned to face them. The early morning sun shone on her pale face as she smiled shyly. "Thanks again for seeing me off."

Enid said, "Are you going to be okay? I mean – with the baby and all?"

Laura said, "I thought about flying but I'm still trying to wrap my head around the fact that I have a family in Oklahoma. They wanted to fly out but I talked them into letting me drive there. I guess it's my way of giving myself more time."

Jack nodded at the baby. "When she's older – what are you going to tell her? The truth?"

Laura said, "If you were her father – would you?"

Jack frowned, unsure.

Laura reached into her purse and pulled out a photograph, held it out to him. "Maybe you want this. Maybe you don't."

Jack took the photo but didn't look at it.

Enid leaned in to see it. It was a black-and-white photo of Eve. Her eyes looked out from the photograph, dark with mystery.

Jack put the photo into his shirt pocket, unseen. He said to Laura, "If you need help, I hope you know you can call me. I can't promise anything – but I can try."

Laura smiled her thanks and got behind the wheel. They said goodbye and Jack and Enid stepped back, watching as the car headed up the street.

Enid said, "Are you going to put me on a plane and send me back to Florida?"

Jack winced. He ran his hand through his hair and walked to his car.

Enid didn't move. "Sixteen," she said.

Jack stopped, turned.

Enid said, "I turned sixteen on February second."

"Happy belated birthday," Jack said.

Enid stared at him, unsure.

Jack hooked his thumb to the car. "I need to deposit the insurance check – for the house. You want to come?"

Enid remained silent, waiting for him to say that he was sending her back to Florida.

Jack said, "I'm going to rebuild. The house, I mean."

Enid said, "The same?"

"No, something new. Better. You want to help?"

Enid looked at him in surprise.

Jack turned and walked to the car, "I hear Florida is humid this time of year."

Enid frowned, catching up to him. "Yeah, my hair gets out of control."

Jack said, "You could hang out in Phoenix for a while."

Enid held her breath, too scared to speak.

Jack said, "When the summer is over, if you like it here and your mom agrees, there's a good high school up the street from the house."

Enid bit her lip, feeling tears burn behind her eyes.

Jack said, "If you want to."

Enid nodded, feeling like her heart was going to burst.

"Cool. Then it's a done deal?" Jack said. "No pressure. We still have to clear it with your mom and I can't promise anything – "

The next thing she knew, Enid's was face was buried in his shirt and she was crying like she was six years old.

"I'll be all right," Jack said, stroking her hair. "I'm sorry. I'm going to try to be a better dad to you."

Enid pulled back, embarrassed and red-faced but feeling as if the world was bright and shiny.

Jack said, "You gonna give me your okay, or keep me hanging?"

Enid nodded. "I'll try too. To be better."

"Then it's a party," Jack said, pointing her toward the passenger side of the car as he got behind the wheel.

Enid hopped into the car. Wiping away the last of her tears, she laughed aloud.

www.ingramcontent.com/pod-product-compliance
Lightning Source LLC
Chambersburg PA
CBHW071202250626
47159CB00001B/174